The Pirate Spy

The 5th and Final Book in the Seductive Spies Series

By
Cheri Champagne

Jacket design and illustrations by Deana Holmes
Editing by Jen Graybeal, Beth Attwood, and Amanda Bidnall

ISBN: 978-1-7777443-8-0

Dedication

For everyone that struggles to fight for themselves.
I believe in you.

The Pirate Spy

Prologue

May 1815

The frigid grip of fear had its talons wrapped firmly around Lady Laura Morris' heart, and nausea churned in her stomach at the pressure of the blackguard's hard shoulder digging into her soft flesh. The brigand paraded her proudly across the ship's upper deck while dark, shadowy figures looked on. Her head ached and swam with faintness, lingering spots danced behind her eyelids, and an icy sweat beaded her forehead and neck.

Her bottom was jutted in the air and her face bounced against the cur's sweat-scented coat with every step he took, her waist-length, curly auburn hair waving down to the man's knees. She wanted grab it, to knot it or pin it up and away from the gaze of these men, but the man had her arms pinned to her sides. Laura had never worn her hair down around a man not her father, and she was mortified that it was happening now, in front of pirates.

Twisting her head sideways, she squinted at the looming figures, and through the darkness of night she saw the faces of her captors, dirty and contorted with lustful sneers. A hard, disquieting pit of terror settled heavily in her abdomen, spreading through to her bound extremities.

With renewed determination, she fought against the man's hold, and his arm tightened painfully around her hips, just as it had when she'd struggled before.

"Now, now, milady," the man beneath her purred. "None o' tha'." He swatted her bottom and she released a shrill, frightened squeal that was muffled beneath the gag that had been tied over her mouth.

"As all of you can see," a new voice called above the din of murmuring voices, "our quarry has been captured. None of you are to have your way with her"—groans rippled through the crowd of men—"until our superiors have given us leave to do so."

The heavy block of ice that filled her now threatened to consume her entirely. Who were these men, and how had they gotten into her father's home? Lord, but she still wore her night-rail and dressing gown!

Her evening had transpired like many others, with her quietly painting at the easel in her bedchamber before she retired—exhausted—with paint-stained fingers. But, unlike other nights, she'd been awoken by material being shoved into her mouth and two men restraining her limbs. She'd fought as they bound her wrists and ankles, and bucked and squirmed the entire way to their awaiting carriage, until she'd been bludgeoned across the temple and knocked unconscious. She'd only awoken as the man beneath her carried her up the ship's ladder, and then she'd been too afraid to struggle lest she fall into the dark, rippling ocean.

"Put her in the orlop," the man in charge grunted to the brute who held her.

With a nod, the man carried her through the small throng of men toward a doorway that led to a ladder. Laura's head gave another throb, and spots swam before her eyes as she attempted to take in her surroundings. They passed a deck lined with cannons, and another with tables. They ventured to the lower decks, but the light was so dim that she couldn't see what occupied them.

The man brought her down more ladders and up another, until he dropped her unceremoniously onto a pile of material in a small room.

He turned to leave, and Laura rose awkwardly to her knees. "Ngh uuung ee eeen!" she shouted, attempting to beseech him through her gag.

With a sneer, the blackguard knelt before her, skimming his fingers across her cheek. She hoped he would remove the gag, so she remained still. He laughed, a waft of his foul breath rushing over her face.

"Yer not goin' anywhere, milady. Yer father, the Duke o' Norshire, better cooperate, or my superiors'll let us have ye. An' I intend t' be first t' get a taste." He pinched her chin, and she reared back. He laughed again, pinching harder as he brought his lips to her ear. "Don't think the duke'll come fer ye, either. We're sailing well away an' awaiting orders. *No one* will find ye." He ran his fingers over her unruly curls before he stood.

A shiver of revulsion rippled through her.

His vile laughter echoed in her ears as he left, the door closing with a hollow *thud*. His words hung in the air, and tears leaked from the corners of her eyes as dread thickened her throat and settled deep in her chest. *No one will find ye.*

* * *

Mid-June 1815

Sunlight broke through the grey clouds overhead and the ship rocked underfoot as Callum McInnis strode toward the frigate's fo'c'sle. His heart full and his mind racing, he breathed deeply of the sea air and turned his face briefly upward toward the sun.

"We've only been aboard this frigate for a sennight, Callum, and you've already made a name for yourself among the other men," his friend and apprentice, Harris, murmured beside him. "Some of them seem to recognize your name. Best hope that the captain doesn't hear of it, or you'll suffer like the others have."

Indeed, if their captain knew of his history at sea, he'd be thrashed for certain, for Lord knew their *esteemed* captain could not abide a man who had more knowledge than he.

Callum's lips thinned grimly. "I'm well aware of what our captain is capable, Harris, but you know what our assignment entails."

He turned to look at his friend, and the young man nodded, his gaze knowing.

Just over a sennight prior, their superior in His Majesty's Secret Service, Sir Charles Bradley—Hydra, to their band of spies—came to them with a request: board a pirate ship, take control, and use the ship to follow and apprehend traitor to the Crown, Sir Humphrey Wycliff. As of yet, they'd managed to complete only their first task. Lord knew how far from their quarry they'd sailed, journeying in the wrong bloody direction as they were, but Callum imagined that they still had some time before Wycliff would reach land in the Americas. The speedy frigate they'd boarded ought to be able to catch up once Callum gained control. But, their ability to sail quickly notwithstanding, the fact that they were behind did not sit well with Callum.

"You're to gain the crew's trust, yes"—Harris nodded—"but you've not yet begun to—"

Callum cut Harris a hard glance. "I'm aware of what I've not yet done. If you'll recall, it is *I* who is training *you*."

The young man pursed his lips. "Well, yes, but—"

"Then allow me to work," he snapped. The dejected pucker in Harris' features cut Callum's ire, and he deflated. "My apologies, friend. I'm pleased to be aboard the ship, but I confess that I struggle with our assignment. I cannot simply take control of the ship without the support of the crew or a sufficient opportunity to—"

A topman strode by, eyeing the pair warily. To avoid suspicion, Callum nodded to the young lad then bent over the taffrail, lowering a wooden bucket down to the water with a rope.

"We look suspicious," he muttered over his shoulder to Harris as he held tightly to the rope, now tugged by the water rushing past. "You're a topman and I'm a mere gunner's assistant. We oughtn't be seen conversing in this way."

"I'm only a new topman, not permitted to touch the lines. I sit on the fighting top and—"

"I know what a bleedin' topman does, Harris."

"*You there!*" A low shout came from behind them, and Callum's gut sank.

He cursed and hurriedly pulled up the bucket.

Harris spun around and saluted their captain. "Yes, sir." He grimaced, and Callum surmised that he felt a twinge of pain from his still-healing shoulder. He'd had three weeks to recover from his gunshot wound, but it likely still ached.

"Why aren't you in the rigging?" The captain strode closer.

Callum retrieved the bucket and placed it on the wood planks at his feet, then spun to salute their domineering captain.

Harris cleared his throat. "My shift's just finished, sir. I was going to retire to—"

Crack! The captain slapped Harris full on the cheek and hissed, "Don't ever speak that way to me!"

Other men paused in their work to gawp openly at the display, and anger flamed through Callum. He resisted the urge to clench his fists, knowing that untamed fury in that moment would do little good. This might well be the opportunity that he'd been waiting for.

"Take him to the stern and fetch my whip," the captain muttered to the men standing nearby, who hurried to do their leader's bidding.

Careful not to make eye contact with Harris, Callum stepped back and allowed the other men to grip his apprentice's arms and drag him across the quarterdeck. The pirates were quiet and sombre as the scene took shape. A sharp gust of cool wind blew past, ruffling the men's unkempt hair and attire and spreading gooseflesh across Callum's skin.

The crowd around the captain and Harris grew as Harris' shirt was torn from his person and his arms were tied around the mizzenmast, his back to the captain.

Callum sidled closely to one of the other men and gingerly divested him of his pistol. Keeping his hand—and the pistol—down and tight against his thigh, Callum made his way toward the front of the crowd.

A thrill of anticipation travelled down his spine and a grin tugged at his lips. Callum lived for this sort of excitement, the pleasurable rush of the chase, the capture of evil persons, and the delivery of justice. It was what kept him waking up every morning, what drove him to always take the next assignment. Working in His Majesty's Secret Service satisfied his intense desire for adventure…for danger. And he was damned good at it.

The captain wielded his whip and raised his arm, prepared to deliver a punishing blow to Harris' back, but Callum leapt forward, catching the captain around the neck with one thick arm and pressing the pistol to the bastard's back.

"Swing that whip, and I'll shoot you," Callum hissed.

With wide, fearful eyes, the men around them silently watched.

The captain sneered. "You'll not get the chance. Men! Take this mutinous wretch off of me."

Callum grinned as he eyed the men surrounding them. None appeared eager to come to their captain's rescue, all having been, at one time, abused and thrashed by the man.

"*Men*!" the captain bellowed. When no movement was forthcoming, the captain screamed, "*Mutiny*! *Cads*! I'll have your heads! I'll see you fed to the sharks! I'll—"

Bang!

Several men cursed soundly as the captain slumped in Callum's arms. One man rushed forward to take the captain's legs, and together they hauled the man over the rail and released, letting him fall to the water below.

"Untie him," Callum grunted, nodding toward Harris.

There would be no other moment. He'd best take it quick, before another man found his cods and tried it himself.

Callum strode back through the milling crowd and leapt atop the wooden roof of the skylight to the captain's quarters, directly beside the mizzenmast.

"Hear me!" he called to the men.

Harris rubbed at his wrists and nodded gratefully to the men who'd released him before turning his attention to Callum.

"We've worked under our departed captain for too long." There was a murmuring of agreement among the men. "We need a captain who will be fair. Who will reward his men!"

Someone called out in agreement, and Callum took it as encouragement.

"That captain failed us." He paused for effect. Another breeze swept past him, pulling at his wavy brown locks and the short growth of hair on his cheeks and jaw. "Did he bring us riches?"

"No!" several men called back.

"Did he bring us glory?" Callum shouted.

"No!" More men joined the first, pumping their fists into the air as they replied.

"We set sail a sennight ago, and we haven't taken a single vessel! *I* can lead you into battle, men. I can lead you to riches. I can lead you to *glory*!"

A roar of cheers and applause exploded in the crowd of nearly one hundred and twenty men, and Callum's heart gave a joyous squeeze.

"*Will you follow me?*" he hollered, feeling the veins on his neck protrude with his efforts.

Another eruption of cheers came from the men, and Callum beamed, his heart thumping with overwhelming elation.

His boyhood dream had finally been realized. Callum was a pirate captain.

Chapter 1

Late June 1815

A warm wind ruffled Callum's hair and tugged at his long, newly acquired, midnight-blue coat. He strode across the quarterdeck, a grin on his lips as he observed his men.

It had been nearly a sennight since he'd become captain, and everything was faring impeccably. He'd led two successful ship raids in which no lives were lost and bounty was acquired.

Unsurprisingly, it had taken some convincing before the men consented to not kill—or maim—the sailors on the opposing ships, but to his relief, they'd listened. It was a weak excuse, he would admit, but he'd informed his men that if no one was left alive—and with enough foodstuffs to take them to land—there would be none to tell their tale. He and his men could gain their riches while simultaneously building their notoriety. It would also allow Callum to maintain his personal—and the Secret Service's—scruples. For as much as he'd coveted this position on the sea, he'd not be able to live with himself if he took the lives of innocent people.

A voice rang up over the din of the ruffling wind, lapping water, and shuffling movement of the men. "They call me hanging Johnnie…"

"Horray, horray!" Callum and the other men replied.

"They call me hanging Johnnie," the first man sang.

"Hang, boys, hang."

"They say I hang for money," Callum sang.

"Horray, horray," the others replied as they worked the ropes and scrubbed the deck.

Callum continued, "But saying so is funny."

"Hang, boys, hang."

"I'd hang the highway robber!" Harris led the verse.

"Horray, horray!"

"I'd hang the burglar jobber."

"Hang, boys, hang."

They stomped their feet in time with the tune, using the rhythm of the shanty "Hanging Johnnie" to synchronise their work. Continuing on, they took turns leading the verse while the rest replied.

Singing sea songs, ballads, and shanties was really the most enjoyable interlude on a ship when one was not engaging in battle. Callum had heard and learned many in his time, but had never thought to write them down. Most sea men—who were not part of the Royal Navy—were illiterate and wouldn't consider the possibility of the songs fading into nonexistence.

"Ho!" one of the topmen overhead called.

Callum's gaze flicked upward to see where the lad pointed, then followed the young man's outstretched finger.

Unhooking his newly acquired spyglass from the leather strap about his waist, Callum dashed to the fo'c'sle and peered through the metal eye.

"A ship," he called. A rush of anticipation pumped through his veins and tightened his gut. Perhaps this would be the ship that Sir Wycliff had boarded. "Let's take her, men! Raise the Jolly Roger!"

The bell began to toll, a flurry of activity overtaking the quarterdeck while men ran to their stations. Callum dashed past several of his men on the companionway and took the helm from Harris, now his second-in-command. The double wheel controlled the tiller, located two decks below, with ropes connecting them that ran through his cabin. He steered the frigate toward their target, which—*hell*—didn't even appear to be moving.

"Run out the carronades!" Callum called to his gunners. Carronades had shorter barrels than the traditional long guns, and they had a narrower muzzle. Those without experience believed them to be inaccurate when compared to long guns, which required higher aiming in order to hit your target, but, in fact, the carronade was *more* accurate. If one aimed them as one did long guns, they overshot their target. "Aim low and true!"

They approached their target far more quickly than he'd anticipated, and Callum narrowed his eyes in consideration. Awareness dawned and, with a grin, he called out to his men, "Their anchor is uncatted, and they're floating listless! A feast of riches ready for the taking!"

* * *

A weak groan echoed in the small room, reaching Lady Laura Morris' ears before she realized that she was the source of the sound. Her stomach ached and her mouth was dry, her lips cracked and coated with dried blood.

She'd lost count of the number of days in which she'd been imprisoned on this ship. Stuck alone in a dark room, days merged into nights without her knowledge. The brutes fed her a paltry amount, scarcely giving her one meal per day—or so she imagined. They filled a small jug with watered-down wine during each of her meals, but it failed to fully quench her thirst.

Her fingers trembled as she curled a lock of hair behind her ear. She was permitted to leave her room only to use the seat of easement, which she despised, for a guard was ordered to observe her at all times.

A sob caught in her throat, but her eyes remained dry; she'd run out of tears weeks ago. She ran a hand over her face and steadied her breath. Despite her constant fear, her thirst, hunger, and the very distressing fact that she'd been kidnapped, Laura was grateful that these blackguards hadn't abused her. *Yet.*

Even in her weakened state, she'd fought her captors, though it was to no avail. They were strong and large, and she was weakening with every passing moment. And, truthfully, if she *did* manage to break free of them, how could she possibly reach land? She'd considered the possibility of acquiring a rowing boat and rowing away, but they must be weeks from shore. Without enough foodstuffs and water, she would surely perish.

Shifting her position, Laura settled on her side upon a pile of folded sails, resting her head in the crook of her elbow. A sharp pain travelled through her hip, and she cringed. Her entire body ached. She'd attempted to make the folded sails softer by placing her robe upon them, but the material was so thin that it scarcely made a difference. Unaccustomed as she was to sleeping on such a hard surface, her body did not take well to the experience. The absence of her luxurious bed, however, was the very least of her worries.

Her mother must be frightfully concerned…but would her father be? *Surely*. Years ago, when her sister Charlotte had gone missing, he'd lost himself in his work and subsequently neglected any relationship that he'd once had with Laura. But he *would* worry for her, would he not? What were the villains' demands? she wondered. Was her father capable of fulfilling them?

A muffled shout came from the deck above her, followed by several other bellows and heavy footfalls. Laura sat upright and trained her ear toward the noise, the movement causing a sharp pain to sear through her back and a wave of dizziness to lighten her head. There were several loud rumbles and thuds, and Laura's heart pounded madly. *Are those the cannons?*

* * *

The *boom* of cannon fire reverberated off the rocking ocean, and a ball arched high overhead to land harmlessly in the water beyond them. Callum crowed, lifting his fist in the air.

"They're going to give us a fight, men!" he yelled. "Take down their main mast!"

One after the other, his arsenal fired their deafening blows. With a loud *crack*, their opponent's main mast skewed to one side, sending men toppling from their rigging down to the upper deck.

"Board her!" Callum roared, a grin on his lips. "Topmen, keep your guns aimed, and shoot only when necessary."

There was a chorus of *yes, sirs* above him as the gunmen on the upper deck swung from ropes over to their opponent's ship.

With anticipation coursing through him, Callum gripped a dangling rope and pushed off the bulwark. Salty ocean air and the harsh scent of gunpowder rushed past him as he swung, and a laugh bubbled up in his chest.

He landed with both feet on their opponent's upper deck, and was instantly set upon. Callum flashed his teeth and yanked his pistol-wielding arm, throwing one foolhardy man over the bulwark and into the water. Callum laughed and punched another man in the eye. Carefully observing the battle that had begun around him, Callum unsheathed his French cutlass and strode determinedly across the deck toward the ladder, eager to reach the hold.

Two more men approached him as he walked, but with quick slashes of his cutlass to their arms, he managed to disperse them. Brushing past one last man, Callum descended the ladder.

Shock rippled through him as he reached the bottom rung and glanced around the gun deck. It was entirely vacant. That would mean that most—if not all—of this ship's crew were on the upper deck. But what the devil was a ship doing with such minimal crew? And floating listlessly in the middle of the sodding ocean? What experienced captain would uncat their anchor when they knew very well that it would not reach the ocean's floor? Something wasn't right.

Cautiously, he strode across the gun deck toward the captain's cabin. Nothing was amiss, though the space was sparsely furnished. He returned to the ladder and descended to the mess deck. He searched the space, but found nothing. Hell, even the galley was devoid of a cook.

"What the devil—" he muttered.

The hairs on the back of his neck stood on end as awareness dawned. These men weren't sailors. They were here *hiding* something. Indeed, there was no other plausible explanation. What sort of treasure would these men have been hiding so far from land?

His pulse thudded wildly as he considered the possibilities. He descended the ladder to the hold, his breath held in his throat as he spun around, anticipating a great treasure. And he stilled.

"*Nothing?*" he breathed in disbelief.

His boots clomped on the hull's wooden floor as he searched. He found the bread room and the cheese storage, spare oars and various ropes, but nothing of significance.

Callum cursed and turned back the way he'd come. Perhaps his conclusion was incorrect. But then, what were these men doing out in the middle of the ocean?

A flash of movement above him caught his eye. *The orlop.* He grinned in triumph. There was a guard set outside the sail room.

Sheathing his cutlass, he slowly climbed the ladder, then paused before reaching the top.

"You've a choice," Callum drawled. "Surrender now and live, or die guarding that door."

"I'll die either way," a low voice replied. "An' ye'll die, too, once our master finds out."

Callum's curiosity was piqued, but he wasn't dissuaded. "Very well." He gripped the rail with one hand and withdrew one of the three loaded pistols strapped to his chest. Aiming over the orlop's floor, he heaved himself upward, careful to keep his aim steady on the large man.

The guard wielded a small dagger, poised to throw as Callum came to stand before him.

With a grin and a raised eyebrow, Callum slid his gaze from the man's small weapon to his fearful eyes. "Do you truly wish to do that?"

"This item is not for ye, pirate. It's not worth the trouble. Ye'd do well t' leave with yer crew and nae look back."

Callum nearly rolled his eyes at the brute's dire warning. He'd grown bored with this exchange. In one quick movement, he stepped forward, arching his arm high, and brought down the handle of his pistol to the man's temple.

With a groan, the guard crumpled to the hard wood planks. Callum nudged the fallen man aside with his boot and reached for the door's latch.

His heart raced and his breath hitched with excitement as he pulled the door open, eager to see the treasures within. Just as soon as it opened, however, his grin fled, his heart sank, and cold fury pumped through his veins. For, curled upon a filthy heap of rotting sails, was a woman.

Chapter 2

The man at the door cursed long and low while Laura kept her face hidden by her arms, willing the ship's hull to swallow her whole and deposit her into the ocean. Fabric swished, leather creaked, and there was a distinct *clink* of metal as he knelt next to her. A gust of air swept over her at his movement, and a shiver of fear travelled over her. Despite herself, she inhaled the scent. The aroma of the ocean, gunpowder, and—amazingly—soap and minted tooth powder reached her senses over the stench of her own unwashed body. As absurd as it was, she wanted another whiff of the fresh fragrance.

"I'll not hurt you," he said softly.

She squeezed her body tighter into her inept ball, hoping that if any blows came, they would not do damage to her head or neck. Her guard had called him a pirate, and surely pirates were not bound by a moral compass. Nor was this pirate and his fellows—for she was certain there were more—bound by any promise to whomever had ordered her kidnapping. They could—and would—have their way with her if they chose.

Laura would not allow that to happen.

"I…" The man cursed under his breath. "I might be a pirate, lass, but I hold myself and my men by a strict code of honour. By my tr—"

Laura lowered her arms from her face, prepared to give him a speculative glare, but his gasp stopped her. His eyes—dark in the obscurity of the space—were wide with recognition.

"God's teeth, you're the Duke of Norshire's missing daughter, Lady Laura Morris!"

She wanted to deny it, but her parents had undoubtedly posted her likeness in every newspaper and magazine across England, and her face was relatively unforgettable. Drat, but the man could hold her for ransom himself, for clearly he knew her father and how very wealthy he was.

He started to reach his hand out to her, but halted when she flinched.

Pain lanced through her at the sudden movement. Lord, but her body ached all over.

Men's voices and swift, heavy footfalls sounded above them, and unbridled terror turned her stomach to ice.

"I haven't time to explain," the pirate whispered. "I give you my word that I'll not allow any of my crew—including myself—to harm you. You'd do best to ignore what I say to my men, for I assure you I'll not mean it." He glanced over his shoulder as deep voices came from the hold, then he turned back to her. "I'm afraid that I'll have to bind you."

* * *

The terrified woman struggled weakly as Callum found rope and loosely bound her wrists and ankles. To his horror, heat prickled over his hands and up his arms at their contact.

"*No,*" she protested.

Callum's heart twisted. "I do wish that it wasn't required, but if I bring you, unbound, to my ship, the men will be suspicious. My character must remain intact." Frustrated with his inability to explain in so short a time, and pained by the fear in her shocking green eyes, he shook himself. "My apologies, Lady Laura. I will explain in due time."

The voices of his men called him from within the hold and he turned to shout over his shoulder. "I've found a bounty, men! But this one I'll claim as my own."

He returned his gaze to Lady Laura's wide, terrified eyes, and the emotional dagger in his heart twisted yet again. "Appearances," he mumbled.

Footsteps drew near, and Callum stood, gripping Lady Laura's arm and pulling her to her feet, as well. She swayed and blinked, and Callum worried that she might faint.

"Ah." A low voice came from the stairs behind him. "Who's this, then?"

With as much of an apologetic glance as he could send Lady Laura, Callum bent and hauled the woman over his shoulder. Hell, but she was light, and far too thin, her jutting bones poking against him with every movement.

"This," Callum said, turning toward his men, "is my prize."

One man licked his lips as her ladyship's bottom pressed against the stained fabric of her thin night-rail. Callum felt ill. There would be no way for him to protect her modesty from here to his cabin. He must walk quickly, then.

"Can we 'ave a taste when yer done wiv 'er?" one man in the growing crowd of pirates asked.

Callum glared and shook his head. "You'll have as many tarts as you desire once we reach port, but this one's mine."

Lady Laura struggled and cried, and despite the painful squeeze inside him, he affected a lust-filled smirk for his men. "Hush, sweetheart."

With long, purposeful strides and painful one-armed climbing, Callum reached the sun-bleached upper deck. Lady Laura's kidnappers—with the exception of her unconscious guard—were bound and breathless on their knees, Callum's men aiming pistols or holding dirks, cutlasses, or swords to the curs' throats.

Callum's gaze travelled over the blackguards' features. He'd instructed his men not to kill them, for Callum could not abide the killing of innocents…but these men weren't innocent. They were hired kidnappers who worked for monsters and would do anything for a bit of coin.

Before he'd left England, Callum's superior—Hydra—had been sought out by the duke for his assistance in searching for Laura. Hell if they'd known why she had been taken, but Hydra had agreed to help. Callum could scarcely believe that he'd found her…but the woman's condition was dire, indeed.

In the likeness that had been posted in the papers, the duke's daughter had a pleasing oval face with neatly pinned hair and penetrating eyes framed by long, thick lashes. Lord, but to learn that those eyes were as green as leaves touched by sunlight… It was enchanting.

Now, however, her oval face was sallow, her cheeks sunken, her lips cracked with layers of dried blood surrounding them, and her hair dark and encrusted with filth. He mightn't have known it was her, but for one very distinguishing trait: an abundance of freckles. The endearing spots were most concentrated along the bridge of her nose and high along her cheeks, then faded up her forehead and down toward her full, pink lips. From the moment he'd seen her face in a shaft of lantern light, he'd resisted the inappropriate urge to run his fingertips along her skin to see if it was as smooth as it appeared.

The poor woman was gaunt, not only in her face but in her body, as well. She'd been lighter than a barn cat when he'd lifted her in his arms. Bloody hell, it appeared as though her body had been consuming itself due to lack of food. The fury that burned just below the surface of his skin threatened to break loose, but he held it at bay. He would reserve his anger for those responsible.

His men watched him expectantly, and eyed the enticing woman slung over his shoulder.

"There is no bounty below," Callum announced in a carrying voice, "but I found myself a prize. She's mine, mind, and no one else's. You can help yourselves to the stores of food, doctoring supplies, the magazine and the armoury." He eyed Lady Laura's kidnappers with distaste, fury burning hot in his gut. "Then sink the ship."

* * *

Laura's skin prickled with awareness as she felt the pirates' gaze on her, but the sun was so bright, she couldn't open her eyes to confirm it. She wanted to fight, to scream, but the pirate captain was too strong, and her voice had grown hoarse and her body so weak. So, instead, she hid her face beneath her dishevelled and matted hair and allowed the large man to carry her away.

Terror, embarrassment, and resignation warred within her. A new captor, new bindings…

He had assured her that he meant her no harm, but while Laura might wish that she could trust him, she knew better than to allow herself that hope.

The pirate captain stopped and muttered something to the man behind the ship's wheel before he descended the ladder to the next deck, moving swiftly with long strides. Laura couldn't see what deck they were on, but the heat from the sun had been replaced with a cool, comforting breeze carrying the distinct scent of gunpowder and beef stew. Her stomach growled.

A low rumble vibrated the pirate's back before he bent, depositing her on a thick green velvet coverlet that stretched along the foot of an enormous bed. Laura squinted at the bright light that shone through the wall of windows behind her, scarcely able to take in her surroundings.

Thump. Click. Laura's stomach sank to her toes as she realized that the pirate had locked them within his spacious cabin.

With her wrists still bound together, she brushed aside her mass of hair and glanced about, her eyes adjusting to the room's brightness.

There must be a way to escape. Perhaps she could break the windows and leap— She cut the thought short as she realized the futility of such a venture. She could not tread water until another ship arrived, and they were weeks away from England's shore. Hell, she could scarcely hold her head up any longer.

With determination and strength of will, she managed not to cower, but she could not meet his gaze. Instead, she turned her gaze down at her lap and the bound hands atop it.

"I sincerely apologize for that display, my lady." The scoundrel strode toward her, and she pulled away, sliding backward on his sinfully large bed. "I'll not hurt you. I mean to untie you."

Reluctantly, she stretched her trembling arms toward him. His movements were swift and his fingers nimble as he tugged deftly at the ropes binding her wrists and ankles. He tossed the ropes aside and ran a hand over his eyes, then pinched the bridge of his nose.

"I'd never thought to find you on this journey," he said. "To be sure, I'd imagined that it was possible Hydra and my fellows would find you and return you to your father. But as a matter of happenstance, in the middle of the sodding ocean, a sennight's sail, at least, from the bloody shore—" His contrite gaze flicked up to meet hers. "My apologies, Lady Laura, for my language. I've been at sea for some weeks and have grown accustomed…"

She inclined her head reflexively, as years of strict training had instilled in her. "Not at all."

The man strode to a large writing desk and pulled the armchair out from behind it, swinging it to face her, then depositing himself in it.

Something that he'd said caught in her mind. "What do you know of my father?"

Chapter 3

The pirate shrugged. "Not much, I'm afraid. He spoke to my superior shortly before my departure from England, requested our compliance with his search and any aid that we could spare. Naturally, Hydra agreed—" He paused, apparently noting her confusion. "My apologies again, Lady Laura. I'm not explaining this very well."

Laura waited for the pirate to speak. He removed his tricorn and ran a hand through his mop of brown curls. His gaze bore into her, and she had an intense urge to settle her filthy skirts over her ankles and pull her hair over her shoulders to hide the shape of her breasts.

Lord, but she felt affright. She'd been denied even the most basic of necessities for so long that her night-rail was stained brown from her last menses, her teeth felt rough against her tongue, and her hair was matted. She wished for nothing more than to return home and feel *clean* again.

"Putting voice to the truth puts us both in peril," the pirate said, "but I fear that it is the only thing that will facilitate trust between us. I also believe that my superior would do the same."

She frowned down at her loosely fisted hands, confusion and exhaustion riding her. "I'm afraid that I do not take your meaning, sir." Her stomach growled pitifully to punctuate the moment.

He sighed. "You're hungry, and you must be in want of some comforts. Please, allow me to provide them before we converse further."

Without another word, the pirate retreated to the door and mumbled to someone beyond it.

"I've requested a meal and hot water for a bath. I'm fortunate that the previous captain was such a monger for luxuries."

She toyed with the filthy material of her night-rail, unsure what to say and whether to give in to the hope threatening to inflate in her chest.

"Since becoming captain of this frigate," he continued, "I have collected articles of clothing in order to build my wardrobe. Among my acquired articles, I found several that were too small to fit me. I'd thought to give them to one of the other men, but as good fortune would have it, it slipped my mind until this moment." The captain placed a folded stack of material at the foot of the bed. "They're not made for a woman, and mightn't be terribly comfortable compared to the fine dresses to which you're accustomed, but they'll keep you warm and covered."

He withdrew once more and Laura peered through the strands of her hair to see him tapping one of the knobs on a chest of drawers. "This is the drawer I've reserved for brushes, combs, and ribbons; you're welcome to use them." He bent to retrieve an item from the bottom drawer and placed it on the surface beside the washbasin. "This will be your toothbrush, and the tooth powder is for your use, if you wish. The towels are in the middle left drawer."

She hastily returned her gaze to her lap before he could observe her.

"I'm afraid that in order to maintain appearances, I'll be unable to vacate the room while you bathe——"

A squeak of alarm and protest escaped her, and his voice softened. "There are hooks on the beams overhead; I shall create a privacy screen of sorts, using bedclothes."

* * *

More than anything at that very moment, Laura wanted to sink into another fresh, hot bath and remain there for days. The boiled sea water, murky with soap and the filth from her body, however, would have to do. It *was* a sight better than how she'd spent her time on the previous ship.

While the pirate had provided her with what he had called his "emergency rations" of cured meat and an apple, her stomach still rumbled with hunger. She was grateful, however, and content at having been fed anything other than stale, hard bread.

Moisture clung to her eyelashes, the scent of soap and salt heavy in the air. Her gaze flicked over to the makeshift privacy screen that the pirate had erected, ensuring that he still could not see her.

She wrung out her freshly untangled and washed hair and scrubbed her body with weak, trembling fingers, using the opportunity of concealment to take in the room. It was rather large and staid for a room on a ship, though she supposed she knew little of how a pirate captain's rooms ought to look.

Across from the grand bed, there were two sets of double doors leading to the deck beyond, and both were closed. Between the doors was a long cylindrical pillar, which Laura assumed was the ship's mast.

To the left of the door was an enormous table littered with a map and measuring instruments and surrounded by chairs. Before the partition had been hung, Laura had glimpsed a large, dark wood desk with papers strewn about its surface, which was positioned to the left of the bed.

The pirate's chest of drawers was adorned with washing and shaving implements. A tall wardrobe, some ropes and fabric stood to the right of the door, and to her immediate right was a door. A sideboard covered in liquor decanters, glasses, and a silver tray stood on the right side of the room.

There was an alcove set into the walls on either side of the room, and ropes and pulleys stretched along the ceiling beams. Lanterns hung from metal hooks along the perimeter of the room. The walls were panelled with wood and painted white, and the floor was chequered in black and white beneath sizeable burgundy rugs.

It was masculine, bright, and shockingly simple for a pirate.

Laura's bath had been positioned at the foot of the bed, within reach of her suit of men's clothes.

Men's clothes! How scandalous! And yet, she would wear them without compunction or complaint; anything was better than what she'd had on.

With another hesitant glance toward the makeshift privacy screen, Laura concluded her bath, dried, and dressed. The tooth-cleaning implements had been laid out, and she quickly made use of them.

Relief flooded her, and she glided her tongue over her teeth with a sigh of satisfaction. Padding on bared feet to the hanging bedclothes, Laura cleared her throat.

"Thank you, sir," she said.

"You're welcome," came his low reply.

The bedclothes moved before the man appeared from around them.

Good heavens, but his eyes were the brightest shade of blue that she'd ever seen. Her palms instantly began to perspire, and her heart thudded faster. The pirate wore a black tricorn hat over dark, curling hair that reached over the rims of his ears. He had a curly brown beard that was shadowed with red, which matched the colour of his straight, neat eyebrows. His nose was slightly bent, his cheekbones were high, and his jaw broad.

By society's standards, this pirate was not handsome. Most assuredly not. But, Lord above, he was unaccountably attractive.

Her gaze slid downward to his attire. He wore a long, midnight-blue coat that was lined with burgundy and embellished by frayed black trim, shining black buttons, and thick cuffs. Beneath, he'd foregone the use of a waistcoat and cravat, letting his greyed lawn shirt billow and drape open to expose his finely hewn neck, hair-dusted collar, and scarred chest.

Heat crept up her neck, and Laura resisted the urge to fan herself. This was a *pirate*, for pity's sake!

Over his shirt were three straps of leather: one that wrapped the width of his waist, another that hung low on his hips, and the last that ran from his shoulder across both of the others toward his hip. All three of them were decorated with elaborately carved silver medallions, and they strapped his pistols to his person. A thick, bright-red sash peered out from beneath his bottom two belts and knotted at his hip while the remainder of the crimson fabric brushed the side of his thick thigh.

Her gaze caught there, and she fought to keep her breathing even. His thighs were barely contained by his tight black breeches, which strained so valiantly she was certain they'd pop open should he crouch. His boots were dulled leather and rose up the length of his calves then folded back on themselves in a very dated fashion.

"The clothing fits." He beamed. "Splendid."

The breath fairly rushed from her lungs, and she coughed to cover the awkward moment. How could a pirate be so beautiful? It was dreadfully unfair.

"Come." He gestured for her to sit and tugged down the makeshift privacy screen. "We have much to discuss."

She retreated to the foot of his bed, waiting patiently while he dragged a chair close and sat.

"My name is Callum McInnis." To Laura's amazement, the blue of his eyes dulled to grey as he spoke. He spun the tricorn in his hands, then deposited it on the desk behind him. "And I work for the Home Office in His Majesty's Secret Service. I was tasked with commandeering this ship in order to follow and apprehend a traitor to the Crown, and return him to England where he will stand trial and hang for his misdeeds. Just before I set sail, your father approached my superior and requested that, if we found you in our dealings, we return you safely and bring the man responsible to him." He paused to lean forward, resting his elbows on his knees and clasping his hands together. "I must beg you to keep silent on this matter. On this ship, among these men, I am the captain. A pirate. They do not know my true identity, nor my true purpose, and they mustn't ever know. Can I trust you with my secret?"

Laura sat numbly, shock thudding in her ears as his words sank in. As vehemently as she wanted to distrust him, his direct grey gaze was sincere and his words held a ring of truth. He'd said awful things to his men, but he'd been kind to her in private. Theirs was a short acquaintance, but if he was who he said, then she should trust that she would be safe.

"Yes," she said, the bud of hope blossoming in her chest. "Does this mean that you will return me to my father?"

"I'm afraid that our circumstance is not so simple. Whoever hired those men to kidnap you will be furious once they learn what has transpired. It is likely that they will seek another means to punish your family. However, with the ship sunk, it is possible that we have some time before that happens."

She could feel the blood leach from her cheeks as her hope fled.

"Additionally, my assignment is urgent in nature. If my quarry reaches the Americas, I'll likely never find him. It is imperative that I continue on in search of him. On the next ship that we encounter that is bound for England, I intend to send word to my superior and your father, informing them of your safety."

"*Safety!*" she spat, her fear and anger rising. "You intend to keep me imprisoned here! The room is larger and the bed more comfortable than my previous accommodations, but I am still a captive." Her hoarse voice rose as her ire heightened. "Am I to share a bed with you, too, sir? Mayhap you would like to guard me while I use the privy, as well?"

Shock and affront lined his features. "I should say not! Why the devil would you—" His sudden scowl was thunderous, his eyes a stormy grey as he cursed under his breath. "They didn't... The men who kidnapped you, did they...?"

He cursed again and rubbed his fingers over his eyes before pinching the bridge of his nose. "I've a hammock in the corner in which to sleep. You may have the bed. And the seat of easement beyond that door shall be for your private use." He nodded toward the door in the wall to her right.

A knock sounded at his cabin door, and the captain spun around. "Damn it."

Quick as a flash, he whipped his coat off, dropping it to the floor. His fingers moved swiftly to withdraw his pistols and unfasten his belts and place them carefully across his desk. The red sash was next, finding a spot on the floor next to his coat.

Another knock came, and the captain growled. "Just a minute, confound you!"

Laura's eyes grew wide as he withdrew his shirt from his trousers while simultaneously kicking off his boots. The absurd urge to laugh with nerves bubbled inside her, but she tamped it down firmly.

In one swift movement, his shirt came up over his head. Laura's breath halted in her throat. His chest was too broad to be aristocratic. His shoulders and arms were large, and his waist narrow. He seemed impossibly strong. Dark brown hairs smattered his chest and narrowed to form a line down the centre of his abdomen, leading downward toward his navel. The small, curling hairs covered numerous scars, and she briefly wondered what had caused them. Laura's pulse sped. His muscles were defined, their sheer size likely the result of labour or pugilism, certainly nothing that one would see on the cossetted and self-important men of the *haute ton*.

His defined muscles and attractive body hair, however, were not what stood out most to Laura's eye. Indeed, it was the thick, inked rope wrapped around and around his right bicep, leading to the anchor on his inner forearm and the crossed blade and pistol tattooed on the left side of his ribcage. Lawd, but she'd known that seafaring men often garnered tattoos, but she'd never once thought that she would see any.

If Laura had been one to blush or faint, that would most certainly have been the time for her to do so, for she couldn't pull her gaze away.

The captain sped toward her. "Recline against the pillow," he whispered. She opened her mouth to object, but he cut over her. "My men must believe that I intend to ravish you. If it doesn't appear so, they'll question my character. Come now," he urged.

Too perplexed to deny him, she reclined, and the man pulled the velvet coverlet up to her chin.

With one last glance at her person, he gave a nod and strode toward the door. Laura peered over the bedclothes, and nearly choked on her tongue. Spanning the width of his back was a ship upon rolling waves, its masts billowed. It was grand in its scale and moved with his body.

Lord, but his back was just as sculpted as his front. His muscles bunched and twisted as he moved, and his rear… Her heart rate picked up speed once more. His bottom was fine, indeed, straining taut against his black breeches.

He pulled the doors wide, allowing his man and the men beyond to see his shocking state of undress.

* * *

Ensuring that his scowl was kept in place, Callum growled. "What the devil do you want? I'm *occupied*."

Harris lifted an eyebrow at him. "I've something that I wish to discuss with you, sir."

Feigning irritation, Callum cursed soundly and stepped aside, inviting him in. Several men in the gun deck snickered as Harris strode inside. Callum swiftly closed the door.

"I'm glad that you're here," Callum said quietly.

Harris' other eyebrow lifted to meet the first. "Are you, indeed?"

"Harris, meet Lady Laura Morris, daughter to the Duke of Norshire." Callum gestured toward the bed.

"Blimey!" Harris hastily removed his tricorn and held it to his chest as he approached the bed. "It's an honour to meet you, my lady."

"Lady Laura," Callum continued, stepping between Harris and the bed, "this is Harris, my first mate and my apprentice within the Secret Service."

Harris' wide eyes swung toward Callum. "You told her—"

"Of course I bloody did." Callum raked his fingers through his hair. "Did you think that she would trust me if I didn't?"

The young woman rose to a seated position, her gaze switching between the two men. His stomach knotted. He'd hoped that the heat of her bath would put some brightness to her sunken cheeks, but, in fact, with her skin clean of dirt, they appeared far paler. His anger roused again, burning deep in his belly, and he ground his teeth against it.

"It's a pleasure to meet you as well, Mr. Harris," she replied softly. There was a brief pause before she continued. "How many of you are aboard this ship?"

"Just us two," Callum answered.

Harris turned to Callum. "What are we to do?"

"We pen a missive for Hydra and the Duke of Norshire and send it with the next vessel we encounter, then continue on after our quarry, of course. Once we have him in hand, we'll return her safely."

Harris' lips bunched as he considered Callum's reply. "This complicates our assignment, to be sure, but oughtn't we bring her home directly?"

"Whoever did this will only redouble their efforts once they learn that they no longer have the control. Even if we didn't have a current assignment restricting our actions, it would be unwise to alert the enemy to her rescue."

"Ah, yes." Harris nodded, grinning. "If our men know that Lady Laura is safe, then they are able to actively work against the enemy without fear for her safety."

"Indeed." Callum clapped Harris on the back then turned his attention back to the lady herself. "You are free to roam the decks, but I must insist that once you leave this cabin, you are accompanied by Harris or by me at all times. Despite my orders, I do not for one moment trust these men with your safety."

To his relief, Lady Laura nodded.

He turned back to Harris. "At the first sign of battle, it is imperative that she be brought below. The captain's cabin is the most vulnerable spot on this frigate; cannon fire would tear right through it. Do you understand your duties?"

"Of course, sir."

"Lady Laura will sleep in the bed, and I will occupy the hammock." He eyed the woman carefully. "Unfortunately, my lady, in order to complete this ruse, we must remain within this cabin for some time before we are free to venture out."

"I have no desire to be seen at present," she said quietly.

Another stab of anger jolted through him. Those bastards had mistreated her dreadfully. "Of course."

"Yes, sir." Harris nodded, and with one last tight-lipped smile to Lady Laura, he quit the room.

Callum waited a beat before he excused himself. "I will be but a moment."

Harris awaited him just outside the door.

"Did you get him?" Callum asked in an undertone.

"Yes, sir. I found a secluded spot beneath the orlop to chain the captain."

Callum inclined his head. "Excellent. Once we've catted the anchor and the other ship is sinking, we will question him. It will also give the lass an opportunity to rest in private."

Chapter 4

Her stomach in knots from hunger and nerves and her heart beating erratically, Laura lightly fingered the ends of her loose hair. Lord above, she'd been saved by English spies! She'd not known whether to truly believe the captain when he'd first told her, but his apprentice, Harris, was so youthful and innocent that Laura felt compelled to trust him.

While she was not particularly eager to remain aboard a ship with pirates, it was certainly better than being held captive by her awful abductors. If her innocence was protected, then she—

Her thought was cut short as the consequences that she would face upon returning home hit her. Until that moment, she'd thought only about being brought home and rejoining society. *But what will happen to my reputation?* Months alone on a ship full of men? Surely that was unforgiveable in the eyes of the *haute ton*. Her father had promised that he would allow her three more seasons in which to choose a husband she cared for before he took the matter in hand and arranged a marriage for her. Would he cut that time short? Would anyone have her?

Fingers trembling, Laura placed a hand over her aching heart. She'd never before considered how truly unfair their world was, punishing women for being abducted or other matters of happenstance.

The door opened, and Laura reflexively clutched the coverlet to her breasts. The captain sauntered in before closing the door behind himself.

"My apologies, Lady Laura." He flashed his white teeth in a grin, and her pulse sped. Goodness, but even while sitting, she could feel her knees grow weak.

God blind her, the man was truly stunning. She'd never before been in the presence of a shirtless man, and this one was certainly a sight to behold.

"Your meal will be along directly." He strode toward his wardrobe and dug among the folded clothes at its rear.

Her gaze slid from his finely hewn back to his perfectly rounded bottom. She wondered what it would feel like to squeeze. Would it be soft and give beneath one's fingers like freshly baked bread, or would it be hard and unyielding?

Goodness, but that was an inappropriate thought! *Shame on you, Laura*, she chided herself. This man was doing his duty to the Crown, no matter his state of undress, and he deserved her respect. Likewise, she was a maiden and oughtn't have such impure imaginings. What was it about him that made her abandon propriety so swiftly?

Laura toyed with the fine material of her borrowed coat. Whoever he'd pilfered it from had an exceptional eye for attire. "It's wonderful. Thank you, Mr. McInnis."

The captain smiled again, and her insides wobbled. "While that is my correct title, it would be against my character to allow you to address me as such. Likewise, it would be dangerous for me to address you by your title while there is a chance that we might be overheard. I wouldn't want these men to think to take you for themselves and seek coin from your father. Best to keep your identity secret."

"Indeed." She cleared her throat.

He cringed. "I hate to force it, but the only plausible form of address that a pirate would use would be some term of endearment. I do hope that it doesn't make you ill at ease."

Laura's heart fluttered. "If it protects my identity, I am content with your choice. Shall I call you—"

"Callum," he interjected. "You may call me Callum."

"Very well, Callum." His given name felt sensuous on her lips.

The captain coughed as he strode toward his chest of drawers and withdrew a fresh shirt.

"I haven't words enough to thank you."

"You are welcome, sweetheart." He faced her with a grin.

Her stomach warbled again, and a knock sounded at the door.

"Your meal, sir," a voice called through the wood.

Laura's stomach growled.

Callum answered the door and accepted a tray, kicking the door closed as he turned back to Laura. "Cook has prepared beef stew, some hard biscuits, cheese slices…and it would appear that we've acquired some more apples from our latest haul." He placed the tray across her lap and braced her back with pillows.

Another wave of warmth spread through her chest, and she whispered her thanks.

His head dipped in a shallow bow, and he donned his clean shirt. "I'll leave you to sup."

* * *

Lady Laura's gaze burned into Callum's back as he bent over the map on his table. He'd thought to continue work on their navigation, but it was a challenge with the distraction of her eating behind him. Her soft moans and hums of appreciation as she ate were nearly enough to unman him.

Christ, but the way her green eyes had widened and heated when she'd gazed at his chest had jolted through him like lightning.

He scrubbed a hand over his face and straightened his spine. A mission was at hand, and a woman was in need of his protection. What sort of cad would lust after the woman he was guarding? *You*, his mind whispered, and he grunted.

The bell signalling the hour chimed overhead, and Lady Laura gasped.

"What in heavens?" she breathed.

A laugh escaped him, and he turned to look at her over his shoulder. "It's the ship's bell. It's housed in the belfry at the aft end of the fo'c'sle."

Her brows knit. "I'm afraid I didn't understand most of that."

He laughed again. "I would be pleased to show you about the ship on the morrow, if you're amenable."

A steady, rhythmic tune grew louder overhead as the men began to sing, stomp, and clap. Callum had the sudden urge to burst into song, as well, but he resisted.

"If this is to be my home for the coming weeks, I suppose I ought to learn the ship's layout. However, I'm unsure if I shall have the strength."

A rush of anger heated the back of his neck, and he nodded. "Of course. Take as much time as you require. I am at your disposal whenever you are ready."

Lady Laura offered him a shy smile. "Thank you, Callum."

His gut jumped at the sound of his name on her lips, but he gnashed his teeth against it and nodded. Bloody hell, it had been too long since he'd been with a woman.

* * *

"I can't tell ye nothing!" the man who'd carried out Lady Laura's kidnapping snivelled, his voice echoing off the walls of the ship's hold.

"You can't, or you won't?" Callum asked, flipping a dagger nonchalantly through his fingers.

The man's eyes shifted between Callum's and the dagger. "I-I didn't get their names, but I know tha' one's a baron and one's a marquess. They want the duke's support on a bill, or someaught."

It made no sense. If they'd taken Lady Laura to gain support on a bill, would they not have told the duke after they'd taken her? As far as Callum knew, the duke hadn't been contacted at all. Additionally, support on a bill was not reason enough to kidnap the man's daughter, let alone spend the moderate fortune that it would cost to have the woman held captive at sea. There was unquestionably more at play here.

With a nod, Callum rose and turned to Harris, who stood several paces behind him. "We shall treat the man as *his* captive was treated, and see if that loosens his tongue further."

He moved to leave, but the other captain cried out, "Don't leave me down 'ere! I can 'elp, I can—"

Callum's voice deepened menacingly. "What did you say to Lady Laura when she begged to be released?"

The man's eyes grew wide.

"What did you say to her when she cried for food or water?" Callum asked, his voice lowering another fraction.

The bastard was silent, the pleading glint in his gaze dimming to hopelessness.

"You denied her the most basic of necessities." He glared at the man. "I ought to slit your throat…"

The man cried, spittle gathering on his bottom lip.

Callum continued, "But I have need of you yet, and I wager that my superior will wish to have a word."

With that, Callum strode away. He couldn't look at the bugger for another moment without giving in to his desire to break his nose.

Chapter 5

His cabin was silent and still, and the lanterns all lit, when Callum entered. The door closed with a soft *click*, his gaze instantly finding the lightly breathing lump in his large bed.

Harris must have removed the tub of water, for it was nowhere to be seen. Lady Laura's night-rail was hung to dry on a hook beside the bed, and though it was still horribly stained, she'd done a fair job of cleaning it. He would wager that she'd never had to wash something in all her life.

Callum strode toward the bed, and his chest squeezed. The filth on her hair and skin had been washed away, leaving her face luminous, and her mass of light brown curls flowing in waves around her head. Her eyelashes were like dark fans gently resting on her freckled cheeks.

Her hands were curled beneath her chin, her muscles relaxed in sleep. Faint stains marred her fingertips, and Callum blinked. Perhaps she was a writer?

Something pulled again in his chest, and he turned away. He'd known the woman for less than one day—they had scarcely exchanged words—and yet there was a mysterious force that drew him to her. Mayhap it was a sense of duty, or a desire to protect her from further harm. Hell, he didn't know. Whatever it was, it had best remain platonic.

* * *

With a yelp of surprise, Laura awoke, sitting upright in bed. For a brief moment, she frowned in confusion at the coverlet twisted around her legs. *Where am I?*

A shouted curse echoed from across the room just as intense, rapid ringing came from above. There was another curse and a heavy *thump* as a man fumbled and fell out of a hammock.

The captain… Callum, she reminded herself. Memories of the day before instantly flooded back.

The ship rolled sideways, and Laura gripped the bed to remain upright.

"What is happening?" she asked.

Callum stood unsteadily, and hastily drew on a clean shirt. "The bell not only announces the hour, but it is also used as a signal during fog, before battle, and to alert the crew in a storm."

"Storm?" she squeaked.

He tucked his shirt into his black breeches. "Stay here. Hold fast to the bed."

A flash of light and *crack* of thunder filled the room. Laura jumped, her pulse racing. What if they capsized? Would lightning strike the masts and cause a fire?

Callum appeared at her side, his hand gently gripping her shoulder. "We shall be fine. I'll be at the helm, and my men know what to do. Remain abed and think of something to distract yourself."

Just as quickly as he'd appeared, he was gone. His voice boomed through the closed door as he shouted orders at his men.

The lanterns in the cabin were all extinguished, leaving the windows behind her the only source of light. Distract herself, he'd said.

The two thick ropes, on either side of the wide post between the sets of doors, creaked and moved up and down. She fell sideways on the bed as the ship rocked. Waves splashed the windows and more shouting came from overhead. Her stomach twisted.

"A distraction." She tapped her chin with a trembling finger.

Her gaze darted about the room, searching for anything that would be diverting, and her attention caught on a book beneath Callum's hammock. Had he been reading when the storm hit? Or had he read last eve to put himself to sleep?

Curiosity drove her forward. She slid her trouser-clad legs over the bed and planted her feet firmly on the chequered tile floor. She took two shaky steps before she was pitched sideways and knocked to her hands and knees. Pain shot up her thighs, wrists, and forearms, and she clenched her jaw. Waves continuously rocked the ship, forcing her weight one way and then the other.

"I must be a fool," she mumbled. "It's probably a book on piracy or the ocean."

Thinking better than to walk again, Laura crawled across the room, finding it decidedly easy without her skirts.

A crashing wave rattled the windows, and more hollers erupted overhead, but she remained focused on her task. The book slid on the floor, and Laura caught it in her outstretched hand. Sitting back on her heels, she glanced at the cover.

"*The Crypt*, by Mr. Mystery," she read. A laugh escaped her, and she covered it with one hand. The pirate spy read gothic novels! Of all the titles that she might have imagined the man would read, *this* was most certainly not one of them. Had he a romantic heart, then? Or mayhap he enjoyed adventure? The latter was the most probable.

Tucking the book under one arm, she made her way back to the bed and curled herself between the bedclothes. Her heart fluttered with an odd sort of anticipation at the prospect of reading the same novel as Callum. It felt amusing, but also intimate—and decidedly naughty.

The ship rocked, and another flash of lightning and *boom* of thunder surrounded her. But she was suitably diverted.

* * *

Ocean spray splattered Callum's face as he navigated the frigate through perilous waters. His men scurried about the deck, tying ropes, dumping buckets of water, and holding on for their lives. Another splash hit him, followed by a hard gust of wind and rain. Gooseflesh spread over his sopping skin. He was soaked straight through to the bone.

In his many years on the ocean, Callum had faced similar storms, but never had he been the captain during one. He'd never had to steer his ship into the deep waves, weather every squall…or be in charge of so many men's lives.

Callum had always craved danger, and was comfortable guiding his men into battle, but the ocean had her own mind. Going against such a fickle woman was fruitless; one must move with her, accept her changes in mood and use them to best advantage. She deserved respect…reverence. No matter your station on a ship, the ocean was in charge, and she knew it.

A crack of lightning shot through the water just off the port side of their bowsprit, and Callum blinked against the blinding light. *Boom!* The thunder reverberated through his chest and spread throughout his entire body, his every hair standing on end. Several of his men cried out in alarm and covered their ears.

"Bloody hell, that was close," Callum muttered to himself.

* * *

London

"Your Grace, two gentlemen await your presence in the parlour." The butler bowed.

Michael George Morris, the Duke of Norshire, waved a hand through the air. "I will be there directly. Thank you. That will be all."

The butler bowed again and quit the study on silent feet.

Michael knew who had come to call, and he didn't particularly wish to see them. The Baron of Beresford and the Marquess of Weston had been vying for his political support for months, and Michael had no interest in backing such a bloody awful bill.

The rules of polite society dictated that he be hospitable and entertain them for the required quarter of an hour, but he'd be damned if he offered them tea. He'd *told* the duchess that they ought to remove the knocker from their door, but she insisted that someone with information about Laura's whereabouts might come calling.

As they had since the morning of Laura's disappearance, nervousness, anger, and gut-wrenching, helpless fear twisted inside him. Someone had come into his bloody home and kidnapped his daughter, for Christ's sake! It was a blow to his gut and his heart, most especially after losing his eldest, Charlotte, nearly a decade prior. Charlotte had married a man beneath her station and disappeared from the life she'd known.

And hell, but he'd searched for Charlotte—and continued to do so—to no avail. He had no leads, and…Christ, but he had no hope.

His stomach dipped, and pain fisted in his chest.

Weeks ago, he'd sought the aid of the Home Office, begging Arthur Wellesley, the Duke of Wellington, for a meeting with Sir Charles Bradley of the Secret Service. Much to Michael's relief, the men had agreed to help in his search. Weeks had passed, however, since their meeting, and Michael had once again lost hope of their finding her.

The soft *thunk* of his elbows hitting his desk echoed hollowly around him, and he dropped his face into his hands.

This was all his fault, of course. He was a powerful man with wealth and connections; surely someone would come forward soon with a list of demands.

Since he'd lost Charlotte, Michael had immersed himself in the war effort. Hell, the Secret Service was veritably funded by him. Why, their school for spies alone—

That thought gave him pause. Could someone have learned of his contributions to the war effort? He'd never made public his association with the Home Office, but he'd also not been particularly circumspect.

Christ, but that bore thinking on. Now, however, was not the time, for he had guests he must reluctantly entertain.

With a sigh, Michael pushed himself to his feet and trod toward his front parlour, where he preferred to receive callers.

Three men rose to their feet and bowed at his entrance.

"Lord Weston, Beresford, how do you do?" He nodded at the third man. "I don't believe I've had the pleasure of making your acquaintance."

"Oh, of course. My apologies, Your Grace." The Marquess of Weston gestured toward the other man. "This is Mr. Ralph Richards. He is a good friend of mine, and the owner of some of the largest cotton mills in all of England."

The man bowed, and Michael nodded in greeting. "A pleasure, I'm sure." It wasn't. Suspicion crept up Michael's spine, and he gestured for the men to be seated.

"To what do I owe the pleasure of your visit this afternoon, gentlemen?" he asked.

"Just an agreeable visit with like-minded men," Weston drawled, lazily crossing one of his legs over the other.

Beresford copied the gesture and leaned back in his seat. "I heard tell that Miss Mary White found herself a protector."

"Indeed?" Mr. Richards said, his eyebrows raised.

The men spoke briefly about actresses, and Michael's thoughts grew troubled. What would happen to Laura once they *did* manage to find her? Despite her station in society before she'd been kidnapped, she would no longer be accepted into the bosom of the *haute ton*. He could pay a man to marry her, surely, but would he be the sort of man that Michael could stomach being associated with? He was unsure. Mayhap if he found a suitable farmer or estate owner in the north somewhere, he and Laura could live out a quiet life.

The men's conversation turned to Astley's Amphitheatre and then to horseflesh and carriages. Michael merely wished for the men to take their leave. He had research to conduct and people to question about the abduction of his daughter.

Michael's ears caught on the latter part of Lord Beresford's sentence.

"…clear the little urchins from the streets."

Weston uncrossed his legs and leaned forward in his seat, his direct, icy gaze boring into Michael's. "We would be very grateful for your support, Your Grace."

"As I've said before," Michael replied, his ire lifting, "I haven't a desire to support a bill that pulls children from their families and forces them into servitude in factories and mills, where they'll earn no pay."

"The children are living lives of servitude already, Your Grace," Mr. Richards put in. "Most are orphaned and live in squalor. My mills are safe, warm, and will provide food and shelter for the lads and lasses—"

"*Safe!*" Michael spat. "More children die working in mills than from starvation. What we *should* do is work to improve conditions for these children and their families by creating shelters and orphanages, and by giving those who work a fair wage to feed and clothe their wee ones. Not make babes work until their deaths."

There was a moment of silence when Weston's steely gaze locked with Michael's, a lazy grin on his lips.

"I must say, Your Grace," Mr. Richards uttered softly, "that I was terribly disheartened to learn of your daughter's kidnapping. Have you managed to find her?"

Alarm spread painfully through Michael's chest, but he kept his face impassive.

Mr. Richards shrugged one shoulder. "I merely inquire because I, too, have a missing relation. My cousin, Colonel Kieran Richards, disappeared several weeks ago and has yet to be found. I…know people, however, who are excellent at dealing with this sort of thing. I've no doubt that he will be found soon."

Anger flared once more in Michael's chest. What connections could this man possibly have that Michael didn't? Who were these people who were able to seek out missing persons?

His spine stiff and unease screaming through his mind, Michael shook his head. "I haven't found her, I'm afraid."

All three men wore matching expressions of false pity and concern, and Michael clenched his jaw. He despised those looks, most particularly on men who clearly didn't mean it.

Unable to withstand another moment in the presence of these abhorrent men, Michael stood and gave them a solicitous smile. "I thank you gentlemen for your company, but I must excuse myself. I've a meeting with my steward."

"Of course, Your Grace. We would not wish to waylay you," Weston murmured as the three men rose.

Michael walked them to the foyer, where his butler opened the door. The bright sunlight shone in, highlighting his guests.

The men bowed and crossed the threshold, but Weston turned to face Michael once more. "I'm certain that we'll have your support eventually, Your Grace." He placed his tall hat upon his head, his thin face crinkling with his smile. "There are many reasons that a man might change his mind."

With that, the men were gone.

"Your pardon, Your Grace," his butler intoned as he closed the door. "This came for you while you were entertaining."

The butler extended a silver salver toward Michael, and he accepted the missive atop it with a muttered "Thank you." He cracked the seal and unfolded it, scanning the tightly scrawled script.

As the words passed through his mind, his blood ran cold, his skin growing damp with sweat. Sir Bradley and Lord Wellington must be informed immediately: his daughter's kidnapping had become a matter of national security.

* * *

Rupert Grave, the Marquess of Weston, rapped on the ceiling of his carriage, and it jolted into motion.

"We've waited long enough," Beresford muttered.

The carriage's wheels rattled over the cobblestoned streets of London, and Rupert gazed out the window. He'd known precisely how their interlude with the duke would transpire, and the man didn't disappoint. He obviously harboured the notion that he loved his daughters—of all the impossibly trite emotions—and Rupert would use that to his advantage.

"It is a fortunate thing, then, that our plan is in motion." He nodded. "We've under a month before parliament closes, and our bill must be voted upon. I'll not wait until next season.

"A sennight ago, I summoned Mr. Piper and Mr. McMann and had them captain our two vessels. One was filled with supplies and the other the trappings of a privateer. They'll fetch the female and aid Wycliff, and once they return, we'll perpetrate the ruse."

The baron inclined his head. "Excellent."

"They'd best not displease me," Rupert drawled, his gaze set on the man across the carriage from him. "I've had enough disappointment with the other fools that joined our cause. Not only did they either fail abysmally or die, but they were also obstinate and noncompliant. I'm absolutely certain that they knew the names of Secret Service *filth*, but they refused to give me the list. It cost us the bloody war!"

The other men frowned and murmured their agreement.

"We'll not allow that to happen again. The messenger will have delivered the missive during our discussion with the duke. Our plan is in place: he will not only support the bill, but he will also help us take down the Home Office."

Clenching his hand into a fist, Rupert hit his thigh, unrelenting determination filling his chest.

* * *

Sir Charles Bradley leapt from his horse and strode up the front steps of Grimsbury Manor, the school for Secret Service spies, his spine stiff with agitation. The front door opened as he reached the top step, and Charles tugged his gloves from his fingers.

"Any news, sir?" One of his skilled men, Colin Greene, hurried alongside Charles as he walked across the foyer.

"No," Charles grunted, crushing both of his gloves in one hand. "I take comfort in the thought that Hugh has been freed, but the absence of communication has me gravely concerned." He raked a hand through his hair. "I have yet to uncover signs of Richards' direction. Whatever path he—or whoever has him—might have taken has long since grown cold."

Greene cursed under his breath. "I'll summon Brown and question landowners."

"Thank you." Charles nodded. "Have you any news about the whereabouts of the Duke of Norshire's daughter?"

"I'm afraid not, sir. I've had the men keep an eye out for suspicious behaviour and for a woman of her likeness, but nothing yet has come of it."

"Blast."

Greene turned back into the foyer and retrieved his tall hat. Charles called after him.

"Yes, Hydra?" Greene asked, using Charles' title among the men.

Allowing his hopefulness to come through on his face, he smiled. "We'll find them. Have hope."

Chapter 6

Light shone against Laura's back and illuminated the pages of the book in her hands. She turned the next page and was part way into a paragraph when realization dawned. The shouting overhead had ceased.

Looking up from the book, she gazed around the captain's cabin. The ropes near the doors no longer slid rapidly up and down, the lanterns' rocking had slowed to a gentle sway, and only a light rain splattered the window behind her.

Heavy footfalls sounded beyond one of the doors just before it burst open. Mr. McInnis crossed the threshold and swung the door closed behind him, his body sopping wet from head to bared foot.

"Lady Laura," he muttered in greeting before shaking his head in a shiver. Rainwater sprayed from his hair and dripped from his shirt. The material clung to him like a second skin, accentuating the muscles in his chest and abdomen.

Laura's heart fluttered. "Callum," she returned.

He paused briefly in the act of removing his sodden shirt, then lifted it high and tossed it toward the door. Gooseflesh spread over his colourfully inked skin, and heat flared beneath her collar. His muscles stretched and then bunched as he moved. Faith, but could a man have any more brawn than he? Callum was no Adonis. Indeed, Adonis was soft and beautiful, but Callum… He was large, rough, and hulking.

In fact, as much as her mind and heart rebelled at the notion, he quite took her breath away.

"The storm has passed?" she asked in an attempt to dispel the tension building within her.

His pale blue eyes locked on hers as he reached for a towel. "Aye, it has. I suspect it will be the first of many on our journey." He pressed the towel to his chest, and his gaze lowered to her hands. The muscles on his arms tensed and his spine stiffened. "Where did you find that?"

Laura glanced down at his book resting in her grip. "You needn't be embarrassed, Callum. Though I confess to being surprised at first, I considered your position on this ship and realized that it rather suited you."

His chest reddened, and he sputtered.

"There's no sense in denying it," she said soothingly, doing a valiant job of withholding her mirth. "You're a man who seeks adventure and has a romantic heart."

"Oi!"

Despite her efforts, a short laugh forced its way out. The man scowled at her, and she lifted her brows in innocence.

"It is plain as day, Mr. Pirate, that you enjoy—"

"It was the only book to hand," he growled.

She laughed again, and he shook his head in frustration before taking the towel to it. Her grin grew at his agitation, and it startled her to realize that she was growing more comfortable in his presence. Certainly enough to tease him.

Laura's gaze slipped once more to his water-glistened body, to the tattoos adorning his glorious skin, and her throat went dry.

"Our cook has returned to the galley and is preparing luncheon." His voice was muffled by the towel.

* * *

The lady's breath hitched again, and Callum's cods squeezed. *Bloody hell.*

He'd only truly realized what he'd done *after* he'd removed his shirt in her presence. She was a duke's daughter, for Christ's sake; she'd likely never seen a man not fully dressed before she'd been dragged onto his ship and he'd divested in front of her. He ought to be more assiduous not to offend her sensibilities.

Now that the sodden thing was in a heap on the floor, however, it seemed absurd to don it once more. He'd best swiftly make himself presentable. Lady Laura might be aboard a pirate ship, but she was still a lady, and her father would expect that she be returned the same innocent lass she'd been when she was abducted.

His gaze caught hers, and she smiled reservedly. Damn, but her green eyes were as bright as sunlight on a meadow.

"You might wish for…" Her voice trailed away as her gaze dipped to his chest.

Fire ignited in his gut, and he silently cursed. He'd best check his emotions swiftly, for his body's reactions to her presence and attentions were far beyond alarming.

She visibly shook herself. "For a modicum of privacy," she continued. "I'll turn away while you dress."

With another glance at his chest, she turned her back to him.

Heat crawled up his spine, and he gnashed his teeth. He needed something to distract himself, for he was perilously close to beginning a torrid fantasy in his mind.

Callum cleared his throat and glanced out the windows. The storm seemed to have passed, the skies clearing until not even a light rain remained. He withdrew a set of clothes from his drawers. "Do you feel well enough to go for a tour of the decks?"

"I do, yes," she said, her voice barely above a whisper.

Making quick work of donning a clean, dry set of clothes and covering that with his belts, sash, long coat, boots, and hat, Callum led Lady Laura from the cabin, ensuring that the letter he'd written lay securely in his inner coat pocket—one never knew when it would be required.

Men darted around the gun deck, all performing various tasks, such as confirming that their gunpowder remained dry and the shot hadn't shifted overmuch during the storm. Air, heavy with the scent of seawater, sweat, gunpowder, and a faint hint of their food being prepared in the galley, filled Callum's lungs.

The men cast curious or longing glances their way, and both in a gesture of protection and a beastly desire to place a claim on the woman, Callum put an arm around her waist and pulled her close to his side.

Lady Laura gasped, and he pressed his lips to her ear. "These men must believe that you are mine, sweetheart, or they'll attempt to claim you for their own."

"Of course," she murmured back, forcing a smile and glancing warily at the men around them.

"As you can see," he said in a carrying voice, "this is our armament. Many of our long guns have been replaced with lighter and more accurate carronades. Our galley is just there." He nodded toward a section of tiled flooring topped with two large ovens, stoves, and a grate for roasting.

Lady Laura hummed and nodded, though Callum could not ascertain if it was feigned or genuine interest.

"Come, there is more to see." He guided her across the gun deck.

* * *

A tingle of awareness skittered down Laura's spine, and gooseflesh spread over her skin. Callum's tight grip around her waist was far too deliciously distracting.

She attempted to focus on her surroundings as they descended a ladder to the deck below. There were fewer men milling about, but Callum returned his arm to her waist once he had stepped from the last rung of the ladder.

"This is the mess deck," he announced.

Along both walls of the ship were tables and benches, and at the end of each were barrels of water, and others with lids. Hanging above the tables were ropes, small canvas sacks, and swinging lanterns. It was darker than the deck above, but the lanterns lent a warm, yellow glow to the space.

"This space was originally designed to feed the sailors on a warship, and down at the end"—he notched his chin toward a closed-off section of the deck—"is the wardroom, where the officers of the warship would mess. Right now, Harris sleeps and dines there, as well as several other men whom I've deemed worthy."

Through an opened door at the end, Laura could see a long dining table and walls of doors that presumably led to the officers' sleeping quarters. "Why are there no officers aboard? How did pirates acquire this ship?"

His eyes glinted deep blue and a smirk tugged at his finely shaped lips. "That's a studious question, indeed." He ambled along the deck, leading her along with him. "We sailed another ship prior to this one. It was slower, and in dire need of repair. The captain who preceded me was cruel, greedy, and foolish; he didn't see to his men's needs, and he didn't have a great knowledge of the sea. After I'd taken the role of captain, I saw to it that we acquired this ship."

"And *how* did you…?"

His grin deepened. "The Royal Navy happened upon us before we could fully prepare, and they fired, taking down first our mizzenmast, and then our main mast. They outnumbered our men and outgunned our ship. But I had a plan. We boarded their ship and forced their men out."

She gaped at him before she caught herself. "Where did they go?"

"I saw another ship approaching—which often occurs when cannon fire is heard, as naval ships usually travel with other naval ships—and I knew that the other crew would be safe. So, I had them take our broken vessel, and we sailed away before the approaching ship could reach us."

Laura pursed her lips and shook her head in admiration. "A fine idea."

His eyes crinkled in the corners, and his right cheek dimpled—how had she not noticed that before? It was painfully endearing. He seemed warmed by her praise.

Breaking his stride, he gestured toward the tables about the mess deck. "The men sleep here, as well. They hook their hammocks above the tables." He cleared his throat between rushed sentences. "This deck is below the waterline, so there are no ports, unlike on some larger ships. It makes the space a mite dim, but we keep it lit with lanterns, as you can see."

They neared the officers' wardroom, and Laura peeked inside. It was devoid of any character, but seemed a serviceable place for the men to dine.

"This is the aft end of the mess deck." He stopped at the top of an inclined ladder. "And this is the access to the orlop deck. Beyond that is the hold. You're welcome to see it, if you like. It is not unlike the ship that you were on previously, with barrels and casks of beer, salted meat, and other stores. There is a bread room and a cheese room, a sail room, and the carpenter's and boatswain's stores. If it interests you, the ship's doctor, the magazine, and the armoury are below, as well as—"

"No, thank you." The mere mention of a sail room made her ill at ease, for she was fairly certain that was the place in which she'd been stored on her abductor's ship. Her knees weakened, and all of the sudden, the air felt too thin. "Perhaps some air?"

* * *

The green pallor of Laura's skin was enough to alarm Callum. She'd only just been rescued; perhaps she was not yet ready for more.

Mayhap she would feel better returning to his cabin, but he would not question her request.

He ushered her through the ship to the quarterdeck, where she took a deep breath of fresh sea air. Lord above, the woman looked exceedingly fetching in a pair of trousers, a cream lawn shirt, and a waistcoat that fit far too snugly for his comfort.

After-storm sunlight shone between the clouds, warming him through his coat. Lady Laura turned her chin up to the sun, and Callum's breath lodged in his throat. The sun's rays caught in her long, flowing hair, highlighting it with bright red streaks. Belowdecks, her hair had appeared brown, or perhaps dark blonde, but, bloody hell, it was a spectacular shade of auburn.

Low, murmuring voices reached his ears, and he quickly pulled the woman to his side, arching a sideways glance at his men. They returned to their tasks, and Callum led Laura to the ship's stern.

"The upper deck consists of two sections, the quarterdeck at the stern through the middle of the deck, and the forecastle—or, as it is commonly termed, the fo'c'sle.

"There are three square-rigged masts on this frigate. This one," he said, gesturing toward the one at the rear, "is the mizzenmast. The middle is the main, and the front is the fore. The sails are hung from the horizontal yards, which are permanently affixed to the masts."

She turned her gaze upward and gasped. "There are so many young men up there!"

Callum nodded. "Topmen are the most prized sailors on a ship. They require strength, agility, and intelligence. One mislaid line, even the most minute misalignment, could cost a battle. There must be at least two dozen on each watch. Most are younger than five-and-twenty, and many were born at sea."

The lady eyed him thoughtfully. "You know a great deal about life aboard a ship, Pirate. It makes one wonder."

There was no sense in denying it. She was a high-born daughter of a duke, and he was the result of his father's whoring while at sea. Hell, he didn't even know which member of the crew had been his true father, but the captain had claimed him and dropped his mother off at the next port once he was weaned, per her wishes.

Callum inclined his head. "Aye, I was born at sea, sweetheart. She's my home, where I belong."

Her lips pursed in thought, and Callum had the absurd urge to kiss them. "And your parents?"

There was no sense in telling her the whole sordid tale, so he settled for, "Long since passed."

"I'm sorry."

He shook his head. "I'm not. But what of you? How was your childhood?"

"Like that of most daughters of a duke, I suppose." She lifted one shoulder in a shrug, but there was something decidedly stiff about the movement. "Strict etiquette education, schooling, rules, and appearances. But beneath it all, my parents were rather lenient with me. I believe they feared that I would leave them and disappear, as my sister did."

"I believe I heard something about that." He nodded. "What happened?"

She swallowed, the small action betraying a deep emotion that Callum was curious to know more about. "Charlotte was—is—a spirited woman, dedicated to following her heart and doing what she believes is best. She fell in love with a man of whom Papa had disapproved, and she eloped, leaving naught behind but a brusque letter for me, and one for our parents. She was certain that she knew what she was about, but after she'd left, Mama and Papa were devastated. Charlotte misunderstood their caution for disapproval, and cut herself from our lives. Our parents have been searching for her ever since." The more she spoke, the sharper her voice became.

"How awful," he said softly. "You must miss her."

She laughed humourlessly. "There's not a moment that I *don't* miss her. She was not only my sister, but my friend, as well." Her lips slid between her teeth, and she worried the soft flesh as though she were stopping herself from speaking further.

"How long has it been?"

Her mouth twisted to the side as she thought. Callum thought it profoundly appealing.

"Nearly ten years," she said with a note of finality.

Callum opened his mouth to change the subject as his gaze slid over her shoulder, catching on Harris whispering something to one of the gunners.

"Oh whisky is the life of a man…" one of the men scrubbing the deck began to sing. "Always was since the world began."

"Whisky-o, Johnny-o," Callum and the others sang in reply. "Rise her up from down below, whisky, whisky, whisky-o. Up aloft this yard must go, John rise her up from down below."

Laura gasped, a smile on her lips as she looked around at all of the men.

Their voices rang out, veritably vibrating through the air.

"Oh whisky is the life of a man, whisky from an old tin can. Whisky-o, Johnny-o. Rise her up from down below, whisky, whisky, whisky-o. Up aloft this yard must go, John rise her up from down below."

Her grin broadened, and Callum felt a surge of pride and excitement that he could share this side of sailing with Laura.

"Now whisky made me pawn me clothes, and whisky gave me a broken nose…"

A laugh bubbled up out of Laura, and it hit Callum directly in the chest.

"Whisky-o, Johnny-o, rise her up from down below, whisky, whisky, whisky-o. Up aloft this yard must go, John rise her up from down below."

A shrill whistle came from overhead, and Callum's body went instantly alert, his gaze darting to the fore fighting top.

"Ho! To the port side!" the man yelled, pointing to the left of the ship.

His heart racing, Callum dashed to the bulwark and unhooked his spyglass from the belt at his waist. He peered through the metal eye, searching, until he spotted it. Rather closer than he'd expected, and coming directly toward them.

Chapter 7

Men tromped along the deck, running past Laura and pulling on ropes. She covered her ears with her hands as one man rang a bell that was not five feet from where she stood.

More sails were raised, and billowed with the wind, propelling them swifter along the water.

Callum crowed, his voice carrying. "Run out the guns, men! Fly the Jolly Roger!"

Some men disappeared down the ladder while others manned the cannons along the upper deck.

"You'd best get to safety, sweetheart." Callum appeared at her side, putting a hand to her upper arm. "Belowdecks with you." Then he was gone, shouting more orders to his men.

Heat travelled up her arm at his touch, but just as quickly as it had come, the warmth was gone. Mayhap she would ruminate on her odd stirring of feelings later, but at the moment her mind was suitably occupied.

It would be wise to do as Callum had bid, but something—fear? curiosity? *madness?*—kept her feet rooted in place.

Men moved with purpose across the deck, nary missing a beat as the other ship approached at a shocking pace. Laura's eyes widened and her heart hiccoughed. Would the other ship collide with them? Just as the thought came, the other ship turned, and fired. The resounding *boom* vibrated through Laura's chest. Her breath froze with a squeak and her heart nigh stopped as the ball sailed through the air and landed in the water beside them.

Callum crowed again, *"Fire!"*

Laura clapped her hands over her ears as cannon fire exploded around her. A ball whirled past, and she crouched instinctively. Their wooden railing splintered, and the men's shouting grew louder.

They drew alongside the other ship, and some of the pirates carried a large plank of wood to the railing, heaving it over to connect the two ships. Almost instantly, the plank grew crowded with men from both sides. Their swords slashed and clanged, their pistols fired, and men fell to the water below.

Her ears were filled with the cacophony of noise, and yet she remained rooted in place. Until once voice broke through to her.

"They 'ave a woman on deck!"

Other men called out their excitement, and the mass of men swelled in her direction. Evidently, her suit of men's clothing and her thin frame did not disguise her.

"*Get below, sweetheart!*" Callum's hoarse bellow sounded over the noise, his voice heavy with concern.

Fear prickled up her spine at the zeal and bloodlust on the invaders' faces. Surely a woman at sea was not so strange a thing? She was unwilling to find out.

Despite the obvious imminent danger, Laura wanted to help; the desire to seize some unknown opportunity was burning within her, though she knew not what to do. She couldn't hide away during the battle.

Her heart thundered in her ears and her fingers shook with fear, but these pirates had saved her. *Callum the English spy* had saved her, and she wanted to repay him somehow. What could she do?

* * *

Callum threw himself into the fray, ordering his men to capture instead of kill. Their opponents were privateers sanctioned by His Royal Highness, and did not deserve to be killed. But then they'd spotted Lady Laura.

No. No, of course they did not deserve to be killed, even if they desired a…well, a very desirable woman.

Despite his fervour for battle, horror swelled in his chest as the men pushed toward Laura. How would she defend herself? What could she do? Callum was too far away to come to her defence, and even should he attempt to rush to her side, there were at least two hundred men and the gap between the ships separating them.

Callum's cutlass clashed against his opponent's, but his movements were instinctive rather than calculated, for his attention was diverted toward his charge. More shouts rose up among the men around Laura, and Callum's chest tightened.

To his surprise, however, his men came to her aid, fighting the privateers back. A smile tugged at Callum's lips as ease settled over him. His men would secure the upper hand in the battle, and Callum would find a way to teach Laura some basics in fighting in the event that she was ever caught amid a battle again.

Meanwhile, Callum had a mission.

He spotted their opponents' captain shouting orders from the quarterdeck, and Callum ran toward him. The other captain's face glistened with sweat and had turned purple with the force of his shouting. He must have realized, surely, that their battle was lost. Callum's pirates were skilled and had already begun tying the wrists of the other men.

The privateer captain's eyes widened as he saw Callum approach, his hands fumbling for one of the pistols tucked into his belt. Before the man could aim, Callum was at his side. He gripped the man's wrists, holding them down lest the man shoot him, after all.

"I mean you no harm, Captain...." Callum hurried to assure the man in an undertone.

The captain scoffed his disbelief. "Captain Taylor. But your men—"

"My men are preventing yours from doing further harm by tying their wrists. Our aim is not to kill."

"But you're pirates!" the captain exclaimed in disbelief.

Callum nodded. "A different sort of pirate." He continued in a whisper, "Sir, I work with the Home Office."

The man's eyes widened yet further, before narrowing in suspicion.

"You mightn't believe me," Callum continued. "But I need your help."

Callum released one of Captain Taylor's wrists, reached into his inner coat pocket, and withdrew the coded letter he'd penned. Men shouted and ran about them, brandishing their weapons. Callum was grateful for the chaos, for he couldn't risk anyone overhearing his discussion.

"But—" The captain accepted the letter from Callum. "This is addressed to Lord Liverpool!"

"Indeed it is." Callum glanced over his shoulder and stepped out of the way of a fighting duo before returning his attention to the captain. "I've directed him to replenish your stores and to pass along a message to my superior. It is of *vital* importance that this letter reach England as soon as may be. I will have my men leave you and your crew enough supplies to last through the journey."

"Well, o-of course, b-but—" the man stuttered.

"Thank you, Captain Taylor," Callum cut over him. "Your country appreciates your service." With that, Callum spun on his heel and returned to the skirmish.

* * *

Laura had lost sight of Callum through the fray some time ago. Men had swarmed her, but to her surprise, Callum's pirates had come to her defence. Mayhap they feared their captain's wrath should anything happen to his "prize," but it had still come as a shock.

Callum's voice boomed from the other ship, and a small sense of relief washed over her. At the very least, the man was still alive.

Many of the opponents now sat bound, though most of the crew had moved their fighting to the other ship. There were, however, still some men clanging their swords around Laura. She leapt aside to let some men pass, then darted toward the ladder. It was within her grasp, when a roar of pain drew her attention. She spun around and saw two men leaning over the railing, one in a defensive stance and the other leaning over him.

The man in a defensive stance pushed his sword against his opponent's, knocking the man back into a hanging lantern. They continued to fight, moving toward the middle of the ship. But Laura's gaze remained on the fallen lantern.

It was as though time itself had slowed to a crawl. No one else appeared to have noticed the fire spreading across the deck, the flames lapping at the smooth wood. Without considering her actions, Laura ran forward. There were buckets of seawater beside each cannon, so she lifted one as she ran—scarcely noticing its weight— and heaved the water onto the fire.

The flames crackled and hissed, but the fire continued to spread.

With her pulse thudding at her temples and in her ears, Laura ran for another bucket, and then another, dousing the flames with each hefty *splash*.

Men shouted and ran behind her, but her focus remained dedicated to putting out the fire. This ship was her home for the moment, and she would not let it burn.

Lifting another bucket, she hurried back to the fire, and heaved. There was another splash of water beside her, and she turned to see young Harris, beads of sweat running down his forehead.

"Thank you, mil—miss," he said, quickly correcting himself. He turned to the men arriving behind him. "Refill the buckets!"

While Laura appreciated his efforts, she hadn't a moment to thank him; she simply nodded with a quirk of her lips and dashed to retrieve another bucket. Soon, more men were refilling buckets and fighting the fire.

Swiping at the beads of perspiration that had formed on her temples with the sleeve of her lawn shirt, Laura heaved one last bucket of water on the charred surface of the deck. Her lungs burned and her body ached. But the fire was out.

A sense of pride at the accomplishment washed over her, and a fatigued smile pulled at her lips.

"Thank you again, miss," Harris said at her elbow.

Laura nodded. "You as well."

Harris' gaze lifted to a spot just over her head, and she turned, following his gaze. Callum raced across the wood plank between the two ships, his gaze darkly intent…on her. *Oh, dear.* Was he angry with her for not going below as he'd said?

He wove his way through his men, not slowing even as he reached her. In one fluid motion, he curled his palm around the base of her head, wrapped his other arm about her waist, pulled her flush against his body, and pressed his lips to her ear.

"My apologies, sweetheart, for what I must do," he whispered, so softly that she almost didn't hear him.

Before she could register his words, his lips came down on hers.

Chapter 8

Bloody hell. When he'd leaned in for the kiss, he'd only intended to show his appreciation for the woman as a pirate might: a show of desire for the benefit of keeping his identity safe in front of these men. But—*Christ*—the moment his lips had touched hers, all rational thought fled his mind.

Lady Laura's lips parted beneath his, and elation stole through him as he deepened the kiss. She sighed, her sweet breath tickling his cheek while she tentatively touched his tongue with hers. His cods tautened and his cock lengthened. Reflexively, his arms tightened around her, and in response, her hands palmed his shoulders before settling in his hair.

He was in dangerous territory with the woman, and, somewhere in the back of his mind, he knew it. But at the moment, he didn't care. The woman was in his arms, her tongue entangled with his and her delicate fists gently tugging his hair.

His heart pounded against his ribs, his gut tightened with desire. Hell, his palms had even begun to sweat. He wanted—

A throat cleared behind him, and he pulled his lips away from Laura's. Her mouth was rouged and her eyes glazed, and more than anything, he wanted to kiss her again.

Only after ending their kiss, however, did Callum notice the low murmur from his men around them.

Damn.

Keeping the woman pressed to his front in an effort to hide his slowly fading passion, he turned his head and addressed his men. "Our opponents have surrendered!" he shouted.

The men cheered, lifting their cutlasses in the air.

"Take what you will from their ship," Callum continued loudly, "but leave them enough stores to return to England! When we meet again, we will once more be able to replenish our hold." He paused. "When that task is concluded, this deck must be repaired."

Finally presentable, he released Lady Laura and retreated a step, his gaze meeting hers. Sunlight caught the red in her hair and brightened the green in her eyes. Freckles danced along the bridge of her straight, narrow nose and high along her cheeks, spreading up her forehead and down to her chin. He wanted to touch them, to trail his lips over each one.

His men dispersed and did as they were told, though Harris lifted a warning brow at him before departing.

Guilt hit Callum hard in the gut. Their kiss had become far more than he'd intended. He ought to apologize…but when he opened his mouth, the words didn't come.

I'm not sorry, he realized. Indeed, his words wouldn't come because that kiss was something to be treasured, not bemoaned. Treasured, of course, because it mustn't happen again. She was under his protection, and he couldn't betray her—or her father's—trust by pressing his advantage.

It was likely that she would not desire another kiss from him, anyway. Once she had time to ruminate over the consequences of such a performance, she would regret her choice—nay, *instinct*—to respond favourably. He'd best distance himself from her intimately, for Lord knew if his role required another kiss, he would want nothing less than a lifetime from the woman.

* * *

Refreshing ocean wind blew through Mr. Cecil Piper's thinning brown hair as he stood on his borrowed warship's forecastle. He followed Mr. McMann's ship to their coordinates, which they were approaching directly.

This kidnapping could—*would*—change the course of history. England's defences would be taken down from the inside. The irony was delicious: one of the very men responsible for funding the Home Office would have a large hand in killing it.

Lifting his spyglass to his eye once more, Cecil squinted. He still did not see their quarry on the horizon, which was meant to hold the woman, Lady Laura Morris. Hooking his spyglass back into his belt, Cecil leaned his hands on the bulwark.

Ahead of him, McMann's ship dropped anchor and began to slow.

Cecil's heart thumped hard, and he spun to yell at the small crew, "Close the sails and drop the anchor!"

The men scrambled to do as he asked, and they soon slowed to a gentle glide. A row boat was lowered from McMann's ship with several men aboard, and it travelled the distance between the two ships. Something must be wrong.

Before long, Mr. McMann appeared over the bulwark, his brows lowered in a scowl. Cecil approached, worry tingling the back of his neck.

"The anchor won't reach the ocean's floor at this—" the man began.

"I don't give a damn," Cecil interrupted him. "This is where they're meant to be. Even if they'd floated off course, we ought to be able to spot them through the spyglass."

"They're gone," McMann announced as he strode forward.

"*Gone?*" Cecil repeated. "Bit tricky to just disappear, eh wot?" He laughed at his own joke. "Where do you suppose they went?"

The man's jaw tightened. "Not gone." He notched his chin out toward a piece of wood floating off the starboard side of the ship. "Sunk."

* * *

Leicester

Sir Charles Bradley lightly squeezed his wife's hand between his elbow and ribs, smiling down at her stunning face. For the sake of modesty, he refrained from putting a hand to her beautifully rounded belly, no matter how much he'd come to adore feeling their baby's movements. He was a fortunate man, indeed, to have such a woman as Bridget at his side. He glanced about the grand parlour at Grimsbury Manor and, their current concerns notwithstanding, another burst of pride rippled through him.

To his utter amazement, Hugh—their missing comrade—had been returned to them, though not without new missions, anxiety, and a great deal of heartache. Remarkably, he'd been found by the Duke of Norshire's long-missing daughter, Lady Charlotte. The duke's relief and joy showed in the brightness of his smile, the flush of his skin, and the lightness of his movement. His eyes, however, were dark with concern for Lady Laura. And rightfully so.

Charles had received word from the duke about the urgency of Lady Laura's abduction. It was troubling, indeed. The past weeks had been tumultuous with activity, but in that moment, at Hugh's wedding breakfast, when there hadn't been any leads or action for some time, the next mission felt far away. At least for the morning, they could enjoy Hugh's happiness.

A quiet midsummer rain fell beyond the brightness coming in the windows, making one feel rather content to be indoors. Hugh's new wife's sons and Charles' adopted son, Henry, played exuberantly in one corner of the room, just far enough away from their mothers to avoid being hushed, Charles imagined.

"Oh! My dear Charlotte!" Her Grace, the Duchess of Norshire, stepped before Hugh and his wife, Lady Charlotte, and pulled them both into her familial embrace. "And handsome Hugh! Oh, you've both made me so happy today. You will have a long and joyous marriage, I am absolutely certain."

"Thank you, Mama." Charlotte smiled.

A commotion arose at the entrance, and they spun toward the sound. Charles' gut dropped as his man, Brown, scanned the crowd, his mien harried and his clothes sopping. He spotted Charles.

"Hydra!" the man called as he hurried forward.

"Brown!" Charles frowned. "What in God's name has you so weary? Were you not in London?"

"I rode from town as quickly as I could." Brown huffed an exhausted breath. "I have news from Callum and Harris. They sent word on a ship bound for London that they encountered—"

"I don't care how the letter came to us, Brown. What did it *say*?" Charles' chest weighted with worry.

The young man's gaze shifted, discomfited, at the guests around them, then returned to Charles. "They've found the Duke of Norshire's daughter, Lady Laura Morris."

Behind him, the duchess gasped and the duke cursed, coming forward. "Someone has found my daughter?"

Brown sketched a discomfited bow, beads of sweat forming on his brow to mingle with rainwater. "Aye, Your Grace."

"Perhaps we'd best discuss this in a more private setting," Charles offered.

The duke's lips thinned as he nodded. Charles knew the man had been searching for Lady Laura since the night she'd been abducted, and clearly he was desirous to learn all he could of her condition. But questioning a sopping man in front of the attending guests was not ideal.

"Please, follow me." Charles led the group to the private offices in the school for spies, well away from any guests.

The suddenly pallid Duke and Duchess of Norshire sat on the edge of a chaise, Lady Charlotte and Hugh sat on identical armchairs on either side of a small, round table, and Brown stood near the cold hearth. Charles paced the length of the green-and-blue brocade rug before halting in the centre of the room.

With his gut knotted, Charles breathed deeply of the scent of leather, books, and old cigars in an attempt to calm his nerves. "Do you have the letter with you, Brown?"

The young man grimaced. "I do, sir, but the rain…" He withdrew a water-damaged note from his inner coat pocket and handed it to Charles. "It was coded, and addressed to Lord Liverpool. His lordship read it and brought it to our house in town. The moment I had it decoded, I rode directly for Grimsbury Manor."

Charles placed the letter on the desk nearest the large windows, laying it to dry.

"Please." The duke leaned forward in his seat. "Where is my daughter?"

Brown ran a hand through his wet hair. "Lady Laura is on board a pirate ship, under the protection of our men, Callum and Harris."

"*Pirates!*" the duchess breathed.

"The men came across her abductor's ship floating a two weeks' distance from London's shore," Brown continued. "They brought Lady Laura on board, along with the captain, and sank the ship. Currently, they are bound for the Americas, sailing after their quarry, Sir—"

"The Americas!" the duke burst out. "Will they not bring her home?"

Charles shook his head. "While bringing Lady Laura home is a priority, our men are on assignment, Your Grace. They must retrieve a traitor to the Crown before he reaches land, and return him to London to stand trial. They will keep her safe, I assure you."

"How can she be safe when she is aboard a ship full of pirates?" The duke's neck reddened.

The duchess put a hand to her chest. "They might be able to keep her protected from now on, but what of her treatment on her abductor's ship? Did the letter mention her state of health when they found her?"

Brown shook his head. "I'm afraid not, Your Grace; merely that she was now safe aboard their frigate."

The Duke and Duchess of Norshire shared a pained glance, and Charles' heart squeezed. He'd experienced similar anguish when his sister had been abducted all those months ago, and didn't wish that feeling on anyone.

"Did Callum tell us the name of the persons responsible for Lady Laura's abduction?" Charles asked, burning to know if these men were somehow linked to traitorous wartime activity. After what had transpired over the past month, they had some notion of the number of men that they were facing, but not their identities.

"According to the captain that executed Lady Laura's abduction, his superiors are a baron and a marquess that have been vying for the duke's support on a bill. He said—"

"Beresford and Weston," the duke breathed. "Those bastards have been welcomed into my home, and *they're* responsible for my daughter's kidnapping?" His voice rose with ire as he spoke.

Charles could feel the rage radiating from the duke, and he sympathized with the man. "There is a high probability that these men are already aware of her rescue and are sailing after them." He nodded to Hugh and Lady Charlotte. "We will conclude this wedding breakfast with civility and congeniality, and on the morrow, our men begin preparations to set sail."

Chapter 9

Water sloshed in the tub as Laura lifted herself out. Using her towel, she hastily dried her still-aching and bruised body before donning her men's attire once again.

Sliding a glance toward the man softly snoring in the hammock in one corner of the room, Laura's stomach gave a strange dip. He'd said that he must get some rest, as it would be a clear night and he needed to chart the stars for their navigation. Laura found it oddly intriguing.

She buttoned her waistcoat and slid her coat over her shirtsleeves, settling it comfortably into place. Men's clothes, while entirely foreign to her, were rather…*freeing*. Always burdened by society's rules, she'd never before considered what it might be like to seek any sort of freedom.

Is that what Charlotte did? A pang of hurt twinged in her chest at the thought of her sister. Charlotte hadn't just sought freedom from society—she'd all but abandoned Laura without a thought.

The Pirate's snoring snuffled to a stop, and he stretched, diverting the maudlin direction of her thoughts. He yawned and scratched at his chest, and, despite herself, Laura felt warmth spread up her neck.

With a shake of her head, she sat upon the edge of her bed and sipped at the stew that was waiting for her. It had been the same fare since the day she'd come aboard: stew, buns, and citrus fruits. It was, however, far superior to what she'd consumed while being held captive. She needed to regain her strength now, and this was food that would help.

"Good evening," Callum drawled, sauntering toward her.

Blimey. The man moved very like the predatory cats she'd seen at the Royal Menagerie at the Tower of London.

"Good evening," she replied, her throat suddenly devoid of all moisture.

He retrieved an armchair and slid it to face the foot of the bed. "I've something to discuss with you."

"Of course." Her abdomen dipped once more at his contemplative and staid mien.

He cleared his throat. "In the few short days since the fire, I've thought hard on a way to see you better protected against potential threats from men."

The reminder of the fire—and the decidedly delicious kiss that had come afterward—made heat build beneath her skin once more. She frowned. "While I agree that protection is good, I struggle to see what more I could do—"

"I have a proposition," he interjected. "I wish to instruct you in some basic combat training."

Laura blinked. "You wish for me to fight alongside you and your men while—"

"Good God, no! My apologies. I meant that I wish to teach you to defend yourself, should the need arise. I believe that it would give us both a sense of comfort, and for you, a great deal of confidence."

Confidence. She would indeed like to feel confident, to be able to stop someone should they attempt to abduct her or harm her again. With the exception of her art, she'd never excelled at feminine pursuits; mayhap *this* was where she would excel. "I would like that. Thank you."

He smiled, and her fingertips tingled. *What in heaven's—*

"Superb! Shall we begin now?"

Shaking off her odd feelings, she nodded and pushed to her feet. He did the same, setting the chair aside and rounding the tub to stand in the more open floor space facing her. Laura followed, stopping several paces away, her stomach fluttering with nerves and anticipation.

"Excellent." He beamed. "Now. One of the first things that I was taught about hand-to-hand combat was to always assume that your opponent carries a concealed weapon. Many hide blades in their sleeves, behind their back, along their thigh, in a boot, or hidden in a cane or walking stick."

"Blimey."

"Indeed. There are other, more clever hiding places, but the *where* is not necessarily the primary concern. *How* to stop the blighter from using it is paramount."

Laura nodded, and tucked a damp lock of hair behind one ear. "Very well. How would I stop them?"

"The best thing to do is run and seek help. If you're in a confined space, however, or otherwise unable to see a clear path to escape, there are two ways to deal with a potential attacker with a knife. Imagine that I am an attacker and I have a blade in my hand. If I keep my arm extended toward you, like so, it would be easy enough to take away the knife. You would simply grip my wrist, like so"—he used her hand to grip his wrist and nudged her with his other, urging her body to spin him away—"push into my elbow, and wrest the blade away using the trajectory of your body."

"Oh!" Surprise widened Laura's gaze. "That was rather simple. Might we try it again?"

He smiled encouragingly and held out his imaginary blade toward her. "Remember to put pressure on my elbow. The more pressure you use with your opponent, and the swifter your movement, the quicker they'll release the weapon."

With another nod of understanding, Laura gripped his wrist and followed his directed movements.

"Very good!" He stepped back into his beginning position. "If, however, I keep my blade hidden with the intent to surprise you, your aim will be to trap the hand with the blade. Grip my wrist—just so. Now, with all of your weight, force my arm toward the ground. Aha! Superb! Trap your opponent's arm, and unbalance them.

"In both scenarios, once you have your attacker unarmed or unable to use his weapon, you need to incapacitate them and render them unable to follow you when you flee. This is when you take aim at the person's eyes, throat, groin, knees, or feet. Anywhere that you can inflict the most damage, really." He demonstrated some jabs, kicks, and gouges with his fingers, which she repeated. "Excellent! There would be naught left but to run and seek help."

Laura gave a breathy laugh. "I believe that I like this!"

The Pirate grinned back at her, his blue eyes crinkling in the corners and making her knees weak. *Curses.*

"Now, if you are being threatened with a pistol or blunderbuss, the protocol is different. If your opponent is standing at a distance, your best option is to seek shelter. If you are out of the person's line of sight, they won't waste their shot. If, however, you are being threatened within arm's reach, you must grab the barrel with the opposite hand that your opponent is using while simultaneously sliding out of range and hitting the person's wrist. Allow me to demonstrate. Hold your arm out. Just so."

In a quick succession of movements, he had divested her of the imaginary pistol.

"Your turn," he urged.

She copied his actions, and while she hadn't moved as smoothly as he and her muscles had begun to tire, the broad smile on his lips made warmth and pride swell in her chest.

"When you have recovered more fully, we will practise further. There are many techniques that I would be glad to teach you."

"Thank you, Callum." She was pleased by his words, but one worry still remained. "What—" She cleared her throat. "What if someone grabs me a-again?"

His eyes darkened with spots of grey, like storm clouds casting shadow across a blue sky. "I can demonstrate several holds, but if someone grabs you, do your best to press your elbow into the person's neck. If you then clasp your hands together, using your other arm to apply pressure to your opponent's neck while twisting away with your hips, you can break free. Come, let us try."

Laura stepped forward, and Callum rounded behind her, wrapping his arms about her waist. And all thoughts of potential attackers fled from her mind.

His body was pressed against her back, his *appendage* snug against her bottom, and his soft breath ruffling the hair at her temple. An involuntary gasp escaped her, and his muscles tensed.

Desire washed over her to gather low in her belly, her skin flushing beneath her clothing.

"I—" he began hoarsely. "I believe we had best continue this lesson once you have recovered further…regained some strength."

Another breathy sigh escaped her as he released her and stepped backward.

He cleared his throat. "I beg your pardon. I'd best return abovedecks to chart the stars for navigation." With that, he gathered his belts and swept from the room, leaving Laura standing alone.

The muscles in her legs grew weak, and she sat heavily on the bed.

* * *

Wind rushed past Callum's ears as he manned the helm. Naught of interest—with the exception of interactions with his markedly alluring cabin guest—had happened over the past few days: no other ships, no wrecks, no inclement weather… It gave him time to think, to *remember*.

The scent of salt water, gunpowder, and cooking stew reached him. Hell, but he'd long since grown tired of the fare while sailing. He enjoyed the battles and was diverted during inclement weather, but as much as he hated to admit it, were it not for Laura's presence aboard ship, he would have grown tired of this assignment already.

Uncertainty waged battle in his chest. He'd always wanted to be a pirate captain, to sail the sea unencumbered by rules or opinions not his own, to be free and contented. And while this assignment met most of those desires, it also brought to mind what life was actually like aboard a ship.

Before being recruited into the Secret Service, he'd only ever known the sea: the long stretches of silence, the glorious wind, the ruthless sun, and the vastness of the sea. Life had known purpose: to sail. But since he'd moved his life to land—to *London*—he had discovered so many of life's pleasures. The food was delectable, the people intriguing and remarkable, the buildings, the business, the *life*! And the friendships… He'd made many a superb friendship.

A smile tugged at the corner of his lips. What would his friends think of his confusing feelings for Lady Laura? Would they commiserate with or tease him? Would they advise him against pursuing a closer acquaintance? He wished that he could ask them.

This assignment had been a truly exemplary experience thus far, but when it was over, what he wanted…what his soul truly desired…was to go *home*. Home to his modest bachelor apartments in London, where he could live out his life as he'd come to know it as a member of the Secret Service. And where he could ask his friends their advice on what to do about his inappropriate and decidedly inopportune feelings for his charge.

Salty air sprayed up over the side of the bulwark, misting the skin of his face. Hope swelled in his chest, and he smiled.

* * *

Callum's eyes snapped open, his instincts on alert. What had awoken him? Had the bell rung? Was it—

A muffled cry came from across the room, and he sat up, the hammock swinging with his movement.

"Sweetheart?" Callum crossed the room on swift feet to where Lady Laura twitched anxiously in the bed. "Wake up, sweetheart."

The room was dark, but his eyes quickly adjusted under the faint blue glow from the moon. Lady Laura's skin was pale, her features drawn, and the bedclothes wound tightly around her.

"No," she mumbled.

Callum's gut twisted at the distress lining her face. She thrashed, and he gripped her arm.

"Laura," he said louder. "Wake up!"

She woke on a silent scream, her chest heaving and beads of perspiration scattered along her brow.

"You were having a nightmare, sweetheart," Callum said soothingly.

Her eyes gradually shifted from glazed to focused as she took him in. "Callum. My apologies for waking you."

"It's quite all right." He sat on the bed's edge and gave her a soft smile. "Would you care for a distraction?"

She nodded quickly. "Yes, please."

"Would a discussion suffice, or would you prefer to leave the cabin? I could teach you about navigating by the stars."

A thin smile crossed her lips. "I would like that."

They hastily donned coats and trousers, Callum gathered his notebook and quadrant, and they made their way to the forecastle.

"There are so few men about at night," Lady Laura noted.

Callum nodded his agreement. "The night crew is designed as such, but they are perfectly capable men."

"Of course."

He looked up, and though thin clouds stretched across the night sky, the stars were mostly unobscured. "Navigating by the stars is largely about mathematics," he said, opening his notebook to show her the pages of calculations. "We gather key information from the sky and put it into equations and tables. The best method is to use logarithms and trigonometry." He held up the triangular device with knobs and a sliding piece. "This is a quadrant. I need it to calculate the angle of a star's elevation."

Her eyes widened as he spoke. "Does it indeed? How do you use it?"

Stepping closer, he lifted the quadrant to the sky and demonstrated its use. Lady Laura's breathing quickened, firing Callum's blood, and he realized just how close they were standing.

He retreated a pace. "One might also use the Little Dipper to tell the time." He pointed to the constellation's position in the sky. "If you'll notice, the handle of the dipper points to the North Star…" he said, quickly explaining the relevance of the "guard stars" and the earth's rotation.

"I knew a girl who once spoke of reading a book on cosmography, and I confess that I thought the notion rather dull." Her gaze caught his through the moonlight, and held. "I find it rather fascinating now."

"Do you indeed?" Callum's heart gave a hard *thump*.

"Mmm," she hummed.

"You must miss it," he muttered hastily. "London, I mean. *Society*."

Her lips twisted. "No. I was never short on activities, and always invited to events. But since my sister disappeared and my parents focused their attention on looking for her, I became the young woman with the missing sister. Daughter of a duke notwithstanding, my place in society was forever changed the day my sister left."

"I'm sorry." A weight pressed heavily on Callum's chest, and he steadfastly resisted the urge to touch her.

She shrugged one shoulder. "Thank you. It is fortunate that I enjoyed my solitude."

"Indeed?" Curiosity nudged him forward.

"I don't consider myself particularly skilled, but I rather love to paint."

Callum's skin warmed at her honesty. Though he ought to have guessed it; her hands had been stained when he'd rescued her.

She covered a yawn with the back of her hand.

"Come," he urged. "I'd best see you back to your bed."

"Thank you, Callum, for teaching me. And distracting me." Without warning, she lifted on her toes and pressed a swift buss to his cheek, then departed ahead of him.

* * *

The scrape of Michael George Morris, the Duke of Norshire's fork against his plate sent a tremor down his spine.

"Lord above, husband, what a sound," his wife whinged.

"Apologies," he mumbled.

The woman sniffed and dabbed at her nose with a handkerchief. "Have the men responsible for taking our Laura been found?"

Michael shook his head. "The ships set sail at first light. Many of the men will join us on the journey to retrieve Laura and see the bastards sunk. It is not known, however, if they are the ones in charge, or if they are simply carrying out orders." He sighed. "The other men shall remain behind and search for their man, Kieran Richards—for as it happens, they suspect that the very same men responsible for Richards' abduction are also guilty of Laura's."

"*My*," the duchess breathed.

"Indeed. Both searches are a matter of national security, I'm afraid."

He looked down at the evening repast on his plate, but he couldn't eat a bite of it. His thoughts were entirely consumed with Laura. He was exultant, of course, to have Charlotte back in his life, and to have two beautiful grandsons to dote upon. But Laura... His chest squeezed.

Men were searching for her, of course, but what would happen upon her return? Would he be compelled to pay someone to wed her? Or would she be so shamed by her circumstance as to require being sent to a nunnery?

He sighed. His poor Laura. What must she be experiencing? She was a duke's daughter, for Christ's sake, and accustomed to the ease of life that that provided. She had servants, countless frocks and fripperies, and the best damned education for a woman that his money could buy. She was not meant to live on board a ship full of pirates, no matter that she was protected by a member of the Secret Service.

She was a *lady*.

Chapter 10

Anticipation bubbled through Laura's abdomen, and she rolled up her shirtsleeves, her breaths coming swiftly. "Again, if you please."

Callum walked around her, his arm at his side, hiding the stick that they'd been using to practise her knife defence skills. His hair and black shirtsleeves whipped about in the wind, and the golden rays of the sun tinted his skin with a slight rose hue.

"Get 'er, Cap'n!" one of the onlooking pirates called out.

Others shouted their agreement while several men cheered for her.

Laura's lip quirked upward. These men were not at all what she'd thought. When Callum had proposed some practice on the upper deck nearly three quarters of an hour ago, she'd balked. Her worry that the pirates would stare or say cruel or libidinous things to her was entirely unfounded. In fact, they'd been rather encouraging.

Abruptly, Callum swept forward, and Laura immediately gripped his wrist. She spun to face outward and gently connected her elbow with his throat.

He coughed and stepped back. Cheers rose up around them, and Laura curtseyed, pride blooming in her chest. This sort of activity, while exhausting, was rather exhilarating. She was very much looking forward to learning more.

"Well done, sweetheart," Callum croaked as she bent to retrieve the fallen stick.

"*Ho!*" a topman hollered, drawing every crewman's attention in the direction he pointed.

Callum withdrew his spyglass and darted for the bulwark to look out at sea. "A ship! *At the ready, men!*"

Laura rolled the small bit of wood between her hands. She wasn't frozen with fear this time, which was certainly progress. Her heart, however, still raced, and her palms grew a mite damp.

Practising with The Pirate had drained a fair amount of her energy, but she still wished to be of help. This ship was her home, too, for the moment, and she didn't wish to see it sunk. Surely there was *something* she could do.

"We need more gunpowder!" a man bellowed from across the ship.

Laura turned to watch one young man race across the deck and go below.

Men ran out the cannons and otherwise prepared themselves, and Laura knew in a moment of realization what she needed to do. She dashed to the belfry and retrieved her coat, then traversed the ladder to the gun deck and hastily deposited her coat in the captain's cabin. The bell ran overhead, signalling the pirates.

She approached one of the men running out the cannons, and called over the din. "Can I offer you help?"

The man turned to her with uncertainty in his gaze. "I donnae ken, lass," he replied in a Scottish brogue. "Ye want te help us?"

Laura nodded, her stomach fluttering with nerves but also steely with determination. *Good gracious, who am I?* She almost laughed. "Yes. Is there something that I can fetch you?"

He blinked, his fingers worrying the material of his loose shirt. "I suppose ye can, lass. We 'ave need o' shot an' gunpowder from th' magazine."

Something akin to pride wove through her, and she smiled. "I can do that!"

He dipped his head in thanks, and she was off.

* * *

Darkness surrounded her, suffocated her. She couldn't breathe. Disembodied voices sneered and mocked her through the obscurity.

Lord, but she was hungry, parched! She searched for a way out, but the darkness continued on.

Then, someone was on her, grabbing her!

"No!" she screamed. "Let go!"

"You're having a nightmare, sweetheart." Callum's soft tone reached her ears, and she stopped struggling.

A nightmare. She blinked her eyes open, and there he was, his finely hewn features bathed in moonlight.

"I'm sorry to have woken you," she said, rubbing the sleep from her eyes.

He shook his head. "It's quite all right."

Laura sat up, and he offered her a cup from which to drink. She took it and drank eagerly, not caring what was within.

"Mmm," she said. "Port."

"When I was a child," he began, "the ship's boatswain would offer me whisky when my father—the captain—wasn't looking."

Her lips tugged in a smile. "How old were you?"

"Seven. Perhaps eight." He gave a short laugh.

"When I was young, Charlotte and I once snuck into our father's study and tasted his liquors."

He huffed a breath. "And what did you think? Had you a favourite?"

"Goodness, no!" She grimaced, recalling with appalling clarity how ill she had felt that night. "They were all positively dreadful, I'm afraid. I henceforth believed my father to have very poor taste, indeed."

His smile lit his face.

"Had you any children with which to play when you were growing up?" she asked.

"Not one. Before my recruitment into the Secret Service, I'd not met a single child."

"*Oh*," she breathed, sadness for the child that he used to be aching her heart.

"I was not without my amusements, though," he hurried to assure her, sliding down to sit upon the floor, his back against the bed. "My crewmates kept me busy. They taught me to play cards, and chess, and we would sing while performing trying tasks. My father, of course, always had a need of me, teaching me to be the best crewman. He wanted me to know everything about ships and life at sea."

Laura settled back against her pillow, tucking the bedclothes beneath her chin. The Pirate Spy had experienced a childhood very different from hers. While he had been battling men at sea and training with a determined father, she had been surrounded by servants, and was desperate for her parents' attention. She admired— and envied—his father's devotion, and the closeness that he'd had with his crew.

She covered a yawn. "Would you tell me another story? Please?"

Grinning at her over his shoulder, he nodded and settled back. "During one particular storm…"

Laura closed her eyes and listened as he spoke, letting the low timbre of his voice settle over her and dance along every nerve.

* * *

Swiping at the perspiration tickling at his temples, Callum returned to his ready stance and faced Lady Laura.

"Very good. Again."

He wrapped his arms around her, and, using the manoeuvre he'd taught her, she joined her hands and used the extra force to press her elbow into his neck while twisting away with her hips. He released her, and she swung a kick to his cods—though, mercifully, she stopped short of making contact. Those crewmen that had stopped to observe applauded her efforts.

"Ach, aye, lass! Tha's th' way te bring a man doon!" one man called.

She laughed, winded, and tucked a lock of her unruly auburn hair behind her ear.

Callum nodded. "Yes. Well done, sweetheart."

Harris appeared at their side and cleared his throat. "Pardon the interruption, sir, but the bath has been drawn."

"Thank you, Harris." Callum faced the crew. "Back to work, men."

He and Lady Laura made their way to his quarters, where a steaming bath awaited his charge.

"*Oh,*" she breathed. "It looks lovely."

"Your training is coming along nicely, sweetheart," he said, hanging her privacy cloth. "And…I'm not sure if I said it before, but I must thank you for helping the men during our last battle. Harris told me what you did."

She gave him a soft smile. "You're welcome."

"Now, that particular battle was rather tame, the other ship having surrendered rather swiftly." He ducked behind the makeshift curtain and sat at his desk. "There are some battles in which cannonballs will break through the sides of the ship or men from the opposing crew will find their way on board. If that happens—"

Fabric shifted, and there was a hearty sigh as water sloshed. Callum's pulse sped, and he hastily continued. "I-if that happens, remain calm, breathe deeply, a-and——"

Another sigh, and the sound of dribbling water came from beyond the curtain. Despite himself, his cock twitched, forcing him to shift in his seat. *Hell.*

"And?" she asked.

"A-and if the battle is brought to you, it would be best if you remained out of sight. Listen for cannon fire from the opposing ship, and stay alert."

"Mmm," she hummed. "And when will you teach me more about fighting? While I haven't the intention of seeking out a fight, I take comfort in the knowledge that I could fell a person should they attempt to harm me."

"Your recovery seems to be coming along nicely, from what I can deduce. I imagine that it will not be long now before I am able to teach you more."

She hummed again, then gasped, and he imagined her tipping her head back into the bath, the curly auburn locks darkening with the water. His cock twitched again, and he cursed internally. He was in trouble, for certain.

* * *

The heavy footfalls overhead told Laura that the pirates had returned from their opponent's ship. Yet another successful battle and subsequent raid. To her amazement, their ship rarely sustained significant damage, and Callum's pirates not only won every battle, but they showed their opponents mercy and left them with their lives and enough food and supplies to take them to land.

She returned her gaze to the blank parchment that she'd smoothed out on Callum's large table before her, but her mind continued to wander.

A fortnight had passed since the fire on the upper deck—and her kiss with Callum—but the time had gone by swiftly. There was constant activity on the ship; when they weren't in battle or fighting through inclement weather, the men did repairs, cleaned and water-proofed the decks, ate, and socialized. She'd always envisioned pirates as bloodthirsty, chaos-seeking blackguards, but the men on this ship were rather more ordinary. Dedicated and honourable to their own code, though also ruthless in their desire for glory.

The light shining in from the wall of windows at her back slowly darkened, and she turned to look over her shoulder. Grey clouds had formed in the sky, blocking out the sun's light.

Mayhap there will be another storm. The thought sent shameful anticipation through her. After every storm, Callum re-entered his cabin with his shirt wet and stuck to his body, revealing the generous bulges of his muscles. She'd always turned and allowed him to make himself presentable, but the sound of him removing his sodden clothing sent wild images and memories of his glorious tattoos flowing through her mind.

It was baffling, but part of her wanted him to think of her in the same way. With each passing day, however, it grew increasingly apparent that he did not. After he'd kissed her, she'd thought that perhaps he might have romantic feelings for her, but even while spending time with her, he'd grown distant and reserved. He was perfectly cordial and gentlemanly toward her, of course; he brought her items that he'd pilfered from other ships—notably writing and reading material—he engaged in pleasant conversation, trained with her, talked to her when she had a nightmare, and went for turns about the upper deck with her when they weren't otherwise occupied. But he'd not sought another kiss.

As foolish as it was, his lack of interest in her was rather painful. When they were alone in his cabin, he focused his attention on navigation at his desk, silently poring over maps and completing equations in his notebook. She'd understood his message perfectly.

On several occasions, in an attempt to feel a boost of pride and accomplishment—that she was lacking at the moment—Laura had aided the pirates during battle. She refused to hide herself away, and instead aided the men in retrieving shot or gunpowder from the magazine or refilled water buckets while the men were fighting. While Laura felt pleased that she'd helped the men who had rescued her, and she was by no means searching for a reward, she always felt a pang of disappointment when Callum failed to give her another kiss.

With a sigh, Laura returned her blank parchment, unused pen, and inkpot to a small trunk and slid it to the floor beside the bed. There was much that she could write, but her focus was decidedly elsewhere.

Small rain droplets splattered the window next to her, and she looked out at the water beyond. The dark ocean swirled with white caps as they sailed swiftly away from the ship floating listlessly not far behind them.

The door opened behind her, and she became instantly alert. She could feel Callum's gaze on her back, but she didn't turn around, knowing what she'd see: a sinfully attractive man in a long coat and shining black boots, a waist adorned with belts, a deep red sash that held pistols to his front, and a cutlass at his hip. And one could not forget the trousers that always fit a mite too snugly to his legs and a shirt that hung open at his collar, inevitably drawing her gaze.

The worst of it was that while she greatly desired more kisses, and she wanted him to like her, she didn't know what she wanted of him beyond that. Heavens, she did not even know *why* she wanted those things. She'd kissed men before but had never felt such an overpowering urge to give pleasure in a kiss in return. Never before had she wanted to explore a man's body, to feel his skin beneath her palms.

His hard, male attractiveness and his raw power made her feel like a mouse in men's attire. It made her miss the gowns that sat in her wardrobe at home; the jewellery and her corset she did not miss, but to feel pretty and feminine in a delicate purple or sweet blue…

"Good afternoon, sweetheart," Callum said behind her, cutting through her thoughts.

Gooseflesh spread over her skin, and her stomach quivered at the affectionate term of address. At first, she'd found it delicious, but knowing it was a hollow endearment had begun to grate on her.

"And to you, Pirate," she returned, closing her eyes against the disappointment that she knew seeped into her voice.

Blast it, why did she have to feel so downtrodden? The man was a pirate and a spy. He had an assignment and must remain focused. She oughtn't feel slighted by his disinterest in her. The lesson, she knew, was that not all men would be attracted to her in the intimate sense. Perhaps he did not care for red hair or freckles.

Lord, but that was a lowering thought, as well.

"I have a gift," he said, closer than before.

Something made a hard *thunk*, and she turned. Her heart paused. The man was holding an easel, several sets of watercolours, paintbrushes, artist papers, and canvases.

Callum beamed at her. "I've brought you painting supplies!"

A hard, sudden wave of homesickness hit her in the chest, the pain heavy and almost unbearable. Before she could even attempt to hold them back, thick tears rolled down her cheeks.

* * *

Alarm twisted Callum's gut as Lady Laura's face contorted in sorrow.

He cursed and dropped the items he'd been carrying. The woman buried her face in her hands, a heart-wrenching sob rising from her chest.

Ballocks. What do I do?

Helplessness wove through him, and he swooped forward, wrapping his arms around her shoulders and pulling her against his chest. Her shoulders shook with the force of her weeping, her lungs expanded with each gasp and quivering breath, and her tears dampened the opened collar of his shirt. It made him ache to soothe her, to remove her sorrow.

"I found some fine tea for you, as well," he said, tightening his hold about her, though careful not to press her against the pistols on his other hip. "Would you care for some?"

Another shiver wracked her frame, and she shook her head against his shirtfront. "Not at the moment, thank you."

He frowned. "If the painting supplies displease you, I would be glad to store them in the hold," he offered, hoping that the suggestion might help ease her.

"Oh," she said, sniffling. "No! I love them, truly. They merely reminded me of home, and I rather—" A sob caught in her throat and she sniffled again, wiping at her tears with her hands. Then she tilted her head back to look at him, her eyes still swimming with unshed tears and her cheeks reddened with grief.

Holy sodding hell, she's breathtaking. His chest tightened, and he swallowed the feeling down.

Her bright-green eyes searched his. It made him feel exposed...*vulnerable.* His instinct was to hide his feelings of affection and desire, to look away, but he didn't. He let her look.

Laura's hair was rumpled from their embrace, the curling mass tugged from the knot that she'd put it in. A ringlet fell over one of her eyes, and he brushed it away with his fingertip, letting his touch trace the pattern of freckles along her temple and down her jaw. *So smooth.*

He'd once heard her bemoan the loss of her hair pins, but despite his constant searching while raiding ships, he'd not found any. If he could, he'd gift her everything she desired. He'd—

His heart slammed hard against his ribs, and for an instant, he thought he might lose the use of his legs, but he held fast. It was as though time stood still as the stark—and utterly alarming—realization of what he'd been doing pounded in his temples. He *wanted* Lady Laura.

Of course, he'd known that he was attracted to her, but he'd not realized how much he'd come to care for her. *This is dangerous*, his mind whispered. *She's a duke's daughter; you have no future with her.*

The shock that rippled through him must have shown on his face, for Laura's brows puckered in a frown. Callum smoothed her forehead with the pad of his thumb, then slid his palm around to cup the back of her head. He'd tried to fight his desire for her, tried to keep emotionally distant. He'd succeeded, too, for nearly a fortnight. But that fortnight had been torture. Every moment of every damned day he'd wanted to do precisely *this*. He wanted her in his arms, against his chest, wanted to kiss her, to touch her. *Christ*, but he'd wanted *her*. Their time together had been wonderful, their discussions long and engaging…but the ache in his soul could not be denied any longer.

His head swam with her alluring scent of soap and honey, filling his mind with lurid images that he determinedly forced away. Breath coming rapidly, Callum languidly lowered his lips to hers, pausing just before they connected and giving her an opportunity to object.

Lady Laura tilted her face upward to meet his, and he closed the distance between them, pressing his lips firmly to hers. Just as it had during their previous kiss, his body instantly reacted to hers. His skin tightened and tingled, and his stomach quivered with need. The woman was like a flame lighting his way home. He needed to follow her, to be with her…to see where her light might lead him.

Chapter 11

The fragrance of soap, ocean, and gunpowder filled Laura's senses. She breathed deeply, pulling the pirate closer. He tasted of minted tooth powder and lingering coffee. *More*, her body urged her. *More!*

With the tip of her tongue, she teased his. The muscles in his arms and back tensed, and a groan rumbled from his chest.

Elation burst through her. She deepened their kiss, tilting her head to allow him deeper access. He followed her lead, brushing his tongue more urgently against hers.

Her time on the ship would soon come to an end, and once she returned to England, it would be a veritable miracle if her father could pay a man to wed her. Indeed, this pirate, this *spy*, could be her one and only chance to experience any form of intimacy. Who better to give her body to than a man with whom she could fully be herself? A man she trusted?

She'd already been taking pains to feel moments of joy. And exploring this man's body would certainly make her happy.

She fisted her hands in his hair and pressed her breasts more firmly to his chest. His belts and pistols jabbed into her ribs, but she cared not. The man was back in her arms, *at last*. It was a delightful confirmation that he felt desire for her.

With another groan, Callum pulled away. Disappointment lanced through Laura as she released him and stepped backward. The remorse in his stormy blue gaze was too much to be borne. Did he *not* feel the same way, then? Did he not desire her? Would he make love to her, if given the chance?

She detested feeling as though she'd forced him into their kisses, and she could not abide the silence any longer. Humiliation be damned, she simply *must* know how he felt.

Bolstering her courage, and bracing for rejection, Laura straightened her shoulders. "Do you find me desirable, Callum?" Her voice came out far softer than she'd intended.

He blinked. "Pardon?"

Laura's stomach buzzed with nerves. For a moment, she considered retreating, feigning that she'd said something else. But she couldn't continue on wondering.

"If you kissed me out of feelings of gratitude, guilt, or pity, then please be forthright with me," she said quietly. "I find myself wanting to be in your company. And wanting t-to kiss you." She swallowed convulsively and gazed hesitantly into his eyes. "I beg you would tell me now if your attentions have been out of genuine attraction, or a…a part of your *façade*."

He cursed under his breath and rubbed a hand over his face and neck before he stepped forward to clasp her hands in his. "Of course I desire you, Laura. I…" He sighed. "I want to show you the respect that you deserve. I've no wish to sully your reputation."

A quick laugh bubbled out of her before she sobered. Her gaze wandered over his short length of beard, his bent nose, his lips, his curling hair, and his stunning eyes.

"I appreciate your concern," she began, "but my reputation was unquestionably beyond repair the moment those men took me from my home. I've been without a chaperone on two ships full of men for nearly three months. I would be very fortunate if my father could coerce and bribe a man to wed me once I've returned to England, most particularly as I'm already on the shelf at five-and-twenty." She swallowed against the nerves that rippled in her stomach.

The pirate's throat bobbed. "Your reputation, perhaps…but your virtue remains intact. I would n—"

"I wouldn't mind being sullied by you, Callum. In fact, I think I would enjoy it very much."

Her nerves revealed themselves in her rapid breathing and trembling fingers while she awaited his response.

His eyes darkened to a colour that resembled the night's sky. She could veritably hear his mind working as he considered her words.

The man was honourable in wishing to protect her, but she didn't want to feel fragile. She'd weathered far more than she'd ever imagined she could, and she liked to believe herself stronger for it. As long as her heart did not get involved, Laura could withstand anything.

His lips pursed in thought, and Laura saw an opportunity. Lifting on her toes, she surged upward and pressed her lips to his.

Each time her skin met his, it felt as though she'd rubbed her toes on a rug for too long and her hairs stood on end, igniting a little spark. He made her body tingle and shake, and she desperately wanted more of it.

He responded immediately, his mouth hungrily taking hers. Heat pulsed through her, gathering low in her belly and spreading over her thighs and through her core.

A long, low groan rolled through his chest and he dragged his lips along her jaw. "Will you permit me to give you pleasure, sweetheart?"

He pulled the lobe of her ear into his mouth and gently wiggled it between his teeth, sending a jolt of desire through to her. She gasped, her breasts feeling abruptly too confined beneath her borrowed waistcoat.

The answer was swift and emphatic. "*Yes.*"

* * *

More than anything, Callum wanted to touch her, to trail his fingers, his lips…his tongue, all over her body, to give her pleasure and hear her cry out with her peak. But no matter what he did, or what she desired, he couldn't take her innocence. Of course, there were plenty of ways for one to find climax without taking a woman's virginity.

With a smile that he was certain appeared wolfish, Callum unhurriedly removed his coat. Laura's gaze followed his movement, and anticipation rocked him. He wanted to take his time, to commit every single moment to memory: her scent, her figure…her flavour.

Next, he gently removed his pistols, spyglass, and belts and placed them upon the table. The sash, boots, stockings, and shirt swiftly followed, leaving him only in his trousers. Laura's eyes widened as she took him in. She had much the same expression that she'd had the first time she'd seen him thusly. It made his pulse thrum with need. He liked it very much.

"Now you, sweetheart," he murmured.

Her gaze met his, direct and full of want. Callum moved to touch her, but she stepped just out of his reach.

"Allow me." Her lips curved in a grin, and Callum's already rigid cock twitched.

With slow, deliberate movements, she unbuttoned the waistcoat that was snug against her generous curves, and tossed it aside. *Christ,* that left her in just an oversized shirt and trousers. Through the thin material, he could see her dusky nipples and the shadow beneath them, the dip of her waist, and the swell of her hips… He wanted to taste each of them.

She tugged the bottom of her shirt from the waist of her trousers, and slowly lifted. Callum's breath held as her skin was exposed one small portion at a time. She moved excruciatingly slow, her lips grinning and her hands trembling.

Laura paused before fully exposing her breasts, prolonging the moment. Finally, the veil of thin material was gone, up over her head and tossed to the floor, and the top half of her body was gloriously revealed.

"*Sweet Jesus,*" he breathed, his gaze sweeping hungrily over her exposed skin.

Freckles dusted her chest and shoulders, slowly fading over her breasts until they were nearly gone at her navel. He wanted to lick every one of them.

"You're beautiful, sweetheart," he growled.

Meeting her striking green gaze, Callum reached for her. Thankfully, she didn't pull away this time. He wrapped his arms around her waist, pressing her skin against his and relishing in her heat.

He bent, licking the rim of her ear before whispering, "You bewitch me." For, he realized, she well and truly did.

Unable to wait a moment more to have his hands on her, Callum lifted her in his arms and deposited her on the bed. She squealed, then laughed breathlessly, and his gut squeezed.

Callum knelt at her side, revelling in the sight of her. Long auburn waves cascaded over the pillows, her eyes bright with anticipation and heavy-lidded with lust. Her breasts were a bounty of womanly flesh, heavy and rippling with each of her movements. His cock twitched again.

He started with a kiss. Hovering over her—just close enough to feel the tips of her puckered nipples against his chest—he plundered her mouth. Laura responded instantly, her tongue moving with his, and her hands coming up to trace the muscles on his abdomen. His stomach twitched and gooseflesh spread over his skin at her touch.

Wanting more, Callum broke off their kiss to trail his lips down the side of her neck while simultaneously lowering himself to one elbow and smoothing his right palm over her hip and thigh. His body wanted more, *begged* him to take more, but he anchored his self-control. As much as he wanted to pull the trousers from her sensuous hips, release his erection, and plunge himself deep inside her slick heat, he couldn't dishonour her with such barbarism, most particularly as he'd promised to return her to her father a maiden.

He kissed her collarbone and licked at the freckles there before continuing downward.

Laura's breath hitched as he reached the sensitive nub of her nipple. He flicked it with his tongue, and she gasped. His erection throbbed, begging to be released from the confinement of his trousers. *Not now.*

He greedily sucked Laura's nipple into his mouth, and she cried out, arching her back and pressing her breast harder against his lips. A needy groan rumbled in his chest, and he squeezed his eyes shut against the waves of blinding passion crashing through him.

Needing her to feel as lust-crazed as he, Callum slid a finger beneath the waist of her trousers, rubbing her skin with his rough knuckles. The muscles on her smooth, pale stomach rippled in a quiver, and he grinned against her breast.

His hands trembled as he unbuttoned her trousers and slid his fingers inside. Despite his nervousness, he deftly found the treasure that he desired. He teased and slid past the lips that protected her pearl, gently circling it with his index finger.

"Callum," Laura breathed.

"Aye," he growled as he moved his mouth to her other breast and gently tugged her nipple between his teeth.

"*Callum!*" She arched against him, grasping his hair in her fists, the pleasure-pain sending tingles down his spine.

He swirled his finger around her pearl, then slid inside her. A low, incoherent moan escaped her, and in a helpless wave of blind passion, Callum thrust his cock against her thigh.

"So wet for me," he groaned, abandoning her breast and rising to take her lips with his.

Her body moved in agitation as she attempted to reach her peak, her hips tilting up in time with his finger's thrusts, her hands roaming his hair, shoulders, chest, and back. She wanted it just as much as he did, to come apart, to feel the burst of pleasure like a ball from a cannon: *boom*, an explosion of light. And he'd give it to her.

"Relax, sweetheart," he murmured soothingly. "Let it come."

Her bright-green gaze met his, half-lidded and glazed with need as he added another finger to her sheath. She gasped his name and went rigid. Her back arched, and her mouth dropped open on a silent cry. He could feel her tighten around his fingers with each wave of her climax, and his iron-rigid cock jerked in response.

Callum watched the pleasure on her face, the faint flush that spread over her chest and her neck, and the flutter of her dark eyelashes along her cheeks. She made something in his heart ache.

Chapter 12

Callum pressed kisses to Laura's neck and chest as he withdrew his hand from her trousers, sending gooseflesh across her skin. Her pulse began to slow, and her breathing gradually returned to normal.

When Callum had told her to "let it come," she certainly hadn't expected *that*. It had built, and she knew that she was reaching for something, but the fireworks that had danced behind her eyes and the throbbing explosion that had rocked through her body was like nothing she'd ever experienced.

Her married friends had vastly understated the sheer delight that one might experience with a lover.

One thing that she knew for certain, however, was that Callum hadn't experienced the same feeling. Her friends mightn't have sufficiently described the blissful climactic moment, but they'd certainly mentioned that a man released a white, sticky mess—his seed—when he found his completion. And she understood that there were ways for him to find that release without the use of her…er…body. She just wasn't certain *how*.

His teeth grazed the side of her neck, and a shiver went through her.

"May I touch you?" she asked.

Callum lifted up on his elbow to look down at her, a question— and stark, needy passion—shining in his blue eyes.

Instead of answering his unasked question, she removed a hand from his back and slid it down his front, relishing the hard ridges of his abdomen, until she covered the solid weight of his erection with her palm.

His throat bobbed, and a helpless groan escaped him as his eyes slid closed. "Please," he begged. "Touch me."

To her surprise, a tremble of desire rolled through her, and warmth settled in her core once again. The mere thought of touching

Callum in such an intimate way sent prickles of anticipation through her.

With nimble fingers, she unfastened the buttons of his falls, releasing his member into her hands. Her eyes widened. He was far thicker than she had thought a man could be, and his length surpassed that of her hand.

She wrapped her fingers around his girth, squeezing gently, and Callum hissed. Releasing him immediately, she muttered an apology.

"Didn't hurt," he grunted, clasping her hand in his and guiding her once more to the velvet stiffness of his erection. "Like this."

He slid her hand up and down his shaft, and she marvelled at how impossibly hard his appendage could be, how engorged with thick veins, and yet how smooth.

"Harder," he urged, releasing her hand to let her pleasure him without his guidance. "*Shite*, yes. Like that, sweetheart."

He gritted his teeth and hissed another breath as she stroked him. A responding swell of moisture gathered at her core, and she shifted her legs agitatedly.

Apparently sensing her burgeoning desire for his touch, Callum crashed his lips down on hers, and his hand slid once more inside her opened trousers. He found her sensitive cleft immediately, and began to swirl his fingers around it. Laura's breath came in quick pants as her passion instantly returned, building and building, leading her back toward that burst of fulfilment that she knew was coming.

Callum thrust into her hand while she stroked him, his movements uneven and stuttered.

He groaned into her mouth, and as his fingers swirled faster about her cleft, she did the same, gliding faster and tighter around his shaft. Her body felt hot, her skin too tight as the spring inside her was coiled. Her heart raced, and her hand pumped Callum's member.

Then, she broke. Her jaw dropped and her body trembled as another earth-shattering rupture of light erupted throughout her body, throbbing and tingling down her arms and legs.

If it were possible, Callum's erection grew harder, thicker in her hand, and a low, hoarse grunt emanated from his chest. He stiffened and lifted slightly as his member bobbed, spilling his hot seed onto her stomach until there was none left.

Spent, his breath coming in great gasps, Callum lowered himself to the bed beside her. He wrapped an arm about her ribs, pulling her close.

"Sweetheart," he whispered into her hair.

He peppered kisses into her mass of curls, then along her jaw and cheekbone.

"That was…" she breathed, unable to find words enough to describe the miraculous fulfilment and perplexing euphoria that she felt.

He nuzzled her neck. "Aye."

The bell above sounded the hour. With a groan, Callum released her and rose from the bed.

"More than anything, I wish to remain abed with you, sweetheart, but luncheon will soon be served, and it wouldn't do for us to be in this state of undress when it arrives." He held a halting hand out to her. "Just a moment. I will fetch a cloth for you."

Striding to the washbasin, he dipped a cloth in the water and returned, his trousers just barely holding on to his hips. Laura watched as his now-softened member flopped about while he walked. She nearly laughed. Never would she have imagined that a man's privates would jiggle so much when he moved. She feared that she'd not be able to see him walk about without that image popping to her mind.

He glanced down at himself, following her gaze. "I'm afraid that it's much more impressive when standing at attention."

"I rather like it like this, as well," she admitted.

He flashed a grin before wiping his seed from her abdomen. She gasped at the cold, and he murmured an apology, then aided her to her feet.

Sending her another warm, lingering glance that put a flutter in her chest, he fixed his trousers and donned his clothes. Laura followed his lead, pulling her shirt and waistcoat back on and knotting her hair at her crown.

Callum stepped forward and pressed a kiss to her forehead. "I apologize that I haven't yet been able to acquire a gown for you."

Laura lifted one shoulder and looked down at her men's attire. "This is better than my ruined night-rail. And I daresay the men's clothing is better suited to life aboard a ship. I am able to traverse the ladders, spar, and aid the men during battle without tripping over my petticoats." She smiled sheepishly at him. "They're also rather freeing, I must admit."

"Quite so." With a laugh, he fastened his last belt, returned his pistols, spyglass, and cutlass to their places, then leaned over and lightly touched his lips to hers. Laura's heart fluttered once more.

* * *

Callum couldn't seem to keep his mouth away from Lady Laura. His chest tightened every time he looked at her, and the only thing that seemed to ease it was a kiss.

Bloody hell, but that moment of intimacy with Laura had been far more satisfying than sex with any woman before her. He couldn't imagine what sort of ecstasy he might have felt if he'd found his completion inside her. Hell, the thought of it was enough to get him half-hard again.

Their interlude surpassed his expectations—nay, not just his expectations but his *hope*. Laura was extremely receptive to his attentions, her body responding naturally and exquisitely. Her instincts were very well, indeed.

"Would you explain your notes to me?" At some point in his musings, the woman had found her way to his desk.

"Of course." He strode to her side, placed a palm on his desk's surface, and pointed at the map with his other hand. "We are here, and this is where we are going." He dragged a finger across the map.

"You mentioned that you are pursuing someone."

"Yes. He set sail more than four-and-twenty hours prior to my departure with Harris from London. If we had followed the traitor directly, it's unquestionable that we would have returned him to London by now." *But I would not have found you.* He cleared his throat. "Unfortunately, we tarried far too long before I became captain of this ship, and we fell behind in our search. Our ship is swift, so I imagine that we are not far behind now."

Laura pointed to a spot off to one side of their route. "What is this?"

"A rock formation."

"An island?"

Callum shook his head slightly. "Not precisely. This would be much smaller than an island, and likely just a grouping of tall or jagged rocks."

"Mmm."

He watched her lips twist in thought as she scanned the map, the rhythmic shanty being sung on the deck above them scarcely registering in his mind.

The woman had just allowed him incredible liberties and had alluded to the difficult prospect of finding a husband upon her return to England. She required protection, and he very much wanted to be the man to provide it.

Callum's reaction to her was strong; he craved her presence, even if they merely sat in silence. Being around her was like being in the morning sunlight: warm, fresh, and stimulating. Would she be receptive to a courtship in truth? Would *he* wish for one if his cock wasn't doing the thinking?

Being a spy in His Majesty's Secret Service consumed much of his time, and danger was prevalent in his position. He knew, however, of Secret Service men and women who married and had families, and they lived fulfilling, happy lives. Hydra himself had wed during a time of war.

The notion of a courtship, however, was impossible. Not only would her father—the sodding *duke*—likely forbid a man of Callum's station and low birth from marrying his daughter, but his superior—Sir Charles Bradley—would probably prohibit it, as well. In fact, they would both despise the intimacies that had already transpired.

He sighed, guilt gnawing at him.

Have a care, Callum, he warned himself. She could easily damage his heart when they returned to England and she returned to the bosom of her family. Would that his heart not get swept away when she left him, as well.

"I failed to thank you properly for the painting supplies," she murmured. "They're wonderful." Laura put a hand to his shoulder and lifted on her toes, pressing her lips lightly to his. Tingles prickled up his spine.

Chapter 13

The pirate's mien was adorably discomfited, his neck flushed, his breath shallow, and his eyes a light grey. Laura found it all terribly endearing.

He'd not said as much, but part of her wondered if his gifts, their intimacy, could be leading toward an offer of courtship. What they'd just done was…truly remarkable, but it did not necessitate an offer of marriage. There could be desire on his part, certainly. Their dalliance, however, had been very much her idea; she'd nearly forced him into it.

He is a spy, her inner voice reminded her. *He will be sent on assignments, possibly for long stretches of time at sea. He could be killed—heaven forefend—or worse, he could grow bored of you and take on a mistress.* The thought sent a pang of anguish through her midriff. She could not be abandoned. Not again.

She couldn't allow him to hurt her in such a way. Indeed, she could—and would—willingly offer her body to him, but she could not give him her heart. Her life had changed the moment those men had entered her bedchamber, and she'd been given a long while to think. She'd often said no to outings and society, eschewing activities in which she felt vulnerable. But now, she had been thrust into a life of unexpected adventure, and she found that she craved more.

"Thank you, Pirate."

He beamed at her, and her heart skipped in response. Pulling her into his embrace, he nuzzled his face into the crook of her neck, sending prickles of heat across her skin.

His eyes were again a bright blue, and soft in the corners. "When we return to Lon—" He halted, his gaze flicking up toward the windows, and staying there. He cursed. "My apologies, sweetheart, but I must go." Pressing a quick buss to her lips, he released her and strode determinedly from the room.

Laura stood numbly for several heartbeats, dumbfounded by his sudden departure, before she turned to follow his gaze to the windows. A light haze gathered around the ship, swirling along the air as their ship passed through it. *Fog.*

The bell overhead began to ring rapidly.

With quick steps, Laura swept from the cabin and ascended the ladder to the upper deck. The pirates had grown silent, and the bell's ringing abruptly ceased. Callum stood at the helm, his hand lifted high in the air, his fingers spread wide.

A gentle wind ruffled his hair and tugged at the edges of his long coat. Laura thought he made a dashing pirate.

The gentle haze turned quickly into a thick, dense fog, and as though in one great wave, silence washed over the frigate. One could scarcely see from the port to the starboard side of the ship! A slight panic sped Laura's heartbeat, and she strode carefully across the deck until she reached Callum's side.

She lifted on her toes and whispered in his ear, "Why is it so quiet?"

His mouth quirked upward in a grin as he leaned sideways, pressing his lips to her lobe. She shivered as tingles found their way from her ear to her toes. "In fog, ships ring their bell in timed succession, in order to alert other ships of their presence. If we are silent, we will hear other ships in the vicinity."

"Mightn't we wish for them to hear *us*?" she returned.

Callum's grin deepened, and he winked at her. She understood his silent message. If they alerted other ships of their presence, they would not be able to approach them unheard and take them by surprise. The pirate was cunning.

They sailed through the dense fog, an eerie silence settling around them. If it were not for the gentle breeze, she would not have known that they were moving. A disturbing calm surrounded the ship and settled over the crew.

Gooseflesh spread over Laura's skin and anxiousness seeped into her bones as she glanced through nothingness, a shiver travelling up her spine. The ocean was still, and the men were silent, as though holding their collective breath. She held hers, too.

Desperate to calm her disquieted nerves, she slid her hand into Callum's. He was a source of strength, warmth, and comfort that she needed just then. Gently, he squeezed her hand and brought it to his lips for a kiss. His beard tickled her skin, and she was grateful for the small distraction.

The silence stretched as they traversed the thick fog. Then, she heard it: a faint ring in the distance.

* * *

Callum's heart soared. *A ship.*

With great force, he stomped twice on the deck, alerting his men to ready themselves for battle. While it pained him to do so, Callum released Laura's hand and gripped the wheel.

"Best seek shelter below, sweetheart," he whispered to Laura. "A battle is about to begin."

He steered them in the direction of the bell's ringing, anticipation bubbling beneath his skin. This thrill was precisely what he sought, what he *craved*.

Another peal came from just ahead of them, and Callum turned the wheel, aligning their ship with the other. He could sense the men on the other ship trying to focus through the fog. They were entirely unsuspecting of the attack they were about to defend against. It was devious and underhanded, but, damn it, he was a pirate.

This was it. This could very well be their last encounter with a ship before they reached the shores of the Americas, for Callum was certain that land was but a few nautical miles ahead of them.

"*Fire!*" he shouted, the sound echoing off the water.

Boom! Boom! Boom! The carronades fired their balls amid flashes of light. The acrid scent of gunpowder and the horrified shouts of their opponents filled the air.

"Ready!" Callum called, stomping hard on the deck. "*Fire!*"

Boom! Boom-boom!

A long, loud *crack* rent the air, followed by a heavy *crash* as their opponents' main mast fell. More shouting ensued. For a brief moment, guilt hit Callum. Such was battle at sea, but he would find a way to ensure that their opponents returned home safely.

The loud booming of return fire echoed around them, but the shots missed, sailing between the masts and landing in the water beyond them. Callum crowed.

"Fire!"

Their carronades were fired once more, and his men prepared the planks to bridge the ships.

Boom! The bulwark splintered behind him, and one of his men cried out.

Callum spun around, his gut plummeting. A gust of wind blew the fog in a whirl, revealing a hint of what lay beyond. He cursed. Their opponent wasn't alone.

"*To the port side, men!*" he hollered. "Run out the guns! Fire at will!"

He couldn't tell if it was a warship or one meant for transporting goods and passengers, and that was to their opponents' advantage. If they employed the correct tactics, they could force Callum and his men to surrender, even without knowing whether or not they were outgunned.

Boom! Wood splinters flew through the air as a ball sailed past.

Shite. Where did Laura go? He spun on his heel and squinted through the fog on the deck.

Boom-boom! Boom!

Damn it, he ought to have known. Most ships that weren't privateers or pirates sailed in pairs or groups, though they were often far enough off that he could attack a ship and sail away before being forced to face the others. But this fog was so bloody thick, it was logical for the ships to sail near to each other.

"Harris!" he called, hoping that the man was nearby. "*Harris!*"

Boom!

The ship trembled, and the air was heavy with gunpowder mingled with the tang of blood.

"Here, sir!" Harris stumbled, but made it to Callum's side.

Relief rushed through him. "Find Laura and bring her below to safety."

"*Laura,* sir?"

Callum gave the man a terse nod, unwilling to explain his use of her Christian name at such a damned awful time. "Aye. Find her. Keep her safe."

Harris' lips thinned. "Of course, sir." He dashed away, disappearing quickly into the fog.

"Keep firing, men!" Callum shouted.

Boom! Boom!

* * *

Laura handed a sachet of gunpowder to the gunner's assistant and then covered her ears as another carronade fired. Callum had instructed her to keep safe in the hold, but she couldn't be idle when she knew that these men required help.

Lifting the crate that she'd filled with sachets, she continued on to the men stationed at the next carronade. "Gunpowder!" she said loudly.

The men nodded, and took a sachet. She moved to the next, and a hand came down on her shoulder.

"La—er—*miss*," Harris raised his voice over the din. "The captain has charged me with ensuring your safety. Please, come with m——"

Crack!

Harris screamed and fell to the ground, a large piece of the ship's wall protruding from his arm. Laura's heart lurched in her chest.

"Don't touch it!" Laura hurried to stop him from pulling it out. "I'll fetch the surgeon."

With that, she ran.

The men's shouts, the firing carronades, and the beat of her heart echoed loudly in her ears. Smoke obscured her vision and made her cough as she ran. At last grateful for the trousers that she wore, she swiftly descended the ladders until she reached the surgeon's room.

She halted abruptly as she entered, struggling to catch her breath. A small grouping of men awaited the surgeon's attention, and all of them looked up at her entrance.

"The first mate," she said breathlessly. "He's on the gunner's deck with a large piece of wood in his arm."

The surgeon gestured helplessly to the other men, some bleeding, others with crooked limbs. "Aye. Many men are injured, miss, but I 'aven't the 'ands to tend them all at once. 'E must wait."

"The injured men merely require aid enough to staunch their injuries so it is safe for them to come to your room to be tended properly. If you come with me and teach me what to do, *I* will help you."

Chapter 14

It felt as though time had slowed. The surgeon knelt beside Laura, walking her calmly through the steps to aid Harris.

"You must ensure that no splinters are left inside 'is arm," he reminded her. "If there are, it can cause infection."

Laura nodded and searched the jagged gash for splinters, the man's blood pouring over her fingers.

Harris clenched his teeth and hissed.

"I'm so sorry, Harris." Her stomach knotted at his pain, though not, she was shocked to admit, at the sight of blood.

Boom! Boom!

"Very good, miss," the surgeon urged. "Now wrap 'im up with the bandage."

Laura followed the surgeon's guidance, wrapping Harris' arm.

"Tightly, now. If 'e's to come to my room, 'e can't die on the way. Must keep 'is blood staunched."

She nodded, pulling the bandage tight. Harris hissed again, and she sent him an apologetic glance.

"Thank you, miss," he gritted out.

Her lips quirked in a wry smile. "'Tis not much, Harris, but I am pleased to have helped." She squeezed his hand in hers.

"That arm needs stitching," the surgeon said, rising to his feet and aiding Harris. "Go directly to my room. I will aid the miss 'ere and will join you shortly."

Boom!

Laura cringed. The men continued to fight, filling the carronades around them with balls and gunpowder. A man cried out on the deck above them, and Laura gazed at the ceiling.

"I hope that your recovery is swift," Laura murmured to Harris, giving his hand one last squeeze before turning to call above the din. "Are there any more injured men on this deck?"

"Aye," a voice creaked. "Over here!"

Hefting the doctor's assistant's basket in her arms, she followed the voice, winding her way around the other pirates and squinting through the gunpowder smoke.

* * *

Boom!

"Keep firing!" Callum couldn't see through the fog, but he had a feeling that they outgunned their opponent. He detested that they were harming innocent men, but if they didn't shoot, he and his men would die, themselves.

Boom! Boom-boom!

Another loud crack came off their starboard side. Terrified shouts erupted from the ship they'd first opened fire upon, and splashes followed.

"They're sinking!" Callum hollered. "Gunners to the port side! Let's finish this!"

Elation tingled through his body. The end was in sight. They would win this battle!

Their ship had sustained significant damage, but not enough to slow them down. They had more carronades and they shot more precisely, but their opponents had also taken several accurate shots. Callum and his master carpenter, sailmaker, and boatswain would have to inspect the damage once they were well enough away from the battle. And this damned fog.

Boom-boom! Boom-boom! Crack!

The shots hit their target, and their opponents' men hollered from the other ship.

Now is our chance. Callum placed a finger and thumb between his lips and let out a shrill whistle that echoed off the water. "Get the planks, men! We're boarding her."

* * *

Laura ascended the ladder to the upper deck as the carronades stopped firing. The battle must have concluded, for now the only sounds were that of men's voices aboard another ship.

She hefted the basket of rags awkwardly on one arm and scanned the deck for injured men. The fog was still so dense, she could scarcely see a few feet in any direction.

A groan came from just ahead, and she followed the sound. The cooper's assistant came into view, gripping his knee, agony streaked across his features. She hurried to his side.

"My knee," he ground out.

Blood seeped from a deep gash just above the bones in his knee.

Laura put a hand to his shoulder. "I will bandage it to staunch the bleeding, then you must go below to the surgeon to have it stitched."

He nodded, sweat and dirt streaked across his brow.

Setting to work, she bandaged the man's leg, ensuring that it was tight. The pirate growled and gritted his teeth against the pain. Once she'd tied the bandage off, she aided him to his feet.

"Thank ye, miss."

She smiled at him. "You're very welcome, sir. Are you able to ascend the ladders on your own, or would you care for assistance?"

"I can make it on me own." He limped away toward the ladder, cursing under his breath with each step.

Laura continued her search for other injured men, training her ears on what she couldn't see. The upper deck was perilous in the fog, so she walked slowly, making sure to not trip, and avoided carronades and the chunks of wood that had broken from the railing.

She came across a plank that went out across the water toward the other ship, and she paused, training her ears.

* * *

"Are *you* the captain?" Callum asked, irked that it had taken so damned long to locate the man.

Their opponents' men sat along the bulwark while others climbed, sopping wet, over it, having come from the other ship. Callum was amazed that they'd been able to locate it in the bloody fog.

"Aye." The captain nodded, dampness dripping from his grey moustache and over his beard.

Finally. He scanned the upper deck, and though he wasn't able to see much, he was able to ascertain that this was not a vessel designed for battle. "You are a merchant ship, aye?"

The captain visibly trembled. "Aye."

A chill travelled up Callum's spine, and he frowned. Something was different about this ship. He had a strong feeling that this was precisely the one he'd been searching for. "Do you have a man aboard who is not a member of your crew? A passenger?"

The man's eyes shifted.

"I'm searching for a gentleman named Wycli—"

Bang!

* * *

Laura cried out as she saw Callum fall. Something had compelled her feet forward once she'd heard his voice, but now, she ran. His men scrambled around, keeping the other crew at bay. Laura ignored the scuffle and went directly for Callum, kneeling at his side. Blood soaked his shoulder.

"Callum?" she asked, her gaze scanning his face.

His eyes widened in alarm, and the colour leached from his cheeks. "You should not be here. Quick, return to my cab—"

Laura yelped as she was yanked to her feet. An unyielding arm wrapped around her waist, while the sharp edge of a blade pressed to her neck. She lifted her chin and grabbed at the arm holding the blade.

Terror clawed its way through her, and memories of her kidnapping flashed through her mind's eye. *Not again.*

"Let her go," Callum growled, rising to his feet. A fierce scowl marred his handsome face.

The man holding her cackled, the sound piercing her ears. "Not a bloody chance."

Callum stepped forward, and the man pressed the knife deeper into her neck. Laura winced at the sharp pain. When Callum had trained her, they'd not used a weapon and a hold *together*. What did she do? Did she use the hold manoeuvre, or did she attempt the knife hold? Neither made particular sense when the blade was cutting into her throat. *Think, Laura!*

"Don't do this, Wycliff," Callum urged, putting a hand out in a placating gesture.

Wycliff. Laura's mind whirled. This was the man—the *traitor*—Callum had been searching for! He needed to return the man to England, and he couldn't do that if the man absconded with Laura.

Wycliff behind her shouted something, but Laura couldn't hear him over the blood pumping in her ears. She'd had enough of men carrying her off. She was a woman, not a sack of potatoes, for Christ's sake! Indeed, she was a woman who had spent the past weeks aboard a pirate ship, helping men in battle and now bandaging their wounds. She was capable, strong, and bloody brilliant.

She wouldn't allow this man to control her, and then torture herself with regret. She would simply have to improvise, using what she'd learned from Callum and what the pirates had shouted to her as they'd observed her practice.

Acting swiftly, Laura released a feral growl and leaned her head forward, before smashing the back of her skull into Wycliff's face. Her neck and head ached something fierce, but as soon as he let out a howl and released her, she spun to face him and kneed him in the cods with all of her might.

The blackguard went down hard, landing on his back and gripping his nethers as blood spurted from his nose.

Callum cursed and unknotted the burgundy sash about his waist, hurrying toward her.

Laura turned to grin at him, her heart racing with elation and pride. "I did it!"

Alarm spread through her chest at his ashen complexion. He reached for her, and she gave him a puzzled frown.

"*Where is the surgeon?*" he shouted.

He gripped the back of her head with one hand and pressed his sash to her neck with his other.

"What are you doing?" she asked, pulling away.

Callum followed her movement, pressing his sash harder against her neck. "You're bleeding."

She eyed his shoulder. "*You* are bleeding."

"I'm fine," he muttered. Turning toward his pirates, he hollered, "Apprehend the bastard and put him in the hold! Then take only what you can carry from the ship. Leave enough for them to make it to land."

With his sash still pressed to her neck, and his grip on her getting tighter, Callum guided Laura back to the plank connecting both ships. She stumbled in the fog, and he cursed.

"Must you walk so quickly?" she asked.

"You've been injured, sweetheart."

Her heart still thundered with the exultation of her success, but she wasn't in a great deal of pain. "I am well enough," she asserted.

Pausing his steps, Callum carefully peeled the scarf away from her neck, revealing a glistening crimson stain. Laura blanched.

Callum pressed the material once more against her neck. He cursed again, his voice deep with concern. "Decidedly *not* well enough."

Chapter 15

Hellfire and damnation. Callum had never been so petrified in his life. His heart beat nigh out of his chest, his knees were wobbly, and his hands trembled as he guided Lady Laura through the fog. It was so curst dense that he nearly lost his way to the ladder.

"Hold the cloth," he said gruffly.

Her complexion pale and her lips lined with worry, she silently did as he asked. Callum wrapped one arm about her waist and lifted her, grunting as pain seared through his shoulder. With great care and concentration, he brought her down the ladder and placed her on her feet on the gun deck. He glanced around, searching.

"Where is Harris?" Callum muttered. He needed the man's help taking the helm and organizing the men on the upper deck while Callum provided aid for Laura.

"He's with the surgeon getting stitched."

Callum's chest tightened, and he stopped walking. "He…*pardon?*"

She paused to face him, her skin far paler than he'd like. "Harris came to speak with me, when a blast from one of the other ships put a hole in our wall. A piece of wood lodged itself into Harris' shoulder, and I helped bind it so that he could go below with the surgeon."

Callum cursed, and resumed guiding Laura to his cabin. Harris had just finished recovering from a gunshot wound in his shoulder. This would reset his recovery to the beginning. He needed to check on Harris, but first, Laura was in need of his undivided attention.

They entered his cabin, and he kicked the door closed behind them.

"Sit, please," he instructed curtly, worry seeping into his voice.

Laura sat heavily on one of the chairs surrounding the large dining table, and Callum rummaged through his chest of drawers in search of cloths, tinctures, and bandages. He preferred to doctor himself when he could help it, and he'd certainly gained plenty of experience in the Secret Service.

"Oughtn't I go below to the surgeon?" she asked.

Callum shook his head brusquely. "No." He ignored the lift to her eyebrows, and refused to elaborate. Hell, he wasn't entirely certain, himself, why he felt compelled to bandage her neck, rather than bring her to the surgeon. He just…couldn't.

"What of *your* wound?" she prodded. "Truthfully, the crimson stain on your coat is terribly alarming."

He tugged his long coat off, wincing at the twinge of pain in the muscle between his shoulder and neck. "The ball is not inside; it went clean through the muscle." He'd wash the coat and mend the holes after he'd administered to his wound, but at the moment, his thoughts were only for Laura.

Collecting what he required, he swiftly returned to Laura's side and deposited the supplies on the dining table. He spread the items out, then rolled up his sleeves and walked to the washbasin. *Remain calm.* He repeated the words in his mind, but his stomach twisted sickeningly and his fingers refused to keep still. Callum washed his hands, then emptied the water out of the gun port. Willing his nerves to calm, he returned to Laura's side.

"Please remove the cloth," he said, his voice surprisingly measured.

With a grimace, she peeled the material away from her neck. Her reddened skin tugged, reopening the shallow wound. A foreign tingling sensation spread over his insides, and he attempted to cough the feeling away. It didn't work. Laura's neck was crusted and bleeding, and it made him decidedly ill to see her in pain. It was distinctly off-putting.

* * *

Laura hadn't truly noticed the pain in her throat until the moment she removed the soiled cloth. The jubilation of successfully felling Sir Wycliff was waning, and she was beginning to feel the aches in her body.

Callum winced and blanched as he examined her cut, swaying naturally with the motion of the ship. He pressed a finger to the skin on her throat, and a strange, painful burning seared through her.

"I do not believe that you will require stitches," he said, his voice low and soft, like the purr of the leopard that she'd seen at the Royal Menagerie.

Gooseflesh spread over her skin, and Callum frowned.

"You're cold," he said.

"I am warm enough."

His lips thinned. "The cut is shallow, but it is bleeding persistently." He splashed water into the washbasin that now rested on the dining table, then dipped a cloth inside. "I'm afraid that it requires cleaning and sterilizing. And it will hurt."

Unable to find her words, Laura nodded. She'd had her share of scrapes as a child, but after the loss of her sister, Charlotte, Laura had been so cossetted that she'd scarcely sneezed without someone being there to offer a kerchief. But while Laura was no stranger to pain, this felt decidedly unnerving.

Callum reached toward her, and she lifted her chin. The water was cool and refreshing but the abrasion of the cloth stung. She closed her eyes against the pain and allowed him to clean away the dried blood.

"Please hold this to your neck," he murmured softly.

Laura held the wet cloth to her wound as he released her to open a jar of salve. He stirred it with a finger, then scooped some of the oddly sweet-smelling mixture into his hand and leaned toward her.

He was so close, so warm. His face was wreathed with concern and his brows were knit in concentration as she lowered the cloth. A lock of his wavy brown hair fell across his forehead and Laura burned to brush it away. The man was sinfully alluring.

Tread carefully, Laura. While she would permit herself to feel desire for the tempting pirate, she had best have a care with her emotions. This man could be dangerous.

"This tincture ought to slow the bleeding and help heal the cut." His fingers dabbed lightly along her skin.

The Pirate's captivating scent of ocean, gunpowder, soap, and minted tooth powder mingled with the sweet and citrus aroma of the salve, creating a distinctly pleasing bouquet.

He pulled away to retrieve bandages from among his supplies, then wrapped them about her neck. His mien was detached and sensible, and his actions swift and efficient. Finishing the last knot, he stepped back to examine his work.

"Thank you," she said, her voice oddly breathless.

* * *

Callum's gaze caught hers, his pulse throbbing in every vein, and his gut knotted. "You're welcome, sweetheart."

He'd startled himself with the strength of his concern for her. The cut was shallow, but on such a sensitive part of her body it bled heavily. The bastard, Wycliff, ought not to have held a blade to her neck. Callum would make certain that assaulting and injuring a duke's daughter went on the bastard's list of crimes when he was sentenced to hang.

Now that Wycliff was in custody, their destination was London, and while that meant that Laura would be in more comfort and his prisoners would face the result of their poor decisions, he was unsure how he felt about leaving the ocean…or the intimacy of his cabin.

His gaze lifted to meet Laura's, and his chest warmed. Her hair—which glowed like fire in the sun—framed her beautifully freckled face with fallen curly locks. And her eyes—*Christ, her eyes!*—made him long for spring picnics and sunlit walks through gardens, like a sodding gentleman.

A knock sounded at the cabin door, breaking Callum from his bewildering reverie. Mentally shaking himself, he answered the door.

"Harris!" He crossed the threshold and closed the door behind himself, eyeing his friend's bandaged and slung arm. "Laura informed me that you were injured. Has it aggravated your previous injury?"

The man lifted an eyebrow and spoke in an undertone. "The previous wound is unaffected; a bit of the ship punctured my arm, is all. I've been stitched up, and feel fine, but the surgeon ordered me to use this sling." He notched his chin downward toward the bit of fabric that tied about his neck and held his arm in place. "If not for the young miss, I would have fared far worse. She's a remarkable woman."

Callum warmed at the praise for Laura. "I'm glad to hear that the damage is not worse. I hate to see you injured, particularly so soon after…" He left the words unsaid, and the other man nodded.

"I would be pleased to watch the door while you pay a visit to the surgeon." Harris looked pointedly at Callum's shoulder.

"No," he replied brusquely. "The ball went through, and it does not pain me greatly. I will manage on my own. If I require aid, I will ask Laura for help."

Harris glanced quickly over his shoulder, then bore his gaze into Callum, his youthful features carefully blank. "You've become quite close with the young *miss*, sir. Ought I—"

"Do not dare to besmirch her name—"

"What else am I to assume, sir?" Harris hissed. "You spend a great deal of time locked in your cabin, you held her hand in the fog, and you parade around the decks with your arms around her! I care about our purpose, as well, sir, but you've overstepped—"

"Enough!" Callum whispered hotly. He gnashed his teeth and took several deep breaths in an attempt to calm his racing heart and the fiery anger that abruptly burned in his gut. "You do not know of what you speak."

"Then explain it, if you would."

As much as it pained him, Callum had to grudgingly admit to himself that the man was right about his flagrant disregard for Laura's reputation. He sighed. "You're right. My attachment to Laura is…inappropriate due to our difference in station."

Harris' eyebrows lifted to his hairline. "At least you have the cods to admit it. Have you thought of her father's approval? Of *Hydra's*? You're not a member of high society, Callum, and she's a…" His lips thinned. "Well, surely there is a more sensible option for her future—"

"She has been alone with men for above two months," he ground out, feeling the need to defend his actions, despite his clear wrongdoing. "Her reputation has already experienced irreparable damage. Even with her aristocratic blood, the *haute ton* will not forgive such an absence without a chaperone. She is ruined. And while I'm by no means a gentleman, I imagine that her father—"

"Will be glad to accept *you* as a suitor," Harris finished for him. He paused, narrowing his gaze, and whispered, "You're a decent sort of man, Callum, but what could you possibly offer the woman in marriage?"

His jaw clenched. The question irritated Callum like a burr in his boot. "I don't have to explain myself to you," he growled. But the man was right, damn it. He'd already posed these arguments to himself—why was he debating the topic with Harris?

Because you want him to encourage you to seek a courtship. You want approval and hope…

Harris' eyes narrowed further. "Do you have feelings for the woman?"

Callum flicked his gaze pointedly beyond his impertinent apprentice's shoulder to the men on the gun deck, then frowned at Harris and spoke in an undertone. "I could just as easily ask if you had feelings for the gunner that you've been tupping, but I don't, because it's none of my damned business."

Harris had the good sense to appear abashed as heat rose up his cheeks. "But, sir, what you're implying is a sin and a punishable—"

"*Shite*, Harris, I don't bloody care. Have at it, for Christ's sake. I'm *saying* that you needn't explain yourself to me. And I damned well don't have to explain myself to you."

"Very well. Point made, sir." Harris' ears grew increasingly red, and his throat bobbed. "And thank you. I think."

All at once, Callum's agitation evaporated, and he mentally kicked himself for being so ham-fisted. *I'm an insensitive arse.* He softened his tone. "I apologize, Harris. I oughtn't have brought that up as I did. You could have said something, you know. Our professional association aside, I do hope that you would consider me a friend. Know that you may confide in me."

With a short nod and a small smile, Harris said, "Thank you…again."

Callum nodded and transitioned to a more pressing matter at hand. "Now that we have Wycliff, we must come about and return to London. We will use the desire for full repairs to convince the men. For the present, have them search the merchant ship for books, painting supplies, and dresses for Laura."

"Yes, sir."

"Once I'm bandaged, I will take the helm. Have the men ready to set sail in ninety minutes."

Harris nodded. "As you wish, sir."

Without waiting for his apprentice to leave, Callum entered his cabin and locked the door.

Laura looked up at his entrance, sitting in the same spot in which he'd left her. His chest ached with surprising force as he took in her appearance. Her borrowed shirt, waistcoat, and trousers were frayed and covered in blood, dirt, and Lord knew what else. Guilt hit him like a fist to the face.

He cleared his tight throat. "Luncheon was postponed due to the battle, but Cook has returned to the galley and will begin preparing the meal shortly. Once the stove is hot, I will have a bath drawn for you."

"I would like that very much," she replied softly.

Callum nodded, tugging his shirt's hem from his trousers. He carefully bared the upper half of his body, and refreshed the washbasin water, cloths, and bandages, before settling in to clean his wound.

Chapter 16

Grimsbury Manor, Brampton

Bridget Bradley rubbed a hand affectionately over her large belly as she sipped on some tea in the spy school's parlour. Several of the school's students filled the room around her, some studying and others enjoying games of cards or chess.

Jones, Bridget's husband's valet and most trusted man, sat on the settee across from hers, eyeing her carefully. The man had been tasked by Charles—or as his fellow spies called him, Hydra—to watch over her and Henry while the spies set sail on their assignment.

"Lady Bradley!" Eleanor, one of the school's newest recruits, hurried into the room and sat in a nearby armchair. Her eyes were bright, and her smile wide. "Your demonstration today was truly inspiring."

"Ill-advised, you mean," Jones grumbled into his teacup.

Bridget slid a sideways glance at the man before turning her attention to Eleanor. "Thank you. My form has changed since the pregnancy, but my regular practices have aided my range of movement."

"So modest, dear Bridget," Oliver Dove, Bridget's greatest friend and sparring partner, said from his seat beside her. "You're a fine swordswoman, whether you're *enceinte* or not."

She smiled affectionately at her friend and patted the hand that rested on his knee. "Thank you, love."

"How long did it take you to learn?" Eleanor asked. "I heard that you bested Hydra!"

"I did." Bridget nodded. "It took several years, but my lessons were sparse. With Oliver as a new instructor at the school, you will learn far swifter than I."

Eleanor beamed.

"Pardon the interruption." One of the acting footmen, Ferris, entered, holding out a folded piece of parchment to Eleanor. "A letter has arrived for you. The messenger informed me that it is urgent, and you must share the contents with everyone here. Should I summon Mr. MacLean?"

Mr. Lachlan MacLean was always second in command at the school, but often took the role of headmaster whenever Colonel Kieran Richards was on assignment or recruiting more students. Now that Richards was missing, however, MacLean had slipped fully into the lead role.

"Yes, please, Ferris," Eleanor replied, accepting the folded piece of parchment.

The acting footman sped away, and Eleanor glanced at the direction.

"It's from my cousin, Caroline Newport, in London." She glanced at Bridget with a slight frown. "What could she have to say that Mr. MacLean must hear?"

"Something important, I'll wager." Jones leaned forward in his seat, resting his elbows on his knees.

Bridget's stomach rippled with movement. Her babe was no doubt reacting to the sudden nerves that travelled through her.

In but a few tense minutes, Mr. MacLean entered, followed by Ferris, Hugh Haddington, Dr. Simon Claridge, and his wife—Bridget's sister by marriage—Lady Emaline. They gathered around the seating area, the men standing and Emaline sitting next to Jones on the settee. The gathering drew the curious attention of several of the other students in the room.

"I've been informed that an urgent message arrived for you, Eleanor," Mr. MacLean said, his voice low.

She nodded, and Mr. MacLean gestured for her to open it.

With slightly shaking fingers, Eleanor tore the seal and began to read aloud.

Eleanor,

> *As you are aware, despite my proper education, no household would hire me as a governess due to my low birth, and I became a nurse to help the physician at the Bethlem Royal Hospital. I have met a man—a patient not like the others—and we have formed a friendship. During a discussion about our families, I mentioned you, Eleanor, and, to my great surprise, he claims to have met you at a school…*

She stopped reading, a gasp on her lips as she lifted her wide-eyed gaze to Mr. MacLean.

Jones' curse was echoed by Mr. MacLean, and Bridget placed a hand over her rapidly beating heart.

Eleanor continued on in a rush.

> *The doctors and other nurses here are absolutely certain that this man—my friend—is mad like the others, but I can assure you that he is not. It is in his eyes, Eleanor. His eyes are full of pain, betrayal, fear, and great intelligence. And I believe him.*
>
> *He has told me that it is not safe to write his name or give too much detail, but he has asked that I write to you requesting help from you and your friends, whoever they might be. And do please hurry. Someone is attempting to do him harm; I have found him injured on several occasions.*
>
> *I miss you, dear cousin.*
> *Affectionately,*
> *Caroline*

Mr. MacLean's spine stiffened as he addressed the room in a booming voice. "We will need a group to act as a skeleton staff here at the school. The rest of you will journey to London with me. Colonel Richards needs our help, and we're damned well going to give him the best we've got."

* * *

No matter how many times Laura read the paragraph, the words wouldn't make sense. The Pirate Spy had removed his shirt and cleaned his wound, and was now bandaging it over the tincture that he'd applied. He didn't appear put out in the least, his countenance entirely unmoved by the small bleeding hole.

She'd attempted to distract herself from his ungentlemanlike but remarkably attractive physique, but the small leather-bound book that she held in her hands was not sufficiently distracting. More than anything, she wanted to run her fingers over his body once more, to trace each tattoo with her lips and see gooseflesh rise up over his skin, to kiss him wildly and soothe any pain that he felt.

Her gaze slid upward to the brass bathing tub that sat in the middle of the large cabin. It had arrived not five minutes prior, and Callum had assured her that he would not be much longer dressing his wounds, and would give her privacy to bathe. But while the desire to remove her filthy clothing and slip into the steaming water was almost overwhelming, the enjoyment that she felt just being in The Pirate's presence was even more powerful. It was a vexing problem, indeed.

The rustle of clothing filled the cabin, followed by the *clang* of his belts' buckles. Callum strode toward her, and she hastily stood, tossing the book aside on the table. Her insides quivered at his nearness, and she took a shuddering breath.

"The cabin is yours," he said softly. "I must man the helm, at least until we are out of the fog, and then I must oversee the ship's repairs. There is a fresh set of trousers, a shirt, and waistcoat for you in the chest of drawers."

Laura nodded slightly.

His light blue gaze bore into hers, and she felt tempted to lose herself in their depths. A ring of grey bordered his irises, while the outer blue grew more intense. They were truly magnificent eyes.

An odd groaning sound escaped him, and he swept forward, wrapping one arm about her waist, his hand clutching the back of her head. Anticipation rushed through Laura as he held her there, his gaze locked on hers. Refusing to wait for him, she rose up on her toes and touched his lips lightly with hers.

Callum groaned again and deepened the kiss, crushing her lips. Laura gripped his arms tightly as they squeezed around her. She opened her mouth to his searching tongue and a responding heat spread through her.

She wanted—*needed*—that same release that she'd felt in his arms that morning, and more than anything, she hoped to give him that same pleasure. Her pulse sped, and her feminine core throbbed with desire. Callum broke their kiss, and it was Laura's turn to groan…until he pressed his lips to the underside of her jaw.

A quiver of delight danced across her abdomen as he trailed his mouth along her skin.

He broke off with a curse, pulling away from her. His skin had grown ashen and his chest heaved as he stared at her neck. Did her bandage offend him?

Laura reached for him, but he stepped further away. Hurt cut through her chest at his rejection.

"What is the matter?" she asked, detesting the quiver in her voice.

His throat bobbed, and her eyes were drawn to the movement. "I'm afraid that our—er—activities have caused you more bleeding."

Laura touched her fingertips to the bandage at her neck, and Callum hastened to halt her.

"No," he said gruffly "Don't. Keep your heart rate down and let it heal." He retrieved the pistols and spyglass that he'd placed on the table, and tucked them into his belts before striding purposefully across the room.

Gripping the cabin's door handle, he turned, opening his mouth to speak, but nothing emerged. Instead, he clenched his jaw, yanked the door open, and stepped through. The door closed with a resounding *slam* as he left.

Unbidden, tears sprang to her eyes and a heavy ache settled in her chest. She blinked, and twin tears rolled down her cheeks. Swiping them away with a sob, she began to undress.

It was foolish, being weepy, when she knew that he was right. They'd both just been injured and required rest and time to heal, but his reaction stung nonetheless.

More tears burned trails down her cheeks as she disrobed and stepped into the hot bath.

* * *

The upper deck was a flurry of activity as men struggled to navigate their way through the fog, their arms laden with pilfered items. A cool breeze swept past, carrying the sound of the ocean lapping against the ship's hull. Callum's boots crunched on debris as he traversed the deck toward the helm.

Even through the fog, Callum could ascertain that they would require extensive repairs. The gun deck alone was a bloody mess.

"Remove the planks!" Harris' voice carried through the fog toward him. "Put your items in the hold and return to your stations!"

Callum reached the helm, placed his palms on the smooth knobs of the double wheel, and looked out toward the forecastle. He couldn't see a damned thing, so he trained his ears. Men hollered, water splashed, footfalls thumped along the deck…and somewhere in the distance, he could swear that he heard the high-pitched trill of feminine crying. His gut knotted with guilt, even though it must be his imagination—*surely*.

Lady Laura could not be hurt by their exchange, could she? Jaw clenched, Callum stood thusly for several long heartbeats, considering the possibility. *No.* She must see the rationale in his refusal to keep kissing her. The woman required rest, and her wound was still bleeding; he couldn't risk worsening her injury and causing loss of blood.

"Captain!" Harris hastened toward him, drawing him from his distressing thoughts.

"Are we ready to set sail?"

"Yes, sir."

Callum nodded. "Then let's get out of this sodding fog."

* * *

Following the lady's trail was easy enough for Cecil Piper and Mr. McMann; whoever she was with engaged in battle at every opportunity, leaving a trail of damaged vessels in their wake.

The moment they'd realized that the ship upon which they'd held her had sunk, Cecil had boarded McMann's ship—taking on the title of first mate—while his ship and crew returned to London to report to Beresford and Weston. Those gentlemen had no doubt boarded the ship and were even now sailing after them.

Cecil's gut burned with the desire to catch the woman. They'd best have her in their clutches before their superiors reached them, or there would be the devil to pay. For everyone.

The question was, who had taken her, and why? And, of course, for how long would the bastards be tortured?

McMann approached. "We've found more debris off the starboard side."

"Another battle, eh wot?" Cecil replied. He gazed out over the ship's bow, damp wind biting at his cheeks.

"I feel as though we're close," McMann muttered. "Perhaps a sennight behind them; however, at our speed it could be mere days, particularly with their desire to fight everyone they meet."

Cecil nodded, but something teased the back of his mind. "They're skilled at battle, wot? Likely have ample artillery—"

"We will take them on," McMann asserted. He nodded toward the debris floating in the water. "They're probably running low on ammunition and powder, and their ship cannot be in the best of conditions. We will easily overtake them. And when we do, we'll take the woman back with us, and kill everyone else on board."

* * *

Gradually coming out of sleep, Laura rolled to her side, her still-damp curls rubbing between her cheek and the pillow. She groaned. Her abdomen and her back hurt something fierce. Mayhap she was hungry; Callum had informed her that the cook was preparing a meal that should be ready soon.

Pain throbbed through her hips and Laura curled into herself, hugging the aching muscles across her belly. It was subtle, but the motion caused dampness to gather at her nether region. Her eyes snapped open, and a soft exclamation left her lips.

Her courses had begun.

Leaping out of bed, she turned to examine the bedclothes. The moment she stood, however, her trousers were ruined in a humiliating flood.

Panic began to build in her chest as she gazed frantically about the room through misted eyes.

What could she do? The pirates would not carry such female necessities as the proper cloths, and she could not very well tear up the sheets that graced the beds.

Bandages, her mind whispered. She swiped at the dampness around her eyes. The surgeon! He would have ample supplies for her, and it wouldn't mortify her to speak discreetly with him about the matter.

With swift movements, she removed her stained trousers and used them to wipe at her thighs, then donned a clean pair, setting the stained pair aside to be washed once she returned. Slipping her feet into the slightly overlarge boots that she'd been borrowing, she hastened across the gun deck toward the ladder. Only a few men stared curiously at her before returning to their duties, but thankfully, none said a word.

She descended the ladder and made her way to the surgeon's room, the ache in her stomach and back almost too much to bear.

The surgeon looked up at her through his spectacles as she entered. A smile lit his face. "Miss Laura," he cooed, but his gaze sobered as he noticed the sudden flood of tears in her eyes and the bandage on her neck. "Why, what's the matter? Ye've been 'urt!" He stood and came toward her.

Swiping once more at her damp eyes, she whispered, "The captain cleaned and bandaged my wound, but that is not why I am here."

"Then what is it?" His eyes were large and a warm brown behind his spectacles. For a pirate surgeon, the man was remarkably kind.

Her lips quivered distressingly. "My courses have begun. Have you any bandages that I might—"

His face cleared, but reddened slightly. "Oh, of course. Not to worry, miss. I 'ave just the bandages that will 'elp you." He turned and rummaged through a barrel and a crate, before he returned to her side, his arms laden with torn cloths. "This amount should suffice, but if you 'ave need of more, I 'ave plenty."

Relief rushed through her, bringing forth more heated tears. "Thank you, sir."

"If you 'ave need of pain management, I 'ave that, too."

Laura had attempted to use syrups given to her by her family's doctor, but they made her dizzy and tasted awful. The pain only lasted two days and, severe though it was, she could withstand it.

"My thanks again, sir."

"Just call me 'Enry." He smiled at her.

"Thank you, Henry." She returned his smile with a small one of her own.

With a small dip of her head, she turned and hurried toward the ladder. She held the bundle tightly in one arm and was reaching for the rung, when a voice stopped her. The hairs at the back of her neck stood on end, and a chill ran down her spine.

"I'm right pleased to see you, Lady Laura…"

Chapter 17

The longer Callum manned the helm, the more his shoulder burned. Keeping his bearings was increasingly difficult in the dense fog, and it concerned him. The upper deck was silent but for the gentle rustle of their sails, the creak of wood, the rush of wind, and the spray of water on their hull.

Callum reached into his pocket, withdrew his glass-encased iron compass, and flipped open the lid. He adjusted the wheel until they were sailing in the direction that he desired, and then he returned the compass to his pocket.

Laura hadn't joined him on the upper deck as she often did. He wondered if she had enjoyed her bath, or if she'd been given a tray of food. Perhaps even now she was sitting in their cabin enjoying her repast. His stomach growled. He was famished, and exhaustion pulled at his eyelids. It was difficult to ascertain without seeing the sky, but the ache in his body told him that it was nearly nine of the clock in the evening.

"Captain." Harris appeared at his side.

"Report," Callum replied brusquely.

"Half of the crew have eaten and are sleeping in preparation for the night shift. Once we've cleared the fog, I recommend that you sleep, sir. I can oversee the hull's inspection and the commencement of the repairs."

More than anything, Callum wished to return to his cabin—*and Laura*—and sleep, but his apprentice must be exhausted, as well. "You have not yet rested, Harris, and you're injured. I cannot allow you to take over unless I know that you are—"

"With respect, sir, you're injured, as well. And not properly tended, mind—"

"Shh," Callum hushed him, notching his chin toward the ship's bow. "The fog is thinning."

They were silent as they sailed toward the fog's edge. Dim sunlight glistened on the water beyond, marking the end of the sun's set. Several long heartbeats later, and they were free. His men blinked into the dwindling light.

"Ho!" a topman called.

"Shite," Callum muttered as he withdrew his spyglass, his gut knotting sickeningly.

Harris quickly took over the helm as Callum dashed to the bulwark and looked out though his spyglass. The figure of a ship sailing toward them was just a speck, but it sent a pang of fear into Callum's heart.

Thinking quickly, he marched back to the helm, and Harris moved aside.

"What will we do, Captain?"

Callum's lips thinned. "We cannot engage in battle in our condition. It is a risk, but we have only one option."

* * *

Her body a riot of nerves, Laura turned from the ladder to face her abductor. Lantern light played over his features, flickering shadows over his eyes. The darkness lent him an ominously sinister mien.

"What are you doing here?" The words slipped from her mouth in a bold whisper.

The man sat on the floor several paces away from Wycliff, his wrists tied, and the rope knotted to a metal bolt in a wooden beam that arched across the ceiling.

He sneered at her. "Come closer, and I'll tell ye."

Laura's feet remained rooted to the spot. She hadn't expected an answer from him. In fact, she could hedge a guess as to why Callum had ordered his imprisonment. Like Wycliff, her captor was likely meant to stand trial. That thought didn't ease the fearful trembling that had begun to quake all over her body, however.

"Ye look mighty fine in trousers, wench." He groaned, then bared his teeth in a snarl. "I should'a taken ye when I 'ad a chance."

"Stop," Laura said, inwardly cursing the quiver in her voice.

The man laughed, revealing his yellow-and-brown stained teeth.

"Come closer, love, and I'll tell ye who ordered yer abduction," her captor whispered conspiratorially.

Her eyes narrowed. Why did he wish her to approach him? Something did not feel right. Her gaze flicked to Wycliff, and her stomach sank. One of the crew had loaded a crate full of silver cutlery into the hull, and Wycliff was edging toward it.

* * *

Callum turned the wheel, and cursed. The sun had lowered, and the moon and stars brightened overhead, leaving the ship in a swath of blue light. That meant he couldn't see the edge of the stone. One ill move, and they would puncture the hull.

"We'll not make it around the rocks," he said to Harris, who echoed Callum's curse. "We've only one option if we don't wish to be blown against the stone. Tell the men below to run out the oars."

Nodding his understanding, the young man dashed away.

"We're running out the oars!" Callum called to the topmen.

"Aye, aye!" several hollered back.

The men immediately swung about the masts like monkeys in trees, gathering, folding, and tying off the sails so the wind wouldn't carry them. They had one shot at this, and they had best move swiftly, for the other ship was quickly approaching.

On either side of the ship, wood scraped wood as the ports were opened and the oars were let out. The men were silent, awaiting orders. Wind rustled Callum's clothing, and waves lapped at the hull, and he assessed their location.

"*Port side, row!*" he shouted.

The men on the left sank their oars into the water and rowed. The ship turned.

"*Starboard, row!*" Callum bellowed.

For several heart-stopping minutes, Callum directed them around the side of an enormous rock formation. The ocean on this side was calm, the rocks providing a shield from the wind.

"*Uncat the anchors!*"

Metal clanged and wood scraped as the anchors were released and the oars were brought in. *Splash.* Silence descended on the crew. Not a sound was heard, but for the gentle creak of wood and ripple of water.

On soundless feet, Harris approached. He lifted his eyebrows, winked, pointed to their feet, then put a finger to his lips. It was a strange series of gestures, but Callum grasped his meaning. His apprentice had ordered the crew's silence. They were awaiting orders.

* * *

In an awkward movement, Laura hastened toward the crate of cutlery. Squeezing her legs together so as not to embarrass herself, she wrestled the crate with one hand, dragging it along the wooden planks until it was out of Wycliff's reach.

With a wicked snarl, the man rose to his feet and lunged toward her. Laura leapt backward in fear, even though somewhere in her mind she knew that he couldn't reach her.

Wycliff laughed vilely, his cackle scraping along her nerves.

"Little girl, so afraid," he taunted.

Her abductor joined in the revelry, and both goaded her with abhorrent, suggestive comments. Laura closed her ears to their biting words and straightened her shoulders. They were bound, and she was free. *They have no control over me now. Not unless I give it to them.*

Heart flapping about in her chest, Laura stiffened her spine and faced the blackguards. "Sod off!" The words were entirely foreign on her tongue, but she quite liked how they felt. "Good luck with your trials, gentlemen. I hope that you enjoy your final days."

With that, she spun on her heel and dashed for the ladder, her bandages still thick under one arm. The villains' curses followed her to the next deck, but faded entirely when she'd reached the next ladder.

She kept her gaze directly ahead, focusing on her task and hoping beyond hope that a stain hadn't formed on her trousers, and that the men around her hadn't noticed. The moment the captain's cabin door closed behind her, a deep sob wracked her frame.

Tears formed in her eyes and spilled over her lashes, and she let them fall. Her stomach and back throbbed with hurt, and her heart ached.

Striding across the cabin, she deposited the cloths on the bed and swiftly changed into her last remaining clean pair of trousers, carefully placing some folded rags close against her sensitive feminine skin. She stored the remainder of the cloths in the drawer that Callum had given her, carefully hiding them away.

"Dastardly men," she muttered as a flash of their laughing, sneering faces filled her mind's eye. She hated them both.

Another painful pang seared across her abdomen, and she gazed longingly at the bed. She would lie down, but only after she'd washed her soiled trousers. Her fingers still trembling, she set to work.

* * *

Callum withdrew his spyglass and trod softly to the bulwark. They'd been silent and at the ready long enough. Through the darkness of night, they'd seen the lantern lights of the other ship pass by some time ago.

He looked through his spyglass and scanned the edge of the foggy haze behind them. Satisfied, he turned to Harris. "They're clear. Are you able to man the helm?"

"Yes, sir."

Callum nodded. "Very good. Summon me in four hours, instruct the night crew to keep vigil for passing ships, and tell them *not* to ring the hourly bell. We'd do best to remain hidden here. The rest of the crew must sleep; we'll begin repairs on the morrow."

"Aye, aye." Harris saluted.

Casting his apprentice a sideways glance, Callum made his way to the ladder. His body was abuzz with anticipation. It had been hours since he'd last seen Laura, and he was eager for her company. He needed to know if he'd hurt her feelings by not kissing her—and, by God, he wanted to kiss her!

He leapt past the last two rungs of the ladder and landed with a *thump* on the wooden-planked floor of the gun deck. Several crew members sleepily looked up at him from their tasks, but Callum ignored them and strode determinedly toward his cabin.

Eagerness propelling him, he swung the door open. And froze. Laura stood at the washbasin, scrubbing blood from material. Her eyes were wide and pained as she whirled to look at him. His heart plummeting in alarm, Callum closed the door behind himself and went to her side.

"What's happened?" he asked. "Has your wound reopened?"

Laura's chin dipped low, and Callum caught it with the crook of his finger, forcing her gaze to meet his.

"Christ," he murmured.

Her eyes swam with tears, and a responding panic sped Callum's pulse.

"Where are you hurt?" he demanded. "Shall I fetch the surgeon?"

Instinct driving him, he turned, but Laura's soft voice halted him mid-step.

"I am uninjured."

Callum turned back to face her, his gaze flicking from the stained water in the washbasin to her flooded moss-green eyes. "The evidence would suggest otherwise. I cannot help you if I do not know what is wrong."

The skin between her brows creased, and she shifted her stance.

"Please," he pressed. "You have me concerned. If you are inj—"

"My courses arrived," she blurted.

Stunned, Callum stared at her, his mind working. He could feel a slow heat rising up his neck. Damn, but he was a fool. Of course she would experience her monthly courses while on the ship; he ought to have thought of it sooner. But he'd not even considered it! No woman had ever voiced their condition so bluntly to him. He'd known that there were days in which he couldn't visit his mistresses—when he'd had them—but they'd never discussed…*this*.

"I—" He cleared his throat. "I apologize for not considering your needs before now. Is there anything that I can do for you? Do you require anything?"

To his horror, Laura's face scrunched, and thick, streaming tears leaked from her eyes. A sob shook her shoulders, followed closely by a harsh gasp.

Shite, what do I do? An entirely alarming sense of panic spread through his body. He felt helpless and flustered in the face of her raw emotions.

Relying on instinct, Callum unbuckled his belts with quaking fingers, carefully divesting himself of his coat, pistols, spyglass, and compass, and enveloped her in his unobstructed embrace. He smoothed the palm of one hand over her shoulders and rubbed in small circles as she nestled into his chest, her body still shaking with the force of her sobs.

He glanced about his cabin, desperately hoping for something that might help. *Aha!* A tray of untouched food and tea sat on the table.

"Would you care for something to eat?" he asked, gesturing toward the tray, his own stomach growling at the prospect of sustenance.

She peered over his arm. "I hadn't noticed it there," came her muffled reply as she pressed herself harder against Callum's chest. "I haven't a desire to eat. Unless… Is there any chocolate?"

He grinned and pressed a quick buss to her mass of curling hair. *Christ, she smells like sunshine.* "I'm afraid that we haven't any chocolate on board. Will a cup of tea with sugar suffice?"

Chapter 18

To Laura's continued mortification, her tears were unrelenting, streaming down her cheeks as she sipped at her tea. The Pirate looked alarmed, to say the least; he ate a helping of cured beef stew while watching her with trepidation.

Her family ordinarily ignored her when her courses came, letting her lady's maid take care of her until the worst of it was over. She'd never had someone fuss over her condition, and most certainly never a man, let alone a pirate spy.

She swallowed the last of her tea and swiped once more at the hot tears on her cheeks. The ship rocked gently from side to side, but the feeling was vastly different from when wind was at their sails.

"Why have we stopped moving?" she asked.

Callum swallowed his mouthful of stew. "We are anchored behind that large rock formation that I showed you, so that we might organize some repairs without the threat of attack."

Her tears stopped as she gazed at the imposing man. Even with his weaponry and his coat removed—and his mouth full of food— the man was an impossibly large figure. The material of his shirt's sleeves strained against his muscled shoulders and arms.

"I like you," she said bluntly.

He blinked, a slow grin forming on his sumptuous lips. "Why thank you, sweetheart. I like you, as well."

A sudden yawn caught her, and she covered it with the back of one hand.

"You're tired," he noted, rising. Rounding the table, he held his hand out to her. "Come, I'll bring you to bed."

She wanted to protest, to tell him that she was capable of bringing herself, but a deep, bone-weary exhaustion had settled inside her, and all she wanted was the comfort of his presence, and to sleep. He was being conciliatory and gentlemanly, and she appreciated the thought behind his gesture.

Clasping his hand, she stood, gritting her teeth against the pain in her abdomen. The bed was cool but inviting. A long sigh escaped her as she slipped off her boots and curled between the bedclothes, her eyes closing in satisfaction. She rolled to her side and tucked a hand beneath her pillow.

"Good night, sweetheart," he murmured softly.

"Stay with me," she pleaded, her eyes still blissfully closed. She'd slept alone every night since her sister had left home, and Callum was a source of comfort. "It has been a trying day, and I imagine this bed is more comfortable than yours. It will be better for your injury." He was silent for a moment, and her heart gave a hard thump, urging her to be honest.

She gazed at him over her shoulder. His face was half in shadow, the faint lantern light flickering on the left side of his chiselled features. The slight bend in his nose was highlighted, the sharp angle of his strong jaw more noticeable, and the glittering intensity of his gaze deeply pronounced. A lock of his brown hair teased the line of his brow. He was power and vulnerability, bravery and concern, all in one.

Her throat worked, and she continued on a whisper. "You're a source of warmth and solidity on the cold, unsteady water, Callum. I merely thought that we could provide each other with comfort, but I'll not force you to join me if you do not wish to."

His jaw tightened and he nodded. "I wish to."

Whatever it was that had held him back seemed to melt away. The tension in his shoulders appeared to ease as he rolled down his shirtsleeves. His weight settled on the bed behind her, and his warmth enveloped her back. She'd never slept thusly, but she imagined that he'd done so on many occasions. That was a lowering thought. She frowned, but pushed the unpleasant thought away. This was *her* moment, and she was far too exhausted to allow jealousy into her mind and heart just then.

Reaching behind herself, she found his arm and pulled it over her waist, sidling back against his chest.

"Happy sleep, Pirate," she mumbled drowsily.

His soft breath brushed her temple and sent a wave of gooseflesh over her skin. "Happy sleep, sweetheart."

* * *

"*No!*" Laura's soft cries drew Callum closer.

"You're having a nightmare, sweetheart," he murmured, sitting on the edge of the bed.

He put a hand to her shoulder, and she jolted awake, her eyes snapping wide with fear.

"It's me," he said. "You're well, now."

She groaned and nodded, further mussing her hair against her pillow. "Thank you, Pirate."

He slid to the floor, resting his bared back against the bed and drawing his knees up toward his chest. "Shall we converse?"

"Yes, please."

"Family? Books? Our other intere—"

Her index finger burned a trail across his skin, tracing the curves of the rope inked into his right bicep. He suppressed a shiver, even as gooseflesh spread over his skin.

"Tell me the story of how this came to be," she asked quietly.

He looked down, touching his own fingertips to the anchor on his forearm. "It began with the anchor. If you'll notice, it's slightly misshapen, the black has faded to blue, and the edges are hazy."

"Mmm."

"My father gave it to me on my thirteenth birthday."

"Thirteenth?"

He shrugged one shoulder. "Such was life at sea. Once I'd been recruited into the Secret Service, I decided to return to the docks and seek out a man skilled enough to build it into a piece that I'd be pleased with."

"I like it," she murmured.

Warmth bloomed in his chest at her praise. "Thank you."

"How many tattoos do you have?"

"Six."

Her gaze scanned his body, and he knew what she must be thinking. His lips quirked. "The others are hidden."

The green of her eyes darkened in the moonlight. "Indeed?"

"Mmm," he hummed, rising to his feet.

Without thought, he unfastened his trouser falls and lowered the back enough to reveal the right cheek of his arse.

Laura gasped, and he immediately knew that he'd done wrong. He glanced over his shoulder to see her wide eyes studying the plume of roses that he knew resided on his arse cheek. Clearing his throat, he righted his trousers and sat once more.

"My apologies, Laura. I oughtn't have been so forward."

She swallowed audibly. "The roses are beautiful."

He nodded. "What book are you reading? Would you like for me to read to you?"

With a sigh, she reached for a book, and handed it to him. "I was on chapter nineteen."

* * *

"See to it that the repairs begin immediately," Callum said authoritatively.

"Aye, Captain." The boatswain nodded before barking orders to his assistant and limping away.

The ship's carpenter swiftly took his place.

"Report," Callum grunted.

"The damage is substantial, Captain…" The carpenter spent several long moments describing the extent of the hull's damage. Callum's stomach sank with each word.

"We haven't enough material to complete all of the repairs," the carpenter went on.

"Use whatever you must to repair the hull. I will get us to land so that we might do more extensive repairs with the proper materials, but I'd not like to sink before we get there. Use the oars to fix the bulwark, but leave enough for us to get away from this rock when we're ready to set sail."

"Aye, aye, Captain." The man nodded and strode away.

Another sailor approached, waiting for orders, and Callum grimaced. "If we're to be anchored here for some time, we must do our best to scrape the barnacles from the hull without lifting her from the water. Have we enough rope and able-bodied men to carry out the task?"

"Aye, Captain McInnis." The man tugged on his forelock and hurried away.

Already that morning, he'd met with the sailmaker and the surgeon to assess the sails and their crew. Many men were injured, and one man had perished. But it was one too many. Callum ought to have thought better than to attack a merchant ship in the fog without first considering the fact that it was sailing in a pair.

Striding to the bulwark, he gazed out toward the rising sun and its reflection on the white-tipped waves in the water. Wind rushed past him, bringing with it the fresh, cool fragrance of salt water.

He yawned, and his eyes watered. Hell, he was exhausted. He'd gotten at least five hours of sleep, but he'd not truly rested. Not with Laura's full, rounded arse pressed agonizingly against his untimely erection all night.

Callum scrubbed a hand over his face and through his windblown hair. Yesterday had been one hell of a day. Now, it was time to recover from it and push forward into the next level of his assignment. Return Wycliff to London…and Laura to her family. A heavy stone sank in his stomach at the thought. He didn't want their closeness—torturous though it was—to end.

* * *

Blinking her bleary eyes, Laura re-entered the cabin from the seat of easement. She wanted to sleep longer, but the bright morning sunlight would not let her.

Since she'd awoken, she'd not been able to get the image of Callum's bottom out of her mind. It was just as muscular and plump as she'd imagined it to be, and yet oh, so much more colourful. She wanted to bite it.

Lord, but that man was trouble.

Something glinted across the room, drawing Laura's gaze. An admiring gasp escaped her, and she rushed forward. Draped across the back of a dining chair was a charming walking dress of blue shot silk and elaborate embroidered dark-blue flowers. The long sleeves were gathered delicately, tipped with silk-corded trim at the wrists. Laura ran her fingers over the low, square bodice, in the very centre of which was a sapphire stone that reflected the sunlight.

Beneath the dress was a clean, white shift, short stays, and petticoats with lace sewn along the hem. And on the table was a note. Laura flipped it open.

Sweetheart,
These are for you. There were several styles from which to choose, but I believe this one will not only fit you but suit you, as well.
Affectionately,
C

Laura's chest swelled, and anticipation bubbled through her. It had been so long since she'd worn a gown that she'd almost grown accustomed to the trousers, shirt, and waistcoat.

With quick, eager movements, Laura divested herself of her shirt and waistcoat, and donned the handsome frock. She did not have drawers, stockings, or slippers, so she kept the bottom half of her men's costume on beneath the dress. It served her better anyway, she supposed.

Laura was unable to reach the top buttons at her back, but would happily wait until Callum returned to ask for aid. She felt beautiful. The silk dress outlined the curve of her figure and the light shade of blue was pleasing against her pale, freckled skin.

Grinning, with a lightness in her heart that she hadn't felt in months, she set her easel on its feet facing the sunlight, gathered her supplies, and began to paint.

For the first time since her abduction, Laura truly felt like herself.

* * *

Warm wind ruffled Michael George Morris, the Duke of Norshire's grey hair as he looked out over the ocean from his ship's forecastle. After receiving the missive from Sir Charles Bradley's man, Michael had gathered his resources, his men, and he'd set out after his daughter immediately.

In the past two months, he'd found his daughter, Charlotte, aided in the rescue of his grandsons, and watched his beloved eldest daughter get married to a Crown spy. He would be damned if his good fortune ended there. It was time to take further action and ensure Laura's safe return home.

He turned his gaze toward the spymaster, himself. Sir Bradley stood at the helm of another ship, speaking with one of his men. Once Michael had voiced his decision to take to the seas, Sir Bradley had insisted on gathering his own men and joining in the quest. He'd said that now that the war was over, several of his spies had elected to pursue a business on Bow Street as runners, and this would be the ideal last assignment for them. Bradley had apparently left several of his men in England in order to search for another spymaster, who had gone missing.

The fact that the terrible events of the past year had been orchestrated by the same villains who had kidnapped his daughter and now threatened the very safety of England was enough to trouble any man. But Sir Bradley and his spies were handling the circumstance with admirable aplomb. Not so for Michael. He was nervous as hell.

* * *

Despite the heat of the sun beating down on him, Sir Charles Bradley felt a prickle at the back of his neck. He turned, and noticed the Duke of Norshire's attention. Charles lifted an arm in the air and waved at the man from the great distance between them. The duke nodded in return.

They'd been at sea for nearly a fortnight, now, and though Charles knew that they were going in the right direction, he felt drawn back to England. And to his pregnant wife and son, whom he'd left behind at Grimsbury Manor in Brampton. Lord, but it would be two months at the most before Bridget gave birth.

"Hydra."

Charles turned to see Edward. It was *his* return to duty—and the information that he brought—that had been the catalyst for getting Charles and the other men onto the ocean. Charles had known that they were going to follow Callum and Harris' trail in order to help the duke retrieve his daughter, but he hadn't known how very much they were needed.

Edward had been stationed in Lord Langston's home, until the man had been killed in battle, then he'd been transferred to Baron Beresford's home. Due to security, and fear of his cover being blown, Edward had been out of contact for the past months…until Beresford and the Marquess of Weston had received news and had taken to the seas. Charles and his men had then clamoured to gather additional supplies.

"Yes, Ed?"

"I'm afraid that Mary has another bout of seasickness."

Charles' lips thinned in concern. "Is Gabriel with her?"

"Yes, sir. Also, luncheon has been served on the mess."

"Good." Charles' stomach growled at the mention of a meal. "Thank you for the report."

With a nod, the man returned to his place at the helm, leaving Charles to look out at his men. The crew was small but fierce and capable. He'd left just as many proficient men and women behind in London to continue the search for Richards. Of course, he'd not forced the men to come along; he'd allowed them to make that choice for themselves, and to Charles' amazement, many wished to join the crew, including Stevens, who left his new wife with his sister in London.

This mission was critical, however. Not only were they attempting to rescue the duke's daughter, but they were attempting to capture the men who had been manipulating Charles' band of spies and attempting to take England out of the war. They were traitors, and must stand trial. The war might be over, but that was all the greater reason for them to find the traitors now, as they mightn't get another opportunity.

Chapter 19

"We've used every scrap o' wood that we 'ave, Captain, but it ain't enough to make all o' the repairs," the ship's carpenter said apologetically.

Callum nodded, but his gaze was locked on Laura, who strolled along the deck. "Very well. I've no intent to continue to the Americas, but with the repairs already made to our ship, we will undoubtedly make the return journey to London. It is time to enjoy our spoils!" He grinned at his carpenter before clapping him on the shoulder and striding past him.

His assignment was very nearly complete. He had his traitor—caught mere hours before reaching American soil—and he was bringing him home. It was truly remarkable how good fortune had smiled down upon Callum, for when sailing directly from London to the Americas, it ought to take under one month. But even with delays, Callum had managed to keep his rank as captain on his ship, pillage as his men had desired, rescue Lady Laura, and catch the bastard, Wycliff.

Callum reached Laura's side and lightly bussed her temple. "Good evening, sweetheart."

She turned and beamed up at him. "Good evening, Pirate."

Something in his chest melted. She wore the same blue dress that she'd washed and worn for the past sennight, with the heavy men's boots poking from beneath her lace hem. Her fingers were lightly stained a rainbow of colours, which only served to tug at his heart even more. With the sun slowly lowering, the red hue in her brown hair glowed vibrantly.

More than anything, he wanted to pull her into his arms and kiss her, right there on the sodding deck beneath the setting sun. He settled for clasping her hand lightly in his.

"Would you care for a stroll?" he asked.

She grinned, the bright green of her eyes shining even brighter in the evening light. "I thank you, yes."

A burst of pride spread through him as she looped her arm through his. She squeezed slightly, sending him a sideways smile before they began to walk along the ship's bulwark. With Laura on his arm, Callum felt like a sodding king. The woman was a sunlit garden.

They strode in silence for several minutes, moving with the gentle rocking of the ship. The warmth of the lowering sun slowly faded into a cool dusk.

Callum cleared his throat and prepared to broach a subject that had long been on his mind. "We've spoken about the search for your sister." He deliberately left out her name, lest the other men overhear. "I confess that I am surprised that so many years have passed since her elopement, and subsequent disappearance, without word or success in finding her. It rather worries me."

"It worried me for some time, as well," Laura replied quietly. "But I comfort myself with the fact that if anything untoward had happened, we would have heard about it in the newspaper. Charlotte must be happy—wherever she is." There was a bite to her words that told Callum that there was more to the tale that she was not sharing.

Callum's lips thinned. "What if there was danger surrounding her departure? What if she was forced to leave against her will? Think you that she could have been…hurt?"

Laura's astute gaze lifted to his, and his gut knotted. "Is there something *else* that is on your mind, Callum?"

"Aye, there is," he said grimly. She waited silently while he considered his words. "Two *friends* of mine—Hugh and Kieran— have gone missing over the past months, and despite our efforts to find them…" He shook his head.

Laura placed her other hand over his forearm in a gesture of comfort.

"Another friend, Barrows, was gravely injured," Callum continued. "Even now, he remains asleep in a house in London, slowly wasting away."

"I'm so sorry, Callum," Laura breathed. She pulled her lips between her teeth as she seemed to consider her words. "My aunt Agnes was a very proud, strong woman."

Callum nodded, unsure how to respond to the abrupt change in subject.

"One day, she slipped while getting into her bath, and injured her leg. I loved her dearly, but the woman was too proud to seek help, even though she struggled to walk." Laura's lips pursed. "My aunt Agnes lost her balance at the top of the grand staircase in her home, and tumbled down, severely injuring her head and sending her into a deep sleep."

A painful quiver began somewhere north of his gut, and Callum swallowed, afraid to hope. "What happened to her?"

"She passed away two years ago," she said softly, slicing through Callum. "But not before awakening from her sleep and living out the rest of her days a woman changed for the better."

"How…" His throat closed and he cleared it with a cough. "How long did it take for her to awaken?"

Laura gazed solemnly into his eyes. "For my aunt, it was under one month. But," she hurried to add, "her doctor had said that he'd had several patients that did not awaken for months. In fact, his assessment was that patients had a greater chance of awakening within the first year, but that it was still possible within the second and third. He said that reintroducing them to sounds and smells that are familiar will help pull them back, that they should be talked to on a daily basis, and that they can often hear what is said when they are sleeping."

He nodded again, but couldn't yet speak, a spark of hope blossoming within him. Everyone that joined the Secret Service knew that injury, death, or torture were some of the perils of sneak-work, but it was not easy to face it when it happened to someone you cared about. Their training included all manner of practice scenarios, in which they would endure torture and learn how to handle questioning under duress, but there was no training to teach the men and women working for the Home Office how to endure the suffering of a friend.

"And it's all for me grog, me jolly, jolly grog. All for me beer and tobacco…" a topman sang as he adjusted the ropes.

"Well, I spent all me tin on the lassies drinking gin, across the western ocean I must wander," the other men sang.

"Where are me boots, me noggin, noggin boots, they're all gone for beer and tobacco," Callum sang loudly. "For the heels they are worn out and the toes are kicked about, and the soles are looking for better weather."

"And it's all for me grog, me jolly, jolly grog. All for me beer and tobacco. Well, I spent all me tin on the lassies drinking gin, across the western ocean I must wander…" all of the men joined in.

The song concluded several verses later, and Laura turned to him, smiling. "You have a lovely singing voice, Pirate."

His wide-eyed gaze caught hers. He'd never considered himself as having a *singing* voice, precisely, he'd merely joined in with the singing aboard ships and hadn't thought more of it. He genuinely hadn't any idea of how to respond, so he cleared his throat and said awkwardly, "Thank you, sweetheart."

Her grin deepened. "Have you always sung these songs?"

Callum nodded thoughtfully. "Since my earliest memory, yes. Never on land, mind you. Only at sea."

"And are they always so…" She twisted her lips as though searching for the right word.

He laughed. "Wicked?" he offered helpfully. "Yes, I'm afraid that most of them involve drinking to excess or women. Does it bother you?"

"Not at all. I rather enjoy them, actually. They make me want to dance, but I would not know how."

I'll show you how, my sweet, his mind whispered as a wholly inappropriate and entirely licentious image sprang to his mind. His heart rate abruptly sped, and ill-timed tingles of awareness spread out over his skin. *I must stop this.*

"Captain," Harris greeted as he approached.

Callum and Laura halted their stroll. Poor Harris looked exhausted, Callum noted. The young man's hair was mussed from the wind, his skin was pallid, and dark circles of exhaustion had formed beneath his eyes. His left arm was held tight against his ribs and chest with a length of cloth; even after a sennight of rest the blasted thing hadn't yet healed fully. The poor blighter.

"Harris." Callum inclined his head.

"The night shift is ready to take over; I have already dismissed the day crew."

"Ah. Thank you." Callum nodded. "We had best take our evening meal and retire." He eyed his young apprentice meaningfully. "You, as well, Harris. On the morrow, we set sail for London."

* * *

Callum's words repeated in Laura's mind all through the remainder of their discussion with Harris, their withdrawal to the captain's cabin, and their evening meal. At some point, she must have agreed to a game of cards, for The Pirate had searched about the cabin for several moments before turning with a deck and settling across the table from her. But her mind was decidedly distracted.

They were returning to London. It was precisely what she'd wished for since her abduction. She would return to her home, could have a proper bath, Cook's famous beef, teacakes, and…oh, everything that she'd missed since she'd left. And yet now that her wish was to come true, she felt strangely despondent. A horrid jumble of emotions knotted in her stomach and snaked around her heart. It all made very little sense to her, and seemed rather silly, even admitting it to herself. But she didn't want to lose this closeness with her pirate. With Callum.

"It is your card." The Pirate's deep voice rumbled through the cabin, shaking Laura from her reverie.

She blinked, and realized that she held an unorganized set of cards in her hands, the low, flickering light of a nearby hanging lantern wavering over their surface. Goodness, but she didn't even know what game they were playing!

"Are you well, sweetheart?" he asked, a note of concern in his voice.

"I'm sorry." Laura shook her head. "I fear that I'm a mite tired." At the thought of sleep, a yawn caught her, and she covered it with the back of her hand.

Callum immediately stood and rounded the table to offer his hand. Her mind still suitably distracted, she accepted the man's aid in rising, and went about her evening ablutions. Callum murmured some soft words that she failed to hear and went to his desk, leaving her to ready herself for bed.

The light was so dim that she struggled to locate the tooth powder.

Wearing only her shift with loosened ties, Laura drew down the bedclothes and looked over at the pirate spy. He was frowning at the map currently splayed over his desk's surface as he made a note on a piece of parchment.

Laura smiled to herself and slid onto the mattress, pulling the bedclothes up over her shoulder as she rolled onto her side. Despite the dry burn of her eyes, the sheer exhaustion slumping her body, and the gentle rock of the ship, sleep eluded her.

* * *

The frown marring Callum's brow deepened as he attempted to focus on the map in front of him. Lord knew how long he'd been standing over the thing, staring blankly. He'd begun to map out their return journey—again—but found himself fighting the urge to watch Laura, instead.

She lay stretched on her side, her back facing him. Callum's body screamed at him to go and join her. Exhaustion had long since dried his eyes and drooped his shoulders, but he knew that it wasn't the desire for *sleep* that had him wanting to strip himself bare and join her beneath the bedclothes. His body constantly reminded him that it had been more than a sennight since he'd last kissed her, since he'd cupped her sweet, pert breasts and felt her warm, wet…

He broke off his thoughts with a curse. *Christ*, but he ached for her.

The cockstand in his trousers throbbed, reminding him that his attempts to calm himself were failing. He balled his hands into fists and took several long, deep breaths. This wouldn't do.

With a silent curse, Callum slumped in his desk's chair. As though of its own free will, his right hand found its way to the hard ridge straining his trouser falls and gave it a tight squeeze. His gaze slid upward toward Laura.

Their nights sharing a bed must come to an end.

He wanted Laura as his wife. The war was over, and he'd likely not be sent on such perilous assignments again. Hell, if he wished it, he could join some of the other men and become a Bow Street Runner, as the Secret Service would need only half as many men as they did during the war and there was plenty of new blood to fill those positions.

Indeed, all that he required was a flow of funds to care for Laura, and any bairns that they might have. The thought of children made his heart leap.

With a self-deprecating sigh, he shook his head. *It will never happen.* Laura might be a woman like no other, willing and eager to bravely throw herself into danger and new experiences, but she was still a high-born woman, and he the son of a pirate and a whore. Regardless of her current position in society, her father would never condone a union between them.

His gut burned with the desire to have her for his own. He wanted to brand her heart, just as she had branded his. He wanted the freedom to hold her, to touch her, to claim her in their marriage bed every night for the rest of their sodding lives.

Reflexively, his hand tightened on his erection through his trousers.

The subject of his desire suddenly turned, her bright-green gaze catching his, and his breath caught. *Shite*, she was awake, and he was sodding blushing.

He abandoned the clutch that he had on himself and gripped the chair's arms, instead.

"Will you not come to bed?" she asked, her voice soft.

Chapter 20

A series of emotions played over The Pirate's face: shock, contrition, worry, need... Even through the darkness, she could see the redness creeping up his neck and into his cheeks.

"Are you well?" she asked, turning fully toward him.

He shook his head. "I will sleep in the hammock tonight."

Laura frowned as hurt cut through her chest. "But—"

"I want to sleep next to you, sweetheart, but it isn't right. You're—" He broke off with a curse and surged to his feet. Slowly, he came toward the bed. "Mayhap the past nights were a comfort to you, but they were torture for me."

Her frown deepened as she attempted to understand. Was being close to her painful for him somehow? "I'm sorry," she said softly. "I did not mean to torture you."

"No, you didn't." His words came out harsh, and he grimaced. He paced two steps, and returned, his hands on his hips and a sigh lifting his chest. "Being around you arouses me. Sleeping with you... Hell, I scarcely slept at all for the feelings your nearness stirred in me. You were warm and soft, and more than anything I wanted to pull you into my arms and—" He broke off with another curse. "It's not your fault, sweetheart, and I can control my passions, but it would be best if I returned to sleeping in my hammock."

He stood before her, his chest heaving and his skin reddened beneath the thin lawn shirt that hung untucked from his trousers. Light from the swaying lantern lit his profile, and Laura's gaze caught on the rapid pulse on the side of his neck. He was aroused, she realized; even after his impassioned speech and confession, he wanted her.

And, dash it all, she wanted him, as well. She would never get an opportunity such as this again. If—and that was a rather large *if*—she were to ever marry, the man would be of her father's choosing, not hers. No matter what she told them, they would likely believe her to have been soiled during her abduction anyway, so why not indulge her desires with the man that *she* wanted? This joining would be *her* choice, not her father's or her potential future husband's.

Indeed, that thought was rather liberating.

There was, of course, the possibility of impregnation, but truthfully, that didn't worry her overmuch. Most women took months of trying to get with child before they succeeded—if at all—so the risks were minimal.

The Pirate's lips thinned and his chin dipped, but before he could turn away, Laura caught his wrist, his blue eyes dark with longing.

Without saying a word, Laura rose up on her knees at the edge of the bed, wrapped her arms about his shoulders, and pulled his head down toward hers. Their lips met, but his kisses were reserved, almost polite.

"*Kiss* me, Callum," she pleaded, tightening her hold on his shoulders. Goodness, but her stomach was in knots, twisting and fluttering with nervous anticipation.

His groan vibrated through her chest. "I don't think that I can, sweetheart. I want more, but you must remain—"

"Oh, ballocks!"

Callum's eyes grew wide on a startled laugh.

She grinned at him, tightening her hold once more. Closing her eyes, she pressed her forehead to his. Taking a deep, quavering breath, she whispered, "I *want* you, Pirate. Give me at least one night before I live out a life in isolation. I want to remember this, remember *you.*"

A second groan turned into a growl as Callum captured her lips in a hungry kiss. *This* was what she'd wanted! His arms came about her waist and pulled her tight against him, his hard, thick erection pressing into the soft flesh of her *mons* through the thin layers of fabric.

He released her waist to fist the hem of her shift in his hands, and in one fluid motion, Callum lifted her shift up over her head and tossed it to the floor. For the briefest of moments, Laura felt like covering her freckle-covered body with her arms, but that urge swiftly fled as The Pirate's heated gaze took her in. Her pulse raced with an erotic thrum, and anticipation bubbled through her.

"Bloody hell, Laura," he groaned. "You're beautiful."

Her chest warmed at his praise. "I want to see you, too." She wanted far more than to just *see* him; she wanted to touch him…to taste him. Slipping her hands beneath the hem of his shirt, she rubbed her palms over his torso.

The Pirate's skin was hot and smooth. She let her fingers roam, finding the narrow line of coarse, springy hair that ran from his navel to the edge of his trousers. Another groan rumbled in chest. Laura grinned and slid her fingers along the ridges of his muscles.

"You drive me mad, woman," he uttered in a harsh whisper as his muscles quivered.

She played her lips over his, teasing and tasting, as she slowly slid his shirt over his head in a movement that mimicked his.

Her gaze caught on the red, still-healing wound on his shoulder, and her chest swelled with compassion. She pressed her lips to the puckered skin surrounding his injury, and out of the corner of her eye, she saw his throat bob.

"*Christ,*" he murmured, before tugging at his falls frenziedly.

Laura sat back on her heels and admired his speed, her pulse racing and her abdomen abuzz with nervous flutters. She wanted him to ravish her, she wanted unbridled passion and all-consuming desire. Indeed, she wanted him to want her just as passionately as she wanted him.

In few quick—albeit awkward—movements, his boots, stockings, and trousers were heaped on the pile of fabric on the floor. He stood only briefly before her, but what she saw was truly remarkable. He was large and hard, his skin reddened and hot but oh, so soft.

He eased her back on the bed and hovered on one arm above her while his other hand traced a pattern over her skin. The gentle abrasion of his calloused fingertips on her breasts, waist, and abdomen caused gooseflesh to spread over her. His lips followed his hands, pausing to kiss along the red scar at her throat, to nibble on her earlobe, and to suckle tauntingly at her breasts.

Laura writhed beneath him, clawing at his back and urging him to take more of her. But, to her frustration, he held back. She moaned in complaint, a frown puckering her brow.

"Please, Callum," she begged, lifting her hips toward him. He backed away and another whimper escaped her.

He spread sweet kisses along her shoulder while he swirled his palm over her hip. "Have patience, sweetheart." She could hear the smile in his voice, and it only increased her frustration.

The Pirate wanted to take his time—for Lord knew what reason—but she wanted him to take her like a…a…like a *pirate*!

Well, she would not allow him to decide for her what her first time would be like.

Not wanting to wait a moment longer, Laura reached between them and put a hand around his length. Callum twitched in surprise, then gritted his teeth and hissed a breath as she began to stroke him.

"Sweetheart, I—" He broke off on another groan, his eyes sliding shut.

Now when she urged him over her, he came willingly. Using the tip of his erection, she teased her cleft, delighting in both the jolt of pleasure that heated her abdomen and the erotic swelling of the thick appendage that she held in her hand.

She stroked him again, and teased her cleft simultaneously, and Callum growled, pulling her hand away.

"I can't take any more of that," he uttered hoarsely.

Laura wrapped her arms about his shoulders as he took himself in hand. The Pirate nudged her knees apart, and she eagerly complied, lifting her legs about his hips. He was large—*so large*. He slickened himself on her, then paused as he came over her fully, resting an elbow on either side of her and tangling his fingers in her hair.

His gaze was searching, his skin flushed and damp, and his breath came in erratic puffs.

The question was clear. Laura gave a quick nod and pulled his head down toward hers. His kiss was fervent, his tongue playing with hers and his muscles taut. His short growth of beard and his quick breaths tickled her skin.

Then, in one swift motion, he was fully inside her. She gasped, and he moaned, the sounds muffled by their heated kiss.

Laura marvelled at the feeling of him inside her. It hadn't hurt, like she'd feared, but the thickness of him felt so tight that it almost burned.

Pulling his lips away, he pressed his forehead to hers and grunted. "You feel so damned good, sweetheart."

"So…do you."

His body trembled, and Laura ran her fingers through his hair and tightened her hold on his waist.

Then, he began to move.

He started slow, the friction making her want to squirm. Holding himself up with one elbow, he slid his other hand down her side and cupped her bottom. He moved faster, squeezing her rear with each thrust.

The heated friction of their joining grew to a steady, stimulating blaze. Laura's body was afire for him, burning higher and brighter with each thrust. She knew what was coming, what was building…and she craved it.

Laura rocked her hips in time with his thrusts, lifting instinctively to drive him deeper. Her heart hammered against her ribs. Their panting breaths mingled and their bodies grew slick as they moved.

The inferno of passion within her grew brighter and brighter until, finally, it burst. Her head pressed back against the pillow and her lips parted, but Callum caught her cry with his kiss. White, blinding light pulsed behind her eyelids as wave after wave of pleasure crashed over her.

Above her, Callum grunted, his movements abruptly stuttered. His grunt turned into a growl, his grip tightening on her bottom and his muscles stiffening as his manhood jerked inside her.

They remained thusly for several long moments, panting and kissing. Laura's pulse began to slow, and her body began to relax.

Callum withdrew from her sheath and reclined beside her, pulling her into the circle of his arms.

"I don't know what to say, sweetheart," he murmured against her hair. "You're bloody remarkable."

She turned in his embrace and pressed a swift kiss to his lips. "You're pretty amazing, yourself, Pirate."

Chapter 21

The ship rocked to one side, and Callum blinked himself awake. The dim light shining through the windows told him that it was just past dawn.

He yawned and stretched—and, in an instant, the memories of the night before came flooding back. His blinked again, clearing his eyes of sleep, and looked at the woman in his arms. Laura lay sleeping with her back pressed against his chest, and her soft, full, and beautifully rounded arse pressed against his growing erection. Shortly after their activities, he'd pulled the bedclothes over them, and they'd fallen quickly to sleep.

Holy hell, that was a night to be cherished. He'd had all manner of women in his bed before, but never one so responsive, so fiery, so damned beautiful…so caring, generous, or kind as Laura. No one compared to her.

He'd wanted to make the night last, to make her first time slow and passionate, but she'd taken matters—and his cock—into her own hands. And, shite, he adored her for it.

She stirred in her sleep, nestling further against his chest. The movement caused her arse to rub against his erection, and he inwardly groaned. Was she sore from last night? Would she accept him again? Lord knew he wanted her again. And again.

Sliding himself down the bed so that his face was in line with the crook of Laura's neck, he gripped her hip with one hand and tilted her arse toward him. He nuzzled in her abundance of auburn hair as she stirred once more and murmured.

"You smell so damned good, sweetheart," he said softly.

She murmured again, and rubbed herself against him.

A groan escaped him and he pressed a kiss to her shoulder. "Are you sore, or can you take me again?"

"Mmm." She pulled his hand away from her hip and guided it to her cleft.

A grin of triumph stole over his lips before he shifted her hips backward and entered her from behind.

"Bloody hell, woman," he ground out as his fingers played between her folds and he was fully sheathed within her once more.

Laura gasped as he thrust and swirled his fingers simultaneously. His heart soared as she began to rock her hips in time with his movements. He pressed kisses along her shoulder, teasing her skin with small nips in between. His breath came fast, his pulse racing with his exertions—and excitement.

Her moans grew louder and his rhythm faster. His control was slipping.

Callum twirled his fingers in earnest. And then, she broke. She arched her back, crying out her climax as her hot sheath pulsed around him.

It sent him over the edge. Pumping twice more, he buried his face in her mass of auburn hair, growling his pleasure as he spilled his seed inside her.

Still panting, he grinned. "Ah, sweetheart, you've undone me."

She laughed, quick and breathless. "Good morning to you, as well, Pirate." She looked over her shoulder at him, her green eyes bright and achingly beautiful.

He hoped that their childr—*oh, holy hell!*

Shite, bugger, and fuck, he cursed soundly in his mind, shutting his eyes against the too-tempting sight of Laura. He'd come inside her! *Twice!* He'd not even *thought* about using a condom or withdrawing before spilling his seed.

Hell, but he was in trouble. Neither her father, nor his superior would be in favour of his actions. No matter how "compromised" she was, he'd taken a woman's maidenhead out of wedlock. What if, even now, she were carrying his child?

Nerves and no small amount of excitement erupted in his stomach. His blasted emotions couldn't grasp the difficult situation in which he'd put himself.

He would, without hesitation, take responsibility for both her and their child, of course, should the need arise. Would that she could want the same of him.

His heart gave a heavy *thump.*

Damn, but he must have a care. She could easily break his heart.

The ship rocked, and Callum put a hand out to steady himself.

Laura tilted her head back to look at the windows. "Oh!"

"A storm," he noted. *Damn.* He'd mistaken the sky's colour as early morn, but a heavy storm waged just beyond their stern. "I must go." He bussed her cheek and slipped from the bed.

The bell overhead sounded just as a wave rocked them sideways.

Boom! Callum stumbled toward his table just as Laura tumbled from the bed.

"*Shite*! We're hitting the rocks!"

Callum righted himself, then rounded the bed to help Laura to her feet. His gut knotted, he found his trousers, and hastily donned them, scarcely buttoning the falls before he had the cabin's door open.

He glanced at Laura over his shoulder. *Damnation*, she was a vision: her hair was mussed, her eyes fiery, and her shoulders bared, holding the bedclothes to her breasts as she sat upon the bed. He didn't want to leave her, but if he stayed, they would all perish.

"Hold fast and stay safe."

She blinked her wide and frightened green eyes at him, and nodded. "You, as well."

Callum closed the door and raced along the gun deck, shouting, "Up, up, men! Get to the oars! Cat the anchors!"

Another wave rocked them sideways, and Callum cringed, hating what would come next. *Boom!*

Steadying his balance, he raced up the ladder. Chilled wind, rain, and ocean water sprayed him as he reached the chaotic upper deck. The bell rang haltingly as the man ringing it struggled to keep hold of his footing.

Callum shouted orders, attempting to assemble his men over the din of the storm.

"*Wave!*" he hollered, gripping the wheel tightly with both hands just as another wave crashed over them.

Boom!

Clank-clank-clank. The sound of the anchors being catted was faint against the roar of the storm.

"Port side oars, row!" he called.

A series of shouts echoed his words, and the men began to row. The bow of the ship was nearing the edge of the rock's outcropping, when another wave hit. Callum tightened his grip on the wheel as water crashed over him. Men cried out and sputtered, and another resounding *boom* echoed in the hull.

Harris sped toward the fo'c'sle, his harried and half-dressed appearance much like Callum's: bare-footed, wearing nothing but a pair of trousers, and soaked to the bone.

"*Port side oars, row!*" Callum hollered. The oars moved, pushing them briefly away from the rocks. "Starboard side oars, row!"

The men worked to dislodge themselves from between the crashing waves and the barrier of punishing rocks, one stroke of the oars at a time. Slowly, the sea level lowered, and Callum's heart sank. He didn't want to look out at the water, knowing what he'd find, but his gaze slid that way nonetheless.

A wave grew and slowly approached off their starboard side. No, it wasn't a mere wave, it was a sodding wall of water.

Panic hit Callum's chest, and he bellowed, "*Row! Row, men, row!*"

* * *

Laura clung to the bed as the ship rocked back and forth. Shouts rang out overhead, and the hull echoed with deafening bangs. Fear and helplessness gripped her heart and knotted her stomach. The storm was violent, wave after wave pushing them into the rocks. And it petrified her.

Unbidden images of her family, her home…of her pirate flashed through her mind, taunting her with things that she might never see again. She squeezed her eyes shut against the sting of tears that threatened.

If she allowed herself, she would go mad with worry. What she needed was a distraction.

Keeping her eyes closed, she forced herself to recall the smooth heat of Callum's skin under her searching hands and the dark, coarse hair that trailed from his navel to the dense thatch surrounding his impressive length. His muscles were sculpted and moved lithely beneath his tanned skin—

The ship rocked again and more shouts rose out overhead, and she squeezed her eyelids tighter, trying to keep her thoughts locked on the wondrous things that she and the Pirate Spy had done.

His hands in her hair, tenderly caressing her skin, her—

Boom!

She gasped and flinched at the thunderous noise. Her fear returned full force.

Laura's lower abdomen gave a pang, and she cringed, her gaze sliding toward the door to the seat of easement. She could attempt to tighten her muscles further, or she could risk being exposed to the waves.

Something that had fallen to the floor caught her gaze, and a slight smile stole over her lips. One of the books that Callum had procured for her had fallen from its place on the chest of drawers. If she were to use the seat of easement, she could retrieve the book as she returned to the bed. It was both something to look forward to and a suitable distraction.

Careful to keep her balance, Laura carefully made her way to the seat of easement. It was covered from above, but the waves splashed from beneath. With brusque movements, she completed her toilet and hurried back inside the warmth of the captain's cabin, her bare legs sopping wet.

"Dash it," she muttered. She would need a towel, for certain, but she was grateful that she'd remained in the nude and had not ruined her handsome frock.

The loud shouting on the deck above grew hoarse and frantic, and Laura's heart caught in her throat. She reached a hand out to steady herself as the ship began to turn, but her feet slipped on the small puddle on the tiled floor. The wave hit, knocking her sideways, her feet sliding out entirely from beneath her. Her heart leapt in alarm, and time seemed to slow as she fell.

Despite her efforts to halt her momentum with her hands, the bed's post came up quickly. And then there was only darkness.

* * *

"*Row! Row! Row!*" Callum chanted loudly, his voice hoarse and, he hated to admit, panicked. The wall of water was approaching, and the only way they would survive was if they manoeuvred themselves away from the rocks, and turned.

They were just clearing away from the rocks, thank Christ, but they weren't done.

"Port side, row!" Water sprayed from his lips as he shouted, the rain and salty ocean continuously dousing him, turning his skin into a living, moving river of water.

The men rowed, and they began to turn sharply. They weren't going to make it.

"*Brace yourselves!*" Callum bellowed.

He clung to the wheel just as the wave overtook them. For a brief moment, Callum was entirely surrounded by water, and he feared the worst. Pain shook his body, the weight of the water bearing down on every inch of him. But just as quickly as it arrived, the water was gone, and he sucked in a deep breath of thick, humid air.

Several curses and prayers rang out around him, and Callum shook himself. "Do we have everyone?"

"Man overboard!" one of the topmen called, pointing to their port side.

"Throw him a rope!" Callum hollered.

Five men along the port side gathered to retrieve their overboard shipmate, and Callum returned his attention to the wheel and the waves. He'd have liked to help them, but while they would no longer die crushed against the rocks, the sea was just as ruthless on its own, and he needed to focus on navigating the storm.

"Pull in the oars!" His command echoed across the deck and down to the gun deck as several men repeated him.

Rain battered the side of Callum's face, and he shook his head to clear his sight. *This* he could manage. He'd been through rough storms and knew how to weather the waves. He—

"Ho!" a topman called.

Callum cursed low and dark before following the topman's pointed finger out to their port side.

Not far away was another ship weathering the same storm as they. *Damnation.* He'd have seen the blasted thing if they hadn't been behind the damned rocks.

Harris ran to Callum's side. "Captain—"

"No, we'll not attack, Harris. With luck, this storm will drive us further apart, and once the weather has cleared, we'll have enough of a lead that we'll not be forced to encounter them if they wish to pursue us."

His apprentice nodded. "Very good, sir."

With a cautious eye on the other ship, Callum turned the wheel, aiming them toward London. Despite the squalls, the other ship followed the movement.

Harris let out a low curse, barely audible over the roar of rain and ocean water.

"Take the wheel," Callum instructed, reaching for his spyglass. But his hand merely slapped at his bared chest. The blasted thing was with his belts and pistols in his cabin.

"I've one here." Harris turned and bent, reaching into a small satchel that had been tied to the mizzen bitt directly behind them. The wooden posts were used while running rigging. Harris must have hidden the satchel for moments such as this. He straightened and handed a sodden spyglass to Callum.

A series of foul curses fell from Callum's lips as he spotted the flag on the other ship. "It's the crest of a noble family, and it's not the duke." He lowered the spyglass and looked at Harris. "Laura's kidnapper mentioned a baron and a marquess. I'll wager that they've come looking for their bounty. Go below and question our prisoners. Ask about this ship's firepower, the crest, and their purpose. I want to know if these men would risk their lives in their desperation."

"Right away, sir." Harris nodded, and he was gone.

Another wave crashed over them, and Callum flicked his sopping hair out of his eyes. If the other ship was who he feared, he must get Laura well away. Hell, he'd lower the sails in this storm if he had to, the dangers of such an act be damned. He'd not let them take her.

Chapter 22

A salty wave of ocean water sprayed Callum in the face as he struggled to turn the frigate's wheel. The damned storm wasn't ebbing.

His gaze slid to the side, and his heart hammered faster against his ribs. Despite his hopefulness and expectation, the other ship was gaining on them, using the waves to propel themselves closer.

Boom!

One of their pursuer's chase guns fired but went wide, the ball falling harmlessly into the water.

Callum cursed under his breath. He hadn't a damned choice.

"Lower the sails!" he hollered, and the topmen scurried to do his bidding.

It was an ill-advised plan in this storm, to be sure, but it couldn't be helped. If they were to have any chance of speed, they must take it.

He steered away from a wave, and it only splashed at the ship's hull. The rain was continuous, but it was not as punishing as it had been only moments ago. Hope began to blossom in his chest, and a flicker of confidence swiftly followed.

"*Captain!*" Harris shouted as he reached the upper deck, his brows puckered, his lips thin, and his complexion slightly pale.

All at once Callum's hope fled and his pulse sped faster. Something terrible had happened. "What is it?"

Harris reached his side, his chest heaving. "Our prisoners, sir. They've escaped."

"*What?* How, goddamn it? And where are they now? Have they reached the armoury?"

"A box of cutlery fell over, and they sawed themselves free with meat knives. And I don't know; I came directly to you when I noticed. They could be anywhere by now."

Callum's muscles were taut with frustration and worry, but he forced himself to breathe. There was no sense in bemoaning what was done; they must now focus on how to solve the problem. One thing—one *person*—however was foremost on his mind, and he was certain that she was the target of his prisoners' anger. He wanted to go to her, to leave his post and be damned with the consequences, but he couldn't justify such an action.

"I've no doubt that the bastards will reveal themselves soon enough," Callum said. "But while the men are in large groups and able to protect themselves, Laura is alone in my cabin. Harris, will you—"

"I'll see to it right away, sir," Harris interjected.

Callum gave a tight nod. "Guard her with a pistol in hand until I return. Shoot anyone else who tries to enter."

"Of course, sir." With that, Harris turned and strode toward the companionway.

There was an indefinable pull inside Callum, telling him to follow Harris, but he rolled his shoulders and mentally shook himself. Their night—and morning—had been absurdly satisfying. The woman was not only receptive in bed, but eager and enthusiastic, as well. He wanted many nights like that one. A lifetime of nights with her, as a matter of fact.

* * *

Laura blinked away her blurred vision and frowned, her head throbbing with each beat of her heart.

What happened? With trembling fingers, she tentatively touched her temple and felt the warm stickiness of blood.

"Oh, drat," she muttered. She required aid from the doctor, Henry, but she certainly couldn't leave the cabin in the nude.

Careful not to jostle her head or cause faintness, she lifted herself to a seated position and hissed a breath at the feel of the cool tile on her bottom. The ship rocked, and she stiffened her resolve. On hands and knees, Laura crawled to the chest of drawers and withdrew a pair of her men's trousers and a chemise. Lord knew if she fell again she didn't want anyone seeing beneath her skirts, and the trousers would stop them from seeing something alarming.

With quick, slightly painful movements, Laura donned her trousers and chemise, then crawled toward the dining table chair, where she'd draped her dress. A wave rocked her sideways, and she spread her hands wider on the floor in an effort to keep herself upright.

Her head ached, and her body felt stiff, but she held fast. At last, she was able to reach for her dress and slip it over her head. As she did, she looked down at her chemise and sighed.

"Double drat," she groaned. The blood from her fingers and temple had left crimson stains on her white chemise.

Bang! The cabin's door crashed open, and, waves or not, Laura scrambled to her feet.

"There you are, you bitch," her kidnapper spat, his grin greedy and his eyes full of malice, perfectly matching those of his companion, Sir Wycliff.

Laura's heart all but stopped in her chest as terror gnawed inside of her. It was unconscionable! How had they escaped? And what were they going to do to her if they caught her?

Wycliff stepped forward, and instinct had Laura retreating behind a chair. She knew how to fend a man off, drat it. Though, she'd never practised with *two* opponents.

The man sneered as the other rounded the dining table to trap her against the windows.

"Do not come any closer!" she said, hating the slight tremor of fear in her voice.

The men converged, and Laura's stomach wobbled. She tossed the chair at them then began to barrage them with small objects: her paints, canvases, books…anything that she could find.

Wycliff cursed foully, retrieved one of Callum's pistols from among his things, and aimed it at Laura. Her breath froze, and her skin turned to ice. *Hide*, Callum had said. When at a distance, she must seek shelter. But *where?*

"I've had enough of this," Wycliff muttered.

He pulled the trigger, just as her kidnapper hit the other man's hand sideways. "Weston and Beresford want her—"

Crack!

Gunpowder filled the small room, and it was a moment before Laura realized what had happened. Her hands went to her side, the hot flow of blood passing quickly through her fingers.

"That hurt, you basta…" Her words slurred before both men faded from her vision, and there was nothing but obscurity.

Chapter 23

Callum's gaze snapped up and his chest tightened as the *crack* of a pistol being discharged sounded, momentarily louder than the storm.

Harris stilled at the companionway, his foot on the first step of the ladder as he turned to look at Callum, eyes wide.

Without hesitation, Callum turned to shout at the third man in command. "Take the wheel!" And he let go, running toward the companionway without looking back. His heart thundered in his ears, his lungs labouring as he ran.

That couldn't be what he thought… *It can't be.*

He and Harris darted down the ladder and across the gun deck until they reached the captain's cabin. His heart all but entirely lodged in his throat, Callum burst through the doorway just as Laura's kidnapper heaved a dining chair through one section of the window, the shards glittering down into the ocean's waves.

"*What the devil are you doing?*" Callum shouted, pressure building in his neck and forehead.

Then, he saw her. Lying limp in Wycliff's arms, her blood spreading alarmingly over her side and smearing her head and hands, was Laura. His heart full stopped. *She can't be—*

An alarming, tingling numbness spread across his chest and out his arms, prickling in his fingertips as he processed the scene. A sob echoed in his ears, and he realized dimly that it came from him.

He blinked and raced forward, Harris on his heels. Swiftly retrieving his last loaded pistol as he passed the dining table, he raised his arm, aimed at the bastards, and fired. But the men jumped. Laura's glorious auburn hair rippled in the wind as she fell, and Callum's heart felt as though it was rent in two. He was distantly aware of a low, hoarse, and horrifyingly soul-deep screaming as he ran to the window and looked out at the water below.

It was only when Harris pulled him bodily back that he realized that he was about to follow them out…and that it was him who was screaming. His throat was tight and his eyes stung as he watched for Laura to resurface.

Her dress arrived first, then Wycliff, before the blackguard lifted her head back out of the water and began to swim.

An odd mixture of relief and dread filled Callum. He was glad that Laura would live—only because the scurrilous bastards wanted her alive—but he couldn't countenance what they might do to her.

* * *

Sir Charles Bradley released the wheel, letting his man Henderson take over while he walked to the forecastle. Gabe and Mary—newly married in a rushed ceremony—were standing, deep in conversation with Brown, Stevens, and Greene as they looked out at the worsening storm.

Charles stopped at their side and glanced sideways at Mary. "How are you feeling, Mary?"

Her pallor was slightly on the green side of ashen, but she smiled. "A bit better, thank you, sir."

"There is another ship up ahead." Brown gestured deep into the storm. "When the waves dip lower, you can see it."

Charles withdrew his spyglass.

"Oh!" Mary gasped. "Hydra, the duke is attempting to get our attention."

Turning his gaze to the Duke of Norshire's ship, Charles nodded. "Indeed he is." The man was gesturing wildly in the direction of the other ship, and Charles gave a wave to let him know he'd seen.

"This must be our quarry," he muttered, lifting the spyglass to one eye.

The waves cleared enough for Charles to see the ship…and the flag. "It's the Marquess of Weston's family crest."

Stevens crowed, a grin on his lips and anticipation lighting his golden eyes. "We've got the bastards!"

The same wave of jubilation rippled through Charles. Two ships against one were good odds. They could capture their quarry and put them in irons before continuing their search for—

Boom!

Charles' gut sank and his gaze flew to meet his men's.

Greene blinked away the rainwater that had gotten into his eyes. "Sir, was that—"

"Cannon fire," Charles finished for him.

* * *

Callum's insides wrenched, and his chest ached. He'd never before entered into battle feeling this way, but it could not be helped. *Goddamn it*, his eyes had even begun to prickle around the edges. Lady Laura had apparently gotten under his hide far more than he'd thought possible.

They'd slowed the frigate and turned, ready to attempt to retrieve Laura and free her from that bugger's clutches, but he'd witnessed Wycliff and Laura being brought aboard already. He had only one clear course of action.

He could not allow them to have Laura.

"Run out the guns!" he called to his men. "Aim *only* for their masts. Let's clip this bird's wings."

Callum swiped at his eyes, but he wasn't entirely certain that it was all rainwater, and he inwardly cursed.

"Fire when ready!"

Boom! Boom-boom!

"Ho!" one of the topmen hollered, arm outstretched off the bow of the ship.

Callum followed his gaze, and his heart sank further. "Hellfire and damnation."

Three ships were sailing their way.

* * *

With the urge to retch, Laura coughed, salt water sputtering from her lips and pain slicing through her side.

"I told you the bitch was alive," a menacing voice said.

"Tie her up and put her on a chair. I don't want her getting my bed wet with her sodden clothes," another voice growled.

Her eyes felt dry and full of sand, but she opened them, blinking rapidly to clear them. Three men stood around her supine form, their gazes each holding hatred and such violent vitriol that it made her breath catch in her throat.

Wycliff stood to her left, fury radiating from every sopping line of his body. He and another man lifted her bodily off the floor and deposited her on a chair. Someone had bound her wound overtop of her clothes, which gratefully staunched the flow of blood, but did nothing to rid her of the pain.

The moment she was seated, Wycliff rounded behind her and tied her wrists, and the other man seized her face in a punishing grip.

"You've been very naughty, Lady Laura," the man sneered. "We've been searching for you for some time."

"Here, here, Piper," the third man put in.

The blackguard named Piper squeezed her face tighter, his fingertips digging deeply into her skin. Laura fought against the urge to wince at the biting pain.

"We've a battle to win and your lover to kill," Piper continued, "but once we've done, we'll be back to see you thoroughly punished, eh wot?"

"Come, Piper, Wycliff," the man standing nearest to the door said, his gaze narrowed on Laura. "Leave the whore to fret, and let us get on with it. I've a need to kill some pirates."

With one last smirk, the men left the room, locking the door behind themselves.

Laura's pulse skittered with anxiousness and fear. She'd seen Callum in battle, but would he fight back knowing that she was on board? Would he be overtaken? Lord, it wasn't to be borne. Even if he *did* fight back to the best of his ability, she was in an impossibly horrid position. No matter what happened, she would be harmed and he and his crew would be in danger.

Her only hope was escape. But *how?*

* * *

"It is Callum, sir," Colin Greene said, lowering the spyglass from his eye. "Their ship has taken on damage, and it seems that they've done repairs."

Hydra accepted the spyglass from his man and peered through it. They were close enough now that he could see the men running about the upper deck, preparing the cannons, Callum—shirtless and face reddened from shouting orders—at the helm, and Harris—also half-nude—beside him.

Charles was glad to see them alive and well, but worried about the state of their ship in this battle.

Cannons were fired at the other ship, which Callum's ship had come abreast of.

"They need help," Charles said, lowering the spyglass.

The storm was slowing, but the danger had not yet fully passed. Callum and Harris were on a damaged ship and engaging in battle, when Weston's ship approached.

Charles turned and called above the din of the rain and splashing ocean water. "Run out the guns! Prepare for battle!"

* * *

"*Fire!*" Callum bellowed at his men.

Boom-boom! Boom-boom!

Cannonballs flew through the air, aimed directly at the enemy's masts. Two hit their targets, taking down the fore topgallant yard and the mizzen's fighting top.

"They're getting closer," Harris warned, his focus on the approaching ships.

Callum lifted the borrowed spyglass to his eye and peered through it. The closest ship was the unknown nobleman's, which was preparing to do battle with the Duke of Norshire's ship. The man must have received notice of Callum's letter.

"Thank you, Captain Taylor," Callum muttered under his breath.

The other ship… He swung his spyglass to the side and found the vessel. His breath hitched before a whoop of glee escaped him.

"Sir?" Harris asked.

"It's Hydra," Callum replied. "There are several men on the ship, but I can—*Christ*, there's Gabe and Mary, Greene, Ed, Brown…"

Boom!

Wood splintered behind him, and he cursed.

"Keep firing, men!" he bellowed.

Boom-boom-boom! Boom!

Cannons simultaneously fired from his frigate and Hydra's ship, targeting their enemies.

Their opponent lowered their sails and gained speed. *Damnation.* Callum had known battles to last days this way, but he couldn't risk leaving Laura in their hands for so long.

"Lower the sails, men! It's time to give chase."

* * *

Twisting her wrists, Laura attempted to tug herself free of her binding. It was futile, of course, but that did not stop her from trying. She glanced hopefully about the room. It was much the same shape as Callum's cabin, but it felt devoid of character or warmth. And there was not a weapon in sight.

Laura wiggled, and realized that Wycliff hadn't bound her *to* the chair, merely bound her wrists and ankles together and sat her upon the chair. *This*, she thought, she could get out of.

To avoid detection, she stood and shuffled away from the chair, her ankles chafing dreadfully, before she sat on the floor and rolled to her back. She'd learned during her previous kidnapping that she was able to slide her body through her arms, bringing her tied wrists to her front, but the process could be painful.

She worked quietly, ensuring that not a groan or gasp escaped her, despite the excruciating pain of her wound. She brought her arms around, her gaze continually darting about as she considered her options.

Callum's frigate would not be far behind, so she would likely not be required to swim a great distance before he reached her. But could she make it that long? Her side ached something fierce, and while the flow of blood was staunched currently, the impact of the water might reopen the flood.

Light flickered in the corner of the room, and she paused while getting her second foot through the circle of her arms. *The lantern.* An idea formed in her mind, and she didn't allow herself a moment to doubt it.

As swiftly as she could, she rose to her feet and shuffled to the nearest lantern. She cringed at the pull to her side as she lifted the lantern from its hook. With a glance over her shoulder toward the door, she heaved the lantern up and smashed it on the ground.

A flash of fire erupted from the spilled oil, flames lapping along the floor and up the dining chairs' legs. Careful not to burn herself, Laura retrieved a piece of broken glass and hurried away, sitting down and settling in to saw at her bindings.

Chapter 24

The rain and wind abated, and the large waves had settled into a gentle rocking, but the absence of the threat of drowning in a storm did nothing to calm Callum's nerves. They'd come abreast of the ship that Laura was on and had begun to fire at their masts once more, but now the other three ships were in the fray.

Cannonballs sailed through the air, and, with each one, Callum's heart stopped.

This wasn't him. He wasn't afraid of a fight: he *yearned* for it. He sodding loved his job, and was damned good at it. But one woman—his Laura—had changed all of that. She wasn't with him. She was trapped on his enemy's ship enduring the devil knew what, and he couldn't countenance the thought of her being injured in this fight.

"Captain!" Harris called from behind him, and Callum turned, following his apprentice's gaze.

"Dear God," he breathed. His stomach sank as he saw the bright light coming from the other ship's stern. From the captain's cabin, damn it.

"Fire," Harris confirmed.

* * *

A grunt threatened to escape, but Laura swallowed it down as she lifted the dining chair, her wrists and ankles blissfully free of her bindings. More than half of the cabin was engulfed in flames, and the space was entirely filled with smoke. Her lungs burned, and she coughed, cringing against the pain in her side.

The door burst open just as she heaved the chair over her head and threw, the wood crashing through the window. All at once, the air felt sucked from the room, the flames growing ever angrier, more aggressive.

"*Fire!*" came a shout from the doorway. Wycliff pushed through the flames, his fury palpable.

Laura's breath came in short, terrified gasps, and her pulse fluttered wildly. Without sparing him another glance, she jumped, Wycliff's roar following her as she fell toward the water.

* * *

A chair burst through the window of the captain's cabin, and Callum's heart leapt with hope. *Brilliant, Laura, now jump. Jump!* His gaze was fixed on the same spot, his body alight with the persistent buzzing of nervous energy.

Then, he saw her. A vision in a blood-soaked dress and sodden auburn curls falling to the water. But she wasn't alone. Swiftly on her heels, Wycliff bound after her.

Callum didn't think, didn't for one second consider his plan or the potential consequences as he ran toward the section of broken bulwark. He just dove.

The water felt like a shock of ice to his warm body, but he paid the feeling no heed, forcing his arms and legs to propel him through the slowly calming ocean toward Laura. He moved quickly, swimming hard and fast.

She was close—*so close*—when he heard her scream. Wycliff cursed at her, and they struggled.

Callum's heart hiccoughed, and with a short burst of speed, he had the man in his arms. He hauled the blackguard away from Laura, allowing her to resurface and gasp for air.

"You'll not beat them," Wycliff spluttered as Callum's arm tightened about the man's neck. "They're closer to you than you think."

"What does that mean?" Callum demanded, alarm spreading through him.

The bastard laughed and struggled, attempting to pull Callum beneath the water's surface with him.

Callum tightened his hold in a jostling movement, easily keeping them both above the water. "*What does that mean?*"

The arse laughed again, and spat toward Laura. "Fuc—"

Crunch. Laura squeaked at the horrifying sound of Wycliff's nose breaking, and Callum felt a moment's remorse for having punched the man in front of her.

"I apologize, sweetheart." He pushed the unconscious man away, and swam toward her.

"No, I... It just wasn't something...that I...was expecting." She huffed for breath between her words.

Alarm spread through Callum once more. "Are you able to swim with your skirts weighing you down?"

She was gasping, and clearly struggling to tread water. "I can't—" She gasped again. "My side..."

Rounding behind her, he wrapped an arm beneath her breasts, holding fast to her ribcage, and lifted her out of the water. Then he began to swim.

* * *

Boom! Boom-boom! Crack! Crack! Boom!

Sir Charles Bradley braced himself as a cannonball flew past and mercifully landed in the water beyond their ship. Cannons discharged, and his men were firing their pistols at the men on Weston's vessel.

Chaos had erupted the moment they'd come abreast of their opponent's ship. The duke and his men had already begun their battle, and within seconds of Charles and his spies joining the fray, madness ensued. The air was thick with smoke and gunpowder, and was still humid after the recent rain. His skin felt sticky and decidedly uncomfortable.

Men from Callum's frigate shouted and ran about, though Charles hadn't the faintest idea of what had caused it. He only hoped that his men and Lady Laura were still alive and well.

Callum's opponent's ship was engulfed in flames, the men jumping overboard and swimming toward the battle waging on Weston's ship.

His pistol loaded, Charles sighted down the gun toward a gunner preparing to fire on them, and pulled the trigger.

* * *

Shivers wracked Laura's frame, and her teeth began to chatter as Callum carried her across the gun deck toward his cabin. The warm, familiar scent of ocean, gunpowder, and wind surrounded the man who held her, and she pressed herself into his deliriously wonderful warmth. *How is he so warm?*

"Fetch the doctor," Callum said to someone over his shoulder. "She's lost a lot of blood."

Her heavy eyelids closed of their own accord, and she was vaguely aware of frantic talking as she was placed on a soft, inviting surface.

There was loud banging and the fresh scent of glue and wood.

A shadow passed over her closed eyelids, and she felt warmth at her side. "We've the carpenter repairing the stern gallery window that was destroyed," Callum said. "Odd timing or not, I refuse to have you fall out or be otherwise injured by the broken window."

Laura fought against the pull of sleep and opened her eyes to meet Callum's. His eyes were more grey than blue and turned down at the corners with worry.

"I'm 'ere, Captain." Henry hurried into the room, his arms laden with doctoring implements.

Laura's eyes slid closed once more, and she felt Callum's presence shift further away. Someone cut into her dress and chemise, exposing her abdomen and the bullet wound near her hip, but she scarcely registered the movements. The doctor clucked his tongue and spoke brusquely to her Pirate Spy, but she didn't hear the words.

Time passed quickly as Henry worked. He turned her on her uninjured side and thoroughly cleaned, stitched, and bandaged her wound. The poultice he'd applied felt warm and almost tingly, but through it all, her tired eyes remained closed.

"The pistol's ball went through the flesh just above your 'ip, Miss Laura," Henry said loudly. "And the crack on your 'ead will 'urt for several days, and you've a sizeable lump, but it's stitched and will 'eal."

She hummed in response.

"You lost a great deal of blood, and require rest and sustenance." The doctor patted her arm gently before withdrawing. His voice turned away from her. "Make certain that she stays warm. Summon me immediately if she gets the fever, although the ocean water should 'ave cleaned it enough to avoid infection."

Her Pirate muttered a response before coming to her side. He touched a palm to her cheek, and she nuzzled into the comforting warmth.

"I was so worried, sweetheart, that I didn't know if my heart could take it," he whispered, his lips touching her ear. "Hell, I'm *still* worried, if I'm being truthful. I don't ever want to feel this way again."

His forehead briefly touched her temple. "You're an incredibly brave woman, Laura, and for that you will forever have my admiration.

"Now, I must leave on a matter of justice. Harris will watch over you. Please rest." He discreetly bussed her temple and left.

* * *

Callum's fists clenched involuntarily as he marched back through the gun deck and up the ladder to the quarterdeck. His chest still ached something fierce, the pain having burrowed deep with each of the doctor's ministrations on Laura. *Christ*, that had been difficult to witness. She had been scarcely conscious through the ordeal, but her brow had puckered and she'd groaned and whimpered in agony as he'd cleaned and stitched her wound. And there'd been so much damned blood.

Hell if he didn't want to hang the bastards himself for their crimes against such an innocent, lovely woman. He'd wager that she wasn't their first victim, either, the scurrilous curs. But she'd damned well be their last.

His zeal for battle returned full force, surging hotly through his blood. The man at the helm stepped aside when Callum approached, and he felt another rush of eagerness as his hands touched the smooth wooden handles.

The ship next to them was all but entirely engulfed in flames and sitting low in the water. Men swam frantically away from it, moving swiftly toward Weston's ship.

"Not bloody likely," he rumbled under his breath.

With a glare at the sinking ship, Callum barked orders at his men, leading them toward Weston's. The coward was attempting to flee the duke's and Hydra's ships, its sails unfurled. Callum's gut jolted in anticipation of the chase, his damaged frigate sailing faster than the other two.

"Hold your fire!" Callum called to his men. "Ready the planks!"

They drew up alongside Weston's ship, matching his speed.

"You only have one enemy today, and they reside on that ship," Callum yelled, gesturing toward the common enemy. "Don't harm the men working with us, and you can claim everything in the hull!"

Callum laughed at Weston's unholy curses and angry bellows at his men. Saying that the man ought to be frightened was not nearly strong enough; the man should have been petrified. Callum was going to see his name strung through mud and horse shit before he was hanged for his crimes.

"Board her, men! Disarm and bind," Callum reminded them. "*Do not kill* if you can help it."

With exclamations of excitement and enthusiasm, his men readied their weapons and rope, and laid out the planks between the ships.

Following his lead, the duke's ship neared Weston's other side, and Callum grinned. The hard *thunk* of the planks hitting the bulwarks echoed around them before Callum noticed Hydra's ship sailing along his other side. They were going to use Callum's frigate as a bridge to Weston's, it seemed.

Callum crowed as the tide of men converged on Weston's ship.

Finding himself a cutlass and a handful of rope, which he tucked into the hem of his trousers, Callum joined his men. He waded through the fray, taking down several of Weston's men. But they weren't who he wanted.

His gaze was on the man in charge, the man responsible for the past years of torment on Hydra, his family, and their band of spies. The man who had ordered Laura's abduction and had manipulated a grieving and frightened father to get what he wanted. Weston was responsible for far too damned much treason and violence. He needed to be stopped.

Paving a path to his target, Callum continued on. Many of the marquess' men were already being bound, but others were fighting for their lives and freedom. Cutlasses clashed, pistols were fired, shouts rang out around him, and the air was heavy with gunpowder, sweat, and the metallic zing of blood.

Callum was jostled from behind, but he pushed the man off. A daring man with a sword in one hand and a dagger in the other blocked Callum's path. The man wasn't Weston, but a fight would do him good.

With a quick shout, Callum made the first swing and the man blocked it, the clash reverberating down his arm. He let out a laugh, making his opponent scowl. Their blades moved quickly, and the man's sword caught his cutlass. With a sneer, the man swiped at him with the dagger. Callum jumped back, narrowly avoiding a blade to the gut, when a shadow swiftly passed over their gnashing blades. He moved quickly to the side, his body at an awkward angle as he narrowly missed the new man's blade to the back of his skull. But the man didn't miss him entirely.

Callum roared as the new attacker's blade sliced through the base of his little finger, severing the small appendage from his left hand. He withdrew his cutlass, a string of dark curses falling from his lips.

That was enough playing. He used all of the force that he could muster and out-swung the men before knocking them both unconscious with the hilt of his cutlass.

His gaze flicked up, and he cursed. Weston was no longer at the helm.

Chapter 25

Callum pushed his way through the throng of men, searching for the bastards responsible for Laura's abduction. His hand hurt like the devil, but it was nothing compared to the hatred burning in his gut.

The fighting men parted, and he spotted his target…between Greene and Hydra, trussed and on his knees. *Shite.* Well, he wouldn't let the man get away that easily, and he knew damned well that he'd regret it the rest of his life if he didn't at least say his piece. He switched his cutlass to his injured hand, the hilt growing slick and sticky with his blood.

With determined strides, Callum made his way to the trio, not halting his momentum before slamming his fist into Weston's nose.

The cur's head snapped back. *"Son of a—"*

Callum slammed his fist into the man's face once more. Greene and Hydra struggled to keep the bastard on his knees, both of them uttering rebukes in Callum's direction. But he didn't care. He bent, putting his face in line with Weston's, but far enough away that the man couldn't hit him with his forehead.

"Fuck you," Callum spat, emphasizing each word.

"That will do, Callum," Hydra said stonily.

In one last move of defiance, Callum clenched his fist and slammed it once more in Weston's swollen, bleeding face, knocking him unconscious.

"One more time, but with feeling," Colin Greene said, a smirk curving up one corner of his mouth.

That pulled a laugh from Callum, making his chest feel a bit lighter. "It is damned good to see you all. Thank you for coming to our rescue."

Hydra shrugged one bloodied shoulder before raking his fingers through his mass of blond hair. "It is you that we should be thanking,

Callum. Do you still have Wycliff and Lady Laura's kidnapper…?" The man's question faded away as he noticed Callum's shaking head.

"No, sir. When we entered this storm, they managed their escape. I shot one, and the other is floating unconscious in the ocean, probably drowned or taken down with the blazing ship."

Hydra nodded. "Thank you for your efforts."

"Where is the baron?" Callum asked, desirous to punch that man's teeth in, as well.

Greene notched his chin to one side, and Callum followed the man's gaze.

The battle, it seemed, was over. His men, the duke's, and Hydra's bound the rest and awaited orders.

The Baron of Beresford, the rotter, struggled face down among blood and other prisoners as Stevens pressed a knee into his back. Stevens grinned unrepentantly, his golden eyes veritably glowing with triumph, despite his clearly broken left arm.

"Come now," Stevens called, holding his left arm out to one side. "Would I not make a superior pirate?"

* * *

It was some time later, when they'd gotten their prisoners into Hydra's hull and Callum and his fellows had been seen by the ship's doctor, that they realized the extent of everyone's injuries. Most of Callum's men had suffered only minor scrapes and bruises, with two casualties. His fellows—Hydra's men—had all sustained various blade or bullet wounds, but for Stevens, whose arm was broken, and Henderson, who'd been knocked out by his third opponent.

The duke and his men, however, were significantly less experienced with weaponry than pirates and spies, and had taken on far more injuries. Nearly a quarter of his crew had been killed—a truly substantial number—and the remainder suffered injuries ranging from minor to life-threatening. The duke himself had been both stabbed and shot. It was unclear if he would survive.

Callum swallowed a dram of whisky and placed the snifter back on the table of his ship's wardroom. He'd never dined or even sat there, but he couldn't bloody well hold this meeting in his cabin and risk the other men seeing Laura and disturbing her rest. *Christ*, he hoped she was doing well.

"Will you not give us your report, Callum?" Hydra asked, sipping on his own draught of whisky.

His fellows all sat around the table, sporting various styles of bandaging, with the exception of Brown, who was fighting for his life in the infirmary on Hydra's ship.

"Yes, sir." Callum thought back to the beginning of his journey. "It took a fortnight for me to garner control over this frigate…"

He told them everything, with the exception of his courtship and trysts with Laura. The courtship he would only discuss with the duke, and their trysts… Well, he'd discuss those with no one.

"…which brings us to today," Callum concluded.

Hydra nodded and pinched the bridge of his nose before returning his gaze to Callum. "Holy hell, what a sodding mess. The ocean has not been kind to you."

Callum shrugged one shoulder. *Far kinder than you might think.*

"Your ship's turned to shit," Stevens said abruptly.

"Indeed." Callum smirked and inclined his head.

Hydra swallowed more of his whisky. "Take Weston's ship. The man won't need it any longer, once his neck's been stretched, and it's a damned sight better than leaving the vessel floating in the ocean with no one to man it."

Pursing his lips, Callum considered his superior's thought. Callum's lifelong aspiration had been to captain a pirate ship. As a man, he'd achieved his goal, and it had been very nearly perfect. But something about his superior's offer felt wrong. To be sure, the bastard Weston wouldn't require the ship, and leaving it floating in the ocean seemed a waste, but Callum no longer pined for a life at sea. And he would be damned if he'd leave Laura.

Callum had a position in the Secret Service that he could continue on at, or he could join several of his fellows in becoming Bow Street Runners. Hell, if he desired it, he was certain that he'd be permitted to teach at Grimsbury Manor. Before him were endless possibilities that would satisfy him. In fact, he rather preferred those options.

"Thank you, sir," Callum began, "but I believe that my days as a captain have come to an end. I will gladly advise that my men take the ship and sail on to do as they will."

Stevens cursed, his golden eyes wide. "Hell, Callum. Hasn't this always been what you desired?"

The chair creaked as Callum shifted his weight, discomfited. "Yes, and now I'm done."

His fellows remained silent for several heartbeats, and Callum avoided their searching gazes, choosing instead to stare into the bottom of his empty snifter. They were curious, he knew, but he couldn't discuss his feelings for Laura when he was not entirely certain of them, himself. He wanted to marry her, of that he was confident, and he most definitely desired her, but as for his heart… Damn it, he didn't know what he felt. He needed time to ruminate on it.

"Very well." Hydra broke the silence. "If it pleases them, I will give your pirates privateer status, as long as they continue to avoid killing anyone and are willing to search ships for sensitive documents on our behalf and send them to me if they come across any."

Callum nodded. "I believe they would be very grateful for the honour, sir."

"Now, what of you and Harris?" his superior asked.

Taking a deep breath, Callum steeled himself to voice what he knew would garner questions or knowing gazes from his fellows. "I cannot speak for Harris, but due to the duke's great losses, I would like to seek his blessing to reside on his ship for the return journey. I've experience that I believe will be invaluable to his men."

Hydra's left eye crinkled in the corner before he nodded. "Very well, you may seek an audience with the man."

A wave of relief swept over Callum. One hurdle was over. The next was to seek permission from the duke. While the intimacies that he'd shared with Laura had come to an end, he couldn't imagine residing on a different ship. Hell, it would be difficult enough sleeping in a separate bed.

Shite, but with all of the events that day, he'd not taken a moment to truly think about what had transpired that morning and the night before. He'd made love to Laura, for Christ's sake. *Twice*. And he bloody well wanted to do it again, once his hand and Laura had healed. *It can't happen, man*, he reminded himself.

His stomach dipped, and his chest tightened.

"Thank you again, Hydra," he said. "I will speak with my men and help them transfer their belongings to the new ship. It might take several days due to the crew's injuries, but if you do not mind waiting…?"

"I should imagine not," his superior replied. "Our men require rest and time to recover, as well. The duke would like to see his daughter, of course, but once she's been moved, we can take our time to ensure that everyone is settled before we set sail once more. Our prisoners can rot in the hold for a little while longer."

"Come to that," Mary put in, "did anyone else notice that Weston, Beresford, McMann, and Piper seemed distinctly unmoved by their capture and imprisonment?"

Colin Greene nodded, the bandage about his head slipping slightly. "I did. It is almost as though they anticipated—*planned*—on this."

"We'd best keep an eye on them," Hydra said. "If they believe themselves capable of escape, then so must we."

* * *

London

Bridget's pulse sped as she tugged once more on the too-tight waist of her bombazine frock and knelt against the rear outside wall of Bethlem Royal Hospital, her stomach rolling and her smallsword in her hand.

Jones cut her a sideways glance, his gaze derisive. "You ought to have remained home, milady," he whispered. "This is a dangerous business, and most certainly not the place for a woman in your condition."

Stubbornness made her jut out her chin and narrow her eyes at him, though she must admit the man was right. Being pregnant winded and exhausted her, and her movements were slower than they ought to be for such an excursion. But she'd never say as much to the man. And, blast it, she could be useful, too. She wanted to help, and she damned well would.

The rear door's lock gave an audible *click*, and Hugh carefully replaced the small picking implements in his coat pocket and stepped aside. Mr. MacLean, Milford, and Oliver hurried forward, opening the door on silent hinges and allowing the group of them through. The remainder of the men and women were divided between the hospital's surrounding land and her husband's spy refuge town house with Doctor Simon Claridge.

The guards standing just inside the door—like the ones outside— were swiftly put to sleep, and they all crept silently through the halls. During the men's reconnaissance, they'd learned that several unnamed patients remained behind barred doors at the hospital, and only three of those were considered of higher risk to harm others or themselves. Those men were on the second floor.

Bridget put a hand to her mouth as her stomach lurched. The acrid scent of bile, human waste, and rotting wood was very nearly too much to bear. The floor was uneven, and she clutched at Jones' arm with one hand to keep her balance. The walls were cracked and dripping with some unknown glistening liquid, and all manner of groans, cries, and pitiful wails came from all around them as they traversed the halls.

She and her sister, Kat, often visited the hospitals about London, but had never graced the halls of Bethlem Royal. And now she regretted that fact. These poor souls needed some light, love, and friendship in their lives.

There was a gasp and a scuffle of feet up ahead before they turned down another corridor. They moved slowly now, the men looking carefully into each cell. The unholy scent grew stronger the further into the hospital they travelled, and Bridget was forced to blink the sting of tears away from her eyes.

A low, whispered curse came from Mr. MacLean, who led their group of six, as he stopped at one of the cells. He side-stepped, allowing Hugh through to pick the lock, which gave a scraping *snick* as it opened. Milford greased the hinges with liquid from a small vial, and the door swung open silently.

Inside was a horror. The man within lay broken, swollen, and bleeding on a small square of cloth in the corner of the cell, his one opened eye watching them with first fear, then hope.

"Hugh, Jones, Milford, and Oliver," Mr. MacLean whispered harshly, "help me carry him out. Bridget, lead the way and clear the path."

A wave of pride washed over her as she nodded. The fact that Mr. MacLean trusted her enough to guard them was remarkably flattering, and quite an honour.

With nary a grunt, the men lifted Colonel Richards in their arms and slipped from the cell. Several of the patients—*prisoners, more like*—in the nearby cells noticed the intrusion and began to plead with them. Bridget's heart twisted as she walked away, her smallsword lifted in the *en garde* position.

It wasn't the first time that she'd been on an *assignment*, and she hoped that it wouldn't be her last, but the moment she'd begun moving, she was focused. Her ears were trained ahead of her and to each side, listening for the heavy footfalls of guards.

Two voices came from around their next corner, and Bridget flattened herself against the cool, moist brick, motioning for the men following her to do the same. Jones cursed.

The voices grew louder before two men rounded the corner.

"Wha—" The startled exclamation was cut off as Bridget swung her blade with a *whoosh.*

In four rapid movements and two knocks to the head with her hilt, both men were splayed on the floor, unconscious and bleeding from shallow cuts.

Another low curse came from behind her, and she gestured for the men to follow her. Her heart squeezed once more as Colonel Richards groaned at the jostle.

Eleanor's cousin had been correct: someone wished harm on poor Colonel Richards. Unfortunately for Colonel Richards, they hadn't been swift enough to save him this last beating. She just hoped that the doctor could help him.

Chapter 26

The next four days sped by in a flurry of activity. Callum's first task was bringing Laura aboard her father's ship, where she was placed on a second bed in his captain's cabin. Then he'd manoeuvred his and Weston's ships together and they'd begun the process of transferring goods. They outfitted Weston's ship with the carronades from Callum's and emptied the food stores, gunner's store, magazine, and cabins of anything worth using on the new ship.

By the end of the move, every man was weary and sore. They were very nearly ready to set sail, but there was one thing that Callum had yet to do.

His boots clicked on the gun deck as he approached the duke's cabin. The guard standing at the door watched him expectantly, and Callum steeled his nerves.

"Might I have a word with His Grace?"

The guard's lips tightened. "Allow me to inquire." He disappeared through the door, closing it behind himself.

Callum waited, his stomach bewilderingly in knots. It was a simple question; he really oughtn't be so nervous. He hadn't yet met the duke, even when he'd brought Laura aboard, as the man had been sleeping. As Callum understood it, His Grace was very ill, indeed. He'd been impaled in the stomach and shot through the thigh, but it wasn't just the injuries that kept him abed—it was the infection.

The guard returned and gestured for Callum to enter. Two men flanked the duke's bed, guarding and tending him. Callum resisted the urge to look at Laura's empty bed. *Where is she?* he wondered.

Callum approached the duke's bedside and bowed low. The room smelled like death.

"Come," the duke rasped, his voice barely above a whisper. "I must ask you..."

"Your Grace?" Callum hadn't anticipated being asked anything by the duke in his condition. He'd merely wished to seek a position on this ship for him and Harris—who wished to join him—and request permission to court his daughter.

"My men are"—he rasped a breath—"inexperienced. And many…have died. I need…you to captain my ship…until I am well…again."

A frown puckered Callum's forehead before clearing once more. "Haven't you another man better suited for the position, Your Grace? Surely I am not your—"

The duke waved a hand weakly in the air, but despite the feebleness of the gesture, it held strength of meaning. "You…are the man who…saved my daughter. I saw…you fighting. I saw how…you command your men. *You* are…the man that…I need, Callum…McInnis."

Callum inclined his head. "I would be honoured to take the position, Your Grace, as long as I am able to bring aboard my second in command, Harris—"

"Of…course. Whatever you…wish." The duke broke off in a fit of coughing, which was followed by more rasping breaths and soul-deep groans.

The man's eyes slid closed, and Callum took that as dismissal. With another bow, he turned on his heel and quit the room.

* * *

Laura tilted her face into the morning sun, relishing its warmth. She would take every moment like this that she could, for she knew that when she returned to London, society's rules would once more be the proverbial manacles about her wrists, and she would not be permitted out of doors without a wide-rimmed bonnet. She'd not noticed how suffocating society could be until she'd been free of it. Aboard Callum's frigate, she'd been free to do as she wished, go where she wished… Even aboard her father's ship, she was more restricted. Thoughtful as he was, he'd brought an array of frocks and underthings so that she might be comfortable, but after living months without the binds of a corset, she'd grown accustomed to her ability to breathe and move.

Gripping the sun-warmed bulwark, she looked out at the gently moving ocean, and sighed.

"Are you well, my lady?" Callum's low voice at her elbow sent gooseflesh prickling along her skin, and she turned to face him.

His blue eyes were light and warm, his brown, waving hair windswept, and his devilishly skilled lips quirked upward in one corner. He'd shaved his short growth of beard, revealing several long scars. She thought him devilishly handsome.

Laura's heart gave a heavy *thump* before quickening its pace. She'd only seen him in passing since the battle, and had missed his company very much, indeed. He had once more donned his full pirate attire: flowing lawn shirt opened at the collar, tight black breeches, dulled leather boots that rose up the length of his calves, his bright red sash that knotted then dangled down along his muscular thigh, belts decorated with elaborately carved silver medallions, and his long, dark coat. The man was sinfully attractive.

"I am, thank you, Pirate." She beamed at him, her stomach fluttering wildly. "And you?"

He quirked one shoulder before resting an elbow on the bulwark beside her, his body leaning and one ankle crossed over the other in a casual, comfortable stance. His pistols and spyglass—now returned to their place among his belts—clinked as he moved. Several of her father's men looked askance at her Pirate, but remained dutifully silent as they went about their tasks.

The warm heat burgeoning in Callum's gaze belied the easy grin on his lips. "I heard tell of an invitation to a rather shockingly scandalous evening of dinner, drink, and song in celebration of the new privateers' successes. Hydra—Sir Charles Bradley—gave them their letter of mark just this afternoon to legitimize them. Would you care to join me in the revelry, Lady Laura?"

Part of Laura wanted to protest the use of her title and beg him to call her his sweetheart once more. But she couldn't, and the loss of that small intimacy made her feel unnervingly desolate. *Keep your heart unmoved, Laura*, her inner voice cautioned.

Her lips pursed involuntarily as she thought. She wanted so desperately to say yes, but what would her father think? He was abed—and very ill—in his cabin, and now that she was returned to him, she felt obliged to once more be the dutiful daughter. Her father would never approve a match between them, even should Callum ask, regardless of her recently lowered position in society. He simply would never permit her to wed a pirate, no matter how much she'd come to—*no*. She shook herself internally.

"If you wish it, Harris could act as our chaperone," Callum hurried to add. "And your father's men are invited, of course."

She blinked. "Is that safe? Is there a chance that your crew would say—" She cleared her throat. "What I mean to say is, would our…er…sleeping arrangements be mentioned to my father's crew?"

"My men are loyal to you. They shall remain silent on the matter."

She sighed, and slowly nodded. It was highly improper, but she simply could not resist the temptation to hear him sing again. "I should be delighted, then."

* * *

The sun lowered along the horizon, leaving the sky bathed in pink, orange, and gilt and the ocean glittering in its almost stillness. A temperate breeze took the heat off the air and cooled Laura under her layers of restrictive silks.

She strode across her father's deck and over the plank that linked to the pirate's ship—previously Weston's. Rhythmic thumping, clapping, and an energetic song came from many of the men gathered on the upper deck. Her father's and Sir Bradley's men had drinks in hand and smiles on their faces, some of them stomping or singing along with the pirates.

Then her gaze found Callum. Her Pirate Spy was near the helm, swathed in light from the many lanterns and setting sun, his face bright with merriment and his neck strained as he sang. Laura's breath hitched, and her stomach quivered. It really was quite remarkable how the sight of him still made her feel so…*charged* after their time together.

"My lady." One of her father's men bowed to her as she passed, and she nodded in return.

"Miss Laura!" Henry hurried forward through the other men and put a hand to her forearm.

One of her father's men, who had been leaning on the main mast, straightened to his full height, his gaze threatening.

Henry's ears pinkened and he withdrew his hand. "Though I suppose you're *Lady* Laura, aren't you? 'Ow are you feeling? 'Ave you been changing the bandages?"

Laura smiled at the kindly pirate doctor, ignoring the intimidating man beside her. "Thank you very much for your concern, Henry. I am doing quite well. My father's physician has frequently applied the poultice that you provided, and the wounds are healing."

She felt Callum approach before he spoke. "Good evening, Lady Laura." His voice was smooth and deep, and it warmed her insides like hot chocolate.

The Pirate clasped her hand and bent to brush a kiss to the inside of her palm, causing her heart to flutter.

"Pirate," she breathed.

His grin was wicked and his gaze possessive as he straightened and led her further into the ring of light.

"Look ahead, look astern," a man began singing.

"Look the weather in the lee," the other pirates joined in. "Blow high! Blow low! And so sailed we. I see a wreck to the windward, and a lofty ship to lee, a sailing down all on the coasts of High Barbary. O are you a pirate, or a man-o-war? cried we. Blow high! Blow low! And so sailed we…"

The men continued to sing, their collective voices vibrating in Laura's chest. Light flickered on their cheerful faces—even her father's men seemed to revel in the merriment, joining in on familiar choruses. She spotted Harris in the crush, speaking into the ear of a liveried man.

The song concluded with the last verse: "With cutlass and gun, O we fought for hours three; Blow high! Blow low! And so sailed we. The ship it was their coffin and their grave it was the sea. A sailing down all on the coasts of High Barbary."

Callum's warm blue gaze caught Laura's and his knuckles brushed the back of her hand, before his voice rang out above the cheers. "Be mine, dear maid! This faithful heart can never prove untrue; 'twere easier far from life to part, than cease to live for you." His voice rose and fell with the melody, his gaze still intent on hers.

Laura couldn't look away. She knew what a sight they must be, but surely word had already reached her father's men of what had transpired between her and the Pirate Captain, for they'd not made their trysts secret. In fact, Callum had been openly possessive and affectionate toward her in their time together.

"Then turn thee not away, my love, oh turn thee not away!" His voice rose in volume. "For, by the light of truth, I swear, to love thee night and day, love! The lark shall first forget to sing, when morn unfolds the east, ere I by change or coldness ring thy fond confiding breast. Then turn thee not away. Then turn thee not away, my love, oh turn thee not away! For, by the light of truth, I swear, to love thee night and day, love!"

There was a moment of breathless silence before the men around them erupted in cheers and whistles. But Laura was caught in the intensity of her Pirate's blue eyes, her breath stuck in her throat. Did he know what he'd just done? What he'd just *said*? It was part of the song, she would grant, but the man had quite publicly revealed their intimate association and professed his love for her.

Her heart gave a happy skip, but she internally shook herself. *It was merely a part of the song, Laura.*

Suddenly, Callum was closer, the heat from his body radiating toward her. Oh, Lord, he was going to kiss her. Right there, in front of her father's men! And she was going to let him, blast it. Where was their chaperone?

Another song broke out: "Come, jolly Bacchus, god of wine, crown this night with pleasure…"

Her pirate's hand found hers, and he pulled her closer. Would this be their last night together? Would he join his fellows for the return journey, or would he, perhaps, continue on with the pirates before coming home to London? Her heart gave a hard *thump*, and her insides quivered. She wanted to beg him to stay with her, but instead she clutched at his coat and lifted on her toes.

"Captain." Harris appeared beside them, and Laura cursed the man's timing.

His lips moved, but she could scarcely hear him over the roar of blood in her ears and the loud, raucous singing. She retreated a step from Callum, instantly regretting that she had agreed to join in the evening instead of suggesting that they find a secluded spot to have a moment of privacy.

"Would you care for a refreshment, Lady Laura?" Harris asked louder.

Laura shook her head. "No, thank you." She didn't feel thirsty, and rather preferred tea to ale or grog.

The man darted a glance at his superior and stepped between them.

Another song began. "Oh, Mrs. McGraw, the captain said, would you like to make a pirate out of your son, Ted? With a scarlet cloak and a fine cocked hat, oh, Mrs. McGraw wouldn't you like that?" one man sang.

"With me too-rye-yaah, foddle-diddle-daah, too-rye, oh-rye, oh-rye-yaah. With me too-rye-yaah, foddle-diddle-daah, too-rye, oh-rye, oh-rye-yaah," the other men joined in, Harris and her pirate included, stomping, clapping, and giving little chirps and whistles between the verses.

Despite her ill-timed desire for Callum and Harris' perfectly reasonable interference, the evening was delightful. Countless more songs were sung, the men danced and drank, and Laura had a brief opportunity to greet Callum's fellows. It had merely been an introduction, but she already knew that these individuals, these *spies*, would be fascinating to get to know better.

The hour grew late, the breeze cool and gentle, and the sun entirely gone. The moon was high, lending a blue, milky glow to anything that was not touched by the circle of lantern lights. It was magical.

"Before the men lose consciousness," Henry suddenly called above the din of voices, "and before we pirates—sorry, *privateers*, blimey, what a thought—are too piss-drunk to remember the words, we 'ave a song for our defecting captain." He raised his glass, along with every other man aboard. "To our captain, who taught us restraint, guided us through 'ell, and led us to all the damned riches we could want! To the new—albeit temporary—captain of the Duke of Norshire's ship, Captain Callum McInnis, son of the notorious John 'Lucifer' McInnis."

Calls of "Hear, hear!" and "To Captain McInnis!" mingled with a low, murmuring of voices before the men drank.

Captain of the duke's ship? Laura's startled gaze swung toward her pirate on the other side of Harris, and he shrugged, an unrepentant grin on his lips. *Just a moment,* her inner voice interrupted. *Who, precisely, was his father?*

"Our anchor we'll weigh, and our sails we will set," the pirates—privateers—sang. "Goodbye, fare-ye-well, goodbye, fare-ye-well. The friends we are leaving, we leave with regret, hurrah, my boys, we're homeward bound. We're homeward bound, oh joyful sound! Goodbye, fare-ye-well, goodbye, fare-ye-well…"

Chapter 27

It had been some time since Laura had ventured out of her father's cabin. The duke's fever had broken some days prior, but soon after, she found herself unable to leave her own bed due to seasickness.

The air remained humid and the sparse clouds were still grey with the threat of rain after days of weathering a storm. Laura took a deep breath, grateful for the fresh air, though her stomach still roiled.

Her slippered footfalls were silent on the wood of the deck as she slowly walked, but the men seemed aware of her, bobbing their heads or lowering in bows as she passed. There was only one man that had *her* attention, however. Her gaze slid upward to Callum, where he stood at the helm, his eyes light, his hair windswept, and his attire outrageously screaming *pirate*. Her pulse sped and her breath came quicker at the sight of him, her stomach quivering ever so slightly.

It had been three weeks since they'd almost kissed, and they'd scarcely spoken since. She'd seen him, of course, but he'd always been busy or she'd been aiding her father, and they hadn't the opportunity to speak in depth. Her heart squeezed at that. She missed their discussions, the feel of his body pressed to hers each night… Heavens, she even missed their quiet, companionable silence.

Before she knew what she was about, her feet had taken her toward Callum, her gaze fixed on him. She had exciting news that she was eager to share with him, for while others might listen, they wouldn't care as much as she suspected Callum would.

He turned and said something to Harris, who stood at his shoulder, and left the wheel, striding purposefully toward her. Another quiver rippled through her stomach, and a smile pulled at her mouth.

"Good morning, my lady," he said, stopping just in front of her with a bow.

"Good morning, Pirate."

His eyes flashed with something heated before he raked his fingers through his unruly hair.

"How is your recovery?" he asked. "And your father's?"

Laura put a hand to the bulwark at her side, the slight rocking motion of the ship still making her stomach feel uneasy. "I am very well," she lied. "My wounds have all but entirely healed, and Papa is still convalescing. His fever broke four days ago, but he is still weak and requires much aid."

Callum's lips thinned before he nodded. "I am pleased to hear that he is recovering."

"I've missed you, Callum," she said, low enough that only he could hear.

* * *

The vice around Callum's heart loosened just a bit at her words. "I've missed you, as well." *Sweetheart.* He daren't say it aloud, but Christ, he wanted to. Three weeks without touching her… It had been sodding miserable. And now she was ill.

It was as plain as the ocean around them that she'd been ill; even if he hadn't heard it from Harris, he'd have known just from looking at her. Her cheeks were slightly sunken—as though she hadn't eaten in days—and her pallor was almost green. Seasickness was not uncommon, but she'd been on the ocean for months and had not shown any signs of becoming ill by the motion. Having it come on *now* was highly irregular. And decidedly alarming.

"Will you walk with me?" Laura asked.

Callum nodded with a muttered "Of course," and they fell into synchronized step along the bulwark. His fingers itched to grasp her hand or offer his arm, but he instead clasped his hands behind his back, hating the forced formality between them.

"My sister has been found," Laura blurted.

Callum's surprised gaze swung toward her. "That's marvellous! How do you feel about that?"

She beamed back at him, and his heart flipped over.

"It really, truly is. Papa tells me that she's been through a rather trying time, but he would leave that tale for her to tell me. He's said that she has two sons by her first husband, and that she is very recently remarried." She sighed and briefly squeezed her eyes shut. "I have nephews, Callum, named Quintin and Maximus, aged seven and four respectively. They are apparently delightful, and eager to meet me. I-I confess, I have conflicted feelings: I'm happy, of course, but I'm also curious about her reasons for not contacting me."

"Of course your feelings are diverged," he replied, his voice low and unusually rough, even to his own ears.

Her smile wavered with emotion, and tears welled in her eyes. "Papa told me three days ago, and I nearly burst at the news. I've wanted desperately to share it with you ever since, but I've not had the opportunity before now."

Callum smiled warmly at the woman walking slowly at his side. "I'm sorry that it has taken so long, but I am very glad to hear such happy news. I have rather pleasing news, myself."

"Have you?"

He jerked his chin down in a single nod. "I only spoke briefly to my fellows on the matter, between the battle, the chaos, and our setting sail once more, but I've heard that Hugh has been found." She grinned at him, and he continued. "Indeed, I was rather surprised, myself, but overjoyed that he was alive and well when my fellows had departed London. All they've said was that he had quite the story behind his disappearance. I daresay I will hear it—and the stories of many of my fellows—once we return home."

"I…" She hesitated until his gaze met hers. "I did learn one more thing from Papa."

He watched her with an air of patience, but something about the way she'd said it made his gut knot slightly.

"Charlotte's new husband is named Hugh Haddington."

Callum stopped and spun, his eyes wide. "*The devil you say!*"

There were several disapproving noises around them, and Callum could feel the glares at his back, but Laura laughed, the sound light and lilting.

"I swear it is the truth," she said, attempting—and failing—to hide her mirth.

Callum raked both hands through his hair, then quickly clasped them behind his back once more, steadfastly resisting the urge to touch her. "Holy sodding hell, Hugh is married. I couldn't be happier for the man, but I have so very many questions. I wonder how they came to meet."

"I imagine it is quite the compelling story."

There was an undercurrent to her tone that had him looking askance at her. *Compelling story, indeed. Just as we have.* His countenance must have shown the direction of his thoughts, for her mirth all but entirely fled and her moss-green eyes burned with promise. Damnation, he wanted to pull her into his arms and kiss her right there. It bothered him more than he cared to admit that he couldn't. Far too much was standing in their way.

A man ahead of them shouted something to another liveried man, and the spell was broken. They resumed their walk, and Callum considered Hugh's discovery. He imagined that there was a flurry of activity among the Secret Service, and Hugh was welcomed with warmth, concern, and congeniality.

He was pleased for his friend, and yet still concerned for the others. Barrows had yet to awaken, and Richards was still missing. *Hell's teeth*. No matter how much Callum wanted to remain on the ocean with Laura always at his side, he was eager to lend his aid when they returned to London.

* * *

London

A bead of sweat paved a path between Bridget's breasts, tickling the fine hairs there before soaking uncomfortably into her already damp chemise. She wanted to reach into her bodice and scratch at the faint tickle—and she was almost certain that no one would look askance at her, due to her *enceinte* state—but she determinedly fought the urge, and instead fanned herself more vigorously.

The mid-to-late-August heat of town was almost enough to drive a woman mad. It was no wonder that it was nearly empty of nobility, all the wealthier families having retreated to their more temperate estates. Bridget longed for the Brampton estate where her family and children were residing, with its opened doors letting in the ever-present summer breeze and scent of fresh flowers. Even with fewer residents, London still smelled heavily of coal, sweat, and ever-so-slightly of urine. It was enough to churn her stomach.

She returned her focus to the chessboard and moved her rook, earning a groan from Jones, who sat across from her. They had brought several pieces of furniture from the parlour up into Barrows' bedchamber, hoping that the sound of voices would encourage the man to awaken. For the past months, Thomson—one of Charles' spies—had been caring for the unconscious man. Though poor Barrows looked far thinner than she remembered.

A knock sounded at the bedchamber door, drawing Bridget's gaze along with MacLean's, Jones', and Hugh's.

"We have visitors, sir," Ferris said to Mr. MacLean, who set aside his paper.

"Visitors," Mr. MacLean repeated. "Who would—holy hell." His eyes grew wide as two men entered the room, large, imposing, and finely attired. Mr. MacLean stood and greeted the men with admiration. "Hades, Ares, what a pleasure it is to see you. Welcome, welcome."

Jones appeared at Bridget's side, his hand extended, and she gratefully accepted it, pulling herself to her feet.

"Mr. McKinnon." She strode over, greeting the man called Hades and then turning to the man called Ares. "And Mr. Smith. A pleasure to see you both again."

They bowed in return.

"Mr. Smith, did Camilla come to town with you?" she asked. The man was recently married to the lovely seamstress who worked for her sister, Kat, in her shops.

He grinned wolfishly at the mention of his wife. "I did, as a matter of fact, but she is being kept safely away while she pays visits to Brown and Brown's Modiste and Tailoring shops."

"Very wise," Jones put in, sliding a sideways glance at Bridget.

"Shall I bring you both up to see Colonel Richards?" she asked. "He is conscious, but unable to communicate as of yet. Doctor Claridge determined that Richards' throat was severely damaged and one hand and one arm broken, in addition to countless other injuries, which have rendered him unable to express himself."

Both men nodded solemnly, and Bridget led the way through the town house toward the colonel's rooms, with MacLean and Jones following behind. The bedchamber was still and silent, and smelled heavily of liniment and hopelessness.

She approached the bed and smiled down at the man lying there. "Good morning, Colonel Richards. You have visitors today."

Bridget stepped aside and allowed the two large men to pass. They spoke softly to their friend, reassuring him and offering encouragement.

Richards groaned, and alarm jolted through Bridget. "Oh, Colonel Richards." She hurried forward. "Doctor Claridge says that you oughtn't attempt to speak."

He licked his lips with a grimace, then croaked, "Danger."

"What danger?" Ares demanded.

Bridget shook her head. "Charles—that is to say, Hydra—and a large group of men have ventured out to sea, following lords Weston and Beresford's ship—"

Colonel Richards was shaking his head, his eyes wide. "Not…them."

Chapter 28

Careful not to awaken any of the sleeping crew, Laura crept on the balls of her feet along the darkened gun deck. With so few liveried men aboard the duke's ship, the night crew consisted of scarcely twenty men, all of them on the upper deck. The sleeping men, however, could easily be awoken, and catch her stealing across the ship in her night-rail and robe. Lord only knew what would happen then.

She found her way to the ladder and cautiously stepped down onto the mess deck. There were several loud snores coming from the gently swaying hammocks, and, with a grimace, Laura continued across the deck toward the wardroom. There were more officers' quarters than she remembered, and each one was occupied.

Since she'd walked with Callum that morning, she'd known that she would seek him out that evening. Not only did she require the comfort of his kisses and the warmth of his body, but she also had something that she very much wished to discuss with him.

The lanterns in the wardroom lent just enough light for her to see as she crept. At each door, she lifted on her toes to peek through the slats, glancing only at the clothing that the men had hung on the opposite wall, and not at their sleeping forms. She was invading their privacy far too much for her comfort as it was, but, with a glance at the uniform, she would know whose quarters were whose.

She'd nearly reached the end of the quarters on the starboard side of the ship when a long coat caught her eye. Her heart leapt as she lifted further on her toes to get a better look. *My Pirate.*

With a cautious glance over her shoulder, Laura opened the door and slipped inside, closing the door silently behind her.

Callum stirred. Then, in a swift, fluent movement, he was seated upright, his legs swung over the edge of the bed, an arm outstretched with his cutlass clutched in his hand.

Laura gasped, her pulse skipping. "It is I, Callum," she breathed.

He blinked, cursed under his breath, and placed his cutlass on the small table at his bedside, the blade glinting in the dim lantern light from the wardroom beyond his door. "My apologies. Are you well? Is something wrong?" His muscles stretched and bunched beneath his skin, heating Laura beneath hers.

"I am well," she returned, stepping toward him.

Her Pirate's eyes widened as he took in her attire. "Laura…" His voice had grown decidedly more hoarse and had lowered an octave. "What are you—"

She closed the distance between them, her knees brushing his. His throat worked, and his heated gaze seared over her, trailing downward from her eyes to her lips, neck, bosom, and to her hands untying the knot in her robe.

The fabric fell away and she tossed it aside, then lifted the hem of her night-rail and straddled his hips. She ran her hand through the sparse, springy hair on his chest and along the smooth, warm skin of his shoulders and back.

"*Christ*, sweetheart," Callum groaned, eliciting a shiver of pleasure along her spine.

"I've been waiting to hear you call me that again, Pirate," she whispered against his lips.

There was nothing but a thin piece of material between them, the air hot and musty with the scent of lust. Laura spread her thighs and rubbed herself against the hard ridge of his stand through his bedclothes.

Callum groaned again, his hands fisting the night-rail at her hips.

When she'd first fantasized about joining Callum in his bed in this way, she'd imagined drawing the act out, waiting until they were both breathless and begging before she finally satisfied their need and took him inside her. But she couldn't wait. Her nerves felt flayed, her heart and body aching for comfort and solidity. Indeed, having him was not merely a desire—it was a necessity.

Laura slid the bedclothes out from between them and tossed her night-rail over her head and to the floor. Callum's calloused palms grazed her hips, waist and over her ribs to tease her breasts before sliding back down. The gentle abrasion caused gooseflesh to spread over her.

The world narrowed to just them: their heated, sweat-dampened skin touching, their hands exploring, and their mouths devouring.

Laura reached between them, lifting just enough to position him at her entrance. Her breath came quick, her heart racing as she wrapped her arms around his shoulders and took him fully inside.

Another long groan escaped Callum, and he uttered a few breathy curses as she began to move. He felt tight inside her, but so very right. Laura quickly found her rhythm, kissing him with the same tempo as the rock of her hips. It was steady and exhilarating, the sensation of her climax building quickly.

Callum gasped, breaking off his kiss to press his tongue and teeth to the curve of her neck. "Holy hell, Laura," he breathed. "Please say you'll never leave me."

She rocked her hips faster, nearly ready to reach her peak. "Why would you think that I…would ever…leave you?"

"I'm…afraid." He threw his head back with a hiss of breath, the pads of his fingers digging into her hips as he encouraged her movement. "I'm afraid of losing you."

His confession jolted straight to her heart as she rocked faster. The coil of her climax wound tighter and tighter until it finally snapped, and she whispered raggedly, "I'm afraid I might be pregnant."

Her heart thundered in her ears for what felt like several long moments, her movements uneven as her body rode the waves of her completion.

The kiss Callum gave her was savage, raw, and possessive as he wrapped his arms around her. His hips pumped thrice more before she swallowed his moan, and he spilled his seed inside her.

* * *

Their embrace slackened, and Callum pressed his dampened forehead to Laura's, attempting to catch his breath.

He'd not meant to confess such a gut-churning fear to Laura, most particularly while in the midst of lovemaking, but it had merely slipped out. And so had hers, apparently.

Pulling back, Callum looked into the green eyes scarcely visible in the dim light. "Is it true?" he asked on a hoarse whisper. "Are you with child?"

Laura's lips thinned, and one shoulder lifted. "My courses are late, and I have been dreadfully nauseated."

Despite his internal caution not to celebrate before it had been confirmed by a doctor, his skin puckered with gooseflesh, his stomach quivered, and his heart felt as though it would burst. He wanted to laugh or crow. Hell, he might have cried if he were not exceedingly aware of his sleeping neighbours. Instead, he took Laura's lips in a tender, passionate kiss.

He tangled his fingers into her loose, curling locks and put as much feeling into their kiss as he could.

They must post the banns the moment they reached London, or he could acquire a special license if the duke gave his consent. Callum could scarcely wait. *Laura as my wife, and a child of our own…*

"I take it that this is satisfactory news?" Laura pulled back to ask in hushed tones.

"Hell, sweetheart," he half groaned. "I'm the luckiest sod in the whole of England. If—" He licked at his suddenly dry lips. "If I were to have your father's approval, would you marry me?"

Her eyes widened, then misted over. "If you're asking out of a sense of duty—"

He tightened his hold on her. "I *want* to marry you, sweetheart. I've wanted you for months, but I'd not thought it possible. You've just given me hope. Please say that you'll be mine."

Twin tears slid down her cheeks, and she nodded. "Yes, I'll marry you, Pirate." She pressed a sweet, damp kiss to his lips.

His heart soared. But he knew that this moment must come to an end. "Come," he whispered. "As much as I would genuinely love to have you in my bed all night, you must return to your father or you will rouse suspicion."

With one last kiss, she slid from his lap. Callum followed, retrieving a worn towel and dipping it in the water in the washbasin. They made quick work of cleaning while Callum considered their options. There was no question that he must speak with the duke on the morrow and ask for Laura's hand, but would *she* wish to tell him of her pregnancy, or did she wish for Callum to?

He stepped into a pair of trousers as Laura lifted her night-rail over her head.

"When I speak with your father on the morrow—" he began, but stopped at her small gasp.

"Please do not tell him that I am with child." Even through the darkness, he could see that she'd grown alarmingly pale, her freckles standing out sharply in contrast.

Callum's brow puckered in a frown. "But whyever not? He is your father, Laura. He deserves to know." He finished fastening the last button on his falls, and he wrapped his arms around her.

"I simply…*cannot* have him know, yet."

He pressed his lips to her ear. "I will do as you wish, sweetheart. But remember, you are mine now, Laura." Pausing, he bussed her cheek. "Come."

Silently, he retrieved her robe from the floor and held it up for her to don. She tied the knot, and Callum opened his door, stepping into the doorway with her.

Damn, but he didn't want her to go. Tangling his fingers in her hair once more, he leaned in for one last kiss of the night. Her lips gave easily beneath his, soft and full.

A door across the wardroom opened, and Callum broke the kiss, his heart plummeting to his stomach. His gaze swung toward the movement, and they froze, all four of them: Callum with Laura, and Harris with a man half-dressed in the duke's livery.

For what felt like several long moments, no one moved. The only sounds were that of snoring men, the ocean spraying and splashing—muffled by the hull of the ship—and his own rapid heartbeat drumming in his ears.

Finally, Harris moved. He leaned in and whispered something to his sailor, then pressed a swift kiss to the man's lips. The poor sod's pale chest and face darkened to scarlet before he turned and hurried out of the wardroom.

His eyebrows raised, Harris exchanged a nod with Callum before retreating into his quarters.

"My father's man," Laura breathed, a note of panic in her eyes. "Will he—"

"No. He's likely more concerned about himself."

It was Laura's turn to frown. "For…" Her eyes widened and her jaw dropped. "*Oh.* You mean…sodomy?"

"Yes," he said grimly. "Men hang for less, and without sufficient proof."

Her face scrunched in puzzlement and distaste. "But I wouldn't say anything, and I don't wish for him to be frightened. I don't care who he—"

Callum swooped down and pressed his lips to hers.

"That's a man's life, Callum," she pulled back to add. "I ought to assure him that I—"

He kissed her again, but this time she didn't pull away. She sank against his hard chest and wrapped herself in his warmth.

* * *

Rupert Grave, the Marquess of Weston, picked at a spot between his teeth with his thumbnail, listening to the other men gripe.

"I'm so bloody hungry," McMann groaned. "When will they *feed us*?" The last words were shouted toward the deck above them.

Piper snarled, and Rupert had to suppress a surge of irritation. The man had not stopped snarling since they'd been captured.

"I feel filthy," Beresford complained. "I need a bath and a sodding proper doctor."

"At ease, men," Rupert drawled. "I, like you, am displeased that our plans did not proceed as intended, but do not trouble yourselves. We have not lost, and nor will we. London is only a few days away."

McMann huffed a breath of mirth. "No, we have not lost."

Beresford's eyes glinted, and Piper's snarl turned into a wicked grin.

Chapter 29

The ship rocked side to side, and another wave of nausea crashed through Laura. The room spun around her in the early-morning sunlight, twirling and rolling and making her feel light-headed. A groan caught in her throat and she covered her eyes with a chilled palm, her other clutching the bedclothes under her chin. She breathed slowly in and out, willing the nausea to pass.

Distraction, her mind whispered, and she swiftly brought memories of the previous night to the fore. Callum's reaction to the news of her pregnancy, his confession of fear…

She ought to—*wanted* to—be overjoyed by his obvious pleasure, but…she wasn't.

As a fallen woman, her very last concern would be how society viewed her marriage, but what would she say to inquiries about her husband's position? While Laura found his station rather thrilling, she would not be permitted to speak of it.

Trivial lies to members of the *ton* weren't what concerned her, however. Indeed, she was certain that when her father approved the match, they would devise a planned response to any impertinent questions. No. Her chest gave a breathless squeeze. It was something decidedly more terrifying than society that kept her withdrawn.

Callum's true love was the ocean, and his life was as a spy. She could not take him away from that. He would be sent on other assignments, ones that would pull him from her for extended periods of time, and possibly ones that would take him back out on the ocean. What if he was hurt? What if he *died*? What if he found himself taken with another woman in distress?

Her chest tightened once more, and Laura felt as though the room was suddenly devoid of air. She would marry him, of course—she was no fool—but she could not love him. For if she loved him, and he abandoned her and their babe…she would be broken.

Another swell rocked the ship, and Laura's stomach rebelled. The burning liquid scorched its way up her throat, and she leapt up—already running—and dashed to the seat of easement to cast up her accounts.

It was several long minutes later when she finally strode to the washbasin to brush her teeth, the muscles in her back aching. She'd grown used to the salty taste of the water mixed with the tooth powder, but she very much looked forward to bathing and brushing with fresh water once more.

"Laura."

She turned at her father's voice, dabbing at the water on her face with a towel. "Yes, Papa?"

He sat up in bed, braced by pillows and swathed in shadow by the windows at his back.

"Come here. Sit." He gestured to the chair at his bedside.

Laura nodded. She'd not noticed that he'd sent his men away, leaving just the two of them in the cabin, or that he was even awake. She'd been so absorbed in her own nauseating misery…

Settled in the chair, she sat and smiled at him, willing the warble in her stomach to settle. "Are you well, Papa? Should I summon the doctor?"

His gaze met hers, shrewd and unblinking. Laura's heart sank, but she carefully kept the smile on her lips.

"How are you feeling, pigeon?"

She swallowed. "I am well enough, Papa. I am merely experiencing some seasickness."

The duke's right eyebrow lifted, and his gaze sharpened.

"I assure you, there is no need to worry," she continued. "Since the storm, I've felt off balance, but I am certain that it will pass s—"

"Enough," he interrupted gruffly. "Do not patronize me."

Laura pulled her lips between her teeth and bit down, fighting against the simultaneous waves of nausea and trepidation.

"During both of your mother's pregnancies, she had dreadful sickness. It started early on, and lasted until the third or fourth month, as I recall."

Panic swelled in Laura's chest. "B-but I'm not—"

"*Do not deny it*," he said, harshly cutting over her words. Anger seethed in his light-blue eyes, and his skin grew mottled.

Her pulse skipped, and her palms were cold and damp. She nodded.

"*Goddamned whoreson!*" he bellowed, slapping a hand against the coverlet over his thigh. "I ought to have—"

"It is all right, Papa," Laura hurried to reassure him, reaching out to clasp his hand. "Do not worry, it—"

"No, it is *not* all right, Laura!" His face had turned a deep crimson, and his gaze burned with fury. "How am I not to worry when my daughter carries some scurrilous pirate's bastard?"

"But it wasn't a scurrilous pirate," she blurted. "It was Callum."

Her father's angry eyes widened, and his face darkened ever further. "I'll have his head for this. A man I trusted, a man I *thanked*? I'd thought the blackguard was a decent man, and all the while he'd taken advantage of my daughter!" With a harsh curse, he bellowed at the closed door for his man.

"Papa, no," Laura breathed.

"Your Grace?" the footman said with a bow as he appeared in the doorway.

Her father coughed. "Have Callum McInnis brought to me this instant."

The man left, and her father lapsed into a fit of coughing. Laura stood and put a hand to his shaking back.

"Your health, Papa," she gently admonished. "You ought not to—"

The furious duke batted her hands away while he continued to cough, and Laura's heart sank further.

* * *

With a grim set to his lips, Callum strode across the gun deck toward the captain's cabin. The sound of the duke's coughing echoed through the hull, and Callum felt a moment of concern. He knew not what to expect with the man's health. Could he have declined overnight? Or could something have happened to Laura?

Hellfire. His booted feet moved swifter over the wooden planks. The two footmen stationed at the door opened it as he strode up, and he slipped inside.

The cabin was bright with sunlight, though thick with the scent of sickness. His gaze caught on Laura standing at her father's bedside, her cheeks ashen—almost green—putting her abundance of freckles in stark relief. Her nose and eyes were reddened, her eyebrows were puckered, and her jaw was clenched.

Callum's spine stiffened as he bent in a swift bow. Something was decidedly wrong.

"You summoned me, Your Grace?" he said to the coughing man.

It took another moment for the red-faced duke to gather himself enough to glare at Callum. "You're a deceitful disgrace of a bloody rogue, Mr. McInnis." The duke's voice rose with each syllable, squeezing Callum's chest with its spitting vitriol. "How *dare* you take advantage of my daughter's trust and innocence in such a vile and despicable way?" The man recoiled and batted at Laura's pale, protesting hands. "How did you do it? Did you rescue her from her first prison then abuse her trust to coerce her into your bed, you damned whoreson? Convince her that you were a decent man and then have your way—"

"I beg your pardon, Your Grace, but it was not like that, at all." Callum stepped toward the foot of the duke's bed, fighting against the red tide of indignation and affront crashing through him. "I've asked Laura for her hand in marriage. I'd intended to seek your approval." His gut tightened. He hated the awkwardness of what he was about to say. "As for the lovemaking, Your Grace, I did not force myself on your daughter. I respect her and care for her, and would never wish to importune her with my attentions."

The duke's strong jaw worked as he thought. The man was large and, in full health, Callum was uncertain if he could take the muscular duke in combat. But now he sat, frail and sickly abed, losing the tone and muscle that he must have worked hard to gain.

"Is this true, Laura?" The duke looked up at his daughter.

Callum expected an immediate response, a confirmation of his truth, but when it wasn't forthcoming, his gaze slid to her. She watched the floor, her fingers clutched together. *Good God*, was she going to deny him? Had she changed her mind? He'd thought they had parted on good terms the night before, but could he have done something to upset her?

"Yes, Papa. It is true," she said, her voice soft.

Callum's breath left him in a silent *whoosh* of relief.

The duke nodded and covered a cough with the back of one hand. "I am displeased. Displeased and grieved that you both could not show more restraint." He sighed. "But if this is how it is to be, then I cannot stop it. Mr. McInnis, you must marry my daughter and make certain that your child is not born a bastard. I will see to it that arrangements are made upon our return to London."

Elation rushed through Callum, pumping wildly in his veins. Laura would be *his*. He kept his expression carefully sedate, hoping that the duke would see remorse and contrition in his mien, but inside he was veritably bursting.

His gaze lifted to meet Laura's, and his heart stuttered. She seemed detached, remote, her green eyes dulled. Her lips pulled upward in a tight smile, and Callum felt as though the room flipped on its axis.

Damn, bugger, and hell. She was faking her happiness.

"…Mr. McInnis will journey on Sir Bradley's ship for the remainder of the trip," the duke was saying.

"I beg your pardon?" Callum interjected, uncertain if he'd heard correctly. "I've been acting as your captain—"

"I cannot very well have you bedding down on the same ship as my yet-unwed daughter. I will find an adequate replacement among my men to serve as captain." He pinned Callum with his astute blue gaze. "You *will* abide my decision, I trust, Mr. McInnis. For surely you realize how futile and imprudent going against me would be."

Indeed. The Duke of Norshire's warnings were perfectly clear. "Of course, Your Grace."

The duke nodded and waved a hand. "Send my man in on your way out." He flicked a gaze at Laura. "Both of you."

Callum bowed deeply and turned on his heel, a flurry of undesirable emotions buzzing just under his skin. He scarcely took notice as Laura relayed her father's message, exiting the room behind him.

The man left quickly, and Laura moved past him toward the bustling gun deck, but Callum halted her with a touch to her arm. "Laura," he uttered in a harsh whisper.

She turned, her emotionless gaze still and questioning.

"Are you well? Is something amiss? Or…" Lord, but he felt abruptly insecure in his own skin, as though his clothing were itchy or slightly too tight. "Do you feel upset by this arrangement?"

"Not at all," she assured him with a brittle smile.

Not good enough.

"Please," he said, not at all embarrassed by the pain and confusion that he knew were seeping from his voice. "I can sense the change in you. I know that you are unhappy; I merely do not know why. Is there anything that I can say—or do—that would make you feel better?"

One of the duke's men exited the cabin and gripped Callum by the arm, guiding him away with a mumble about retrieving any belongings and leaving on a rowing boat. But Callum's eyes and ears were only for Laura.

Her bottom lip quivered slightly, and a pang went through his chest. The mossy green of her eyes clouded over with unshed tears before she uttered a cold and conclusive, "No."

Chapter 30

A sennight later—London

Bridget Bradley's stomach quivered, not only with the movement of her babe, but with sheer violent nerves as she directed a maid toward another spot of blood that required cleaning. The bedchamber was bright and cheerful with its yellow furnishings, but the air was heavy with death, guilt, and crippling remorse.

"That makes four deaths," she said disbelievingly at Simon's—Dr. Claridge's—back as he washed his hands at the washbasin. "Four men—servants—from Sir Kieran Richards' home that have been murdered."

"And one woman," Mr. MacLean muttered.

Bridget's shocked gaze rose to meet his. "But I thought that was an accident."

The older gentleman shrugged one shoulder. "I have my doubts."

Jones paced between the door and the fireplace. "It is not safe for you here, my lady. We must return to—"

"But whoever is making these attacks is not entering this house. They're—"

"No, my lady, but they're bringing the broken and bloodied bodies to our door!" Jones' voice rose as the colour drained from his cheeks. "We've not enough men to fight this off, to find out who is doing it. Putting anyone out there is a danger."

What could she say to that? She knew very well that there was nothing. The man was right. With Richards distraught in bed, Barrows unconscious and withering away, and now with these new deaths, hope was very low.

Oliver pushed away from the wall from where he'd been silently and stonily observing. "While I agree that everyone under this roof is in danger, where would we be able to go—to hide Bridget—that these villains would not see? The moment any of us step from this house, we will be targeted. I believe that our best course of action is to remain and wait. We have a better chance of survival behind these walls. And, with luck, Charles and the others will return before we are forced to do battle."

* * *

The scent of stewed beef, buns, and ale filled Callum's senses, drifting down from the gun deck to the ward room, but while his stomach growled, it failed to move him. It would be a meal fit for the finest pub or dining room in England, and likely tasted far superior, as Gabe was their cook. But, he felt broken. Somewhere deep inside, something wasn't quite working.

He felt…bereft—like Laura had been taken from him, despite their impending nuptials. It…cracked his heart, leaving a raw fissure of anguish.

A bowl, plate, and tankard appeared at his elbow, and he looked up as his friends and fellows joined him at the long dining table.

"We will arrive before nightfall," Edward said, sitting across from Callum. "Harris is at the helm."

Harris, ever loyal, had seen Callum being flanked by guards on the duke's ship and ushered into a rowing boat, and he'd requested to join him without hesitation.

Mary took the seat beside Callum, placing her hand on his shoulder in a gesture of comfort. "Only a few more hours."

Callum nodded. "How is Brown?"

Greene shook his head as he swallowed a dram of ale. "Still unwell. His fever broke three days past, but he can only remain awake for short periods of time before he lapses into unconsciousness again."

"The poor young sod," Stevens added grimly, dipping his biscuit into his stew.

"I've missed a great many discussions," Mary said softly. "Tell me, what are we to expect upon dropping anchor?"

Indeed, she'd missed many discussions. The poor woman was not meant for life at sea. She'd not yet been able to find her sea legs, though he supposed she didn't need to, now.

"We will drop anchor before the Duke of Norshire's ship and send a group of men to the docks to arrange the carriages," Henderson began.

Stevens waved a spoon in the air. "I'd like to suggest that Mary be among the first to reach land, but something about our prisoners doesn't sit right with me. They're far too comfortable."

"Too confident," Greene added.

Stevens nodded. "If she's ill, she cannot properly defend herself or our ward—"

"Oi!" she exclaimed indignantly.

"Come now, love." Stevens softened his tone with his long-time friend. "You know full well what dangers you would be bringing upon yourself if you attempted to fight in your current condition."

"My wife will nae be on the first boat te land," Gabe grumbled in his low Scottish burr as he strode toward them. He pressed a swift kiss to Mary's lips before joining them at the table with his own meal. "Battle is one thing, as I ken she can hold her own, but a potential ambush is quite another. I'll nae risk her or our babe."

There was a moment of stunned silence before words of congratulations came, and the others rose to exchange handshakes and swift embraces. Callum followed along in a haze, his heart constricting. Soon, they'd resumed their seats and the conversation continued, but Callum didn't hear it. He stared at his plate and ate the food, all the while thinking of Laura.

He was going to be a father, too. But his affianced was decidedly less pleased by their circumstance than he'd hoped. He wished that he'd had but a few more minutes with her before he'd left, that he'd been able to glean the reasons for her reservation and sadness.

Christ, but he felt heartsick. His chest ached, his skin tingled as if it were too tight, and his lungs felt as though they weren't taking in enough air.

A hand touched his back, and he flinched. The wardroom had grown decidedly quieter, his table empty but for Mary and Stevens.

"Where did you go?" Mary asked softly.

"I'll wager that I know where." Stevens leaned forward on his forearms, his golden gaze astute.

Callum looked down at his half-eaten meal, the chilled soup now congealed around the edges and the buns slightly hard. He put his elbows on the table and lowered his head to his hands.

"Somewhere in the back of my mind, I knew that I was reaching too far above my station, but I'd thought that my feelings were returned." Callum frowned at his plate. "I was *certain* that they were. But the moment our plans seemed to be falling into place, she pulled away. And I've no idea what I've done, or how I can make it better."

He could sense his friends attempting to wordlessly communicate across the table, and he shook his head.

"While our courtship took place out of the customary order," Callum continued, the words flowing, "I made certain that she was amenable…that she would receive my attentions with equal interest. I don't even think that that's the problem, but for some reason I feel like a cad, like I've made some grievous mistake with her virtue. But then that last night… Ah, hell, I've no idea. She'd seemed happy enough. Was it just that her father found out? Was it her illness? Did she expect something of me that I did not deliver?

"Goddamn it!" He slammed his fists on the table, making the cutlery jangle. "That look in her eyes… That sodding look that told me that her world had collapsed haunts me like nothing else has. This whole bloody circumstance has me doubting every one of my instincts, but worst of all, it makes me hate myself because I still want to go through with it. I want to be there when she experiences it all, and I want to be damned good at it, be what I didn't have. It makes me want to say, 'To the devil with her reservations, we'll make it work in the end.' Does that make me a blackguard?" He looked hopefully between his friends.

"I don't—" Stevens rubbed at the back of his neck, looking warily at Mary. "I don't think so. But I'm not entirely certain that I understand—"

"What Bram is trying to say is that you need to trust your instincts," Mary interjected. "You reached a certain point in your relationship believing that you had an understanding with this woman, and you should trust that. Whatever it was that changed her mind about your situation is what you need to focus on. Find out what she's afraid of, what is holding her back, and work through it with her."

The bell began to ring overhead, and Callum's spine straightened. Despite the melancholy assailing him, he felt a tingle of anticipation ripple through his blood.

He pulled Mary into a quick, crushing hug. "Thank you," he muttered into her half-fallen auburn hair, before standing and striding purposefully out of the wardroom.

* * *

Ringing bells echoed along the water as they neared England's shores in the rowing boat. The sun was very nearly gone, the sky a bright mixture of pink, yellow, and orange that was slowly fading into a bluish-grey. Laura sat, with her chilled hands clasped together in her lap and her gaze directed toward the shore. And Callum.

He'd been aboard the first boat to reach land and had begun to prepare the hacks. She watched him from the upper deck of her father's ship, distant though her view was, her heart twisted sickeningly in her chest.

The pain that had slashed across his face at their last meeting was etched in her memory and would not give her a moment's peace. She cringed, as she had done countless times in the past sennight.

Callum's movements were always strong and sure; they were the movements of a spy with years of training and practice. She would not wish for him to feel as though she were holding him back, and she certainly didn't want him to grow bored with domesticity if she asked him to stay with her. Laura could not live with that. Indeed, protecting her heart was the only way to keep their union civil, for she would certainly marry him. She was not a fool.

The rowing boat rocked with the water's motion, and Laura swallowed against the rising nausea in her throat. Her view of Callum's back became obscured as they reached the shore, and disappointment washed over her. She was guided out of the boat and further onto land, but her mind was on Callum.

She wanted to speak to him, to explain her feelings about their upcoming union and make him understand. She'd not intended to cause him pain.

"This way, Your Grace, Lady Laura." One of Callum's fellows led them toward an awaiting hack, his spine stiff and his gaze darting.

He was nervous. All of Callum's fellows were, in fact. They kept glancing at the windows of the local mills and the surrounding buildings, staring into the face of every merchant or sailor, and peering over their shoulders. Were they anticipating resistance of some kind? An attack?

Unable to suppress the urge, Laura mimicked their behaviour, glancing around for any unseen threats. She felt foolish, of course, for she hadn't the faintest notion of what to look for, but she felt better for being aware.

Her lips thinned and nerves fluttered in her abdomen, but she allowed the man to lead her into the hack. She sat in the rear-facing seat and leaned over to look out the window for any sign of Callum. There were so many men—shocking for this time of night—that she'd entirely lost sight of him.

There was a thump on the side of the hack as the man called to the driver, and the hack jolted into motion.

Chapter 31

The hackney lurched into motion on the rough cobblestoned street, the jarring movement pushing Callum into his seatmate and prisoner, the Marquess of Weston. The blackguard had an irksome, haughty expression on his features that made Callum want to knock the sod out. Sadly, his superior sat across from him, and would likely frown upon such harsh treatment.

"On our way, now," Harris muttered, leaning back against the ill-stuffed squabs beside Hydra. "The other hacks are also in motion."

Callum jerked his head in a nod, and Hydra crossed his arms. The air was so thick with tension as to make him choke. They'd known to expect something, but the moment he'd set foot onto the cobblestoned streets just above the shipyard and docks, he'd *felt* it. It was in the wind, in the blue-grey light of late dusk. He could bloody well taste it. The problem was with waiting, and their enemy knew it. Readying for a battle was only successful if you did not become complacent or sloppy, and the longer they waited for the inevitable attack, the greater their chances of failure. Which was precisely why he'd had Laura and her father leave first. With luck, they would be ignored and the attack would fall upon him.

With an agitated sniff, Callum raked his fingers through his hair. In not five minutes, Laura's carriage would turn away from his, heading toward her father's home on Grosvenor Street in Mayfair, while Callum and the rest of the hackneys, carrying his fellows and their prisoners, headed toward Newgate. But he wanted to follow her, to make certain that she reached home safely. Then he'd talk things through with her and they'd spend the evening together. He'd pull her into his arms and kiss her, and then he'd—

Crack! A bloodied hole appeared in the top front corner of their hack just as a horrifying scream filled the air. There was a whinny, and their hack jolted sideways. Callum braced himself, but not quickly enough as their hack toppled. Pain seared through his shoulder, hip, and head, dizzying him momentarily. He dragged in several breaths, attempting to sort out in his mind what had just happened.

The carriage was on its side, and shouting and gunfire had begun just beyond the thin walls of their downed hack. They were under attack.

Callum shook himself and made an attempt to assess the damage. Weston was grumbling about his bound wrists, scrambling to sit up on what was now the floor of the carriage. Hydra had a cut to his head that slowly leaked blood, and Harris cradled what looked to be another broken arm.

"We're lambs awaiting the slaughter in this hack," Callum growled. "Together, we kick the roof on three."

"Why not just use the door?" Weston drawled, gesturing upward toward the door that now acted as their roof.

Callum wouldn't dignify that question with an answer. Clearly the man was trying to get them killed, and acting like a mole poking out of the ground would make for a very clear target.

"On three," Hydra reiterated. "One…two…*three*."

Hydra, Harris, and Callum all stamped their feet on what once had been the hack's roof. There was a great *crunch*, and the roof fell away.

"Callum, grab Weston."

Crack! Crack!

"Gunfire!" Harris yelled as holes began to appear in the hack.

They scrambled out of the equipage and ducked out of view behind the next hack on the south side of the road. He could scarcely see a damned thing in this growing darkness, and their enemy had counted on that.

Weston pulled against Callum's grip, but he held fast as he glanced around. Riders approached from nearly every adjoining street, but his fellows and the duke's men were readying themselves, exiting their hacks and firing back at the blackguards hiding in the nearby buildings. The remainder of their men were still rowing to shore, damn it! Callum hoped that they would reach them in time. Surely by now they'd heard the shots fired and the shouts of injured men. Passers-by ran away in terror, and Callum's gaze was inevitably drawn toward Laura.

He cursed soundly under his breath. Her hack was stopped, but there was no sight of her. *Shite*, she was probably still inside.

A large brute rounded the carriage and swung at him with a meaty fist. Callum ducked and countered with a blow to the man's ribs then a knee to the cods. The enemy landed on his knees with a hoarse groan, and before Callum could withdraw his cutlass and knock the man out, Harris cracked the man on the back of the skull with the heel of his pistol, and the brute fell to the ground.

They were surrounded now, but a quick glance toward the water told Callum that help would be on its way directly. And they needed it.

The scent of London—stale piss, coal smoke, unwashed bodies, and the salty stink of the River Thames—mixed with the sourness of burned gunpowder, the metallic tang of blood, and the cold stench of fear. It was enough to churn one's stomach. But this was battle, and that's just what he'd bloody well do.

* * *

Terror thundered violently through Laura's veins as she listened to the screams and gunfire outside their hack. She'd been right—*they'd* been right—to expect an attack, and it was dashed well happening.

"Why has our carriage stopped?" Her father tried to sound calm, but Laura could hear the underlying panic in his voice. Would that she could see his face through the darkness of the hack. "Why does our driver not run the horses?"

Laura's lips thinned. "Either he is a part of the scheme, or he is dead, Papa."

Memories of her time aboard Callum's ship filled her mind's eye: working to bring gunpowder to the gunners, narrowly avoiding attacks, bandaging wounds. She'd wanted to feel useful—and was— but she'd also learned a great deal from those men. "More will join the attack," she said confidently. "If we remain here, we will be killed." Her father made a sound of protest, but she continued on. "We have a better chance of surviving if we exit and integrate ourselves among the other men, just far enough away from a large grouping that we will not be the main target."

Distant hoof beats on cobblestone grew steadily nearer, and Laura's stomach plummeted.

"Come," she whispered harshly, gripping her father's coat sleeve. "We must go."

Her father blustered. "That battle is no place for a lady, Laura. Most particularly one in your delicate condition."

"I'm already in it, Papa! Can you not see?" The sounds of hoof beats grew louder, and Laura's heart rose to her throat.

"I must see you to safety." The muscles in his jaw jumped as he clenched his jaw. "I cannot lose you so soon after finding you."

She leaned forward and pressed a kiss to her father's pale cheek. "I must see you to safety, as well. You're not half as recovered as you would like me to believe." Her grip tightened on his sleeve as she opened the door and stepped out toward the north side of the road. "Follow me, Papa."

The stubborn man came as Laura dragged him. She crouched low, and just beyond the overbearing sounds of battle was the faintest *hiss*.

"What is that?" she asked, glancing around. Was there a snake just off the side of the road? But that didn't sound quite like a snake. It sounded like… *What?* Men ran around them and shouts rose up, but Laura turned her attention inward.

Her father crouched beside her, muttering his confusion and desire to see her well away from the fighting.

Then, it hit her. The sour, acrid scent of burning gunpowder. She spun to follow the noise with her gaze and spotted an alarmingly large mound beneath their carriage, the line of smoke travelling swiftly toward it.

Without warning, she dropped to her stomach on the cobblestones, dragging her father with her, then covered her head.

Her father cringed at the filth on the ground as he lay beside her. "What the devil, La—"

Boom!

The blast reverberated through her body, just before splinters, bits of fabric, and worn stuffing floated down like snow to cover them.

Someone had blasted a hole through their carriage. It had been a targeted attack, she was certain, and once the enemy discovered that she and her father were alive, they would strike for another attack. She required a weapon.

"Laura," her father breathed. "Are you all right?"

"Fine, Papa. We need to move."

Lifting her head just enough to peer beyond her prone position, Laura scanned her surroundings. A man—not her father's, and certainly not one that she recognized from the ship of spies—lay face down in a pool of his own blood just beyond her arm's reach.

"Have you a weapon, Papa?" she asked, scrambling to her feet.

"I have two pistols in holsters, and a dagger in my boot." He stood, as well. "We must run, Laura. I need to get you far away from here."

She dusted off her dress as she hurried to the fallen man. "I'm afraid that isn't possible, Papa." As quickly as she could, she began to divest the man of his weapons, then looked up at her father. "Whoever this enemy is, they are expecting us to flee on foot. It is dark. We might believe we are going unseen, but watchful eyes could be anywhere. What they are not expecting is for us to fight alongside the other men."

"I see your reasoning, Laura, but I cannot…" He sighed, his jaw clenching as he watched the chaos unfold around them. "Very well, daughter. What do you propose?"

She tore a strip from the bottom of her petticoats, tied it about her waist, then tucked the dead man's weaponry inside. Grinning, she stood to face her father as an idea formed in her mind. "We must find ourselves some horses."

* * *

Boom!

Callum's heart twisted as he spun around. The air was sucked from his lungs, and the chilled breeze around him felt suddenly thick like sludge and impossible to breathe in as he saw Laura's destroyed carriage. His body started moving, his booted feet pounding the slick cobblestones as he ran.

In the back of his mind, he heard someone shout *"Gunpowder!"* and, indeed, the acrid scent hung in the air, taunting him. He slid to a stop as he reached the wreckage, and saw…nothing. There was no blood, no bits of Laura's dress, no evidence that there'd been anyone within, at all.

Hope sprang in his chest and he gulped air, his gaze scanning the area. They'd gotten out, but how? And where were they now?

Harris and Hydra reached his side, dragging Weston by the manacles at his wrists.

"Where—" Harris began.

"Gone," Callum grunted, his gaze still searching. "Do you see them?"

"You two look for them and keep Weston," Hydra said hurriedly. "Find a way to get them clear of the danger. I must help the others, and find Brown. If they're going to blast the hacks—"

Boom!

There was a shrill scream, and the hairs on the back of Callum's neck stood on end. "*Christ*, that sounded like Mary."

Without another word, Hydra was running, disappearing into the fray of fighting men only scarcely lit by moonlight. Callum wanted to follow, to help his superior and his fellows in the aftermath of whatever had just occurred, but…Laura. Not only did his body scream for him to find her, but he'd also been given orders.

Taking the grumbling Weston back in hand, Callum grinned at his friend and apprentice then wordlessly turned. He withdrew his cutlass with his free hand and rounded the damaged carriage in search of clues as to Laura and the duke's whereabouts. The air was heavy with the scent of sweat and blood, though he'd seen startlingly few casualties upon the ground. Callum's heart thundered as a body came into view.

"One of the attackers," Harris noted, nudging the body with the toe of his boot. "He's missing his weapons."

Pride shot through Callum as he nodded, scanning the nearby streets. Laura and her father were armed. But where would they go from here? He looked down the road toward the crush of fighting men. The remainder of their men from the ships had arrived and were swiftly overpowering their enemy. *But who is our enemy?* Callum wondered. How had they known of their impending arrival? The Marquess of Weston had known that he and his fellow traitors were to receive this attempt at a rescue upon their return to England. How had they gotten word back? Who else did they have working with them?

"Sir…" Harris croaked.

Callum turned, and his chest twisted. *Christ.* A man stood at Harris' back, holding a dagger to his neck. It was all too reminiscent of their last assignment, when Harris had been injured because of Callum's inability to hold the enemy's attention. He couldn't let that happen again.

"Drop your weapon and give me the prisoner," the bastard spat, his grip tightening on the dagger at Harris' throat.

Dragging Weston forward, Callum took a small step. "This prisoner?"

He dropped his cutlass at the man's nod, and surreptitiously withdrew the pistol from his coat, the motion hidden by Weston's body.

Callum's pulse drummed out a fast, even rhythm in his ears as he made eye contact with Harris. The young man looked down, then up: their signal for *go*.

Using Weston as a shield, Callum swung his arm up, aimed, and fired in one swift motion, while Harris jerked his attacker's sleeve and ducked away from the dagger. Everything happened at once, leaving the blackguard prone and bleeding on the cobblestones and Harris and Callum breathing heavily.

"Oh, for God's sake," Weston grumbled.

"Well enough, Harris?" Callum gripped the young man's shoulder.

"Well enough." His lips curved upward in a crooked grin.

Callum tucked his spent pistol into one of the belts at his chest and retrieved his cutlass before striding purposefully toward the gradually diminishing fray, leaving Weston in the capable hands of Harris. A man ran toward him, blood on his face and a war cry on his lips, and with but few rapid movements, Callum dispatched of him. His gaze scanned the crowd, searching for auburn curls that would look almost brown in the darkness.

Someone cried out, the sound mingling with the metallic clang of cutlasses and swords, shuffling feet, and the sobs and groans of the wounded.

Several of their opponents fled away down nearby streets, apparently realizing the futility of the fight. *Mercenaries*, Callum surmised. None wore a uniform, and desperate men would do anything for the promise of wealth.

"Damnation," he growled as Harris came abreast of him. His pulse sped faster as his mind raced. Could she have been taken by someone? Was she even now being held captive by another rogue in league with traitors? Would she be hurt? *Touched?* "Do you see her anywhere?" Panic seeped into his voice, but he didn't care. He *must* find her.

"No, sir, I—"

The rumble of horses' hooves cut over Harris' words.

"Another one, just there!" a lilting feminine voice called.

Callum's heart tripped over itself as Laura came into view. She sat astride a horse, her skirts lifted to accommodate the beast, and she pointed to the ground beside a hack. Two of his fellows—Greene, and it looked like Henderson—were focused on scuffing the ground with their feet.

A man approached Laura, his sword raised, and she blithely swatted it away with one of her own before landing a kick to the man's chest and knocking him to the hard ground. Pride swelled once more in Callum's chest. Hell, another such woman could never be found. And Laura would be his.

Chapter 32

Bitter nerves roiled within Laura as she sought trails of gunpowder through the darkness.

Men continuously approached her in an attempt to attack, and though her instinct to strike out in any way that she could seemed to be working, it did not lessen the terror riding her. Her pulse throbbed harshly in her veins and her breath came quick, taking in the stench of the riverside road in erratic puffs.

At some point since they'd commandeered the horses, her father had settled into place behind and to the right of her, his eyes scanning the adjoining streets. She glanced back at him frequently, concerned by his increasingly pallid complexion. He'd only just begun to look well again—though his weight had not yet returned—and she feared that this misadventure would set his recovery back yet again.

Walking the beast beneath her toward the next hack, Laura kept her gaze on the ground as two of Callum's fellows followed her. The moonlight was dim, but she tilted her head to just the correct angle and saw the line of obscurity among the cobblestones.

"Another one, just there!" she called to the men, pointing at the spot.

Immediately, the two men hurried forward and scuffed their feet along the ground, dispersing the gunpowder.

Fast, heavy footsteps clomped on the ground, and Laura's gaze lifted, alarm sweeping through her chest. A cad raced up toward her with sword drawn, his mien malevolent, his eyes red-rimmed and rheumy, and eager for blood. With an inward squeal of fear, Laura awkwardly hit his weapon away with her pilfered one and kicked him in the chest, felling him to the hard ground and knocking him unconscious. Her breath rushed out of her in a *whoosh* of relief, but her body seemed to tremble.

"Laura!" a voice called.

The hairs stood up over her skin and her stomach swooped as she spotted Callum coming toward her, his face slightly puffy from a fight and his long, flowing coat and white shirt splattered with blood. Even from her seat atop a horse, he looked impossibly large, her brawny Pirate Spy.

"Bloody hell, I'm glad you're all right—"

"Language, sir," her father grumbled.

Callum ignored the interruption. "Are you hurt?"

Her mount sidestepped—perhaps sensing her agitation—and Callum gripped its bridle to steady it as he looked up at her. Even through the darkness, she could see that his eyes were wide and full of concern. Her stomach dipped again.

"I am uninjured," she assured him, her voice quivering from the abrupt nerves that swarmed her.

He let out a breath and quickly glanced around them before returning his attention to her. "It looks as though our attackers have mostly fled, and the rest of my fellows are capable of fending off any stray attacks. It is time to take you home."

"I found a horse for you." Laura gestured behind her, where several mounts were tethered.

He gave her a quick grin before turning to call over his shoulder. "Harris. Bring his sodding lordship, will you?"

Together, the men seated the Marquess of Weston on a horse, before Harris awkwardly joined the blackguard in the saddle, sucking a hiss between his teeth and grimacing.

Weston groaned. "Can I not have my own ho—"

"Not a chance in hell," Callum growled as he mounted his own and untethered the beastie. "I'll lead the way."

Callum rode ahead of Laura while her father and Harris flanked her on either side. Laura was more concerned about her father, however. His skin had turned very nearly ashen in the moonlight, and he was exposed to the—

Crack!

Shouts rose up as the men panicked and tried to control their horses. Her mount whinnied and reared back. Laura gripped the beast's mane, struggling for purchase, but it did nothing. They were going down.

* * *

His horse spooked. Callum struggled to regain control while simultaneously turning in his seat to look behind him.

"Laura," he breathed, dismounting as her horse reared.

The beast was dripping blood from its breast, its eyes wild and pained. Laura grabbed hold for dear life and Callum surged toward her. But he was too late. The beast fell hard, taking Laura with it, and her body connected with the cobblestones with a sickening *thunk*.

He wanted to curse, to shout his anger and hurt, but he was silent as he dropped to his knees beside her. Laura's eyes were closed, and a small splash of blood was visible beneath her temple. Callum's heart lurched, and a tempest of helplessness, panic, and sheer, unbridled terror blustered through him. His fingers began to shake and for a moment, he couldn't move, couldn't think, couldn't sodding breathe.

"Laura," he repeated. "*Laura.*"

Harris and the duke appeared at his side, and Callum growled harshly, "Get this damned horse off her leg!" His voice betrayed his panic, he knew, but he didn't care.

The other men moved quickly, with the aid of Callum's fellows and superior, and then, even through the painful heartache assailing him, he was able to let his training take over. He checked for her pulse. *Strong.* Skimming his trembling hands impersonally over her body, he examined her for additional injuries.

"She's not moving," the Duke of Norshire whispered thickly. "Will she live? Where are her injuries?"

Impatience bit at Callum's nerves, but he swallowed them back. The man was in anguish, just as he was.

"I'm not a doctor," he ground out, "but from what I can tell, she has a dislocated shoulder, a knock to the head, and will unquestionably have bruising on her leg and hip. More than that, I cannot tell you." He looked up at Hydra, who was barking orders just beyond his shoulder, but paused to glance at Callum. "I'm taking her to the safe house." She needed a doctor, and he needed to know that she and the baby would be well.

Hydra gave a tight nod, and Callum turned back to Laura. What was once a splash of blood at her temple was quickly growing into a puddle. His stomach sank, and he cursed.

"Your neck cloth, if you will," he said, gesturing toward the duke.

Fumbling, and with shaking fingers, the man did as he was asked. Callum folded the cloth in sharp, decisive movements, doing his utmost to stifle his emotions and let his training do the work, for he very much feared that if he allowed even the smallest crack in his façade, he would crumble.

The quick shuffle of feet sounded behind him, followed by the *crack* of a pistol firing. Weston cried out, and Callum assumed that the man had foolishly tried to get away. At the moment, however, he didn't give a damn.

"Lift here," Callum instructed the duke. "Very good. Sit her up and lean her back against your chest."

"Christ," the duke breathed. "There is so much blood. And her arm, my God, her arm."

With a quick assessment, Callum located the cut on her head and placed the folded neck cloth firmly to it. "Keep your hands here." He guided the duke with his free hand. "Press firmly."

"Is Weston the last of our prisoners?" Harris asked to Hydra over Callum's head.

There was a shift of fabric. "Unfortunately, yes," Hydra returned. "The others slipped away during the mêlée."

More cries, curses, and protests escaped Weston as he was presumably lifted to his feet and returned to the group.

"And I saw—" Hydra cut himself off, then began again. "I *thought* I saw someone that resembled—" He huffed a breath and continued in a quieter tone. "Someone who looked markedly like *Richards*." He ended on a whisper.

Despite the urgency in his task, Callum turned to look at his superior over his shoulder. The rest of the group grew quiet. Richards had been missing for some time, and if he'd turned traitor…

A rough curse escaped Greene, and several others followed.

Callum removed Laura's weapons and unfastened her makeshift belt. He lengthened and unfolded the material, then wrapped it around Laura's arm and body and tied it at the back of her neck as a crude sling.

"I need help to get Lady Laura into this hack," Callum announced, simultaneously standing and gesturing toward the hack behind the duke.

Several men stepped forward, and together they placed her within, the duke holding her to his side and keeping pressure on her wounded head.

Another soft, feminine cry came from a short distance away, drawing everyone's attention.

"Is that Mary?" Harris asked, the worry in his voice palpable.

Hydra nodded.

"Is it Gabe? Stevens?" Greene said, his face paling. "The baby?"

"No," Hydra assured him, his countenance grave. "Stevens lost a finger and Gabe was shot in the arse, but they will recover. It is Brown. Mary was attempting to help him from his hack—had his hand in hers—when it blew. His hand, incidentally, remained with her. I fear it took some effort to take it from her."

Greene cursed again, and a wave of melancholy went through the small group.

"Made her angry as the very devil, though," Hydra continued. "She took out countless opponents after that."

There was a brief moment of silence only broken by the sound of the river behind them and Weston's groaning.

"Harris and Callum, take Weston with you and continue with your orders. Keep him locked at the safe house until I arrive." Harris loaded Weston into the hack while Hydra continued. "We'll sort out a way to bring him to the Tower or Newgate once I'm there. Henderson and Greene, find our injured men—and those of His Grace—and see the duke's men brought to the hospital and our men brought to the safe house. I will help the others to find the surviving mercenaries and bring them to the Tower for further questioning before they're brought to Newgate. Once our tasks have been completed, we will reconvene at the safe house—"

"I'm sorry sir," Callum interrupted, his heart in his throat as he turned on his heel and climbed on the hack's driver's perch, "but I cannot remain here while my affianced is injured and unconscious within. I must bring her to the safe house and to a physician. I *must* know if the baby is well."

He flicked the reins, and the terrified horse jolted into a run, the weight of the hack shifting as Harris hopped on the back.

"What in the bloody sodding hell, Callum?" Hydra called after them. "*What?*"

* * *

It was as though Laura existed merely as a vessel of pain, and naught else. Her head pounded, her shoulder throbbed, and her hip and leg felt as though they'd been crushed by a horse. Quick flashes of memory flitted through her mind's eye, and she mentally congratulated herself on her apt assessment.

"Please, Charles," a woman's voice said in hushed tones, "why do you both not discuss this in the parlour?"

"I'll not leave Laura's side, Bridget." It was her Pirate.

Laura tried to open her eyes, to move, even to say something, but she remained perfectly still. Her head swam slightly, and she wondered if she'd been given a draught of laudanum.

"I cannot believe that you would be so careless," hissed another man, clearly furious. It was difficult to tell while he was whispering in such an angry way, but Laura assumed that to be Sir Charles Bradley—Hydra. "You've gone against your direct orders, against our promise, and you've defiled—"

"Come now," Bridget said softly. "I'm certain that once we've washed up and enjoyed a bracing cup of tea, you will feel more calmly about the—"

"I'm no more pleased with *you*, wife," Hydra growled. "What the devil do you think you're about, coming to London with a motley group of men in your current state?"

"I had Jones, and I can defend myself quite well, thank you. I bested *you*, if you'll recall."

"Aye, I recall, *mi amor*, but you were significantly less pregnant back then. What if you went into labour?" There was a swish of fabric before he continued. "Speaking of labour, what in the bloody hell were you thinking, Callum?"

"I'll have some tea put on," Bridget muttered before her soft footfalls faded away.

"You defiled a duke's daughter and went against our group's moral code. You can bed women, Callum, but not those who are vulnerable and under our protection. Jesus, do you know how that makes you look? How it makes *us* look?"

"It wasn't like that, sir. I didn't *defile* her, and I sure as hell didn't break our moral code. I—"

"Did you not?" Hydra returned. "Lady Laura was under your care, and oughtn't have been a target for your carnal desires, and certainly not a source of relief for your lust."

Laura wanted to protest, to tell the man that their desires had been mutual and that Callum had requested a courtship. But her body still would not cooperate.

Callum took an angry breath through his nostrils. Laura could imagine his jaw tightened, shoulders stiff, and fists clenched. "What I feel for her is more than lust, sir."

"Oh, certainly you feel concern, for right now she is injured, but what of a year from now, Callum? What of ten? Think you that both of you will be pleased with your union once the initial desires have been satiated? You have not thought this through!"

"Yes, I have, damn it!" Callum hissed. "I cannot say for Laura's feelings, but I've thought of little else since I first met her. I know that I'm below her, I know that I don't deserve her, but I'll gladly spend the rest of my life working to prove myself worthy. I love her, sir, and I have every intention of being faithful to her—no matter your low opinion of me and my desires. There is naught that you can say that will convince me that a union between us is anything than what it is: one of love—at least on my part."

Laura's heart gave a hard thump, and her head began to swim. The pain in her body was overwhelming, but something in her chest began to warm. She felt foggy, somehow, as though she were slipping away from the room, either floating into the air or sinking into the mattress. She wanted to protest, but no sound came out.

"Will you retire?" Hydra asked from what felt like a great distance away.

There was a shuffle of feet and someone cleared their throat. "I would gladly do so for Laura, should she wish it. The war is over, and there are other intriguing options for us men that will not be so perilous and that will also keep me closer to her."

Do what for me? Laura wondered foggily.

"There is always a position at the school, should you wish it."

School? Good lord, the room is spinning.

"Tea has been requested, but it will be brought to the parlour," Bridget said from inside Laura's mind tunnel. "Jones and MacLean will wish to speak with you both, and I believe that some of the other men have begun to gather there. Ares and Hades have come to town, as well. There is much to discuss."

The voices faded away, and Laura lay abed in confusion. What had happened? Had Callum been in an argument?

A cold, damp cloth touched her forehead, and she gasped through her nose, still unable to open her eyes. Someone spoke softly to her, uttering calming reassurance, before she slipped back into the abyss of sleep.

Chapter 33

Men sat on nearly every surface in the parlour, an eerie quiet filling the room. The fear in the safe house was palpable. Stevens, Gabriel, Ed, and their other injured men had been bandaged, and sat stiffly in the overstuffed seats about the room. Mary had gathered herself just enough to attend, her eyes puffed and red and a tissue held tightly in one hand.

The others who had fought weren't even clean, lending the room the tangy scent of iron, gunpowder, and the Thames. Several had removed their coats and were clad only in their shirtsleeves and trousers, but it scarcely made a difference.

The men—whether they had just returned from the voyage and subsequent battle or journeyed from the school in Brampton—wore identical masks of worry and tension, their jaws tense and their varied tones of skin tinted the slightest shade of ash.

Three more men entered the room, and Callum nodded to them in greeting. Nearly everyone that he'd known from school—who wasn't on assignment elsewhere, or injured and indisposed—was in this room. The men and women varied in height, size, weight, and race. Several of their spies were Polish, Jamaican, and Spanish. Two, he knew, hailed from Shanghai. And they'd all been recruited by either Hydra or Richards—

Damnation. Callum's gut twisted. The school was Richards' property. If he had turned traitor…

Another door opened, and two of Hydra's fellows, Ares and Hermes, entered. *Christ, what the devil has happened to bring them into town?* Something was decidedly not right.

And yet… While his focus should have remained on his fellows and whatever dire circumstances in which they currently found themselves embroiled, his heart, his mind, and his soul were focused solely on one thing. *Laura.*

At last, he'd come to understand his feelings for her, and had voiced them for the first time only a quarter of an hour past. But it hadn't been to Laura.

The cushion of the chaise dipped beside him.

"I must have a word with you, Callum," Harris uttered in a harsh, disapproving whisper.

His apprentice's hair was dishevelled and his eyes bright with disapprobation.

Callum's lips thinned, and he ground out, "I know what you're going to—"

"You could have picked a better time to announce it. The poor woman is in no condition to support your assertions."

That took Callum aback. He searched the man's gaze again and realized that what he saw was concern rather than censure. For *him*. "Christ, Harris, I thought that you were going to berate me for my 'flagrant disregard' for Laura's reputation."

The man's brow wrinkled. "We had that discussion on board the frigate, and, as I recall, it was concluded. Why bring it up again?"

Callum shrugged one stiff shoulder in response.

"How is Laura?" Harris asked.

"Dr. Claridge assured me that Laura does not have any broken bones, and that the babe will be fine despite the fall. After cleaning her wounds, he put her shoulder back in its socket and stitched her head."

"Jesus," Harris breathed. "Laura is fortunate that she'd not done more damage than that."

Callum knew that Harris was correct, but it did not feel that way. Seeing her in pain—not to mention the sheer amount of blood that she'd shed… No, he didn't like seeing her thusly, at all.

"She's not yet fully recovered from her last injuries, Harris," Callum whispered hoarsely. "Every time one wound begins to heal, another wound takes its place."

"That's not your fault."

"The hell it isn't," Callum objected.

Harris frowned at him. "The woman was kidnapped, starved, and mistreated, Callum. Your rescue might have been unconventional, but you saved her life."

Callum nodded.

His apprentice and friend leaned in closer and lowered his voice to just below a whisper. "What do you think of the new fellow, Oliver?"

The question startled a huff of mirth from Callum. "I thought you were capable of finding your own bed partners, Harris."

"Sod off." He grinned. "I am, but I've never seen him at the clubs I frequent, and meeting a man on a ship is far different than meeting them on land."

"And how is that? Do you not merely solicit an introduction?"

"Very amusing. And no. Men on board a ship are open to pleasure for the sake of it, even when their tastes do not align with mine. Men on land have a choice. And the devil take you if you proposition the wrong man and he takes your, er, proclivities to the magistrate. I've seen friends hang for just such a reason."

"Harris. I'm sorry."

"Thank you for joining us," MacLean's deep voice permeated the still air of the safe house's parlour.

Callum returned his attention to the men around them and realized that several more had joined the group.

"Those of us who have been here in London," MacLean continued, "were given an outline of events leading up to your return to the safe house. What *you* all haven't received is information on what we have been doing in town from the first. Please allow me to do that now.

"Some weeks ago, one of our new recruits, Eleanor, received a letter from a cousin of hers named Caroline Newport. This young woman works as a nurse at the Bethlem Royal Hospital, and was writing to Eleanor at the entreaty of a patient, whom she believed to be sane, and held there against his will. She'd mentioned this man being abused, and stated that he knew Eleanor. Naturally, we gathered our forces and came to London to see for ourselves. And we were right. The poor blighter in bedlam was Colonel Kieran Richards."

"The devil you say!" Hydra pushed himself off the wall and unfolded his arms.

"Indeed not," MacLean continued. "He recovers abovestairs, even now."

Shock and disbelief scrunched Hydra's features, his eyes blinking.

Callum's spine was stiff as he sat on the edge of the chaise. It was very likely that all the men from last night were recalling the same thing: that Hydra had seen Richards—or someone with a striking resemblance to him—during the attack.

"What is Richards' state of recovery?" Callum asked into the silence.

MacLean looked at him. "He remains abed, and has attempted to speak but can scarcely get a word out. The doctor believes that his windpipe was badly damaged."

"Has he someone with him at all times?" Hydra asked.

"Most times," MacLean confirmed.

"And tonight?" Hydra continued the line of questioning. "Two to three hours ago, was he abed with someone watching him?"

MacLean frowned. "Yes, as a matter of fact. I believe Bridget and Jones were with him." He shifted his stance. "Why do you ask?"

"I wish to speak with him." Hydra's voice was low and calculating, but held a breath of relief. "The individual orchestrating the attack this evening bore a striking resemblance to Richards."

A soft curse came from the other side of the room, and several pairs of eyes swung that way.

"When we first arrived at the safe house," Ares began, "Richards warned us of danger. He couldn't say much more than the one word, but made sure to tell us that the danger wasn't from the lords and their men at sea."

Hydra blasphemed under his breath. "Then we must assume that Richards knows of this man, and I must hope that he can at least write his answers down."

The man moved to leave, but Callum's voice stopped him. "Sir, what is our next plan of action? Certainly the mercenaries and the man in charge of them will return. What will you have us do to prepare?"

"Yes, we must expect another attack. It is best to assume that someone followed us here and has reported our safe house's location to their superiors. I believe, however, that we can expect them to take a brief respite to gather their forces, so I would take this time to clean yourselves—should you desire it—gather and load your weapons, and prepare to do battle.

"Barrows, the Duke of Norshire, Lady Laura, and presumably Richards are abovestairs. They should have someone in their bedchambers at all times. Guards—whose *only* job is to report back— will be placed by the attic windows, around the gardens, and along the front walk.

"When the enemy arrives, expect multiple entrance attacks: windows, doors, scullery. We want our attackers to believe that they have the element of surprise, so when you engage in combat with the mercenaries, attempt to keep noise to a minimum so as not to alert their fellows. This means no pistols, if it can be helped. Our men will be stationed about the main and lower floors, near every window and door. Are there any questions?" No one came forward, and Hydra nodded in satisfaction. "Dismissed."

* * *

The sweet scent of honey swirled around Laura, teasing her from sleep. She tried to stretch, but searing pain jolted through her leg, hip, and shoulder, and sudden bits of fragmented memories flashed through her mind. Her eyes snapped open.

"Pirate," she whispered. "My father…"

A pretty woman, with white-blonde hair and emerald eyes several shades darker than Laura's, entered her vision. "Oh, good. You're awake." The woman smiled, the movement lighting her face even through the dimness of the candlelit bedchamber.

"Where—?" Laura began, but suspected that she already knew the answer.

"We are at a safe house owned by my husband."

Laura nodded, rubbing her mass of red curls against the soft pillow. "Hydra. I suppose that makes you Bridget—er, Lady Bradley." She'd heard the name, she was certain, but she wasn't entirely sure where.

The woman's smile deepened. "That's right. But you may call me Bridget."

"Thank you. And you may call me Laura." She cleared her throat. "Can you please tell me what happened? I—I mean, I know that I was injured, but was anything broken? Have I been seen by a physician?" *Is my baby well?*

"Dr. Simon Claridge has seen you, and is confident that your baby is well—my felicitations. And while you might be sore, it would be good for your muscles to move about. Though he did mention that you are not to use your left arm for a sennight, lest the bone in your shoulder pop out of its socket once more. Then he has exercises that you will be permitted to do once per day. I understand that the recovery can be arduous, but you will recover fully."

Laura nodded again, feeling slightly stiff. A quiver of *something* went through her abdomen at the mention of her babe. She'd not gotten the pregnancy confirmed by a doctor, and knowing that she was well and truly with child was rather…liberating, exciting. "Thank you. How is my father?"

"The duke is sleeping in another of our guest bedchambers. I did not glean any details from the doctor, but I understand that your father will be fine. The duchess is on her way to see him."

Laura released a short breath of relief. She was pleased that Papa would be well, and she would be glad to see her mother again. But there was something hiding just beyond her memory that held back her full enjoyment. "Is there something wrong?"

Bridget's white-blonde eyebrows puckered in puzzlement. "Wrong?"

"With the men, I mean. The attack is not over, is it? There will be more battles?"

Bridget idly rubbed a hand over her large belly as she shifted upon the chair at Laura's bedside. "My husband wishes to keep that information from me, but I can only assume so. From what I understand, they've lost their prisoners—save one—and they'll need to retrieve them.

"Mere months ago, some villains learned my husband's true identity and laid traps for him, our families, and me. And when a traitor is desperate, they will stop at nothing to achieve their goal. These men might very well know our names and the location of our safe house. If our spies allow these men to flee, they can return with the power of hate and vengeance, and kill every one of us."

Laura nodded again, a quiver of fear rippling through her. She couldn't remain abed doing nothing. Being on Callum's frigate had changed her, and it wasn't just a matter of not wishing to feel helpless. That was a part of it, of course, but she *wanted* to help, to share in this aspect of his life, even if it was as small a role as providing gunpowder.

Her heart skipped a beat, and Callum's impassioned voice rang in her ears. *I know that I'm below her, I know that I don't deserve her, but I'll gladly spend the rest of my life working to prove myself worthy. I love her… There is naught that you can say that will convince me that a union between us is anything than what it is: one of love—at least on my part.*

Callum loved her. Her Pirate Spy *loved* her! She lifted her uninjured arm to cover her face with her hand, a wave of self-loathing rushing over her. How could she have been so foolish?

When they'd last parted, she'd told Callum that there was nothing he could do to improve their connection, to have her return his affection, and now she merely hoped that she could find a way to take it back. *Oh, Laura, you colossal tit! You deserve this ignominious feeling.*

"I need to speak to Callum," she said. "Please, Bridget, will you help me rise and dress so that I might find him?"

The woman's lips curved upward in one corner in an arch grin, her eyes crinkling playfully at the edges. "I do believe that the doctor said that you must exercise your muscles."

Chapter 34

Laura's body screamed in protest as she walked to face the small bedchamber's mirror. A light sweat had broken out on her brow, and some stray hairs clung to her damp skin. Donning the simple frock was a feat that she dreaded repeating. Bridget had helped, of course, but the agony in her arm had far surpassed that of her hip, leg, back, and head. The deed was done, however, and she thought she looked rather bonny in the dove grey.

"There," Bridget said at her back, gently adjusting the sling over the dress' short capped sleeve. "Now your hair."

Laura swiped at the perspiration on her face and neck with a nearby cloth and shook her head. "I do not wish to prepare my hair." Seeing it now, still matted with her blood in places, she knew that she couldn't stomach an errant tug reopening her sutures.

She almost laughed. The time at sea without the shade of a bonnet brought out even more freckles on her face, which stood stark against her pale skin. But, a duke's daughter being seen with her hair down in public? Covered in *unsightly* freckles that every governess had attempted to remove with minimal time out of doors and lemon scrubs? It was unheard of.

A smile tugged at her lips, and she wiped at the blood with the cloth.

Mayhap it wasn't unheard of for a pirate's wife.

"As you wish, Laura." Bridget smiled back at her in the mirror's reflection. "Your hair is truly glorious. I daresay Callum will be agog."

The compliment warmed her. "Thank you."

"Now, come. I understand that the gentlemen concluded their meeting belowstairs and have dispersed. I do not know where Callum is, but we shall find him." Bridget clasped Laura's hand in hers and walked carefully with her to the door.

The hallway was empty but for faint flickering candlelight, the echo of low voices, and a woman's sobbing.

"Oh, no," Bridget breathed.

Laura urged Bridget faster, forcing her legs to move through the pain. They came to another bedchamber. Inside were the woman spy who had been on Hydra's ship and a man sitting abed and attempting to eat some broth with one hand.

"The danger…" the injured man croaked, "…is my…cousin. R…" he rasped. He tried to swallow some broth. "Ralph." That appeared to be the end of his speech, for he sent an entreating, fearful message through his gaze then returned his attention to his broth.

The woman sobbed again.

Without a moment of hesitation, Laura let her instinct drive her, and she strode forward to place a comforting palm on the woman's shoulder.

"Good evening," she began in an undertone. "My name is Laura Morris. May I sit?"

The man in the bed nodded with a wince and gestured toward the edge of his bed with his spoon. Laura sat.

"Thank you." She turned to look at the weeping woman. "I'm sincerely sorry that you're upset. Is there anything that I can do to help? Would you care for some tea?"

The woman gave a damp smile and shook her head. "My name is Mary." She gestured to the man in the bed. "And this is Colonel Kieran Richards."

"It's a pleasure to make your acquaintance." Laura smiled warmly.

Mary sniffled. "With the constant activity since the first of our battles at sea, I have not yet had the pleasure of speaking with you. I've heard some from Callum, but men do not converse like women. Do tell me, how was your time at sea?"

Mary's gaze held genuine curiosity and warmth, and Laura supposed that the woman wished to draw her thoughts away from whatever was troubling her. If this was what Laura could do to help, then, by God, she would do it.

She started with her kidnapping, detailing the brigands' mistreatment of her, her hunger, and fear, then spoke about the day that she was rescued by The Pirate. With fondness creeping into her voice, she recalled their initial awkward discussion about his position in the Secret Service, his promise of a bath, and of her being forced to wear men's clothing.

From there, she went on to discuss the perils of the sea and their countless battles, as well as Callum's attempts to find her suitable attire.

A thick, callused hand came down on her uninjured shoulder, gently caressing, and Laura turned her gaze upward.

Callum's face was stony, his gaze searching, but he said nothing. Candlelight flickered over one side of his face, casting the other half into darkness.

During her speech, Bridget had rounded the bed to sit on the other side, Mary's tears had dried, and the room had filled with Callum's other fellows and his superior.

"You forgot an important detail, Laura," Harris put in.

Laura turned her attention to the other man, who was propped against the wall behind Mary's chair. "What is that?"

"How you took so naturally to life at sea, to life aboard a pirate ship."

If Laura had been one to blush, she might have done so, then.

"You not only took to it, Laura," Harris continued, "but you excelled at managing those men."

"I didn't—"

"You did. They didn't once approach you or proposition y—"

"That was because Callum had threatened them," she insisted.

With a wry smirk, Harris shook his head. "No. Pirates, even ones who respect their captains, often stop at nothing to seek out their own pleasure. Laura, those men respected *you*."

She blinked. "But why? I did nothing t—"

"Did you not? Laura, in one of our first battles with you aboard, you put out a fire almost entirely by yourself. From then on, you worked during most battles, supplying men with gunpowder and shot, then, once I was injured…you became a doctor's assistant and got those men's blood on your hands trying to save them." He shifted his feet. "Now tell me, why would they not respect someone like that?"

Laura blinked again. "I… I'd never thought that my actions would have such a meaning. I'd just done what I thought was right."

"My point precisely."

Callum's grip on her shoulder tightened slightly before loosening. "Might I have a word?"

Her stomach jumped, and her mouth abruptly turned dry. Was she breathing? Lord, she didn't know if she was breathing. "Of course." Oh, dear, that sounded a bit of a squeak.

With a tight smile to the others in the room, she stood, and painfully began to move.

* * *

The hall was dimly lit with sparsely placed candles and carried the scent of tallow and battle.

Callum's chest felt tight, his lungs labouring as he drew Laura to one side. Hell if he knew what to say to her. He'd thought about it all through the last leg of their journey, when he'd been aboard Hydra's ship, but after the attack at the docks, he'd not had any opportunity to speak with her.

"I've wanted to discuss matters with you since our last parting," he began, his voice slightly trembling, betraying his nervousness.

She stepped closer to him. "Callum, I—"

"Please." He put a hand up in a short gesture then took a deep breath to steel himself. "I promised myself that I would be more open with you, rather than merely honest.

"Being separated from you that day was one of the most painful experiences of my life, and I've suffered relentlessly since." He stepped closer to her and clasped her hand in his. "You said that there was nothing I could do to make things better for you, and I offer you my profound apologies for making you feel that way. I do, however, want you to know that while I respect your feelings, I will not back away from our union. I've made a promise to you, to your father, and to our unborn child, and I fully intend to keep it." His hand tightened slightly on hers. "I vow I will work tirelessly every day to ensure that you do not regret accepting me."

There was a slight waver of the candles' reflection in her eyes before she blinked it away.

"I do not believe that a union between us is a mistake, Callum."

Callum's heart gave a hard *thump* before it fluttered wildly against his ribs as he waited for her to continue.

"I…" She glanced around them at the empty hall before lowering her voice. "I was scared."

He frowned, his gut churning. "*Scared?* Did I—"

"No, no," she hurried to assure him. "You did nothing wrong."

Callum released the breath that he'd been holding. "Then of what are you afraid, Laura?"

Her bottom lip trembled, and she cleared her throat. "I'm afraid of being abandoned."

He frowned again. "But I wouldn't—"

"You might not think that you would, Callum, but there are many ways to abandon someone without deciding to walk away from that person. My sister, if you'll recall, loved me but left to marry her first husband. And while my father did not physically leave me, his heart and his mind did." Her eyes began to ripple with unshed tears once more, and Callum's chest ached at the sight. "What if you grow bored with me and take a lover? What if your assignments take you away, or, in order to protect me from some villain, you must attempt to hide me away? What if you are taken to sea once more, or you are killed, or…or you end up like your friend, Barrows?" Her chin quivered.

Callum's chest squeezed with a disheartening combination of emotions: worry that he might never win her heart, and joy that he might have already begun to break through her walls. "There is—"

"Callum." Milford stepped into the hallway, appearing discomfited as he glanced between Callum and Laura. "Hydra requests your presence in the front parlour."

Callum nodded, and, just like that, his opportunity to make things right with Laura disappeared. His gut sank. At the very least, he felt like he understood her reasoning, but that wasn't enough.

"There is much that I need to say," he said, his voice a rough whisper as he clasped her hands tighter. "Will you permit me to visit you in your bedchamber later, once this business has concluded?"

Her gaze searched his, the green of her irises dark in the dim light of the corridor. "Yes."

Lips quirked in a thin grin, Callum tightened his grip on her hands. "Thank you. Now, I must see you someplace safe while I meet with my superior."

"Your friend Barrows," Laura began. "Is this home where he resides, or has he been placed in a hospital?"

"He is here."

"Might I meet him?"

Chapter 35

The bedchamber was still, the air heavy with thick, stale air, and the candles and hearth fire flickered dimly. Laura's gaze focused on the narrow form on the bed, her heart in her throat. The poor man.

"There is usually someone here to tend him, but I believe that they have been called away to aid in the preparations for battle," Callum said behind her.

"I am here to tend him now," Laura said confidently as she strode toward the bed.

A chair was positioned at his bedside next to a table with a pile of books, a pair of reading glasses, and two candelabras.

"Hello, Barrows," Laura said in a strong voice. "My name is Laura Morris. I hope you do not mind that I have come to spend some time with you." She sat on the chair. "I am new to this home, so you will not know me, but I feel as though I understand you. You see, I had an aunt that was in quite the same circumstance as you. It was frightening and emotional for us, her family, but even more so for her. She explained to us once she had awoken—for she *did* awake— that she was conscious during the entire experience, but unable to move or speak or let us know that she was there, at all. It was truly harrowing. She would grow bored when no one was near, she felt discomfited when the doctors and maids changed her bedclothes, and, more than anything, she wanted to open her eyes and see how we children were growing."

Callum shuffled around the bedchamber behind her, but she kept her gaze on the sickly man's face. He looked so young. She could imagine him full of life, his face animated in discussion. Compassion swelled in Laura's chest, and she took the man's hand.

"If you can hear me, Barrows, I wish for you to know that there is always hope, you are not alone, and you needn't be afraid." She patted his hand. "I shall return on the morrow with a book to read aloud."

With that, she quit the room with Callum, passing Mary as she entered.

"This is precisely what occurred with my aunt," Laura said softly as they strode down the corridor. "She began with opening her eyes and tensing her muscles, and over time she was able to speak, then move, then walk again."

"It's remarka—" He broke off as a sharp cry rent the air.

Despite her pain, Laura turned around and strode as swiftly as she could back into Barrows' bedchamber. Mary turned wide eyes over her shoulder at them as they entered.

"His hand tightened in mine!" she said with excitement.

Callum strode forward. "What—" He fell silent as he saw Barrows' and Mary's clasped hands. "Jesus, Mary. I don't think he's done that bef—*Holy sodding Christ!*"

Barrows' eyes snapped open, unfocused and dilated, staring directly at the room's ceiling.

Without a moment of delay, Callum turned and dashed from the room, bellowing down the corridor for the doctor and Hydra.

Slowly, Barrows' eyes slid closed, and his grip on Mary's hand loosened, and she sighed with a gusty *whoosh*. The bedchamber suddenly flooded with activity. A man Laura presumed to be Dr. Claridge entered, and settled his large black bag on the table on the opposite side of the bed. He was followed by Hydra and several of Callum's fellows.

The doctor bent over Barrows, feeling his forehead and opening his eyes to peer at them. "Would you please tell me what happened?"

Mary spoke quickly, explaining every detail.

The doctor nodded. "Thank you." He turned his attention upward to encompass everyone in the room. "Barrows should have someone with him at all times to make the transition to wakefulness as smooth as possible. This could take days or weeks, but I believe you may be optimistic that he will regain consciousness."

"I will gladly remain here for the rest of the night, unless Mary would prefer the first shift," Laura offered. "I daresay I couldn't sleep a bit if I tried."

"I will remain for a short while with you, Lady Laura, but I cannot stay the night."

Hydra nodded. "Very good. This is pleasing news, indeed. And, damn it, we could use some good news tonight. Thank you, Doctor. Come, men. I require you belowstairs."

As quickly as they'd arrived, the spies filtered out. All, but two.

Mary sat with her back to them, her hand in Barrows' once more.

Callum tentatively threaded his fingers through Laura's mane, careful not to disturb the hair around her stitches. "Our discussion is not over, sweetheart," he whispered, bending quickly to take her lips with his, not giving her a chance to respond. But she quickly forgot, for his mouth played hers like a pirate ship in the fog.

"Stay abovestairs—in this room. It will be the safest place during an attack."

With that, he was gone.

* * *

Breathing through the stiffness and pain in her shoulder, hip, and leg, Laura focused her energy on holding Barrows' hand. The man had opened his eyes once more since Callum and Mary had left, but he'd swiftly returned to sleep. She continued to talk, to tell him stories of her time at sea, of her family and her relationship with Callum.

Laura kept reminding herself that he did not know her, and she certainly did not know him, but she felt proud that her connection with him had begun his process of recovery—even if it was not entirely true. So, she kept revealing her inner self while he slept.

She wanted to sit and fantasize, to imagine what a life would be like with Callum…and about his whispered, *Our discussion is not over, sweetheart*. But now was most certainly not the time for such musings.

The house was tense and quiet, as though everyone were holding their breath in anticipation of the attack that they were sure was to come. Laura's skin veritably tingled with worry.

A strange scraping noise came from beyond the window, and Laura started, turning her gaze toward it. The rear of the house was nearly three floors above ground—impossible for someone to scale, surely.

"I must check on something, Barrows," she said in an undertone. "I will return directly."

She released his hand and stood, wincing at the pain darting throughout her body. With quick, awkward movements, Laura doused the candles throughout the room and peered out the window.

All that was left was the low light emanating from the hearth, but it still made it difficult to see past her own reflection in the window's glass. But she *did* see.

Someone—a man—was indeed scaling the wall. And he was aiming for Richards' bedchamber. Even through the midnight darkness, Laura could see the prostrate forms of two men on the ground below the windows. Worry stabbed through her abdomen. *I have to warn someone.*

Her body cried out in protest as she hurried back to Barrows.

"Something calls me away, Barrows, but do not worry. I will return the moment I am able."

She scanned her gaze about the room, searching for a weapon of some kind. With one arm not working, she could scarcely swing anything heavy, but neither was there a pistol to hand. Even if there were, she could not load it. *Blast it all.* With a sigh, she ran to the hearth and selected the heavy iron coal shovel and awkwardly hefted it over her uninjured shoulder.

"I have faith in you, Barrows," she said just above a whisper before hurrying into the hall.

* * *

The night was dark and still, and the air in the safe house's morning room was stifling. Callum waited with several other men in the unlit space, watching for potential attackers through the windows toward the front walk.

Anticipation hummed just beneath Callum's skin. It had been some time since he'd felt that familiar zeal for battle, but it was there now, buzzing and vibrating through him. Lord knew when he would once more engage in battle for the Secret Service, for that was one thing about which he must speak with Laura. This could very well be his last battle, and he would damned well enjoy it.

Naturally, he was disappointed that he'd not had the opportunity to conclude his discussion with Laura, but that only made him more eager for the battle to be won. He would prevail and properly express his love for her, the woman carrying his child. *Holy Christ, my sodding child.*

A bubble of joy fluttered in his chest. No matter what it took, Callum would return to her that morning, and he would set things to right.

Someone slunk along the walk across the thoroughfare, and Callum's eyes narrowed. Was that a man in his cups making his way home, or was it, perhaps, a carefully laid distraction meant to draw the men away from the rear of the house?

A soft hiss came from behind him, and Callum spun around. Henderson stood in the doorway, his eyes wide and his breath coming quickly.

"A fire has been lit in the alley," he whispered harshly. "Prepare for an imminent att—"

His words were cut off by a hoarse shout toward the rear of the building. Several men darted toward the sound, but Callum, Henderson, Ares, and Greene held firm in the morning room.

The mercenaries would not attack from only one entrance.

"*There*," Callum hissed, notching his chin toward the window.

Dark figures darted between shadowed alcoves across the thoroughfare. Then, as though on some signal, the men tore over the cobblestones toward the town house.

Ares appeared at Callum's elbow. "This is it. God speed you, gentlemen."

"Likewise," Callum replied, his pulse racing even faster in anticipation.

"Remember," Greene put in, pulling back the hammer of his pistol, "these are the same men that we fought at the docks. Most of them are likely injured. Look for weakness in your opponents and exploit it."

Henderson nodded. "Make this fight not worth their promised payment."

"And whatever happens," Callum added, "remember the plan."

Ares put his hands to the window's sash, and, with a quickly uttered "At the ready, men," he lifted, opening the room to a rush of cool night air.

Rapid footsteps hurried nearer, and Callum crouched, putting his shoulder to the wall and aiming his pistol out the window.

Crack!

* * *

With the coal shovel's shaft digging into the muscle of her uninjured shoulder, Laura crept down the vacant corridor. She quickly made her way to the top of the stairs, searching for someone to alert.

Men shouted and pistols fired as chaos erupted on the ground floor. Laura's breath caught, and she retreated a step, remaining out of sight as two men tumbled into the foyer, blades drawn.

Her stomach plummeted and a weighty sense of doom smothered her. No one would help her. Sparks of nervous energy sizzled throughout her body, tingling just beneath her skin to prickle painfully in her fingers, toes, and lips. *I am alone. I am forgotten.* No, she corrected. Not forgotten, merely put away to be protected. But what if one of the attacking mercenaries saw fit to venture abovestairs? What if the man scaling the wall was successful and reached Richards' bedchamber? Come to that, how did he know where the man was sleeping?

Be a pirate, her mind whispered. *Be a pirate.* What would a pirate do if someone scaled their ship? She shook her head. The answer was simple: he would blast the man from above with a pistol, or he would kick him in the face or chest the moment he crested the bulwark.

Laura straightened her spine, ignoring the flash of pain that it caused, and forced the sense of foreboding aside. She'd been on a pirate ship during battle, for pity's sake! She could most certainly guard a window.

Fear crackled the air around her as she hastened to Richards' bedchamber. Without a moment's hesitation, she strode past the bed, where Richards lay, and the chair beside it, in which Mary dozed, and made directly for the window. Not wishing to alert the man outside to her awareness of him, she hissed and clicked her tongue in an attempt to wake Mary. The woman didn't stir. *Blast it.*

A faint scrape came from beyond the window, and Laura's breath froze. She hadn't the time to rouse Mary; the man was here.

The shadowy figure of a man lifted the sash and put a hand on the sill. For a brief moment, Laura considered slamming the window on his fingers, and lifted her coal-shovel-wielding arm to do so, when a pistol appeared in the opening.

Her stomach turned to ice, and she remained still, hoping beyond hope that he wouldn't notice her. The man was moving so slowly— *too* slowly. Her arm began to shake and beads of sweat slid freely down her temples and between her breasts, tickling the fine hairs. She wanted to itch at them, wanted to move, to breathe. But she waited, trembling and gritting her teeth.

The intruder lifted a leg over the sill and planted his foot on the carpeted floor, his pistol still aimed toward the bed.

Just a little more.

With his body folded in half, the man brought his head inside.

Now!

Finally giving relief to the trembling ache in her arm, Laura swung, adding force with the weight of the coal shovel. It connected with a satisfying *clang*, first with the man's outstretched arm, and then with his face in the follow-through.

Bang! The pistol was knocked wide, and a low shout filled the room.

Just as she'd hoped, the intruder lost his balance, and slid back through the window, only narrowly catching himself on the frame. Gritting her teeth to bite back at her pain, Laura lifted the shovel with her shaking arm once more and swung.

The man howled and cursed, and Laura lifted the shovel to strike a third time, but she never reached her target. A pair of piercing, furious blue eyes rimmed with thick black lashes—so much like Richards'—caught her gaze just as his hand gripped her shovel and yanked.

Laura yelped, thrown off balance, and landed on the floor with a jolt of agony. Blinking away the spots that danced in her vision, she sat gasping, shaken by the impact.

The intruder's gaze was murderous, but no longer on her. It was on Mary. The remarkable woman positioned herself between the intruder and Laura, as Laura attempted to squirm away. Her back bumped painfully against a chest of drawers, and she hissed.

Mary gripped the intruder's cravat and yanked. The man clambered through the window before Mary slammed his back upon the ground. Laura's gaze was transfixed as they fought, both of them grappling for the upper hand and both striking with several harsh blows. But, Mary was losing.

"Get out," she growled at Laura as the intruder's hands clamped around her neck. "Get to safety."

Laura couldn't. Her eyes were wide, her heart twisting in her chest…and she was incapable of moving. She wanted to help, not flee, but what could she do from her position? Her pain was too great, and her desire to be of aid all but debilitating.

"*Run!*" Mary's face grew red, and the intruder laughed maliciously.

With a grunt, Mary gripped the man's wrists and twisted, wrenching a cry from his chest before she rammed her forehead into his face. Blood spurted from his nose, spraying across Mary and splattering Laura's frock. Mary staggered to her feet, her red-rimmed eyes narrowed on the intruder.

She reached for the coal shovel, but before her hand could touch it, the man had gripped Mary's ankles and pulled her back to the floor. With her winded, the man stood, withdrew a blade from within his coat, and heaved Mary's back to his chest.

The intruder spat blood on the floor, holding Mary's arms at her sides with one of his and pressing the blade to her neck with his other hand. "Now I have you," he said, winded. "And now I'll kill the lot of you."

Chapter 36

A sword swung past Callum's face, and he inwardly cursed, twisting sideways to avoid being struck while simultaneously jabbing his opponent in the ribs with his cutlass. The mêlée was fierce, but the number of their opponents was dwindling.

Callum gasped, filling his lungs with the scent of candles, gunpowder, blood, and sweat as he removed his cutlass and kicked the groaning man away. He darted through the doorway of the parlour into the foyer and clashed his blade against Henderson's opponent's, narrowly saving his fellow from losing a limb.

His movements were swift and efficient, and each *clang* of his cutlass was echoed in the space by several others. Men grunted, their feet shuffled and stomped, and there was the distinct thumping of combat as men punched and grappled.

A man appeared in the doorway across from Callum, hair mussed, clothing in disarray, and blood splattered across his person. *Piper.*

With a toothy snarl, the man ran at Callum, sword raised. Calm determination settled through Callum as he lifted his cutlass to knock the sword away. He was not pleased about the prospect of killing Piper. He would much rather the bastard stand trial for his crimes, but he wouldn't bloody well hesitate to end his life if the man gave him no other option.

The older man's movements grew desperate, his face sweaty and his breathing huffed. Callum's cutlass clanged against the blackguard's sword. The moment was very nearly right… *There.* With a swipe of his weapon to distract the man, Callum hooked the booted toes of one foot behind the villain's calf and pulled, toppling Piper to the foyer's marble floor with a *whomp* and a *thwack.*

Callum stepped forward to peer down at the unconscious man, then bent to check the pulse at his neck. *Alive.* That was rather easier than he'd thought. With nimble fingers, he unknotted the cravat at his neck, slid it from around his shirt collar with a *snick* and, turning Piper onto his stomach, tied the bastard's wrists tightly together. He couldn't have the man awakening and slipping away to do more harm.

Crack! The muffled sound of gunfire and a man's shout from abovestairs drew his attention. *He's here.* With several more well-placed slashes and jabs to approaching mercenaries, Callum made his way across the foyer and dashed up the stairs and into the vacant hall.

The men who had been stationed in the corridor had likely joined the fray belowstairs, and while Callum knew that Mary was fully capable of performing in this portion of their plan, he disliked the thought of the other bedchambers being unguarded. With his lips thinned and his breathing under control, Callum moved quietly toward Richards' bedchamber door, placing his back against the wall as he listened.

He heard their hand-to-hand combat, which was precisely what they'd intended, much to Gabe's dismay and protestation. Mary was the proverbial worm at the end of the fisherman's line, but this worm was meant to take their enemy by surprise. Once their leader was removed, the mercenaries would disband, and Callum could seek out Laura's company and figure out how to make things right again. Then he'd take her into his arms and—

Have a care, Callum, his inner thoughts rebuked. *This is neither the time, nor the place.*

There was a feminine cry of alarm, and Callum's gut clenched. Mary was a skilled actress, he knew, but her fear sounded very real, indeed.

She muttered something, growled beneath her breath, and Callum leaned closer to the doorway, straining to hear.

Warmth filled the dark space beside him, and he knew without looking that one of his comrades had joined him.

A man's voice spoke within the bedchamber, his breath hitched from exertion. "Now I have you. And now I'll kill the lot of you."

There was the sound of shuffling feet, and a light gasp.

"Do you see what you've done?" The man spoke again. "Do you see what you have made me do, cousin?"

The villain must have addressed Richards in the bed.

"Your father was the younger," the man continued. "He shouldn't have inherited the estate. That land was my father's to claim and *mine* to inherit."

There was a croak. "Your father was a—" Richards began.

"*He was not a bastard!*" the other man shouted vehemently. "Our grandfather claimed him just as he claimed your father. You don't deserve the land, especially since you've abused it so sorely. Your *school*," he spat, "will soon be returned to its rightful owner and reclaimed as a grand home."

Confess, Callum urged silently. *Tell us where your evidence is.* He needed to hear the man's confession, blast it, before he could rush the room. Someone needed to speak at the trial, and with a myriad of paid mercenaries and titled lords behind Ralph Richards, it was very likely that he would survive the trial and cause more problems for the Secret Service—and Kieran Richards in particular. The poor blighter had gone through enough as far as Callum could see.

"Despite the feeble actions of your pitiful *spies*, I will get what is rightfully mine, cousin."

There was another feminine whimper, and a rasping "No, don't!" from the bed.

Callum's gut twisted. What if his confession never came? What if Ralph Richards decided to forego the soliloquy that many villains preferred, and go directly to murder? Perhaps Ralph wasn't the type of man to wish for glory, recognition, or a challenge in his actions before he disposed of his prey, after all. *Damnation.*

Tightening his grip on his cutlass, Callum prepared to rise and charge into the bedchamber.

"What sort of man betrays his country for a piece of land?" Laura asked incredulously.

Her voice stopped Callum cold. How the devil had she gotten into Richards' bedchamber? Carefully, he peered around the door's frame into the room. She sat upon the floor, her arm still slung, a grimace on her beautiful lips. Callum retreated once more and received a nudge in the ribs from Harris.

"*Was that Laura?*" he mouthed.

Callum nodded, then trained his ear once more on the bedchamber while Harris relayed the message to Oliver, who crouched beside him.

* * *

Laura could scarcely believe her ears as the intruder droned on about family and duty and what he was owed. Her stomach fluttered with nerves, but she'd put herself in that circumstance, and now must find her way out.

"You're completely mad." The words slipped out before she could bite them back.

The man turned an alarming shade of purple as his lips worked silently. "I am *owed* this!" he spat, tightening his hold on Mary.

What if she could anger him into releasing Mary? Could Mary then regain the upper hand? It was rather worth the try, for what else could Laura do? The fluttering in her stomach intensified.

"Owed a piece of land and an old building?" she returned. "You must see that your paltry desires could have easily been resolved with a family solicitor, possibly a steward, and the law? Why would you go to so much trouble? This seems obscenely theatrical and petty."

He shifted, gripping Mary's neck with one hand and waving the blade at Laura with the other. "How dare you!"

"You're a fool if you think that attacking your cousin in his bed will earn you his land and his money," Laura continued, unabated.

The man sneered, his mask of confidence slipping firmly back into place. "Indeed not. I intend to gain a title! Once I've my title and I've reclaimed my land, I'll continue my work in luxury."

Her eyebrows rose, and she carefully began to shift her legs beneath her. "How—"

He laughed derisively. "By working for the French, of course! For years, I've been intercepting my cousin's letters, feeding their generals information, and receiving payment, all while plotting to take down Kieran's organization. Once my plan was in place, it was just a matter of putting it into action.

"It began with putting spies of my own into his friends' homes, letting them believe that the plan was theirs, and then watching the chaos unfold. There was treachery, deceit, and a delightful amount of death, which I'm rather proud of." His blue eyes grew steely. "It might not have all gone according to my plan, but I evaded notice until I decided it was time for Kieran to know the truth."

Laura's heart beat wildly in her chest. She'd thought him outlandish and almost absurd, but how wrong she was. His gaze was steady, unflinching, and his tone was sure.

"Our mighty Kieran Richards mightn't have a title," he continued, "but that does not change the fact that what was entailed belongs to the rightful heir. *Me.* Our country is divided not only by money and one's standing in society, but by *legitimacy.*" He spat the word, as though it tasted foul on his tongue. "My entire life, I was known as the son of a bastard. Not truly worthy. What sort of country is this that our brothers and sisters are treated in such a way?"

Despite herself, a sliver of pity crept into Laura's heart. As a woman with little power of her own, she understood his plight. She recognized that their laws were unfair, that they promoted superiority, but murder and treachery were not the way to achieve the aims he sought.

She struggled painfully to her feet, keeping her gaze on Mr. Richards and the blade that he had trained in her direction. Her body howled at her to retreat, to find a soft place and lie down until her wounds had healed and every villain had been taken to the Tower. But her heart wouldn't let her back down. This man was in so much pain that it had driven him into madness.

"You're correct," she capitulated. "Our laws aren't fair. But surely you could attempt to do something about that by influencing those in Parliament, or writing—"

He scoffed. "Fomenting sedition would have me thrown into the Tower, just as—"

"It would hardly be fomenting sedition if you were to go about it properly," she replied hotly. "Not like *this*, not by betraying everything and everyone."

"I do not betray everyone. Not myself. I am doing precisely what needs to be done for Kieran to see—for *London* to see—what is done wrong. I am settling injustices while simultaneously receiving a tidy profit. It is truly an ideal situation."

Settling injustices. The words echoed in her mind. The man's logic did not make sense, and the longer she remained there facing him— the more intently he gazed at her—the colder she felt. Icy fear was crawling through her veins, thickening her pulse to forced, heavy thumps.

"You'll not succeed," Colonel Richards' rasping voice said from the bed.

The madman turned his head, and Laura didn't think—she just acted. As though she were transported back to the schoolroom with her sister, Charlotte, childishly fighting over a piece of lace that they'd pilfered from Mama's sewing basket, Laura gripped a mass of the dark, waving hair at the back of Mr. Richards' head and yanked it backward.

He let out a surprised yelp, his arms lifting as he stepped back, attempting to catch his balance. Mary gasped as she collapsed upon the bed, holding her neck.

It felt to Laura as though time had slowed. The blade in Mr. Richards' hand glinted in the dim candlelight, and Laura released his hair, leaping back as far as the small room would allow as he began his upward swing at her.

A low, deep roar filled her ears, and suddenly Callum was there, directly in front of her. Mr. Richards' arm finished its arc, and a splash of crimson sprayed across her forehead.

All at once, there was a hoarse shout, Callum was on his knees, and Mary was at Mr. Richards' side. She gripped his forearm, and in one swift—and seemingly effortless—motion, he was flipped through the air and splayed upon his stomach. Harris and another fellow leapt upon the blackguard's back, holding him down as they began to truss him.

Laura scarcely managed a breath while the flurry of activity took place, but she knew where she belonged. Her pain notwithstanding, she dropped to her knees at Callum's side.

She put a hand to his shoulder, and he groaned behind his hands.

"Callum." She spread her palm over his person, feeling for injuries. But she suspected that she knew where he'd been injured, and her stomach plummeted with fear for him. "Callum, let me see your face."

He wobbled on his knees, and Laura shifted, guiding him back to rest against her thighs. Her breath caught. Blood seeped from between his fingers and trailed down his jaw to drip from his chin. *So much blood.*

Laura looked up at the others, fear pounding through her. "*Harris.*" She waited until she had his attention. "Summon the doctor, please." Laura marvelled at the calm in her voice, when her insides were anything but.

With a tight nod and a worried glance toward Callum, Harris darted from the bedchamber.

"Callum?" Laura stroked a hand through his soft hair. "Please allow me to help. I believe that you might require pressure to staunch the flow of blood."

His fingers trembled, but he removed them with a grimace. Laura swallowed down the gasp that threatened. His face was almost entirely covered in blood, flowing steadily from the deep gash that ran from his right cheekbone to the centre of his forehead, crossing directly over his eye.

"I can't…" Callum's breath came fast and he swallowed hard. "I can't…" He blinked his left eye rapidly before it widened in panic. "I can't see."

"Shh, shh, darling. The doctor will see you, and he'll set you to rights." Laura clenched her jaw against the prickle that began at the backs of her eyes as she unfastened her sling. She balled the fabric and hastily pressed it to Callum's face.

He groaned and bared his teeth. His breath came in ragged, hissed bursts as he attempted to manage his pain.

"You'll be all right," she assured him. Lord, she hoped that it wasn't a lie. Could an eye survive being cut in such a way? *Would* he be able to see again? Would he get the fever? Would he… No, she couldn't allow herself to think that way. Oh, where was the doctor? The moment the thought went through her mind, she felt like taking it back. There was a battle waging belowstairs. It was very likely that the doctor had several—if not, many—patients to see to tonight.

"I can't see," Callum whispered, his left eye watching her, dark blue, and covered in blood.

"Everything will be fine, Callum."

He reached for her hand with his bloodied one, and Laura turned her palm up into the grip, ensuring that the back of her wrist kept pressure on his wound.

"I have to tell you." His voice grew hoarse as his slippery fingers scrabbled for purchase on hers. "I don't want to die and not have told you this."

She shook her head as her heart jolted with worry. "Oh, Callum. Do not trouble yourself. Rest now. You can tell me later."

"Love always comes with risks," he continued, unabated. "But those are risks that I am willing to take. *For you.*" He blinked, then grimaced in pain, and Laura's chest gave a responding pang. "I cannot guarantee that I will not be run down by a carriage or thrown from a horse, but I can certainly take precautions when it comes to my position in the Home Office. If that is your fear, I'd intended to speak with you on the matter anyway. There are other—safer—options for me moving forward, but I believe that you and I can discuss those at a more leisurely pace once the danger of this night has passed.

"As for your other concerns…" He grimaced again and gripped her hand tighter. "I can safely assure you that I will never take a lover, and nothing is important enough to take me away from you. By my troth, I will not be like my sire, single-minded in the pursuit greatness and deserting you as soon as the babe is weaned. The man was a devil…" His voice trailed off, and his eye grew distant.

"I believe you mentioned that he was called 'Lucifer,'" Laura added helpfully, her voice tight with worry.

His lips thinned, and his glazed gaze roamed up toward her once more. "He was. The notorious John 'Lucifer' McInnis, a devil of a pirate and devil of a man."

"I always knew you were the son of a devil," she jested, her throat thick with emotion.

Callum's grin turned into a grimace. "He might have instilled in me a love of the sea, but I have no desire to become like him. The man was respected by his men but feared by everyone else, including every woman he came across. He was a brigand and an abuser of women, and would not have hesitated to continue what those kidnappers had done to you, had he been in my place. My sire was quick to forsake anyone he felt could no longer serve him, sweetheart, and I'll not allow anyone to feel that way by my hand. You and our children will always have me."

The prickle in Laura's eyes grew to a burn, and she attempted to blink it away. Here the man lay, supine, bleeding, and very possibly blind, *reassuring* her. She wanted to pull the fool into her arms and kiss him, for in that moment, his words were the balm to her heart that she'd desperately needed.

He lowered his voice, his breath still coming rapidly. "Will you open yourself to me, sweetheart? Will you permit yourself to be loved and love in return? And will you marry me out of a desire to do so, rather than out of a sense of obligation?"

A tear slipped over her lashes and slid in a heated path down her cheek as she gazed at him. Beneath the drying blood that had sprayed, smeared, and dribbled down his face, his complexion was pallid. She was amazed that he'd put together such coherent thoughts when he must be in great pain.

"Yes, I will," she whispered.

The room abruptly flooded with men, shouting and jostling, and Laura realized that she'd been so absorbed in her moment with Callum that she'd entirely forgotten their audience.

Hydra appeared at her side, curses flowing from his split lips as he made room for the doctor.

"What happened?" the doctor asked.
"I can't see…"

Chapter 37

There was a brief moment of silence as Laura put the newest of Mr. Mystery's novels down on her lap and attempted to turn the page with one hand. Her shoulder had been in the sling for nearly a sennight, and yet the dashed thing still pained her as though she'd just fallen from that horse. The skin on her hip, thigh, and back had turned an alarming shade of purple, but it was not nearly as painful as her shoulder.

"Do you require help?" Callum asked softly from his position across the table.

She glanced up at him, and her stomach quivered. He most decidedly fit the position of a pirate now, no matter his change to proper attire. The deep, angry wound on his face had been treated, and a band of black cloth had been tied diagonally across his head to cover his eye. Dr. Claridge said that the cut to his eye had not been terribly deep and would heal eventually, though it was possible that Callum would require spectacles. Laura found that terribly endearing.

"I will manage. Thank you." She continued to fuss with the page.

There was a burst of laughter from across the parlour, and Laura glanced over her shoulder at Harris and Oliver, where they played a game of chess. Morning light from the windows shone in and glinted through their hair, putting part of their features in shadow. But their mirth and happiness were entirely apparent.

She leaned closer to Callum. "Do you suppose—"

"Leave it alone, sweetheart," he grumbled, attempting to arrange some cards in his hands while squinting with one eye. "I can't blasted well get my depth perception correct. My eye cannot heal soon enough, I say."

"Why not?"

He turned his gaze up at her incredulously. "Because I should very much like to see."

"No, no. I meant with Harris and—"

Callum dropped his hands to the table with a noise of exasperation. "The man can manage his own affairs. You needn't meddle. Besides, Oliver's…*preferences* mightn't align with Harris'. You'd be best to leave it well enough alone."

"It wouldn't be *meddling*, Pirate, it would—"

"Oh, good." Mary appeared at the table and took the seat between Laura and Callum, a wide smile on her lips. "I've found you. You will never guess, so I shall tell you. Barrows spoke to me today."

"Did he, indeed?" Laura's eyebrows lifted and a grin quirked her lips at the look of relief on Callum's features at the change of subject.

Mary nodded. "Said, 'Good morning, Mary,' smiled, and promptly fell back to sleep." She sighed shakily. "You know, I believe that he will make a full recovery."

"I'm so pleased to hear it."

"Damned good news," Callum put in with a crooked grin.

Good heavens, when he grinned like that, Laura wanted to haul him into a hidden alcove and kiss him breathless. They'd not had a moment alone since before that battle a sennight prior, and she'd not had an opportunity to tell him just how attractive she found his proper London clothing when she knew that a pirate's heart lay beneath it.

Oh, how she anticipated their wedding. Papa had returned to his town house—insisting that Laura remain with the spies, who he said would keep her safe—and he'd begun the arrangements and procured a special licence. Laura did not know when, precisely, she was to wed Callum, but she knew that it would be soon.

Callum had been secretive, as well, during the past few days, though Laura expected that his private meetings were more about his work in the Home Office than their nuptials.

Laura almost sighed aloud. Lord, but she was eager for them to wed. Once they were married, she could touch him when she liked, share a room with him…a *bed* with him without feeling obliged to excuse or justify their behaviour. And, of course, there was the added joy of sharing the news that she was with child. She was almost certain that all of Callum's fellow spies knew the truth, but it was very hushed and secretive.

There were deep voices in the corridor before Hydra and two other men entered. They nodded to Harris and Oliver, striding over to speak quietly with them. Laura followed their movement through the bright room, once more in awe of how swiftly the spies' town house had been cleaned. Mere days ago, this room—and all others on that floor—had been splattered with blood and littered with the dead and injured. Today, it was a bright and sun-filled parlour with pretty paintings hung on the walls and trinkets on several surfaces.

With smiles, the three men turned, selected armchairs, and brought them over to the table at which Laura, Callum, and Mary sat.

"We've just returned from the Home Office," Hydra announced as he settled in his seat.

Laura closed the book that she'd been reading aloud to Callum while he played cards and placed it upon the table, her heart abruptly in her throat.

"Our questioning has concluded. The trials for Ralph Richards, Lords Weston and Beresford, Mr. Piper, and Mr. McMann are to begin in a sennight. In that time, we will finish organizing our notes, for we have rather more than I'd thought we might, particularly after the questioning of Mr. Richards' mercenaries." Hydra pinched the bridge of his nose then raked his fingers through his blond hair. "The man had a web through London that was shockingly thorough, though many of his contacts did not know of his traitorous allegiances."

The sound of the front door's knocker echoed from the foyer, and they all ignored it.

Hydra turned his gaze on Laura. "If you're still amenable, Lady Laura, we would be much obliged if you would present your case as a victim."

Oddly, when each harrowing event had happened, Laura felt as though she had handled them with aplomb. She'd thought that once she had reached London, had returned to her homeland, she wouldn't feel the fear any longer, that the nightmares would stop. But she'd been wrong. The night after the large battle, another nightmare had woken her: flashes of gunfire, suffocating ocean waves, and hazy fog had filled her with dread. Logically, she knew that it was in the past, but her fear didn't seem to care what she thought.

A hand gripped hers, which sat fisted upon the table, and she glanced up into Callum's strong, encouraging blue gaze.

She blinked. "I—yes. I will."

With a note of thanks, the others continued the discussion around her, but Laura's attention was narrowed on that one bit of comforting contact. Her Pirate.

"Tell me, Callum." The voice of the man they called Ares broke through her thoughts. "Have you considered what you will do now that the battle is over? Many of our agents"—he nodded at Mary—"Gabe and Mary included, will move on from active duty after the funerals for our fallen comrades and the traitors' trials. I understand that there are options before you."

Even though Callum had the use of only one eye, his gaze was intent on Laura, and it was entirely captivating. "We've not yet had the opportunity to discuss it in detail, sir, but I imagine—"

Callum's words were lost among the flurry of voices coming from the hall. Laura recognized her father's deep baritone and rose to her feet.

Chairs scraped along the floorboards as the men around the table stood, as well, only a heartbeat before her father entered.

"Papa," Laura breathed, hurrying forward to embrace him in a one-armed hug.

He was tall, and far too thin for his frame, and his skin was still pale from his illness, but his eyes were bright and he seemed to move without stiffness.

The Duke of Norshire pulled back to look at her. "It seems that you are recovering well, Pigeon. Are they properly caring for you, then?"

Laura smiled. "You know they are, Papa."

"Your Grace," Callum said solemnly, bowing once he'd reached Laura's side.

Her father inclined his head in return, a ghost of a smile on his lips. "Mr. McInnis. I trust everything is in order?"

"As promised," Callum returned with a grin of his own.

Laura glanced between the two of them, and her eyes narrowed. "You two have plotted something. What is it, and how many years of my life will it—"

"I'm sorry, Papa," came a soft voice from the doorway. "I know that you asked me to wait until everyone had had an opportunity to recover, but I couldn't wait any longer."

Gooseflesh spread across Laura's skin as she gazed at the sister that she'd not seen for nearly ten years. And she promptly burst into tears.

"Oh, my darling!" Charlotte swept forward and pulled Laura into a familial embrace. "I'm so sorry. Papa explained everything to me. My husband had wanted me to be dependent on *him*, and he'd destroyed all of my correspondence. I believe that left us *both* feeling rather abandoned."

Shock rippled through Laura as her sister's words sank in. Charlotte had not meant to abandon her at all!

More tears fell, and she pulled back to look at her sister. Charlotte was older, of course, with knowledgeable blue eyes, rounder hips, a softer belly, and a dusting of freckles that hadn't been there when they were aged fifteen and sixteen. Laura marvelled at how beautiful and how vibrant Charlotte was. Her brown hair was pinned up in a smart knot at her crown, and several strands had slipped loose. She looked happy, even through the rippling tears blurring Laura's vision.

With a choked sob, she pulled Charlotte close once more. Though her shoulder pained her, it wasn't the pain that had her frustrated— it was the blasted sling keeping her arm between them when she wanted to have both arms about Charlotte.

"I've missed you so," Laura said into the loose strands of her sister's hair.

"Oh, Laura." Charlotte sniffed, pulling away to look at her. She ran her fingers over Laura's mane of curls, which had been left unbound to allow the stitches time to heal, and then clasped her hand. "I'm so sorry, dear sister. I ought never to have left like I did."

Warmth spread through Laura's chest, but before she could reply, a tall man and two young boys entered the parlour.

"Apologies, my love," the man said to Charlotte. "They would not be held back any longer. They're rascals, to be sure." The fond look that he sent the boys belied his words, and Laura felt a pang of longing in her chest.

* * *

Callum cursed under his breath, his eyes wide on the man.

Lady Charlotte took another step back and accepted the man's arm. "Darling, meet my sister, Lady Laura. Laura, this is Mr. Hugh Haddington, my husband."

Callum rushed forward to clasp Hugh's forearm in greeting, while the other agents took their time to greet their fellow who had once been missing.

"Damn, but it is good to see you again," Callum said.

Hugh tilted his head, a smile on his lips. "You, as well, Callum."

There was a shift of movement behind him, and Callum turned to watch Laura with one of the young lads. The boy poked the elbow that sat in her sling.

She looked down into his openly curious face. "Hello. My name is Laura."

"Hi! My name is Quintin, and I'm seven."

The younger of the boys bounced on his toes. "And I'm Maximus, and I'm four and a half."

"It's a pleasure to meet you both."

"Did you break your arm?" Quintin asked, poking at her elbow once more.

Laura shook her head. "I hurt my shoulder."

Maximus' eyes grew brighter. "Were you set upon by highwaymen?"

"As a matter of fact, I—"

Quintin's sharp intake of breath stopped her, and she followed his gaze toward Callum. He grinned roguishly at the three of them.

"It's a pirate," Maximus breathed, his soft brown eyes wild with excitement.

"No, no, boys," Charlotte hurried to reassure them, concern written on her features as she glanced toward Callum. "My sincere apologies for my sons' behaviour, Mr. McInnis. They are prone to fanciful imaginings. Boys, express your regrets to Mr. McInnis. He is your aunt Laura's affianced."

"Oh, but I *am* a pirate," Callum said in a conspiratorial voice as he crouched to their level.

The boys gasped again, their eyes going wider.

"Are you really, *truly* a pirate, Mr. McInnis?" Quintin asked, his bright eyes a delightful mixture of brown, green, and an almost red-brick colour.

Callum nodded. "Born and raised on the sea."

Maximus jumped on the spot, then shook his brother's arm. "A pirate, Quin!" He turned to Callum. "Have you ever marooned someone on an island?"

"Aye, but I was only *on* the ship. My father was the captain at the time, and it was he that did the marooning."

"Have you ever *killed* someone?" Quintin asked on a whisper.

Charlotte clucked her tongue.

Quintin reached out a hand and poked at the skin on the side of Callum's neck, just above his shirt's collar. "Do you have a tattoo?"

"I have several."

"Glorious," Quintin breathed. "When did you get them? And where?"

"Tell us a story!" Maximus exclaimed.

Quintin squealed. "Do you know any sea shanties?"

"Perhaps," Charlotte said, interrupting her sons' barrage of questions, "if it isn't too much trouble, we might inquire after luncheon if Mr. McInnis has any tales that are suitable for your young ears, but we must at least give him a moment to consider. Come, boys, we must wash our hands while your aunt and grandpapa speak."

The boys groaned as Charlotte took their hands, and Callum's heart pulled. To think, in under five years, the babe growing inside of Laura would be Maximus' age. So full of energy and curiosity. He could scarcely wait.

Soon, the room was emptied, leaving Callum with the duke and Laura, who stood frowning at them. Callum's stomach suddenly buzzed with nerves, and he felt far too warm.

The duke smiled and clapped Callum on the shoulder. "I'll leave this to you," he said, then pressed a kiss to Laura's forehead. With that, he left, closing the parlour's door behind him.

"What in heaven's name is happening?" Laura burst out.

His heart lurched, and he clasped her hand in his.

"This week has gone by so quickly," he said, ignoring her question, "and yet I feel as though I've scarcely had a moment to speak with you."

"I feel the same way." Her voice had gone soft, and her green eyes warmed.

Callum cleared his throat of the disquieting lump that had settled there. "I feel proud, and bloody fortunate, to have you by my side. I confess I haven't quite been able to grasp why you've chosen me, but I'll not squander such a precious gift." His hand tightened slightly on hers. "You're to make me a father, sweetheart, and I truly have few words to say but these." The lump returned to his throat, and he found it suddenly very difficult to breathe. "I love you, Laura. I have for some time." His voice came out hoarse and warbled with emotion, even to his own ears.

Laura's green eyes misted over before she surged upward on her toes, gently brushing his lips with hers. It wasn't a kiss of passion—though Lord knew she stirred his blood regardless of how much contact they had—but one of affection. Her lips played over his softly, reverently, before she pulled away.

"I love you, too, Pirate."

Callum's heart felt positively buoyant. His chest heaved with his rapid breaths, and his grin could not be repressed. "Then marry me. Today."

With his free hand, he reached into his inner breast pocket, withdrew a small velvet pouch, and fumbled awkwardly with the drawstring. His fingers trembled as he removed the simple golden band from within.

Callum returned his gaze to Laura. Her cheeks reddened beneath her freckles, and tears gathered at the corners of her eyes. Good God, she was exquisite. He cleared his throat. "I'd commissioned a proper ring with stones for you, but it has yet to be completed. Your parents and I have arranged everything else for today: your dress, the flowers, food, guests, and the parson with the special licence, if you desire it."

She released his hand to cover her face on a sob. Alarm spread through Callum.

"Shite. I'm sorry, sweetheart. If you don't like it, we can post the banns and do it properly. I'm sure your mother won't mind; she enjoyed wedding planning far too much, I believe." He put his arms around her as she wept. "Come now, love. I will gladly wait for whenever you are ready." He scattered kisses into her glorious mass of auburn curls, taking in her fresh scent of soap, sunshine, and air.

Laura swiped at her eyes and sniffled, lifting her head to meet his gaze. With a smile, Callum carefully brushed his knuckles over her tear-stained cheek, not wanting to miss or press too hard—*damned depth perception.*

"There we are," he murmured, kissing her temple.

"No," Laura whispered.

He'd offered to postpone the wedding, but even so, hearing the word on her lips stung deep. "Very well, sweetheart. I'll inform His Grace—"

"*No!*" She clutched at his coat with her good hand. "That is not what I meant. I love you, Callum." A breathy laugh bubbled up with her smile. "You know, I believe I shall never tire of saying that. I love you. And I want to marry you today. It merely struck me, just then, that you truly know me.

"I am not adept at feminine pursuits—in fact, I rather despise them—and planning a wedding would be…simply *awful.* You've given me not only the gift of your heart, Pirate, but you've relieved me of any painful obligation. I am well and truly happy."

Callum grinned down at her. "Do you know what this means, sweetheart?"

She hummed her response, pressing her body against his and stirring his blood.

"Tonight is our wedding night." He skimmed his hands down her hips and around to her bottom, then squeezed.

"Then we shall make it an early evening."

With a laugh, she pulled his head down for another deep kiss.

Epilogue

December 1816—More than a year later

Laura held a sombre black coat next to Callum's shockingly bright blue waistcoat, and he shook his head.

"No, that one will not do."

Her shoulders sagged. "Why not choose a different waistcoat?"

Their bedchamber was heavy with humidity from their delightfully sensual shared bath, and was filled with the scent of soap and Callum's shaving cream. Their bedchamber was large and well-appointed, and it suited the rest of the town house. Much to Callum's chagrin, her papa had aided in its purchase, but Papa was insistent that it was part of Laura's dowry.

She clucked her tongue at him. "You ought to have let your new valet dress you this evening. Most particularly for such an important night."

Callum grumbled. "I've never in my life had someone dress me. I do not understand why I must now."

Laura gazed at him, disbelieving. "You're the Earl of Suffolk."

"It's a purchased title." He cringed, as though the words tasted bad. "I work on Bow Street, sweetheart. Hardly respectable for an earl."

She tossed the coat over a chair and cupped his face in her hands, admiring how delectably rakish he was with the scar streaked across his face. "First, my handsome Pirate Spy, *you* do not work on Bow Street—*we* do. If anything, it is far more distasteful for a duke's daughter and countess to sit behind a desk doing paperwork and dealing with clients while you and the other men are out on adventures.

"The title mightn't matter to you, but it will matter to William once it has passed down to him." She ran her hands down his chest.

"I'm afraid that you will have to put up with the small annoyances." Leaning forward, she peppered kisses along the underside of his jaw and down the column of his neck to tongue the edge of his tattoo.

He groaned and gripped her hips, swaying closer to her.

"Now," she whispered against his skin, "you will wear the grey waistcoat with silver and blue embroidery, and the black tailcoat."

His pulse sped beneath her lips, and he groaned once more. "You deserve more paints."

"Indeed I do." She stepped away and retrieved the waistcoat. "I believe the dinner party this evening shall be diverting."

Callum accepted and donned the bit of clothing and began fastening the buttons. "A farce, you mean."

"It is a celebration, my love, of the trial's completion, and the end of any dealings with Napoleon Bonaparte's spies in England."

He sighed. "It *is* a relief, I grant you. But your father and Lord Wellington were far too generous. I daresay most of my fellows, retired or not, haven't the faintest notion of what to do with themselves, now. A duke's dining room full of men with newly purchased titles… They will feel as out of place as—"

"As a lady on a pirate ship?"

His fond blue gaze lifted to meet hers.

"As a lady in a pirate's bed?" she added, stepping nearer.

With a growl, he grasped her hips and pulled her close against him. "Careful, sweetheart, or you'll find this pirate in your bed now, and we'll be late for dinner."

"We wouldn't want that." She laughed. "Tonight, then. And Callum," she purred, stroking her palms downward to his thighs, "wear the pirate coat."

* * *

"To a successful trial and an even better year," Charles said, his tumbler raised in a toast.

The people that were once his beautiful band of spies lifted their glasses in response with a loud, "Hear, hear!"

Pride swelled in his chest as he looked at each of them in turn, sitting around his grand dining table. Bright, flickering candlelight lit the room with a warm glow while snow fell quietly beyond the windows.

"Despite the slight ache in my chest at missing the days that were," Charles continued, "I am mighty pleased at how far you all have come in the past year. Whether you have decided to remain on with the Secret Service, teach at the school in Brampton"—he nodded at Gabe, Mary, and Barrows—"become runners for Bow Street"—he nodded at several others, including Greene, Callum, and Stevens—"or begin an entirely new runner service for women"—he smiled at Grace (once Lucy, Eliza, and several other pseudonyms)—"I am proud of all of you."

There was a murmur of thanks and clinking of glasses as Charles' spies—his *friends*—congratulated each other, as well.

It was a fitting end to their adventures, with the war over, new families being formed, and new life experiences on the horizon. He could scarcely wait to see what came next.

Author's Note:

I spent quite a bit of time researching songs for my pirates to sing, and, as you see, I found some! While the lyrics mightn't be grammatically correct, and aren't spelled correctly, they are true to the time and the sources from which I found them.